A NOTORIO

ROUGH AND RAW

HAYLEY FAIMAN

Rough & Raw
Copyright © 2016 by Hayley Faiman

ISBN-13: 978-1533287441
ISBN-10: 1533287449

All rights reserved. Without limiting the rights under copyright reserved above, no part of this publication may be reproduced, stored in or introduced into retrieval system, or transmitted, in any form, or by any means (electronic, mechanical, photocopying, recording, or otherwise) without the prior written permission of both the copyright owner and the above publisher of this book.

This is a work of fiction. Names, characters, places, brands, media, and incidents are either the products of the author's imagination or are used fictitiously. The author acknowledges the trademarked status and trademark owners of various products referenced in this work of fiction, which have been used without permission. The publication/use of these trademarks is not authorized, associated with, or sponsored by the trademark owners.

Editor: Rosalyn Martin, Another Pair
Cover: Cassy Roop, Pink Ink Designs
Formatting: Champagne Formats

Jeremy —
You inspire me every day with how wholly you love me.

Desperation is the raw material of drastic change. Only those who can leave behind everything they have ever believed in can hope to escape.
- William S. Burroughs

prologue

Brentlee

Five Years Earlier

I make sure the bathroom door is locked. Not that a lock would stop Scotty from breaking the thing down. *He'd done it before.* For a man who is slim and works behind a desk all day long, he has some serious strength.

I sit down on the closed toilet seat, pressing my hands to my face. It happened again. I have lost count of how many times Scotty has slapped me, punched me, kicked me, or raped me.

My entire relationship is a farce.

I hate him, but I married him because my parents encouraged it. They *love* that I married a man with a fantastic career. I hate myself for being weak.

My father scowls when he sees the yellowing bruises on my face, but he never says a word. My mother pretends to be oblivious to the hell that I live in.

I let my mind drift back in time, *not for the first time*, to the one and only man that I have ever loved.

Bates Lukin.

I fell for Bates when I was just fourteen years old. He was the older bad-boy, and I loved everything about him—the thrill and the danger that surrounded him.

I pursued him, relentlessly, and eventually he took notice. We spent one year together before he went away to Marine boot camp. One beautiful year where I gave him everything. My love and my virginity.

"I won't ask you to wait for me, Brent. I know you're still enjoying high school, and you deserve to have fun," Bates murmurs as he cups his hand around my cheek. I wrap my fingers around his wrist holding onto him.

"But I love you," I say, my voice trembling with emotion.

"I don't doubt that, Brent. I love you, too; but I'm not coming back here. I have no clue where they'll send me, but I don't want to be anywhere near my father. You need to have fun in high school. Sitting around on Friday nights alone isn't your style. I wouldn't ask you to do that for me," he says, his dark eyes roaming over my face, taking me in, memorizing me for quite possibly the last time—ever.

"I can stay faithful; do you think you won't be able to?" I ask challengingly, angrily.

"For you, I could do anything, Brent. For you, I would do anything. But you're young and I can't hold you back like that."

He sighs pressing his forehead to mine.

"You're breaking my heart, Bates," *I whisper, unable to hold the tears at bay.*

"I know. At least you have a heart. I gave mine to you," *he murmurs, running his nose along mine before pressing a closed mouth kiss against my lips.*

"You can't have it back. I'll be waiting for you," *I cry.*

My fifteen-year-old heart was shattered the day Bates left for boot camp.

I would have waited for him.

I would have waited a lifetime.

Months went by without news from him.

He abandoned me.

I would beg his sister, Mary-Anne, for *any* information she had. At first, she obliged, sharing letters he sent to her. Then suddenly, she stopped. I knew he had told her to let me move on. He was *forcing* me to move on.

In my anger toward Bates, I turned into someone I didn't recognize. I began drinking and became promiscuous. That lasted for about three years, until my best friend's brother came back from college— law school.

He saw me as a woman, and he wanted me.

Scotty and I were engaged mere months after we started dating, and our marriage was rushed. I was nineteen and he was just beginning his career. We were going to be the perfect couple. Even if I didn't love him, I thought I could learn to, eventually.

Our perfect couple status lasted until our honeymoon. The truth crashed through my little bubble with a vengeance. It was the first night he hit me. I had embarrassed him because I drank too much at our reception. *I was a stupid whore, a slut, and I was lucky he took pity on me and married me.*

I *felt* stupid at the time.

I felt stupid for falling for all of his shit—for not listening to my sister, Kentlee, when she tried to advise me to steer clear of the man. He didn't need to point out that I had been slutty. I owned that slut inside of me, but I wasn't that girl anymore. I was a wife, completely ready to devote my life to my new husband.

I resigned myself to the hell I had bought into, that I had allowed.

That was, until I saw Kentlee with her new man in the grocery store. I was eight months pregnant and had just survived another brutal attack by my *adoring* husband. I didn't lie to myself; I didn't believe anything he said when he apologized to me profusely every time he beat the shit out of me, but I was scared.

Kentlee looked happy and her man, a monster, looked *scary*; yet when his eyes landed on my sister, I watched them soften before my own.

"Get your no good, whore ass out here," my husband bellows from the other side of the bathroom door.

I suck in a breath and grasp the handle of the door, opening it to face my hell, my nightmare—*my husband.*

Sniper

I lie in the dark *alone*.

I hate sleeping *alone*.

The nightmares always return.

Nightmares about the months I spent in the scorching, dry desert while I was in the Marines, followed by my self-created nightmares about leaving the only girl I have ever loved—*Brentlee Johnson*.

Fifteen was too young for me to tie her down. She deserved to experience life. By the time I found my way back to her, it was too late. She was engaged. I watched her from a distance, angry at the way her demeanor changed after her marriage, knowing exactly *why* it had changed, too.

My father abused my mother my entire life. She refused to leave him and I watched as he hurt her, hurt me, and hurt my sister—*repeatedly*.

I kick the sheets off and find my pants, pulling them up my legs, not bothering to button them. I won't be wearing them long. Living in the clubhouse has its perks. *Pussy available twenty-four-seven.*

I need something to exhaust me for a few hours. I won't fool myself into thinking I'll get a full night's sleep, but a couple hours would be nice.

I walk into the room where the clubwhores hang out and sleep, noticing it's pretty empty, except for a sweet young thing that showed up a few weeks ago. I don't pretend to know her name. I'll never use it, and I'll never need it. She has long brown hair and brown eyes. Her body is thin, but curvy. She could look like Brentlee — *if I squinted, were drunk, and high.*

I lift my chin toward her and hold out my hand. She quickly comes my way, wearing a bra and a pair of short shorts with platform flip flops. She's more covered up than most of the girls here, who choose to lounge in just thong panties.

"What do you want?" she asks in a little girl voice once we

get inside of my room.

I hate that shit. I guess it's supposed to make chicks sound sexy, but I can't stand it. Brentlee had a low rasp to her voice. With one word, my cock would be hard as nails—*every time*.

"You don't talk," I grit out through my clenched jaw. "Get on your knees and suck my cock," I order, smirking when she does as I say.

I watch her sink to her knees before she shoves my jeans down with her little hands. Then she slides her hot mouth over me. She sucks me like a goddamned pro, and it feels fuckin' fantastic.

I wrap my hands in her hair and hold her still before I start to fuck her mouth. I want to come, but not like this. I need to fuck or I won't be able to sleep. I pull out of her mouth and order her to strip. She does it slowly and seductively, but I couldn't give a fuck. She's skinny with big fake tits. I prefer long and lean. *I prefer Brentlee.*

The girl doesn't even ask how I want her. She crawls to the center of my bed—head down, ass up. I slide on a condom before I grab her bony as fuck hips and slam my cock inside of her. She's a little wet, but she cries out at first. *I don't stop.* She's here to take my cock. I don't have to do fuck *for* her.

"You want to come, you'll have to make yourself," I say sounding bored, because I am. This bitch is just taking it, making screeching noises that are fake as shit.

Once she starts touching her clit, her voice goes a bit deeper and I feel her shudder underneath me as her pussy starts to swell around my cock.

I close my eyes and imagine it's Brentlee. It's been almost eight years since I've been in her pussy, but I'll never forget the way it felt. Nothing else could compare.

I start to pound into her harder. I know I'm going to bruise her up, but I can't find a fuck to give as I feel my nuts tighten. Finally, I come. I don't stay inside of her even a second after my release. I pull out and yank the condom off of my cock, tying a knot in it and throwing it in the trash can.

"Gonna hit the head; be gone when I get back," I bark as I leave the room.

When I come back, the bitch is gone. I climb back into bed and I close my eyes. Sleep finally takes over, but it isn't dreamless. It's full of Brentlee.

"I love you so much, Bates," she says, kissing my neck down my chest and just above my jeans.

Fuck, I feel like I'm going to blow my load right here and now.

"Love you, too, baby," I whisper, trying and praying that I can hold it together for a few more minutes.

"I want to suck you," she murmurs as she begins to unzip my pants. I swear to Christ my prayers are answered in this second.

I wake with sweat covering my body, remembering the first time Brentlee took me in her mouth. I embarrassed myself, coming within seconds, but she took it all and then she smiled as I wrapped her in my arms.

Brentlee wasn't my first lay, but she was the best. Even now, a decade later, nobody can compare.

I told her once that I didn't have a heart because I gave it to her.

She still owns it all these years later.

Always has and always will.

Three Years Later

Sniper

It hasn't been nearly long enough since the last time I laid eyes on Brentlee.

My heart picks up at the sight of her, and for whatever reason, I stupidly want to see more. It's like I want to punish myself further, but it's Brentlee. I'll never pass up an opportunity even just to watch her.

I look so much different now than when she saw me last. I'm nothing like the boy she knew, so I cross the street and follow her into the store she's slipped into. I trail behind her, close but not too close.

I watch as she picks up the ugliest fuckin' puke green dress I think I've ever seen in my life. Then, she sighs and it goes straight to my dick. *Fuck*, I remember how she would sigh as soon as I slid my cock into her tight cunt. *Fucking beautiful.*

"*Hello*," she whispers lightly into the phone. Her voice is deep and husky, another thing that makes my dick hard.

"Yes, Scotty, I understand. No, no, everything will be ready on time. Yes, I'll be presentable," she murmurs gently, too fuckin' gently—as if she's afraid.

Fear.

I know that emotion well. I've lived it my entire life, and to hear it come from Brentlee's lips makes me sick. I move around so that I can see her from the front, and when I do, I feel rage fill me from head-to-toe.

She's done a good job trying to hide it, but she has a black eye. It isn't fresh either, probably a day or two old. I know because I watched my mother sporting the exact same bruises my entire childhood.

I choke down the bile that threatens to rise. I left her all those years ago and I told her to live, I never thought she wouldn't live and live happily.

I want to turn and leave, but I'm frozen to my spot, watching her every move—her every tentative move. She's a fucking shell of a person. Nothing like the girl she was when I loved her.

My *tigritsa* no more.

I watch as she pulls out a credit card and pays for the god awful dress before she walks out of the store. Then, after a few minutes, I follow, leaving the store. I throw one leg over my bike and I head toward the clubhouse, toward my brothers—my family.

I need a good fuck and some booze.

How did she let herself get mixed up with this piece of shit? *This dirtbag.* She deserves so much better than him, than how he obviously treats her.

I close my eyes for a beat.

I need to not think about how I fucked up Brentlee's life. It was me—my fault. She would have still been mine, she would have waited for a fucking eternity for me, had I not pushed her away. I pushed, and I even made sure Mary-Anne started ignoring her.

I thought I was doing it all for the best, but she's living in fear with some piece of shit, and I'm the one to blame. If I would have kept her, she wouldn't have chosen him, she would have always—*always*, been mine.

"Woah, slow down there, brother," Fury chuckles as I

practically run toward the bar once I arrive at the clubhouse.

I don't slow down. I growl to the prospect behind the bar that I want a bottle of Jack, and I want it right-fucking-now.

"The fuck is wrong with you?" Fury grunts as he slides up next to me.

"I didn't know," I mumble.

"You're gonna need to fill me in," he urges.

I unscrew the cap and start to guzzle the liquid, letting it burn my throat before I turn to Fury, my friend and brother. He doesn't know much about me. I keep my shit wrapped up tight, but this I can't keep in.

"I saw Brentlee," I confess.

"Kent's sister? Okay…" Fury says.

I can see the confusion written all over his face, and I don't blame him. I would be, too; especially since I haven't said fuckall about Brentlee to anybody. I haven't spoken her name since the day I left this town five years ago. It hurt too fucking bad.

"Loved her. *Love* her. Fuck, I don't know," I mutter. "I saw her today; I think her man beats her."

The words put a bitter taste in my mouth. I hate uttering them out loud.

"You want to go and get her?" he asks.

I arch a brow, but he doesn't waiver. The crazy fucker is serious, which makes me think he's more serious than I thought about LeeLee—Brentlee's sister.

"Nope," I say, shaking my head once before I take another huge swig of liquor.

"We got muscle, brother," he offers.

"Won't matter. I know women that are abused, they never leave," I say as I start to stand.

"You writing her off, then? Woman you love?" he asks.

"You gonna claim your woman?" I ask, shutting his pussy ass up.

Fury calls my name after I've already started walking away, but I can't give enough fucks to turn around and acknowledge him. I need to fuck this feeling away or I'll have nightmares all night. I can already feel that panic rising in my chest.

I see a couple of whores hanging out by the pool tables and I lift my chin to both of them. Quickly, and without question, they stand and teeter on their high heels as they follow me. I open my door and let them walk into my room, but I don't close the door behind me. I could give a fuck if anybody sees me with these two bitches.

"Naked," I grunt as I take another healthy swig of Jack.

I watch as they strip and take note of their skinny frames, the blonde has no tits, and it makes me think of Brentlee and her long, lean body. I try to shake her image out of my mind as I take my own clothes off, but I can't.

I walk up to her and look into her blue eyes, not lifeless yet, but dulled. One day she'll have completely dead eyes, especially if she stays here long enough.

"You ever been fucked in the ass, sweetie?" I ask her, my eyes staying focused on her.

"Once," she whispers before she licks her bottom lip nervously.

"We'll make it good for you. Her and me," I promise as I run my thumb over her thin bottom lip.

"How," she whispers shakily.

"You'll see," I grin before I press my lips to hers.

I spend the next several hours exhausting myself, and the

two whores, completely out. I decide not to kick them out quite yet, I might want to fuck one, or both, of them later. Usually they get booted out right after I come, but tonight I might need more physical relief. I close my eyes and will myself to sleep, all I need is a few hours.

What feels like minutes later, I crack my eyes open to find two arms slung over me. One across my chest and the other across my stomach. They belong to two separate women, and I cringe at the thought of letting them stay in my bed until morning. Not something I would ever do, normally. Last night I was beyond hammered; I don't even remember everything that happened. I blacked out right after I fucked the cute little blonde's ass.

"Up," I murmur as I throw their arms off of me, earning nothing but moans and groans.

"Get your asses up," I grunt a bit louder. I smack each of them on their bare asses, hard, watching the immediate handprints form on their skin.

"What the hell?" blondie shrieks as she rubs her ass.

"Up and out," I bark, immediately regretting it. It makes my head pound.

The girls grumble and mumble but eventually leave me alone. I sit on the edge of the bed, naked, with my head in my hands—not because of my screaming hangover, but because the memories all flood back.

Brentlee—bruised. My guilt feels like a heavy brick in my gut. It's all because of me. She's being hurt because of me.

Because I left her. I pushed her away.

She won't leave him. Women in those situations never do. I know. I tried to make my mom leave time after time, and she refused every single one. No matter how much she agreed that it wasn't right, that *he* wasn't right. Brentlee will be no different. She'll either live her life barely surviving, or she'll die by his hand, and there's nothing I can do to save her.

I can't save anybody.

All I do is destroy.

I pick up the empty bottle of Jack and throw it across the room, watching it shatter against the wall—feeling *nothing*.

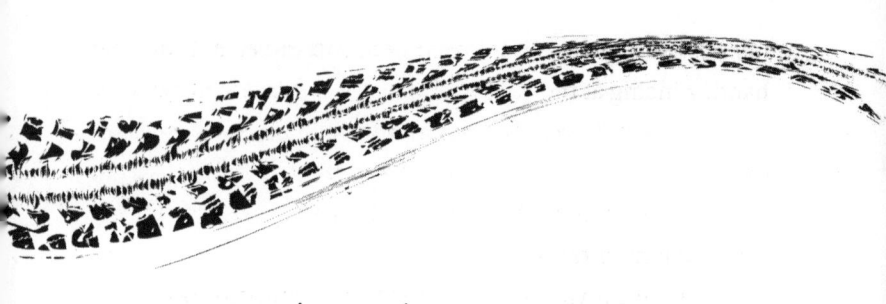

chapter one

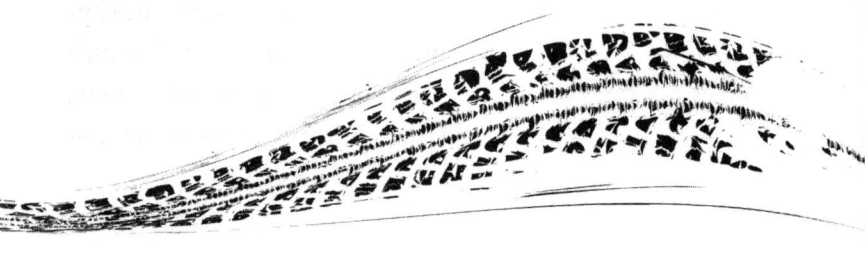

Present Day

Brentlee

It's time.

There is no way around it. There is no more denying that my relationship is abusive and toxic. It will never improve. Last night was the *last* time. Scotty laid his hands on our daughter, and that shit will never—*ever*—happen again.

I quickly throw some clothes into bags and make sure to pack Stella's favorite toys and her sleep lovie blankee.

Stella, my three-year-old, little, innocent girl, is watching Mickey Mouse, oblivious to what is about to happen. I call her name as I turn the television off, and she stands up and runs toward me as if she hasn't seen me in years. I take her hand, wincing at the dark bruise that has formed on her arm.

That asshole grabbed her and shook her so hard yesterday, I was afraid she'd have shaken baby syndrome. I stayed up with her all night, vigilantly waiting and watching for the slightest hint of trauma.

"Where going, mama?" she asks, noticing our bags.

One rolling suitcase for me and a duffle bag for her. Six years of my life has dwindled down to *this*. I couldn't be happier, though. I don't want anything he's bought me. The small stack of cash in my purse is the only thing of monetary value that I'm bringing, and that is only because money is a *need*—not a *want*.

"To see your Auntie Kentlee," I announce. Her eyes widen.

I have told my baby girl all about her beautiful Auntie and her big, strong uncle.

I take her hand and we walk; we walk all the way to the bus stop. I refuse to take anything more from him than I need. A car is a luxury, and it is in his name anyway. I don't need a damn thing from him, except our daughter.

I've never been on public transportation before, but I would ride on the city bus for the rest of my life if it meant I wouldn't have to see that asshole, Scotty, again.

Stella fidgets beside me as the bus slows and stalls at each and every stop, regardless of if there are people waiting to get on or not. I watch as our small city disappears and we are let off at the edge of town.

The last bus stop.

It's deserted out here, but I know what is at the end of the winding dirt path.

Salvation.

Dragging my suitcase with one arm while I hold Stella's hand with the other, we slowly walk toward our destination. She's solemn. She can sense a change, and I hope that whatever happens, I don't scar her for life. Not that she hasn't already been scarred in her short three years of existence. She's seen more hell than a child her age ever should.

The gates appear at the end of the road, and I know that we have reached our destination. I can only pray that Kentlee was sincere when she said her man, Fury, would help us and protect us. I have a feeling we're going to need every bit of protection that this man and his club can offer.

"Help you?" A man's voice calls out as he walks toward the gate.

"I'm looking for Kentlee," I say softly as my eyes widen.

The man is huge, built like a brick wall. He has long, black hair and a long beard. He looks frightening, and I feel Stella's hand grip mine tightly in what I can assume is fear.

"She know you're comin'?" he asks, narrowing his eyes on me. He doesn't open the gate.

I see suspicion swirling in his eyes. Six years ago, I would have given him some smart ass answer, but that smart mouth has been beaten out of me.

"No. I'm her sister," I murmur. I then watch the man's eyebrows shoot straight up.

I look on in anticipation as he pulls his phone out of his pocket and hits a few buttons before he places it at his ear. I'm unable to listen to him as Stella has decided to pull on my arm. I bend down and get to eye level with her.

"Where we are, mama?" she asks in her sweet voice.

"We're going to visit with Auntie Kentlee," I say.

I know I've already told her, but this is all new—a complete culture shock to her. Dirty country roads aren't something she's ever seen before; neither are bikers.

"Who's dat man?" she asks, scrunching up her nose.

"Auntie Kentlee's friend," I explain, hoping she won't say anything embarrassing. She's three—I can't stop half the shit that flies from her mouth.

"He looks like a big grizzly bear," she points out. I try to hide my smile.

"That's why they call me Grizz, little darlin'," he explains.

I turn my head around to look at him. He's got a huge smile on his face, and I'm so thankful he didn't take offence to my little Stella.

"Kent ain't here, but Fury is. He said to let you all in," the big man, I now know as Grizz, says as he opens one side of the gate.

"Thank you," I murmur.

"Let me take your bags, yeah?" he asks as he reaches for our luggage and takes it swiftly from my hand.

I inhale deeply and try to relax as I follow this giant toward the building I know to be the *Notorious Devil's* clubhouse. A place horror stories often come from. My sister is immersed in this life though, and if she can handle it, then so can I. She's softer than I am, always has been; sweeter, too.

I have seen horror and hell while encased in a gorgeous home. Nothing can be worse than what I have already endured.

"He'll meet you in the bar, just wait for him there," Grizz says, pushing my bag against the wall of the entrance.

"My bags?" I ask, looking from him to the luggage.

"Ain't goin' nowhere. They'll be fine right here, babe," he

grunts. I nod.

"You aren't going in there with me?" I ask, wiping my sweaty hand on my tight jeans.

I'm wearing a pair of skin tight, legging jeans and a scoop neck tank top. It's a casual outfit that I had hidden from Scotty because, as his wife, I was not allowed to be casual any longer. Dresses and suits were all I was permitted to wear. I hated them. *Despised them*. I'm only twenty-five years old. I love cute skinny jeans.

"Nope, I gotta get back to the gates. You're good, babe. Place is dead during the day." He winks and strolls away as if he doesn't have a care in the world.

I take another deep breath before I curl my fingers around the door handle and pull it toward me. This is it. I am leaving my husband. It hasn't felt real. Packing our luggage, the bus trip, or walking through those gates didn't feel real.

Now, as I step inside of the dimly lit bar, it hits me. This is all real.

There is no going back. Scotty would kill me without hesitating if I did.

Now, maybe I can *live* instead of just *survive*.

"Brentlee," a gruff voice booms from a seat at a table.

The room is eerily empty, except for *him*. His hair is pulled up into a man-bun and his face is covered in thick scruff. Not a long grizzly beard, but there's definitely a generous layer of hair hiding his face.

"Fury," I say as I walk toward him on shaky legs.

"Sit down," he grunts.

I pull Stella with me. Once I'm seated, I put her into my lap. I don't want her on the floor of this place. I can't even imagine the things that have landed there.

Well… that's not true. I could imagine the disgusting things that have landed and happened on the floor of the Notorious Devil's clubhouse, and I definitely don't want my sweet baby to ever touch it.

"I left him. Kentlee said if I ever needed to leave him, you could help me," I ramble, unable to look anywhere but his throat.

"Calm down, babe," he murmurs. My eyes move to his. He is serious, but his eyes are soft and focused on Stella.

"Why now?" he asks. I swallow loudly.

"He hurt Stella," I whisper. I then watch as his jaw hardens and his teeth grind.

"Then you have my protection, and the club's," he states.

"I have nothing, Fury. We have nothing but a small suitcase each. I have no skills." My voice trembles as tears fall from my eyes.

"We'll set you up and get you work, Brentlee. Not gonna let my woman's sister and my niece suffer another fuckin' minute," he growls.

I blink the tears that have begun to form away and stare at him in awe.

"I'll do whatever I need to do, Fury; whatever you want from me, you have it," I say, meaning every single word.

"You'd dance?" he asks, tipping his lips. I know what he's referring to. He's referring to the strip club they own. *The Devils Club.*

"You protect Stella and me from him, and I'll be your fucking star," I confirm.

"Might hold you to that, babe. It'd get you guys a nice bank account balance, but it's not anything we need to worry about now. I'll call Kent to come and get you. You two can stay with us until we sort out a place for you," he murmurs, taking his phone out of his pocket.

I place my hand on his and he freezes, his eyes crashing with mine.

"Thank you, Fury. I didn't stand up for Kent when I should have, and here you both are helping me. I don't deserve it, but thank you. I don't want to put you guys in danger. I don't want to stay with you. I can imagine it will be one of the first places he goes."

"Only other option is staying with a brother or staying here. I can't have Stella stay here, babe; so with a brother is the only way. Can't imagine you'd feel comfortable staying with a stranger, though," he says.

I don't want to stay with a stranger either, but I can't stay with him and Kentlee. I can't put Bear or their toddler daughter, in danger.

"They can stay with me," a deep voice says from the shadows.

I turn to look at the voice. My mouth automatically drops open and I stare in shock at the man who stands before me. A man I never thought I would lay eyes on ever again.

It isn't possible.

It can't be.

Bates Lukin.

"Bates," I whisper harshly, my eyes locked onto his.

He looks so different. If I saw him walking down the street, I wouldn't recognize him. Perhaps I have done so, walked right past him and not realized it. His voice is the same—harsher, but familiar.

Gone are his boyish features. He has a dark beard now that covers his cheeks and chin. His hair is short and clean cut, but messy on top. *He's massive*, at least double the size he was when we dated. He's no longer the eighteen-year-old boy of my dreams. He's a man now.

I watch as his eyes flick from me to Stella, then back. He takes a few steps toward me and the abrasiveness of his features startle me. His eyes look haunted, so haunted, it's eerie.

I wonder what he's *seen*. What he's *done*.

The sweet boy that held me and told me he loved me is but a memory compared to this hardened man in front of me. I exhale as my eyes stay focused on him. My body tingles as I continue to take him in, it hasn't forgotten how Bates made it feel all those years ago. One touch and I would probably combust.

My skin heats at the thought of his full lips on mine. A million years could pass and *Bates Lukin* would still make me burn hot. Make my belly flip. Make my pussy clench with just the memories he left me with.

Fuck.

No way can I live with him.

I haven't had an orgasm in years, and he's like a walking advertisement for multiples.

Nope.

This cannot happen.

"I don't think…" I say, trailing off before Bates' hand is held up to shut me up.

"No, you really don't. You'll stay with me. I'll keep you safe from that piece of fucking shit," he growls, making the hairs on the back of my neck stand up.

The anger pours off of him and I can't help but inwardly smile. There is no doubt Bates can handle Scotty. He has fifty pounds of pure, bulked muscle on my asshole husband.

"Okay," I rasp.

Sniper

I stand back. Leaning against the wall.

Listening.

Watching.

Waiting.

She's so fuckin' gorgeous, even as nervous as she is, and she still takes my breath away. A piece of me wants to take her back to my room and shove my cock down her pretty throat, then fuck her until she's screaming my name and all memories of the man she married are erased.

Brentlee Johnson.

I'll never think of her with that asshat's last name. *No.* She'll always be my little Brentlee Johnson.

Her raspy voice tells Fury that she's left her husband. She's done and she needs help. He hurt her for so many years, but he has now laid hands on the beautiful little girl in her lap. He's an animal, and he needs to be put down.

I grin to myself. I'm going to be the one to make him disappear. I'm going to be the one to lay him down. But not until I've claimed his wife, not until he sees that she's mine, not his, and that she never was.

My eyebrows shoot sky high when she agrees to dance at the club. My cock twitches at the thought. It shouldn't. I should be angry that she's willing to show off her fantastic body to the world. But Brentlee, naked and on stage? It would be hot as fuck.

Nothing but white hot lust rolls through me at the thought of her baring it all to a room full of men and knowing that everything they're fantasizing about is all mine. *She is mine, too.* From this moment on, she's in my house, in my bed, and at my side. I refuse to let her slip through my fingers again, not now that she's decided to *live*.

I step forward and offer to let her stay with me. When she hesitates, I don't even allow her to finish her thought. She's staying with me. I *need* her to. I need to keep her safe, and the only way I will know that she is one hundred percent safe is if she is under my roof.

"You sure, brother?" Fury asks as he turns to me, a smile twitching on his lips. I want to flip him off, but I don't.

"Yeah," I grunt before looking back at Brentlee. She is staring slack jawed at me. Her little girl's eyes are wide and bright as she takes me in.

"Come on, beauties, let's go," I murmur.

Stella doesn't hesitate as she jumps off of Brent's lap and walks right up to me. I feel like the pint-sized creature is looking past my exterior and straight to my soul as her eyes take me in, as if she's sizing me up and deciding how she feels about me.

I hope she can't see too deep into me; it's not a pretty place to be—full of demons and monsters.

After a beat, she reaches her tiny hand out and wraps it around mine. I look down at her little girl hand wrapped in my big, calloused one and just stare.

I squeeze her hand in mine, a reflex, and she smiles up at me, bright and happy and all Brent. She should've been mine. I'll protect her now, because she deserves it; because she's Brent's; and because if I would've had my head outta my ass, she would have been my baby.

"Mama?" I murmur as I watch Brent's eyes meet mine. Her mouth snaps closed.

She stands but doesn't take my hand. I don't let it bother me. I'll have her beneath me soon enough. Her hand, mouth, and cunt filled with my cock before she can even blink.

I load them up in the dirty pickup truck that I usually only use in the winter. I, along with most of the other brothers, leave our winter vehicles here at the clubhouse all spring and summer long, until the snow comes and we can't ride.

The drive to my place is quiet. I can practically taste the nerves pouring off of Brentlee, but I can't seem to find any words for her. I want to reassure her that everything will be okay, but I can't. Nothing sounds right in my own head. So I keep my mouth shut and drive.

I pull into my driveway a few minutes later, and Brentlee gasps next to me.

"This is your house?" she asks, turning to face me.

My eyes roam over her face, and when they lock in on hers, I fuckin' melt.

Those honey eyes own me.

Always have. Always will.

"Yeah," I grumble as I swing the door open. My whole body stills when I feel her hand on my forearm.

"Thank you, Bates. Thank you *so* much," she says, her voice deep and raspy, just the way I remember it. The sound goes straight to my dick.

"C'mon, baby," I murmur, sliding out of the truck and walking to the front porch.

The house. *My* house. I bought it after the fight with Fury about living with LeeLee when he was in the pen. When I lived with her, I discovered that I liked having a place to unwind, a place that was away from the club and the drama that comes with it.

This house is away from town, out in the country. I own the ten acres of land that surrounds the house on all sides. The house is a little three-bedroom country home, complete with a wraparound porch. Only thing I need are some big ass rocking chairs to complete the country vibe.

"It's exactly what I always imagined," Brentlee whispers under her breath behind me.

We talked about getting a place of our own one day, away from town, away from everybody. A place where we could cocoon ourselves in our own little world. I know she's recalling our dream as she takes in the surroundings.

"I ain't done much to the inside. We'll have to get a bed for the princess and some shit like that. I don't have much furniture or anything. It's a blank canvas for you, Brent," I mutter.

She stays silent as she walks inside of the living room. I chance a look back at her and watch as tears stream down her face. I make my way over to her and cup her cheek with my hand.

"Brentlee," I mutter. She sucks in her bottom lip.

"It's so perfect, Bates. It's everything we ever talked about. I ruined my whole life and here you are, living your dream," she sobs.

I want to hug her, but I don't. Affection isn't something I've handed out a lot since I left her. Instead, I look down at her before I speak.

"It made me think of you, Brent. That's why I bought it. Everything I do is for you," I murmur.

"Mama, don't cwy," the little voice at my knees says.

"I'm okay, honey. They're happy tears," she says, stepping away from me and wiping her eyes before leaning down to be at Stella's level.

"What do you say to Mr. Bates for letting us stay here with him?" she asks.

The little girl looks up at me, scrunching her turned up nose. "Do I get my own room?" Stella asks. I hold back a laugh, nodding. "With Elsa sheets?"

"Stella!" Brentlee scolds.

"You want Elsa sheets, princess? Whatever they are, they're yours, pretty girl," I offer, watching as she rewards me with a huge, beaming, beautiful smile—a smile that looks exactly like her mama's.

"Bates," Brentlee murmurs. I step in her space, my body almost touching hers.

"Think she'll be goin' through enough shit, Brent. She wants some fuckin' Elsa sheets, she can have 'em," I inform her.

I watch as Brent sucks her bottom lip between her teeth. *Fuck,* I want that lip in my own mouth. I need to get away from her before I fuck her into next week right in front of her daughter.

Instead of fucking her like I want, I show them the place. It isn't much, more like completely bare, but its mine. I hope that it's good enough for Brentlee.

I drove by the house she shared with her husband and it was big and perfect on the outside. This little place isn't perfect, never will be, but I hope she can be happy here with me.

"It's untainted, untarnished, and better than I could have ever imagined," Brentlee says softly as she wraps her hand around my forearm. "This whole place feels like a home."

I tell the girls to relax and take a nap while I set up delivery of a bed for Stella. In all honesty, I need some fuckin' time to myself.

I hate that they've gone through hell, but I don't deny that a part of me is fuckin' pleased as shit they are now here.

Soon, they'll both me mine, too.

chapter two

Brentlee

This can't be real.

It has to be a dream.

I hold Stella in my arms as she drifts off to sleep in Bates' queen sized bed. I close my eyes, imagining that if he were in here with me, he'd have to hold me close. He'd practically be on top of me just to fit in it together. I suppress the shiver that threatens to roll through my body.

He looks good, too. *Damn good.*

The love of my life just strolled in and saved me.

Bates Lukin. The man of my dreams.

I've just turned my life completely upside down, leaving everything I know, all of my familiarity and my family. I'm running away from my husband and my parents; running and hiding, and so damn scared.

I know that leaving Scotty wasn't a mistake, I'll never think that it was, but I don't know how I'm going to provide for my daughter, or what will happen in the next hour, let alone next week or next year.

My heart feels like it's beating a thousand miles a minute, and Bates, oh god, *Bates*. He's here to watch my fall, the crash and burn of my life. He's the one to help pick up my pieces.

I can't let myself fall for him.

Having him and losing him again would kill me.

Completely decimate me.

I'll take the help, because I would be a fool to turn it down. I'm too desperate for that, and my daughter means too much to me to refuse it. I also can't put my sister and her children in danger. So this—I'll take this help he's offering, but nothing else.

I can't think about his huge body; how his arms bulge with muscles I have yet to see; how his solid chest fills out his tight t-shirt, or how absolutely huge his legs look. I can't think about how firm his ass is, or how his beard would feel caressing my body.

I *definitely* can't think about his lips and how I already know what they feel like on my entire body.

Nope.

I can't think about him at all.

Not like that.

Not ever.

"Babe." A voice startles me from my sleep and I sit straight up, completely disoriented for a moment before my eyes land on the hazel ones of Bates.

I quickly look down at Stella, who is sprawled out asleep on the bed. I quietly slide out from between the sheets and quickly walk toward the door, squeezing past Bates, who gently closes the bedroom door behind me.

"What's up?" I ask, my voice scratchy from sleep.

"I, uh, I got a twin mattress, headboard and footboard comin'. It had a matching dresser and nightstand, so I got that, too. It'll be here in about thirty minutes. Then we can go and get her sheets and shit," he informs me. I blink once.

"Where am I going to sleep? I thought we would be sharing a bed?" I ask, completely confused. I can't even process what he's said about the dresser and nightstand.

"You'll be in my bed, Brent, where you belong," Bates announces. I stare at him, slack jawed.

"Are you *crazy*?" I hiss.

"You walked back into my life and I'm not letting you go, Brentlee. You're mine. You've been mine since you were fourteen years old," he informs. It floors me.

What the hell?

"You *are* crazy. I'm not going from one crazy man to another."

Bates growls and wraps his hand around the back of my neck. His sudden move makes me flinch and I downcast my eyes in an automatic response.

"Look at me," he commands.

Bates' voice is deep and low, his hand still around the back of my neck, and his chest now pressed against mine. I can feel his hard body touching every part of me.

"Your mine. I'll never lay a hand on you, Brent. I'll never hurt you like he did. *Ever*. I'll take care of you, the way I was always meant to. I ain't gonna fuck you tonight, or even tomorrow, but know that I will. We'll be together, eventually, and we'll be happy. Just gotta get you to good again, *tigritsa*," he murmurs as his fingers massage the back of my neck.

Tigress.

I haven't been a tigress in years—too many years.

"I am not a tigress anymore." I say the words in a whisper, unable to recall the girl that he used to call his *tigritsa*.

"You will be, Brent. You will be again. If I have to kill myself to make you that strong woman, I will. You will always be my *tigritsa*. Always," he says, his eyes pinned on mine, and his lips mere inches from my mouth.

I want him to *kiss* me, to *touch* me, to *own* me again. But I can't let him. It would be a disaster, and I can't allow myself to be hurt anymore. *I'm done.* I'm done with men and I'm done being hurt.

A knock on the door has me jumping out of his arms. Bates doesn't say a word. He smiles before he walks over to the front door, then checks the peephole before pulling it open. My eyes widen when I see a group of three men in matching leather vests standing on the porch.

"Hey, Brentlee," Johnny Williams says with a grin.

I haven't seen him in years. He looks good, really good. I slept with him once, when I was in high school. By the look in his eyes, I can tell he hasn't forgotten. His gaze drags down my body and he licks his bottom lip before Bates steps right in front of him.

"We gonna have a problem, brother?" he asks Johnny.

"You claimin' her?" Johnny asks.

I wish I could see their faces, but Bates' back is to me and standing directly in front of Johnny. His mass covers Johnny's entire body.

"Yeah, she's mine, so keep your fuckin' eyes to your goddamn self," Bates says. I suck in a breath. *His*. What does that even mean? I can't be and I won't be.

"Better patch her ass if you know what's good for you, then. Lotta brothers would like inside there," Johnny laughs. I close my eyes tightly.

I should be disgusted by his words; I should be offended, but I'm not. He remembers me the way I was after Bates left me—he remembers the *slut*.

"Just unload the fuckin' truck," Bates growls before turning to me. "You stay away from him," he grunts, his eyes focused on mine.

I don't tell him the truth. I don't tell him that after he left, I gave myself to anyone and everyone for years. The whore of Bonners Ferry High, until Scotty came around.

I quietly move to the corner of the living room as the men start bringing furniture in. My mouth falls open at the sight of the all-white dresser, nightstand, and bed. It's beautiful, and it's so fitting for my little Stella. It all looks brand new, too.

I can't believe this man.

I choke back tears as the men set the furniture up and then quietly leave. Bates informed them that Stella was still napping, so they were virtually soundless. I didn't know four big ass bikers could *be* so quiet.

Once the men leave, I follow Bates back into the bedroom.

It is so dainty and feminine. Perfect for my little baby girl.

"Bates," I gasp before I turn to face him. "It's lovely."

"Anything for you two. Whatever I can give you, I will," he mutters, stepping closer to me.

I hold my breath as his finger trails my tear tracks. I can't stop myself from crying. It's all too much. The house of my dreams, the man of my dreams, and he's giving my daughter something that's beautiful—a space to call her own and something pretty in the midst of all the ugliness surrounding us.

"I don't know what to say," I whisper as my eyes search his, finding nothing but that sweet adoration that I don't deserve shining in them.

"Don't say anything," he shrugs.

"Bates, you're doing so much for us, and you don't have to."

"You're LeeLee's sister, my president's sister-in-law, and you're mine," he smirks, as if it explains everything he's just done for Stella and me.

"I'll repay you, I swear," I offer.

"I don't want money," he grins.

"What do you want, then?"

"Say you'll be mine again, one day. Not today, not tomorrow, but one day. Don't give up on there being an *us* again just because you married that asshole," he says softly.

The gruffness of earlier is gone and only sweet, soft, murmured words surround me. I want to forget about everything and be that woman for him, that girl that I was, but that's not possible.

"I'm not giving up on you. I don't want anybody right now. Maybe not for a long time. I need to learn how to stand on my own two feet, not just for me, but for Stella, too," I explain.

Bates nods once before he leans in and presses his lips to my forehead. His lips are warm and the contact comforting.

"Mama," Stella's little voice breaks through our tender moment and I step away from Bates to see her walking toward me, rubbing sleep out of her eyes. I scoop her up and cuddle her close for a moment, relishing in the feel of her sweetness.

"Did you sleep well?" I ask as she tucks her face into my neck, a move she's done since she was a tiny baby. A move I love.

"Long nap," she mumbles. I laugh softly.

"Did you see your new room?" I ask. Her head pops up, her curly blonde hair bouncing as her head moves from side-to-side, taking in the space.

"It so pwetty. Elsa sheets," she squeals. I can't help but smile, and I turn to Bates, who's lips are tipped in a smirk as he looks on at Stella's excitement.

"Let's get you to the store for these damn sheets, *malyshka*," Bates chuckles.

I watch as my daughter beams up at him with her dimpled smile. He's already won her over with just the promise of sheets.

"What does it mean?" I ask after I send Stella to the bathroom and start to gather my things to leave.

"Baby girl, little girl," he states, grabbing his phone and keys.

I had forgotten this about him. Bates' father is Russian. Though Bates himself doesn't speak fluently, he knows a few words. I was always his *tigritsa*, his tigress. Now my daughter, *malyshka*, baby girl. It warms a part of my heart. I don't want it to, but it does, and he knows it.

He knows how his whispered words in Russian affect me. No woman in her right mind could ignore *that*.

Once Stella is out of the restroom, we leave. I'm afraid to be seen in public. Our town is small, *miniscule,* and if Scotty doesn't see me himself—someone he knows will.

I can't stop my leg from shaking in the truck, or my fingers from twisting together with nervousness. I don't want him to find me. Not yet, and honestly, not ever. Though I know that won't ever come true. I have to file legal divorce papers, and he'll know where I am after that happens.

I've looked up the process. It's daunting, but I don't want a damn thing from the man. Not spousal support, *nothing.*

However, I know that he'll fight me with custody of Stella. He'll probably win, too. The asshole. Rich lawyer asshat.

"I'm taking you to the next town, babe. Stop stressing," Bates calmly states.

"You are?" I ask, turning to him.

"If he knows you're gone, he's on the hunt," Bates says. I nod.

Yeah, he'll be on the hunt, all right. *The hunt to bring me home and kill me.* His possession. His punching bag. His *whore* of a wife.

"He'll hunt," I whisper, turning to look out the window.

"He won't get you. Either of you," Bates grunts.

"He'll get custody. He has money and his family is very influential. I'll lose her," I say, not turning away from the window, but instead watching the scenery pass by in a blur.

"Then we'll fight. My *tigritsa*, you will fight for her. *We* will fight for her," he says.

I whip my head around in surprise. "Why would you fight?" I ask in disbelief. She is not his daughter—she's mine.

"No person should live with that monster, especially an innocent child. I will fight for her because she deserves to be with her mother, who will treat her with love and kindness. I will also fight for her because she is yours, and she makes you happy. Your happiness means everything to me, Brent," he says, blowing me completely away.

I open my mouth to respond, but am interrupted by the sound of his phone ringing. I watch as he gives one-word answers and his eyes turn black at whatever the person on the other end is saying. Then, he turns slightly toward me and I gasp. He looks scary, mean, and rough—all rolled into one giant package.

"Got eyes on him. He's home from the office, and apparently he's called the police," he grunts as he continues to drive.

"You're taking on too much with us," I murmur as he turns into a parking spot at Target.

"Never. Nothing is too much for my girls," he mutters before he slides out of the truck.

I can now see past the hardness, the haunting from earlier. Sitting beside me, promising me everything I could want, is the Bates from my childhood.

My breath completely leaves my body.

Nothing is too much for my girls.

My girls.

Sniper

I walk into *Target*, my hand wrapped around Brentlee's. She has Stella in her other hand, and I can't help the feeling of pride bursting through my chest knowing these girls are with me. *They're mine.* They were always meant to be mine.

Doesn't matter that that piece of shit is Stella's sperm donor—she's mine. One look at her little, round face, and I've fallen hard for her. I take my hand from Brentlee's and slide it to her lower back. She's a bit fuller than she used to be, but still long and lean; her tits are a little bigger, and so is her ass. *Motherhood looks damn fuckin' good on her.*

I walk straight over to a cart and start to push it, but a little hand tugs on my leather cut. I look down and see Stella looking up at me with wide eyes.

"I wide," she pleads. I can't help the smile that forms on my lips.

"I'll get her," Brentlee says, but I bend down and pick the *malyshka* up and set her in the cart carefully. She rewards me with a big, bright smile.

"Okay, gorgeous, let's get your sheets, yeah?"

"Yes," she hisses as she giggles.

With one hand on the cart, I snag Brent's hand with the other. Together, all three of us walk through the store.

I have never been one for shopping—*ever*. I fuckin' hate it. With Brentlee and Stella, I thought I would despise it. Maybe later in life I will; but for now, I'm in awe. Stella is a ball of excitement. Everything she sees is new and she lights up every single time her eyes land on something she wants. Just one sweep down the little girl bedroom aisle and the cart is full.

"Bates, this is all way too much," Brentlee says as she holds a purple lamp with hanging beads in her hand.

"It matches the bedding," I shrug.

"Just keep a tally so I can pay you back once Fury puts me to work somewhere," she mumbles.

"What I buy, you never have to pay me back for, Brent.

I'm buyin' it because I want to, and for no other reason," I state before I watch her mouth fall open.

I don't let her say another word. Instead, I just walk away.

"*Bates*," she hisses once she catches up to me.

"Let's get Stella some movies and then you need to get whatever it is you need. I know that little suitcase couldn't even fit half of your bathroom shit in it. Don't give me any lip, either," I grunt as her hand goes straight to her hip, ready to give me some of that tigress she carries deep down inside of her.

"Thank you," she whispers instead of bitching me out.

It's not satisfying.

I want her attitude. At this point, *I fucking crave it*. I want her back to *her*. Back to the girl I remember; the girl who had fire in her eyes and said *whateverthefuck* she wanted to say, consequences be damned.

The rest of the shopping trip is quick. Brentlee fills the cart with lotions, creams, soaps, and a few clothing essentials for both her and Stella. She's trying to be low maintenance, but I know her.

Brentlee likes expensive things, she always has. It has never bothered me, and it never will; but I'll let her make this play for now. When she's back in my bed, underneath me and completely mine again, then I'll make sure that she knows she gets whatever she *wants*. Whatever she *desires* is hers. I'll give her the fuckin' world on a platter.

Fuck, I'm such a pussy.

I grin.

Only for this girl, though—always for this girl.

chapter three

Brentlee

Bates goes through a McDonald's drive thru for dinner. I cringe at the thought of putting the salad that I ordered in my mouth, but Stella is as happy as can be with her chicken nugget meal and toy.

I look out of the side of my eyes as Bates takes a big bite of his burger and chews. Like a total creeper, I watch his throat work the food down and I find myself getting hot.

Fuck, even his throat turns me on.

How am I going to live with him and not throw myself at him?

I'm a lost cause. Destined to be beholden to a man the rest of my life. Taken care of and owing men, never being independent.

I don't want to be that, though. I want to be a woman Stella can be proud of. That is another reason I can't just hop into bed with Bates. I don't want to be that woman who hops from man to man. I want to be a better person.

Even if I strip at the *Devil's Club*, I want not only Stella to be proud of me, but I want to be proud of myself. Stripping isn't the best feel-good job I could have, but it will put money in our bank account and it will help me be able to afford a decent lawyer—which I'll need if I stand a chance at fighting Scotty Corbin.

"Eat, *tigritsa*," Bates murmurs. I turn back to my warm salad. It will probably make me sick later, but I'm starving, so I eat.

The hour drive back to Bates' country home goes by quickly. Once we are back, I get to work, washing Stella's new Elsa bedding. Then, I begin to put all of our purchases away. Bates brings all of my bathroom items into the bedroom and drops them on the bed.

"I'll just take these to the other bathroom," I mutter. He wraps his hand loosely around my bicep to stop me.

"This is your room and your bathroom," he says.

"No, I told you, that's not happening," I state firmly. Bates just smiles and shakes his head.

"I know it's not happening—*yet*. But this will still be your space, Brent. I'll take the couch for now. Better if there's another barrier between you and that asshole anyway," he says, his eyes completely focused on me. Too focused.

He can see too much of me.

How badly I want him, how lost I am, and no doubt how hurt I've been.

I nod, unable to speak. I spend the rest of the evening with Stella. I get her room all put together and I bathe her and read her a story before I tuck her in for the night.

"Mama?" she asks as I am standing up from her new bed.

"Yes, sweet girl?"

"I wike Bates. I wike it here. Can we stay foreva?" she pleads with wide eyes before she yawns.

"We can stay as long as you like, sweet girl," I whisper, trying to hold back my tears.

"Good," she mumbles before her eyes close and she passes out asleep.

I leave her room as I wipe the tears from my eyes.

I walk into the living room, heading toward the kitchen for some water, when I hear Bates on the phone.

"They're mine, brother. I'm claimin' both of them. That fucker can try to get them, but I'll just gut him if he even attempts to take them from me," I hear him growl. I press myself against the wall, trying to disappear.

Claiming us—this is the second time he's said it. I don't know exactly what it means, but I think I do, and I'm sure it's not what I want right now. Maybe not ever.

"Thought I'd be okay with it, but the more I think about it, I can't handle that shit, brother," he says before he drops the phone on the coffee table a few seconds later.

"C'mon out, *tigritsa.*"

I step away from the wall and into the living room.

"You don't want me stripping?" I ask.

Instead of answering me, he takes my wrist gently with his fingers and tugs me into his lap. I shiver when his fingertips run up my spine and tangle in my hair.

"Thought I could be okay with men watching you as long

as you came home to me. I can't. Just thinking about any man seeing your gorgeous body makes me want to murder and maim," he explains, his eyes dead serious and focused on mine.

"I need to work, Bates. I need money. I need independence," I explain. He nods in understanding.

"I know you do. I could take care of you, but you wouldn't be happy with that. Baby, I want you so fuckin' happy you couldn't imagine being in any other man's bed the rest of your life," he murmurs as his nose slides along mine.

I feel that way right now.

I've always felt that way with him.

I have never been as happy in my entire life than in this man's arms. At fourteen years old or today. It is as if time stood still for our bodies, our hearts, and our souls.

I just wish I could allow myself to have him, and to keep him.

"What will I do then?" I ask on a shaky breath.

"At the clubhouse we always need someone to clean and run the bar. Get orders together, serve the guys, and clean up. You'd be the safest there, surrounded by brothers constantly," he says as his eyes stay focused on mine.

"Cleaning and running the bar, that's all I would have to do for them?" I ask.

I have images of me having to *service* them in other ways running through my head. I know that they keep women around whose whole job is to screw them. At least that's the rumor I've heard throughout town.

"You askin' if you have to fuck them?" he grinds out through clenched teeth.

I don't answer. Instead, I stare at him, waiting for an answer.

"You think I would really hand you off to be fucked by dozens of guys when I just told you I couldn't handle anybody else *seeing* your naked body?" he balks.

I shrug, avoiding his penetrating gaze as I look down at my shoes.

"Baby, any of my brothers even looked at you funny, I'd lay them out. Nobody will ever touch you but me, ever again," he murmurs, tugging on the back of my hair to tip my head back so that my eyes meet his.

"Why do you still want me? I'm a mess," I admit. He grins.

"Because you're my *tigritsa*. You aren't ready for more yet; you've made that clear, and I'll wait for you. I'll always wait for you," he breathes. His hot breath fans my face and I know that if I leaned in just a few inches, our lips would touch.

I can't do that, though. Kissing him would lead to me spreading my legs for him. I can't. *I won't*. No matter how badly I want it.

"What if it takes years for me to be able to be yours again, Bates? What if I never heal?" I ask, voicing my fears.

I don't know that I can ever trust another man again. I don't know that I *want* to ever trust one again.

"Then I'll wait forever."

I don't respond. I can't. It is all too much. Instead, I choose to ignore his words. I'll deal with them... *never*.

"What will I do with Stella?" I ask as I stand and straighten my shirt.

"LeeLee can watch her can't she?" he asks.

"I don't want her in danger. He'll know exactly how to get to her, and he could hurt Kent in the process," I explain as I chew on my bottom lip.

"Got it. LeeLee used to have this woman, Tammy, watch Bear when she worked nights at the club. He'd never find her at Tammy's. She has nothing to do with the club, just an old neighbor of LeeLee's. She's a great lady," he explains. I nod. It could work.

"You trust her?" I ask.

I have never left Stella alone with anybody except my parents. Not even with Scotty. I haven't trusted him since the day I married him. No way would I leave my baby alone with him.

"Yeah, she's a good lady—grandmotherly and very sweet. Bear loves her, and LeeLee trusts her completely," he explains.

"Okay," I say, nodding my head.

"Go to bed, yeah?" Bates mutters.

I don't say another word. *I need sleep.* I can't think about Bates or my life for a moment longer.

I change into an oversized shirt and leave my jeans in a pile on the floor before I crawl into Bates' bed and slide beneath his cool sheets. My eyes flutter closed the second my head hits the pillow, and I fall into a dreamless sleep. Thoughts of Scotty, of his abuse and the fear I hold, disintegrate.

I am safe.

Stella is safe.

Bates has us, and no way would he ever let anything happen to my girl and me. Of that, I am certain. Even if I can never fully give myself to him as a lover. I can't be certain that he'll stay if I give myself to him ever again. He ran from me, and now I have a child, running from the both of us would damage not only me, but Stella too. He was right when he said she'd been through enough, she has.

I will always have faith in Bates as a protector. He's changed, he's hardened, and through all that, I can still see that there is that boy he used to be, all those years ago, deep down, somewhere.

Sniper

I rub my hand over my face.

Fuck.

This girl breaks me.

Everything inside of me is calling to claim her, but she isn't ready. Not even close to it. I don't know if she ever will be. At this point, all signs are pointing to *never*. She has to heal and get free from that fucking dickwad's hold over her. I don't know what I'll do if she never lets me back in there. I want to believe that I could talk her into giving herself to me again, but she's so fuckin' damaged right now.

I'll be there for her every step of the way, anyway she wants me.

Now, if I could only tell my dick that. He's ready to be buried inside of his home—*Brentlee's body*.

My phone rings and I frown at the name flashing on my screen.

"Fury," I say.

It's late. Since he's been home from prison, he doesn't stay up late. He's always home with his wife and family.

"He came lookin' for her. She was right," he mumbles into the phone. I already know he's called the cops to his place; Vault informed me earlier tonight when he did a check on her old place.

"And?" I ask, wondering what's next.

Scotty's an abusive piece of shit with ties to people high up in the community. He not only doesn't want to look bad, he doesn't strike me as a guy who would easily give up on something he thought was his.

Win at all costs.

Not that I'm any different, I just won't beat Brent's ass to get her to come to heel.

"Told him I didn't know why the fuck he was lookin' for her here since we ain't seen or talked to her in six fuckin' years," Fury grunts. "He didn't buy it. He's suspicious and I wouldn't be surprised if he shows at the club or the clubhouse soon."

"I'll be ready for him," I grunt.

"No, Snipe, this guy is an asshole. You'll be no good to Brent in jail, trust me. We play this smart and legal. I already contacted a lawyer today. We meet with him tomorrow in Boise," Fury says. It shocks the shit out of me.

"That's almost a full day's drive," I point out.

"We're all goin'. Call it an overdue family fuckin' vacation. Kent wants to take the kids to the zoo or some shit. We're leaving at eight in the morning. Make sure you got your girls ready and we'll meet at your place and take off from there. I think that fucker has eyes on my house just waiting for Brent to show. I ain't givin' him a chance to catch her," Fury growls.

I know he's doing this for Kentlee, but he's also doing it because he's watched a young girl get beat the fuck down and that shit ain't right.

"Eight, we'll be ready," I say. "She isn't workin' at the *Devil's Club*," I announce.

"Didn't think you'd allow that shit," Fury chuckles from the other end of the phone.

I sigh, because it's so hypocritical, since I'm the one who pushed his woman into working as a cocktail waitress at the strip club.

"She's going to manage the bar at the clubhouse. Clean and order booze and shit like that. She'll be safer inside there than anywhere else," I say, waiting for Fury to deny me.

"What're you gonna do when a brother wants to tap that?" he asks with a hint of amusement in his voice.

I'm not fucking amused in the slightest.

"She's claimed. She's mine. Nobody touches her but me," I growl.

"She wearing a patch saying she's yours? She gonna have your name inked on her body?"

"Doesn't matter, brother. She's been mine since she was a kid. Any other man looks at her with anything other than sister affection, I'll kill him. *Slowly*," I state. Fury bursts out laughing.

"You're a fuckin' goner for this bitch," he says.

"Always have been," I murmur into the phone.

"All right, brother. I get it. Got the other sister spread out in my own bed," he says laughing.

"Brother," I groan trying not to picture LeeLee spread out in any bed.

"Fuckin' fact. Pussy's the best I ever had; figure that's a family trait, since you ain't had it in a decade and you're ready to give up every other cunt on earth for her without a second thought," he says, laughing uncontrollably, like he's a goddamned comedian. *Asshole*.

"See you tomorrow, *fucker*," I grind out, hanging up the phone without waiting for a response.

I stand up from the couch and start to shut down the

house. I check every single door and window before I go to the coat closet and open my safe. I didn't want to have any guns just lying around with Stella in the house, but I won't be able to get to my safe in the middle of the night very quickly, so I'll need my handgun available. No way is that asshole getting the jump on me. I take my favorite nine mill out of my safe before locking it again and shoving the gun in the back of my waistband.

I go back to the couch and sit down. I'm not tired yet. Horny, but not tired. If I could sink myself inside of Brentlee, I would in a hot minute; but I'm not about to fuck up my chance with her.

This is a second chance to make her permanently mine. I have to play it right. I have to make her *want* me, not *need* me. She's been through enough hell, and I want to give her a taste of heaven.

I hope I don't fuck up.

I'm not that boy I once was.

I'm not good or kind anymore.

I'm rough.

I'm raw.

I need things now that I never needed back then.

chapter four

Brentlee

I feel my body being shaken awake and I suck in a breath before I open my eyes in a panic.

Shit, I missed my alarm and I'm late making Scotty's breakfast.

Once my eyes focus on the figure in front of me, I let out a sigh.

It's Bates.

Not Scotty.

I lift my shaking hand to my eyes and moan.

"You okay?" he asks, concern etched on his face.

"Yeah, you startled me," I semi-lie, sitting up.

"Get ready and pack an overnight bag. We're taking a

road trip today," Bates orders with a grin.

"Road trip? To where?" I ask, my heart beginning to beat quickly in my chest.

"Boise. We're all going with LeeLee, Fury, and the kids. Fury set a meeting up with a good lawyer and then we're just going to chill, spend some time at the zoo with the kids," he says with a shrug, like he isn't telling me something beautiful.

A *family* day.

A day with my sister and her babies.

Tears prick my eyes and I suck in my trembling bottom lip.

"He really did that? For me?" I ask as tears completely fill my eyes and then begin to fall.

"Yeah, baby. He loves LeeLee and she loves you. Get ready because you've got a huge pack of bikers at your back now. I'm making damn sure that asshole is never touching you again. We start the legal way," he says. It sounds as if there is more to that sentence, but I don't want to know what it is.

I don't even want to think about Bates doing something illegal for me. Something that could take him away from me. I wouldn't survive it. *God, I am so pathetic and needy.* I can't allow myself to feel this way—ever again. But I don't know how to stop it.

I quickly shower and pack a small overnight bag before I dress in a pair of cream shorts and a dark blue tank top. I feel lighter today than I have since I was a teenager. I can feel Scotty's heavy cloud of doom lifting away from me, and it makes me smile as I style my hair in the mirror.

Having Bates in my life again is a wonderful thing. Even if nothing ever develops between us, I'm just thankful to be away from Scotty—to have Stella away from that horrible man. I hope that whatever this attorney says today, I can have some reassurance that Stella will be safe. In the end, she's the only one that truly matters to me.

I grab my purse and sling it over my shoulder before walking into the living room. I expect to see Stella sitting in front of the television watching a movie and Bates in the kitchen, maybe. What I don't expect to see is Stella and Bates sitting next to each other at the kitchen table, eating breakfast and talking.

"I wike your big muscles," Stella whispers as she stares at Bates' bulging bicep in awe.

Jesus, I like his big muscles, too. In fact, I'd like to trace them with my tongue.

"Thanks, *malyshka*," he murmurs gently.

"How much do you eat to have muscles that big? Mama says I have to eat to get stwong," she explains. I put my hand in front of my mouth to keep from giggling at her question.

"A lot. I eat a lot. It took me a long time to grow," he explains to my sweet girl.

"*Wow*," she says, still in awe.

I take a step toward them and Bates' head pops up to see me in the kitchen. His eyes soften as they graze over my body. I feel the heat from his gaze touch all of my exposed skin, as if his fingers are touching me instead of his eyes.

It's too much.

The lingering looks are already driving me into sexual overdrive, and I'm only on day two of living with him. I can't let this happen between us. I'm not the same sweet girl I was at fourteen; and by the haunting look in his eyes, he is nowhere near the *boy-man* he was back then, either.

It will never work between us. At one time, he was the

only man I ever knew. He wouldn't want me now if he knew the truth, if he knew how many men I have been with since he left me. Maybe I'll tell him so that he can get rid of this infatuation he seems to have with me.

"Ready, babe?" Bates asks, breaking me of my thoughts.

"Yeah," I murmur as I take a step toward Stella. "Time to get dressed sweet girl."

I take Stella by the hand and lead her into the brand new princess bedroom, which Bates went over and above on, and I dress her quickly. I can't look at the décor in this space. The gestures are too sweet, too soft, too perfect. If I even think about the kind hearted way he took us shopping last night, or the way his eyes lit up every time Stella got excited about any little thing in the store—I'll throw myself at him.

Once I dress Stella and pack her a little overnight bag, we walk hand-in-hand into the living room to wait for Fury and Kentlee. I hold my breath as Bates steps toward me, his big body crowding my space, making my stomach quiver with want.

God, I *want* him so badly.

I want him more than anything I have ever wanted in my life, but I know one taste will never do. I'll want to keep him and then he'll break me again. I'm destined to be the girl who is forever broken. I don't deserve his kindness, his lust, or his affections. If he only knew. If he only knew the truth.

I jump when there is a loud pounding on the door and watch in shock when Bates pulls a gun out from the waistband of his jeans. He holds his finger in front of his lips, signaling me to stay quiet. I squeeze Stella's hand and look down to see that she is staring at Bates with awe. I tip my head to the side and watch as Bates looks through the peephole. His shoulders immediately relax.

I let out the breath I had been holding with relief when the door swings open and Fury's huge body fills the space. For an older guy, he's smokin' hot. *Scary as shit*, but smokin'. Less than thirty seconds later, I watch as my sister squeezes past him and starts to run toward me.

A peace washes over me as Kentlee's arms wrap around me.

My big sister.

A hug from my big sister.

Timeless and epic all wrapped together.

"Brent," she whispers as her body shakes.

She's shorter than I am by at least five inches, but she's comforting, soft and warm—and *home*.

My big sister was my best friend for so long when I was little. I've looked up to her my entire life. I wanted to be exactly like her and failed miserably at every single turn. She is the best, bravest woman I have ever known.

"Kent," I murmur relishing in her hold.

"We gotta go," a gruff voice says from across the room. I lift my head to see Fury standing, uncomfortably, still in the doorway.

"We're going to get through all of this, Brent," Kentlee says, ignoring her husband's command to leave.

"I hope so," I say, not convinced in the slightest that I will survive this split from Scotty.

"We are. These big assholes won't have it any other way," she says with a wide smile.

I can't help myself, I break out into a fit of giggles at her words. I hear both Fury and Bates grunt from the other side of the room, but that only makes us laugh harder. The situation isn't funny by any means, but what's the saying — *laughter is the best medicine.*

I need that medicine like you would not believe.

Sniper

Brentlee takes my breath away on a normal day, but when she's laughing — *speechless*. I watch as she reunites with her sister. Years in the making. Beauty surrounds them. Not only are they gorgeous women, but this reunion is beautiful as well. I readjust myself just to make sure my cock is still attached, because apparently I'm turning into a woman with all this estrogen that has surrounded me the past two days.

"We need to jet now," Fury grumbles beside me. I lift my chin.

"Girls," I say, loud enough for them to hear me.

I focus on Brent and dip my chin. Her back straightens and she solemnly nods before taking Stella's hand in hers and bringing her a step forward.

"Stella, this is your Auntie Kentlee," she announces. Stella looks up at LeeLee in awe and then launches herself at Kentlee's thighs. She wraps her little arms around Kentlee tightly before she speaks.

"Thank you for saving my mommy," Stella whispers.

Beside me Fury clears his throat and I follow suit. To have Brentlee give thanks is one thing, but to see this tiny *malyshka* prove her understanding of the situation is a completely different story. It just proves to me that their situation was beyond horrific. It was probably exactly like my own childhood.

I could be pissed at Brentlee for bringing a baby into that environment, or I could praise her for leaving—something my own mother never did. I could hold my own shit over her, but I wouldn't do that, not when it's my fault she was even in that situation.

Had I never left her, had I come back for her, had I been strong enough to keep her as mine — none of this shit would be happening now. She would have never married that prick. She'd have always been mine. She would have never been hurt and her baby, it would have been my baby, not that piece of shit's.

Fury and I gather the girls and put them in his big ass SUV. Normally, I wouldn't let anybody drive me, anywhere; but I know Kentlee and Brentlee need some time together, and I didn't want to split them up between vehicles.

Once we take off down the road toward Boise, I chance a glance back at the girls, at *my* girls.

They *are* mine.

Stella's little blonde curls and sweet smile.

Brentlee's long, straight, dark hair and lithe body.

Mine.

"You're fucked, brother," Fury murmurs beside me. A fact he's already pointed out to me, just last night.

"Yup," I admit.

"Magic fuckin' pussy, I swear to Christ," he chuckles.

I ignore him. Brentlee's already made it clear I won't be getting in there anytime soon. I don't want to push her, but I don't want her to friend-zone me either. Something I could easily see her trying. No, I'm giving her a few weeks then I'm stakin' my claim on her body, and she's not going to have a fuckin' choice. I only hope she comes willingly to me. It'll be a fuck've a lot easier than me forcin' the issue.

"He's had someone watching our place. You cannot come over to visit," I hear Kentlee whispering to Brent in the backseat. It doesn't ease my mind on the Scotty issue. I want that fucker buried and gone.

"He won't give up," Brentlee says. I can hear the fear in her voice.

I wish I could tell her to stand up and believe that she's strong. She is so fuckin' strong. Her walking out of that door and asking Fury for help, getting herself and her daughter out of that environment, it shows that she has more strength than most women. More strength than my own mother, that's for fuckin' sure.

"Let him come at us guns blazin'," Fury barks loudly.

"*Pierce*," Kentlee hisses.

"I ain't walkin' on eggshells, baby girl," he announces. I almost laugh at his *I-don't-give-a-shit* attitude.

"Well, maybe not in front of the kids then," Kentlee mutters.

"Stella knows what she's seen. She's not dumb. Just proved that shit not an hour ago. That fuckwad wants to come at me and my family, he'll get exactly what he's beggin' for. No bones about it. Brentlee and Stella are under our protection. They're family," he states.

"Fury," Brentlee chokes out.

I can't look back at her. I can't see the tears that I know are streaking down her cheeks. Not because of that piece of shit. Not because she has to rely on people for help. Not because she's penniless and alone. Not because I left her and created this life for her. But because I'm the reason all that fuckin' shit happened to her. The guilt of it all bubbles inside of me.

It's all my fuckin' fault.

Every bruise he ever gave her is my own goddamn fucking fault.

chapter five

Brentlee

Everybody is asleep in the car except for Fury and me. Even Bates is passed out with his head against the passenger window and his mouth slightly agape. He looks younger when he's asleep, softer. Like he hasn't been through hell and back.

"You're teetering on the edge there, darlin'," Fury rumbles.

"What do you mean?" I ask, looking down at my hands.

"You're thinking about running from him."

"I am running from him, you're helping me," I say, confused at his words.

"Not the piece of shit. Sniper. You've got it written all over your face. I know the look. I fuckin' saw that shit in the mirror every day for three goddamn years," he explains. I exhale shakily at his observation.

He's completely correct.

Bates scares the shit out of me.

"It would be better if he discovered I wasn't the one for him. He's living in the past," I coolly remark, not believing a damn word of it myself.

"Bullshit."

"Excuse me?"

"Bullshit, Brentlee. You're scared shitless, as you should be. Snipe ain't the same kid he was before the Marines. I never met that version of him, but I know the man he is now, and sometimes he's fuckin' terrifying. You *should* be scared. But he ain't gonna let you run from him. You gotta know that, right?"

I don't answer him. *I can't*. Fury is right. Bates will never just let me run from him. He's already made it perfectly clear that he wants me, wants a relationship and wants a family. He knows Stella is part of the package and he's accepting of that, accepting of her, and accepting of us. Pushing him away is going to be one of the hardest things I've ever done.

"I am scared, but not of Bates. I'm scared of myself," I admit.

"Are we there yet?" Bear's tired voice calls out from the back of the SUV. He's sleepy and groggy and ready to get the hell out of the car.

I'm thankful he woke up before I confessed just how scared I truly am for myself. How I fear that once Bates discovers just how I behaved when he left me, he won't think of me as his sweet Brentlee anymore.

He'll discover the disgusting, weak woman I am. The de-

pendent woman. No man as big, strong, and capable as him wants some weak, broken woman at his side.

"Yeah, buddy, we're here," Fury says from the front seat. I watch as everybody rustles around, stretching and yawning with the news.

We're in Boise, and now I'm to discover my fate and the fate of my daughter. Will the attorney tell me I'm a lost cause? That I am destined to be under the control of Scotty? And my Stella? Will she be ripped from me and given to that sick fuck?

"I'll go with you," Kentlee offers as we pull in front of the attorney's office. It's a big, tall building, and that in and of itself is intimidating.

"I'm goin'," Bates announces immediately.

"No," I practically yell. "I need to do this on my own."

Fury's eyes meet mine in the rearview mirror and I see what must be his form of pride, possibly, looking back at me. Kentlee wraps her hand around mine and squeezes gently. Bates doesn't say a word. Instead, he gets out of the car and opens my door for me. He's too fucking nice. Way too nice for a person like me.

"Bates," I say once I step out of the car and close the door. I don't need anybody else to hear me. I don't *want* anybody else to hear me.

"You ain't doin' this alone, Brent. That's the end of the discussion," he growls wrapping his hand in mine as he takes a step toward the doors. I plant my feet firmly to the sidewalk and tug my arm back.

"This is my shit, Bates. My problem. I caused it and I'm going to deal with it by myself," I yell.

I look like a crazy person yelling at this bad ass biker in

the middle of the sidewalk. He's in boots, tight jeans, a tighter t-shirt, and his leather cut—I made the mistake of calling it a *vest* while shopping in Target, and he put me in my place on the proper name for it.

"This *was* your shit, you're right. But you're mine now, so it's *our* shit," he announces.

"I'm not yours, Bates," I counter back.

I don't sound convincing, I probably never will when it comes to him. I'll never convince myself that I don't belong to him, because I've belonged to him since I was fourteen years old.

"You're mine. Been mine since I laid eyes on you over ten years ago. I gave you your first kiss, your first orgasm, and I popped your cherry Brent. Ain't no other woman on this earth that's made for me but you, *tigritsa*," he murmurs as his nose slides alongside mine.

Fuck, I have no will power. None. Not when he's close, not when he slides his hands to grab my hips and hold me. Not when his scent surrounds me and his breath fans my face. I melt close to him, pressing my chest against his and tipping my head back to look up and into his eyes.

Fuck.

Those eyes.

Those beautiful, haunted eyes.

"Okay," I say breathlessly.

"There's my girl," he murmurs before he takes his thumb and sweeps it across my bottom lip. I almost touch my tongue to it, just for a taste, but I refrain.

One taste wouldn't be enough.

"Now, let's go and get this shit done with. Fury and LeeLee are going to take the kids out for some food then we'll all crash before an exciting day at the fuckin' zoo tomorrow," Bates grumbles. For some reason, picturing him and Fury at the zoo makes me giggle.

They'll be at one with their animal brethren.

"C'mon," Bates mutters, throwing his arm over my shoulders as we walk toward the big glass doors of the attorney's office.

Walking inside of the building makes me all too aware that I am not dressed properly. Scotty would be furious if he knew I was out in public, let alone walking into a meeting wearing shorts and a tank top. I should care, I really should, but I don't. I'm a mess from the inside out. I don't have to pretend to be anything I'm not anymore.

Maybe I'll just allow myself to be a mess for a while.

We walk up to the receptionist's counter and the perfectly coifed woman behind it widens her eyes in surprise. She must not see bikers and disheveled homeless looking women in here too often. She opens her mouth to speak, but Bates is faster.

"Here to see Stan Jones," he grunts. She presses her red painted lips together with suspicion.

"Do you have an appointment with Mr. Jones?" she asks.

"Nope. But Brentlee Johnson does," he says.

"Brentlee Corbin," I correct before I hear him grunt next to me.

"I'll call Mr. Jones and let him know you're here," she murmurs, picking up her phone.

I step back from the desk and walk over to the reception area. I can't sit down, I've been sitting in the car for hours, but I can't stand still either. So I pace.

"Mr. Jones will see you now," the receptionist calls out.

Bates stands quickly, wrapping his hand around mine.

"Calm down, *tigritsa*," he rasps against my neck before placing a gentle kiss there.

We walk toward the elevator and I hold my breath all the way up to the fifth floor. Once the doors open I see — *Family Law* — printed in bold letters on the wall. I never thought my life would come down to this. Hiding from an abusive piece of shit and visiting an attorney halfway across the state in secret.

An older, clean cut gentleman with a neatly pressed suit is waiting as soon as we turn the corner. He has gray hair and kind, rich brown eyes. I watch as he smiles and brings his hand out to greet us.

"Bates Lukin and Brentlee Corbin, I presume?"

"Yes," I say shakily, taking his hand.

"Yup," Bates grunts, lifting his chin. Mr. Jones just smiles before waving us back to his office.

"Please, sit. Is there anything I can get you to drink before we get started?" he asks. I am taken aback by his kindness.

The only attorneys I know are Scotty, his father, and their colleagues. Not one of them is approachable or kind. They are all intimidating, mean assholes with serious inferiority complexes. They also don't think women have brains or rights. *None of them.*

"No, thank you," I answer for both of us and sit down.

I want this meeting over with. I want the truth quick, fast, and in a hurry. Like a band aide. Just rip the fucker off.

"Tell me the situation. I have to know it all before I can answer any questions or give any advice," he says, getting straight to business. I like that. No fluff and no muss.

I take a deep breath and exhale before I begin. It's going

to be ugly. I tell every single detail of my marriage to the attorney. The mental and physical abuse, the rapes, and then I tell him about his handling of Stella the day before I left.

"Do you have any documentation of any of this to back you up? I believe you, but we need to show the judge some type of physical evidence," he says. I nod.

"I, uh, I had to go to the emergency room a few times," I admit.

"For? And which one, so I can subpoena the records."

I don't look over to Bates. I can't. He's going to know the truth now, how disgusting I am.

"Scotty... uh... He raped me anally one night and I bled, *a lot*. I also miscarried a baby when he beat me another time. I was twenty-weeks pregnant. The police came both times and filled out a report, but I was too scared to actually press charges. All of the other instances were small things, fractures and bruising that his family physician treated me for. I don't think he kept records of it, though."

Mr. Jones gives me a sad look once he's finished writing everything down, and then asks for a list of dates and times when all of these instances occurred.

"I can't remember all of them," I confess.

"Well, the big ones. Can you write down the big ones? Take tonight to think about it and then just drop it off to my office tomorrow before you leave town. I'll get started on this immediately. In the meantime, I'm going to petition to have an emergency restraining order placed against Mr. Corbin," he says. Relief floods my body.

"What about custody? I don't have a job, and I have no education," I admit, embarrassed.

"Don't worry, honey. With the types of abuse you suffered, no judge in his right mind is going to place your little girl with him. If he gets any at all, it will be supervised. But I'm pushing for you having sole custody and spousal support so that you can get an education and enter the workforce. It's extremely common in cases where one parent stays home in the marriage. He'll pay."

Mr. Jones' eyes darken a bit and I bite back a gasp. Until now, he's been so kind and gentle, understanding even. I see a darker side to him, a side he must not show often, and I'm glad he'll be next to me in court, fighting *for* me.

"Okay, I will have the list to you tomorrow. Thank you again, so much," I gush as I stand and shake his hand.

Bates shakes his hand as well but doesn't say a word. He hasn't the entire time, and I wonder if the truth disgusted him as much as I thought it would. At least now I know. It's better that he finds out now the types of things that have been done to me. It's better he knows just how weak I am, just how Scotty has destroyed me. He'll never look at me the same again — and it's all for the better. He needs to find a girl, a good girl, someone whose body hasn't been used and abused since she was fifteen years old.

In silence, we leave the attorney's office. We ride the elevator down and pass the snooty receptionist on our way outside. I expect to see the SUV waiting for us, but it isn't there. Bates doesn't stop. His hand wraps around mine as he walks straight down the street. I try to pull back, but he's on a mission. I blindly follow, unsure of our destination, but trusting him too much to worry.

When we stop, it's in front of a beautiful red bridge that has a walkway underneath it. I look around for the first time and am surprised to see that we are in a park. There's even a pond. Bates doesn't say a word as he sits down and rests his back against a tree. He tugs my hand and I follow suit, sitting right next to him.

"He did all that shit to you, for years?" he asks, his voice low, deep, and gravelly.

"He did," I admit, unable to look at him.

"Never again will a man touch you without your permission. Never again will a man lay his hand on you in anger. Never again will you feel fear like that, Brentlee. No wonder my *tigritsa* is hiding her claws," he murmurs before he turns to face me. I gasp when his rough, calloused, palm cups my cheek. "No man will ever hurt you again, Brent. I fucking swear that shit to the depths of my goddamn soul."

I can't speak.

Tears stream down my cheeks and I wonder how in the hell this man is real. This rough man who is so fucking raw. He's everything I could want. Any other woman on this planet would fall to her knees and suck his beautiful cock—just from his words alone.

Any other woman but me.

I'm too damaged to ever deserve this man.

Too broken.

Too grotesque.

chapter six

Sniper

Brentlee is crying, and there is nothing I can do to stop it. Breaks my fuckin' heart to see her upset. My vow to her was meant to be comforting, not make her cry. I wipe her tears away, but more just follow in their path. I don't know how to comfort her.

"Brent," I murmur before I dip my head and press my lips to hers.

The kiss is meant to be friendly, sweet—but it takes a turn as soon as our lips meet. I run my tongue across the seam of her lips as I wrap my hand around her tiny waist. She gasps in surprise and I take the opportunity to slide my tongue deep into her open mouth.

Fuck she tastes good.

Sweet.

Just like I remember.

I turn my body and plant my knee between her thighs as I guide her back down to the grass. The park is empty, not that I give a fuck. I do what I want, where I want, consequences and prying eyes be damned. I slide my hand underneath her oversized shirt and wrap my fingers around the cup of her bra before I yank it down, freeing her breast.

"Bates," she whispers as she throws her head back.

Fuck.

All that long, dark hair is splayed out around her head on the grass, and her eyes are closed. She looks like a goddamn dream. My fuckin' dreams come to life.

I pinch her peaked nipple and tug as my lips devour her neck. She moans again and the sound goes straight to my dick. I'm so fuckin' hard for her, I think if she just touched my cock, I'd come. I feel her cool hands slide up my arms and then one of them tangles in my hair and grips me tightly. Making my scalp scream with pain. My *tigritsa* is back.

I moan against her skin and then sink my teeth into her neck as my grip tightens on her hard nipple. I feel her warm pussy against the thigh of my jeans as she rubs against me.

Fuck, my Brent—hot as ever.

"No," she whimpers as I continue to lick, suck, and nibble her neck, my fingers working her soft tit.

"Brentlee," I groan. Her body goes still and she pushes against my shoulder.

"No, Bates," she says more firmly. Her tone causes my head to snap up.

"No?" I ask, not removing my hand from under her shirt.

"No, I can't. We can't. *Ever*," she mutters as her eyes fill with tears.

"*Why the fuck not?*" I bark, harsher than intend as I remove myself from on top of her.

I want her so damn much, it aches. Only two days into this and I can't stay away from her. No way could I wait months to have her. She's my woman and I'm going to have her.

"How can you want me after everything I said in there?" she asks, backing away from me and sitting up.

"It'll always be you, Brentlee, my *tigritsa*," I admit.

I'm such a fucking pussy for this girl. She owns every piece of me.

"All the things he's done to me, Bates, how can you not be disgusted by me? How could you still stand to look at me, let alone touch me?" she asks. My eyes widen.

He has beat her down, every single part of her. I thought she was coping okay. She's been strong, and the way she confessed everything to the attorney, I thought she was good. She's so far from good, it's almost laughable.

"You ask him to do any of that shit to you?" I bark. I then watch with anger as she lowers her eyes at my roughness.

"No, never," she concedes.

"Then that's why I'm not disgusted by you. Nothing about you is disgusting, Brentlee. You're beautiful, sexy, and sweet. One day soon, you'll see it, too. I'll help you with that," I say before standing up.

I hold my hand out to her. Hesitantly, she slips her hand in mine before she stands and then adjusts her tits back inside of her bra. I almost whimper, I wanted them in my mouth. I could practically taste them, too.

"C'mon, everyone's waiting," I mumble as I tighten my

fingers around her hand.

I want her close. No, I *need* her close. If I can't fuck her and claim her, then she'll have me glued to her goddamn side until I make her completely mine. No way am I ever going to put her life or our future in jeopardy — *ever*.

I spot the SUV waiting for us as soon as we make our way out of the park and onto the city sidewalk. Brent untangles her fingers from mine as she walks toward the backdoor. I let her. She needs to feel as though she's in control of something, even something as small as this. I watch as she slides into the backseat of the car.

Before she closes the door, her eyes focus on mine. I see so much hurt and sadness swirling in her pretty honey eyes. I want to take all of that away; I want to make her happy again; and I want to kill that piece of shit for making her feel anything less than fucking perfect.

Brentlee

He sees too much.

He wants me, even knowing the things that have been done to me.

I don't understand him at all.

I try to push Bates out of my head, but it's hard when he keeps touching me.

Last night, it was all I could do to eat dinner before I passed out.

Stella and I slept in one bed while Bates took the bed opposite us. I thought it would be strange, sleeping in the same room, but I felt oddly comfortable and safe. I knew that with him right next to me, nothing bad could happen to us. He wouldn't ever let it.

Now we're at the zoo, and Bates won't stop touching me. They aren't sexual touches, just his hand on my lower back or running his thumb along my knuckles. Every single little touch makes me want him that much more. I want to climb his huge body and force him inside of me. I want more of his calloused fingers on my skin. I almost came yesterday just from his fingers on my nipples.

"So, Pierce says you'll be working at the clubhouse?" Kentlee asks with wide eyes.

"Yeah, that should be interesting," I say, not looking at Bates. He is playing with the bottom of my hair as he talks to Fury.

"Just… be prepared, okay? Crazy shit goes down there, Brent," she warns, wrapping her hand around my forearm.

I sigh, looking at the giraffe's as they eat from a huge tree out in the middle of their habitat. Stella is standing right in front of me, her focus nowhere but on the animals in front of her. I run my fingers through her blonde curls before I turn my head to face my sister.

"I'm not a naïve virgin, Kent. I've seen and done some shit. I doubt they're going to do or say anything that I haven't either done or seen before," I admit, trying not to go into detail.

"They have sex in public," she says, scrunching up her nose. I almost laugh that she's so disgusted by it.

"Well, I didn't think they were choir boys," I admit.

"It's gross. Do you know how many of their dicks I've seen in action?" she asks before she sticks her tongue out and pretends to gag.

"I'll be fine, big sister," I laugh as I lean my head down to rest against her shoulder.

"Are you?" she asks. I know she isn't talking about seeing all of the Notorious Devils' dicks in action, she's asking about me.

Am I fine?

No.

Will I be?

Probably not ever.

My hell *with* Scotty is over but my hell *without* Bates is just beginning. He isn't going to make rejecting him easy. I can already tell. I'm going to have to *prove* that I'm no good for him. *Prove* that he doesn't really want me, that I am as disgusting as I've tried to explain to him more than once. *Prove* to him that he can do better than me. Prove to him that Scotty has ruined every piece of me.

"Yeah, I am," I lie.

Kentlee doesn't say a word. Instead, her eyes narrow and I know that she can tell I'm lying. She's always been able to see right through me.

"Where's Missy these days?" she asks, inquiring about my ex-best friend and my current sister-in-law.

"Married," I say with a shrug.

Missy's husband is as much of an asshole as mine, except he doesn't abuse her quite like Scotty did me. No, Darren doesn't hurt her with his fists or rape her. Instead, he withholds from her, all the things she loves. Money, freedom, and affection. I felt sorry for her for a while, when she would confide in me.

Then, I became brave enough to tell her of my horrors.

She called me a liar. She didn't believe that her brother would do any of the things I told her about. I didn't even explain the worst of the things he did to me, yet she didn't believe a word. I had the bruises to prove it, too. She refused to believe it. That was truly the end of our friendship. I haven't spoken to her in over four years. Not even at family gatherings. I keep my distance and she does the same.

"You're not close anymore, then?" Kentlee asks. I can tell she's becoming frustrated with my one word answers.

"She's married to an asshole. He's not as bad as Scotty, but he's still abusive in his own right. I confessed a few truths to her about my own marriage and she called me a liar. She was the last friend I was allowed to have. I haven't spoken to her in over four years," I all but yell in annoyance.

"Brent," Bates' low voice warns.

"No, Bates, I was prodding when I shouldn't have been," my sister admits before she turns to me. "All that shit's done and over with now, Brent. You have a big, huge, group of family and friends now. You're never going to be alone again, no matter what."

I smile, like I should, and nod, as if I believe her. I don't. I used to be popular. I was a mean girl in school, who slept around after Bates left. I've never had a true friend, someone I could count on through thick and thin. Only Kentlee, and I am the one who didn't support her. *I'm the bad person here.* I'll always be that mean girl deep down. It's as if it is part of me. Once my true colors and my true actions take over, Bates won't want me and none of the men's wives will want the clubhouse whore as their friend. Which is exactly what I'll end up being.

My fate was sealed a long time ago. Bates needs to see all

of me for what I am. He'll run before I even have to tell him to leave. That will be the easy part. The hard part will be watching him fall in love and make a family with a good woman he deserves. It's going to kill me when it happens, but I'll just do what I do best. I'll fake it out, I'll fuck it out, and I'll drink it out. I'll try to focus on Stella and being the best version of myself in front of her that I can be.

"*Tigritsa*, don't," Bates says as he wraps his arm around my waist and pulls me into his side.

"Don't what?" I ask defensively.

"Whatever crazy shit you're thinkin', you need to stop it now. Enjoy today with our little *malyshka* and your family. Push the crazy shit to the back of your mind, just for today. We'll deal with it later. For today, have fun," he murmurs against my ear. My belly quivers at his words.

I want him so badly; I want to put all the crazy shit behind me. But I can't. All that crazy shit is screaming loud and proud in my head. I still nod once and offer him a big, fake, smile.

The rest of the day is drama free. We spend it as a family, and it's nice.

Too comfortable — but nice.

Too good — but nice.

Too fucking sweet.

My heart races at the thought of him, at the thought of being owned by any man again. I'm not even divorced and Bates wants a part of me, what's left of me. I don't have much left to give, and I'm not sure I want to give it to any man. Scotty didn't just abuse me, beat me down physically and mentally, he ruined me. Completely and totally ruined me.

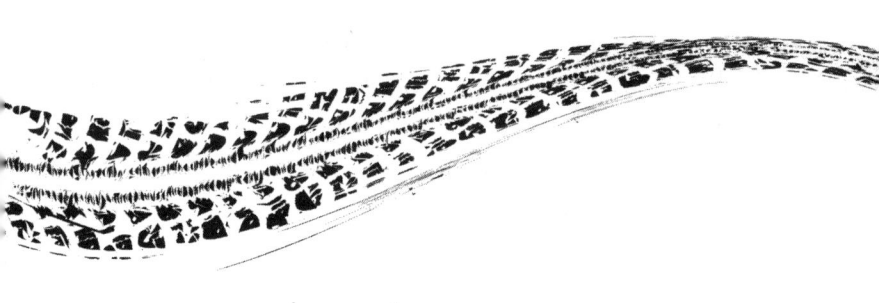

chapter seven

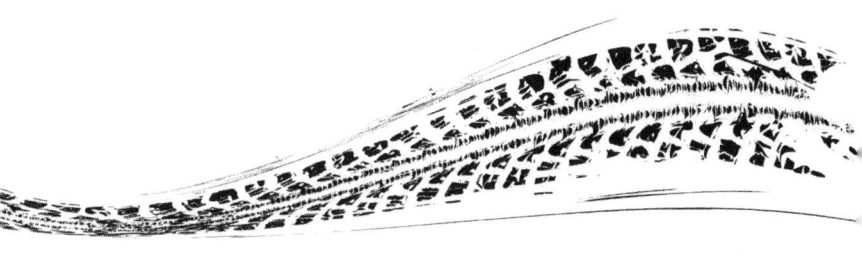

Brentlee

The zoo day ended up being awesome with the Duhart family. I couldn't have asked for anything better to take my mind off of my current depressing situation. After the long day at the zoo, we packed up the kids and drove back to Bonners Ferry. The kids slept the entire way, and we adults enjoyed the peace and quiet. I could tell that Bates wanted to talk, he had things to say to me, but I couldn't hear them. I wouldn't hear them.

Now, it's two days later and I have officially avoided him at all costs. It's worked, too. He's pissy and growly, but I can't be near him.

At least tonight I start working at the clubhouse. I was

under the impression it would be a daytime gig, maybe a big party here or there. Unfortunately, it's Thursday through Monday *nights*, and then all day long on Wednesdays to take and order stock. I'm going to see these dirty men in all of their glory. I don't know whether to be frightened or excited about all of that.

"Tammy's gonna be here in ten, and I'm taking you down there tonight before I head to the club," Bates calls out from the other side of the locked bedroom door.

I also don't want to think about Bates working down at that strip club almost every single night. I know that there has to be freebies that come along with the views of naked women night after night.

I know he's been with a lot of women; he has to have been. A member of the *Notorious Devils* and the manager of a strip club, no way is he not getting ass every other night of the week. I couldn't keep him in my bed for long; and if I did, no way would he be one hundred percent faithful to me. No matter how much he thinks he loves me, no man could keep his dick in his pants with pussy laid out in front of him every night like that.

I shake the thoughts of Bates and women out of my head as I smooth down my tight tank top. It's red and scooped so low in front, you can see the lace of my push-up bra peeking out of the top. My shorts are tight and hit just below my ass cheeks; and my shoes, extremely high heels that I borrowed from Kentlee's cocktail waitress days. I leave my hair long and straight down my back, my make-up dark and heavy. If I'm going to work in a biker bar, I need to look the part.

I hear voices as I open the bedroom door before I slide my coat on. I don't know this Tammy woman too well, but I don't want to give her a heart attack in my skanky outfit, so I try to cover up as much as possible. Kentlee has told me a ton about her. She trusts her implicitly, and from the meeting I had with her, I can tell she's a nice woman.

"Stella usually goes to bed around eight. She has already had dinner, but if she wants a small snack she can have something and a cup of milk…" I hear Bates' instructions float through the house and it makes my breath hitch.

He already knows our routines. He helps tuck Stella into bed every night before he goes to the *Devils Club,* and he's home each morning when she wakes up. He'll be an amazing father to his children one day. I wish that they were children we would share, but that won't ever happen.

"Hello, Brentlee, darling," Tammy says as I walk into the room. I smile shyly, extremely uncomfortable in my outfit.

"I don't have a phone…" I start. I stop when Bates holds out his hand and my eyes go to a brand new iPhone resting in his palm.

"Bates," I murmur. He shakes his head.

"You need a phone, if for nothing other than you and Tammy to be able to stay in contact when you're working."

I look at him in surprise, but quietly take the phone from him. It's slim and sleek, but in a floral hard case, making it feminine and … *me*. Bates informs me that he's written my number down for Tammy already.

I thank her for all of her help and give her my own instructions before I give Stella hers, along with a big hug and a kiss goodnight.

I feel a pang in my heart as soon as the front door closes behind me. Bates wraps his hand around my waist from behind and lowers his head so that his lips brush my neck with every word he speaks.

"She'll be fine, babe. I got a man on the house, she's safe," he says.

"A man? Where?" I ask as I look around in surprise.

"He won't go anywhere near the house unless there's danger. He's here, watching our girl, keeping her safe," he murmurs. I want to melt into a pile of goo at his feet. Sweet heavens, the man is too hot. *Our girl*. Dammit, I want him.

I pull away from him and unsteadily walk toward his beat up pickup truck without saying a word. I'm not mad at him, not really, I'm angry at myself. Why can't I turn off those feelings for him? Why, after ten years, do I still shake when he's near me? Why does my pussy clench and my legs want to spread at the sight of him? *Fuck, I'm never going to be able to move past him.*

A voice inside of me tells me I'm stupid, that having feelings for him, allowing myself to be controlled by him would mean repeating bad mistakes from the past—but that voice can shove it up her ass. That voice doesn't remember what having Bates and then losing him felt like. I can't go through it again. I would just rather not have him at all.

"Tonight will probably be tame," Bates says as we drive toward the clubhouse. "No big parties, just a regular Thursday night. I won't be here, so if anybody says or does anything to make you feel uncomfortable, just call me or Fury and we'll be right down."

"I'll be fine," I say, staring out the window.

"I don't think you realize what these guys are like," he says. For some reason, I am overcome with anger.

"Are they guys that like to fuck anything with a pussy, mouth, or ass?" I ask. The truck swerves to the side of the road and Bates slams on his breaks.

"Brentlee," he says, his tone harsh and sharp.

"I know what kind of men they are, Bates, because they're like *every* man. They want to fuck and be fucked hard. They want to come, and drink, and have a good time without some bitch nagging at them. It's fine. Don't worry about me. I've probably seen and done everything they could do. I'm not worried, so neither should you be," I announce before I turn my head to face the window again.

This is over between us. Whatever crush he has on me needs to end. I need to make sure it's decimated.

"Look at me," his voice is low and deep, rumbling throughout the cab of the truck. I refuse his request. I can't look at him. He's too handsome.

I feel his fingers wrap in the back of my hair, and then they tighten before he forces my neck to turn my head toward him. It burns. It fucking hurts. He's never been this rough with me before in my life. I choke back the tears and try to keep my spine straight and my body taught, ready for whatever is to come next.

"Whatever the fuck you're thinkin', fuckin' stop that shit right now. I've given you days to pull away from me since Boise. You've had your time to stew and come up with stupid shit in your head. Stupid shit that ain't gonna work. You're mine, Brentlee. Every single one of those fuckers knows you're mine. You try anything fuckin' dumb, and they'll all rat your ass out," he announces. I should be scared. The haunted look in his eyes should terrify me, but for whatever reason, it doesn't.

"I'll do whatever I want, Bates. I'm tired of being told what to do," I breathe.

"I'll spank your ass, Brentlee. I'll spank that perfect fuckin' ass of yours if you do anything stupid tonight," he warns.

"You'd hit me?" I murmur.

"Never."

"You just said you would," I say. I try to shrink back, but his grip in my hair is too tight.

"I said I'd spank you. I would never hit you, babe, *never*. I'd paint that pretty ass a nice shade of pink, but you'd be begging to come, not begging me to stop. So please, don't fuck up tonight. You're not ready for that yet," he murmurs right before his lips press against mine in a hard kiss. He then releases me and takes off down the road again, as if our conversation didn't just happen.

My chest is heaving as I breathe heavily, and I stare at Bates' profile in the moonlit truck cab as he drives toward the clubhouse. I press my thighs together, trying to alleviate the ache he's given me. The thought of being bent over his knee while he spanks my bare ass is too much. I know Bates would never hurt me, so I also know that this spanking he's promised for a later date is going to be shit hot.

Luckily, before I can think too much more about it, we pull into the clubhouse parking lot. *Thank goodness.* I hurry out of the cab of the truck and quickly make my way toward the door. Bates' long legs catch up to me, and he throws his arm around my shoulders before he yanks me close to his side. I feel his beard tickle my ear.

"Remember what I said, Brentlee. Don't do anything fucked up tonight. I'll have eyes on you, my *tigritsa*," he whispers before he lets me go and opens the door for me.

The room is smoky and smells like booze, cum, weed, and cigarettes. *I'm going to go home smelling like a brothel ev-*

ery single night. I shiver in disgust, but I try not to let it show. I'm grateful for the opportunity. Truly, I am.

I know that I said I would strip, but in all honesty, I don't think I could do it. This is scary enough for me. I slip off my coat and shiver when all eyes glance in my direction. I feel naked enough in my tank and shorts, no way could I literally be nude.

"Brentlee, baby, how're you doin'?" Johnny Williams asks me, a cigarette hanging between his lips. He's added a little bulk since school, but his frame is long and lean, and his muscles are the same. He's built nothing like the massive tank of a man behind me.

"Claimed," Bates growls. I almost laugh.

"I'm good, Johnny. It's been a while," I say softly.

"Too long," he murmurs, licking his lips and staring straight at my breasts.

"Eyes and hands fuckin' off, brother," Bates grinds out. I want to laugh, but I don't. If he knew the truth, if he only knew, maybe he wouldn't want me so badly.

I turn to him, ready to tell him that I've fucked Johnny, but one look in his eyes and I can't. *I can't purposely hurt him.* Not directly. I need to find a way to make it hurt as passively as possible. I close my eyes and leave him standing there. I walk straight to the bar and a boy-man around eighteen winks at me before he introduces himself as a prospect.

Sniper

I watch her go behind the bar. Dirty Johnny is smart and

doesn't follow the sweet view of her ass in those tiny shorts. Instead, he keeps his eyes on mine. He smirks like he has a secret and I'm about to find out just what it fuckin' is, too.

"What is your deal with her?" I growl.

Fuck, I feel like I want to claw my own fuckin' skin. I can't take it anymore. She's right there, right in front of me for days, but I can't have her. *It's killing me.*

"You really don't wanna know. I forgot you had history," he mumbles. I take a step toward him, my nose practically touching his.

"Tell me, lay it out," I demand. He sighs before he shakes his head once.

"You'd find out eventually, anyway. Your girl was a whore after you left her, man," he says. My eyes fly from his to Brentlee as I take a step back.

"What do you mean?" I ask. Blood starts pumping throughout my body as anger fills me.

"She fucked a lot of dudes, what do you think I mean? You gave her a chin lift, and she'd spread. I hate to tell you, but that's the fuckin' truth," he grunts. I look back at him, unable to focus on anything really.

"You fucked her?"

"Brother," he starts before he clears his throat, "I was a punk ass kid. Wouldn't matter what a girl looked like. She offered up pussy, I was gonna take it, and Brent's always been hot as fuck. Of course I fucked her."

Without thinking, I storm right for her. She's sliding a bottled beer over to Torch, but the only thing I can see is her. *The whore.* The fucking slut I'm in love with.

I haven't been a monk, but hearing that Brentlee spread for countless men, including members of the club, it does something to me. It pisses me off. I'm pissed at her and myself. I'm just furious.

"Get your ass over here," I bark from the side of the bar. Brentlee's head pops up and a look of confusion crosses her face until her eyes meet mine, then I see nothing but guilt.

"Bates," she murmurs slowly walking toward me.

I should take her into Fury's office, but I'm so fucking mad, I don't think. Instead, I speak, and I fuck up.

"So you turned into a whore after I left, I hear," I yell out angrily, loud—too loud. She flinches as if I've backhanded her.

"Bates," she says as her lips tremble—her pretty red painted lips, lips I want wrapped around my cock, even knowing what I know now. Nothing's changed, except my pride, and that's a mean fucker, because he won't let me forget everything I've just heard.

"You did. How many of the men here did you spread for? I'd like to know how many of my brothers have put their cocks inside of you," I growl. It's feral and mean sounding, even to my own ears.

"Bates," I hear Torch's voice behind me, but I can't look at anything but Brentlee.

"It doesn't matter. Now you know the truth, so you can stop acting like I'm yours, like this will ever work between us," she yells.

"Maybe you should be living here then; become a whore for the few guys you haven't fucked yet," I grind out before I shrug Torch's hand from my shoulder and turn from her.

I can't look at her.

Not right now.

I leave, but before I make it to my pick-up, Torch is behind me.

"You're a fuckin' dick, man," he announces.

"Yeah, the woman you love fuck a bunch of your brothers as soon as you leave?" I ask, turning my anger toward him—my only target.

"You were gone. It doesn't matter what she did, she wasn't yours at the time." My jaw clenches with my regret. He's so right. I left her. I told her to have fun. I didn't expect her to fuck anybody else, I didn't want her to. *She's mine, always has been.*

"I won't be back tonight. Make sure she gets home," I mutter, getting into my pickup and speeding out of the parking lot.

I'm fuckin' *done.*

I need a drink and my dick sucked after all this shit. I drive straight to the *Devil's Club* in hope of drowning my sorry ass in booze and pussy.

chapter eight

Brentlee

"You all right over there, darlin'?" Grizz calls out from the other side of the bar.

I watch the front door swing as Bates leaves and I sigh before turning to the big grizzly bear of a man. I give him a weak smile and a nod as my only answer before I go back to work, washing a million disgusting shot glasses.

A few minutes later, Paxton Hill, or as the guys around here call him, Torch, appears in front of me from across the bar. He looks at me with concern and maybe pity, I'm not sure which.

"I'm gonna take you home tonight, okay, babe?" he announces. I feel my stomach clench.

This sealed the deal. This information about me got Bates to give up. Had I known it was so easy, that he'd walk away without a glance back at me, I would have confessed everything the first day. I would have never known how indescribably sweet he could be toward my daughter or toward me. He would have just simply been *the-one-that-got-away*. A sweet memory of the boy he used to be. I knew it would drive him away.

I got exactly what I wanted.

"Yeah, that sounds like a good idea. Thanks, Pax," I murmur.

"He'll cool down, babe. You aren't kids anymore; he can't expect that you stayed true to him all these years. You were married, for fuck's sake," Paxton cries, taking a bottle of beer that I slide toward him. I have about seven more hours of work, he deserves at least one beer for dealing with me and my shit.

"It's better this way. Really, it is. I am who I am, and nothing can change that," I shrug before I go back to washing shot glasses.

"That's bullshit," Paxton says before he takes a swig of his beer.

"No, it's not," I counter.

"You were a fifteen-year-old kid who had her heart broken, so you turned to other punk ass kids for attention. That's what being a kid is, making stupid as shit decisions. He was a stupid kid who broke your heart because he thought he was being noble, or some lame ass shit like that. Doesn't make what he did right; doesn't make what you did wrong, either. I don't recall in the past six years you fuckin' anybody but your husband, have you?"

"Never," I whisper. Not only would Scotty kill me, but I wouldn't cheat on my husband, no matter how much I hated him.

"You and Bates work your shit out, you gonna fuck his brothers on the side?" he asks. My head shoots up, my eyes connecting with his.

"Never," I say firmly. He nods once before he winks.

"You're a good girl, Brentlee. Been dealt some shitty hands, but all-in-all, you've always been a good girl," he murmurs.

"Doesn't change that I'm a slut, Paxton," I point out as someone calls for a beer. I quickly pop the top and hand it to the beastly man.

"So you fucked a few guys when you were a kid. *Jesus Christ*, do you even know how many girls Bates has fucked?"

"Um, no, and I don't think I want to," I grumble as I continue to wash the never ending shot glass pile.

"You really don't; but let's just say you're like the virgin fuckin' Mary, if we were to do a comparison," he says. He then turns and walks away from me, leaving me standing there, behind the bar, with my mouth wide open.

"Gonna catch flies, or maybe a swingin' dick with your mouth open like that, babe," a man says. I shut my mouth quickly, which causes him to start laughing. "I'm Vault, by the way."

"Brentlee," I offer with a smile.

"Know your sister real well. She's good friends with my wife, Rosie," he grins.

I spend the rest of the evening serving beers and shots of hard liquor to bikers and whores alike, trying to not stare as the night progresses and people get drunker and drunker. The women are naked, the men are getting sucked and fucked, and then there's me, serving drinks to them all. It's nothing I haven't seen before, but it still makes me slightly uncomfortable to watch.

"Shifts over, Brent. You ready to head out?" Paxton asks, coming up behind me and wrapping his fingers around my hip with a squeeze.

"Sure," I offer with a smile. I step away from him to grab my coat and purse.

"You'll have to be on my bike, Don't have a cage," he says with a shrug as we walk out of the bar.

Luckily, it's not too chilly out, so I agree and climb on the back of his bike after him.

"Gonna have to hold on tighter, and closer than that," he chuckles, I scoot even closer to him, my crotch nestled into the small of his back, and my arms tight around his trim waist.

I hope Bates doesn't come home tonight. I don't think I could handle the way he looked at me again, shock and disgust marring his features. I am so obviously not *his* anymore, and now he's perfectly aware as to why. I'm not the good girl I once was. I'm just some damaged slut now. Its better this way.

Sniper

It was a dick move to leave her the way I did, I think as I take another shot of tequila. I usually don't drink the stuff, but tonight, I need it. I watch as a pretty blonde named Jordan shakes her tits on stage. They don't move, and for whatever reason, I find that shit hilarious tonight.

"You're so fucked up over that girl, its ridiculous," I hear a familiar voice say behind me. I turn around as Fury sits down at the bar and motions for a beer from Candy.

"I am. Turns out, she fucked a whole lotta guys after I went off to boot camp," I announce as Candy walks up to us, handing Fury his beer and me a water.

"You been a saint for ten years, so that shit matters to you?" Fury asks, taking a pull from his beer. I notice Candy hasn't left, and isn't going to. *Nosey little bitch*.

"You be all good with LeeLee fuckin' other guys while you were in the pen, then?" I slur.

"Not the same thing and you know it. But, I'd get over it; I'd have to with the way I treated her. We all make our beds of roses or shit and have to lie in them. You broke up with her a decade ago. Who or what she did after that is not something you can get pissed at her for. Just like all those bitches you've fucked she can't say dick to you about. It's a two-way street, brother," Fury points out. He's right; he's so fucking right, but I don't want him to be. I want to be justified in my anger with Brentlee.

"Not to butt in or nothin'," Candy begins, butting in. I roll my eyes because she's always up in my shit. "You can't expect her to sit around and wait for you for ten years. I mean, even the best good girl on earth ain't gonna waste all her youth doin' that shit."

"You don't know shit," I mumble, taking a shot as Candy throws her head back laughing.

"Yeah, asshole, I don't know a damn thing. I know that I've wasted plenty of my time and youth on jerks, cheaters, and liars. You cannot get pissed that she didn't stay your one pure love while you abandoned her and did whatever the fuck you wanted to. Don't think I haven't seen you in here, fuckin' two girls at once. You think she's gonna be cool with all that? That she should be fine and accept that? But you don't have to accept that she slept with a few guys when she was young? You're just pissed because you know who the guys are. All you assholes are the fuckin' same," Candy announces before she turns and walks away from me.

"She's right," Fury agrees before he finishes his beer. "Come on, I'll take you home."

I don't protest. I wanted nothing more than to fuck a bitch tonight, to fuck the thoughts of Brentlee away, but I can't. She's all I can think about. Even now, knowing she's fucked at least two of my own club brothers, I want inside of her. I want to claim her for the world to see, I want to shove it in every motherfucker's face that—she.is.*mine*.

Once I step out of the SUV, Fury tells me that he'll be by sometime in the morning to take me back to the club for my truck. I wave him off and stumble to the porch. I open the front door and Tammy is sitting on the sofa, knitting and watching an old black and white movie. Her head comes up and she awards me with a gentle smile.

"Stella's been asleep four hours. What a sweet girl," she says. Her same smile instantly falls as I stumble toward the chair in the room. "You're drunk. You didn't drive did you?"

"Nope, Pierce brought me home," I grunt. She nods once as she packs up her shit to leave.

"You'll be okay here alone?" she asks, eyeing me, probably afraid I'll do something insanely stupid. I wouldn't, not with Stella in the house.

"I'm good, Tammy. 'Preciate you watching Stella tonight.

Send me a text when you make it home safe, yeah?"

"Okay, Bates, I will," she says, giving me her soft smile again before she leaves. I listen for her car to start and then she's gone and it's quiet, except for the low hum of the voices coming from the television.

Once Tammy is gone, I make my way outside for some fresh air. It's too fuckin' hot in that house, and I can't turn the A/C down because I don't want to disturb Stella. I lean my forearms on the bannister and breathe.

I'm trying to wrap my head around what Candy and Fury said. They're right, of course. How can I get pissed off over something that happened years ago, and when we weren't even together? It's so fucking irrational. But I'm still pissed. I don't want any other man on earth, especially my brothers, knowing what her pussy feels like.

The sound of a motorcycle breaks my thoughts, and I see red as it pulls up my drive. Brentlee is holding onto Torch like she's trying to climb inside of his body. Her tits and pussy are pressed up against his back, her long arms wrapped around his waist, and her long dark hair is blowing back behind her.

Fucking hell.

As they come to a stop and he kicks his stand down, I walk down the porch stairs toward them. I can't take my eyes off of Brentlee's long as fuck legs as she steps off of his bike. The way her hand grabs onto Torch's shoulder for balance and support. She shouldn't be on the back of *his* bike, not when she belongs on the back of *mine*.

"The fuck is going on here?" I bark with a sway. *Fuck, I'm so drunk.*

"Givin' Brent a ride home, like I said I would," Torch explains with a shit-eating grin.

"Get in the house, Brentlee," I order.

I watch as her back straightens and one of her hips pops out as her hand rests there. Gorgeous defiance written all over her.

"No, I haven't told Paxton thank you for the ride home yet," she says sticking her chin out. *Tigritsa*—one hundred percent.

"Tell Torch thank you and then get your ass in the house," I bark.

"Thank you so much for the ride home, Paxton. I really appreciate it," she says sweetly. Her husky voice washes over me, turning me on, and pissing me off because it's directed at him and not me.

"Anytime, babe," he winks. I growl.

Brentlee doesn't utter a word as she walks past me and toward the house. I don't watch her go. Instead, I stay focused on Torch.

"Stay away," I warn. He chuckles.

"Brother, you made it clear you didn't want in there. Why in the fuck would I stay away? I know what kind of woman she is," he says as he steps off of his bike and stands nose-to-nose with me.

"I told everybody she's mine, I never took that back," I point out, sounding like a toddler fighting over his favorite toy.

"You better make her believe she's yours then, because the way you treated her tonight, not fuckin' cool. She's a good girl. She deserves better," he scolds.

"She deserves whatever in the fuck I give her, not you, and not anybody else. So stay *the fuck* away," I grind before I spit on the ground next to his boots.

"Then man the fuck up, Sniper, and you won't have to worry about me. I know just how good of a girl she is just remember that," he remarks. Before I can respond he gets back on his bike, and before I can say another word, he's gone.

I turn around and start to stalk toward the house. Brentlee is watching me from the front door. As soon as our eyes connect, hers widen and she takes off toward the bedroom. The time has come. I can't wait another fuckin' minute. It's time she realizes that she's mine, that she's always been mine, and that she will forever be mine.

I'm going to stake my motherfucking claim right here, and right now. She hasn't been in love with that asshole she married for a long as fuck time, if ever.

Me? She's been in love with me since she was fourteen years old.

I've waited ten long years to have her underneath me again. I can't wait a minute longer.

chapter nine

Brentlee

The ride home was exhilarating. I had never been on the back of a motorcycle before, and it was even more exciting than I had ever imagined. My body pressed close to Paxton's, the wind in my hair as we sped down the dirt roads leading to Bates' country home.

I watch as Bates gets in Paxton's face, and I am so embarrassed. Paxton doesn't want me, and neither does Bates, not really. He just doesn't want any of his friends to be with me. Maybe I should just leave. Stella and I could disappear, maybe go to my brother's on the east coast.

Connellee hasn't been home since the Christmas after Kentlee was disowned by our parents. They made it unbearable for him and he refuses to be part of the whole family. I don't blame him. Our parents can be judgmental assholes. I haven't even attempted to contact them, and for good reason. They would tell Scotty and urge me back to him. Connellee would help me, though. I just know he would.

I hate to move Stella again. She's so happy here with Bates in his county home. But if push comes to shove, I won't have a choice, and she'll understand—*eventually*.

Bates turns as Paxton gets on his bike and roars out of the gravel drive. I can't look anywhere but Bates' dark gaze. He looks feral, livid, and so fucking sexy. I clench my thighs together before I bite my lip, causing myself pain so I don't run to him, so I don't wrap myself around him. I turn and run away from him, into the bedroom, closing the door behind me.

I should be healing from leaving my ex-husband. I shouldn't be lusting after Bates. But I am. I haven't loved Scotty ever, maybe. I don't know. If I did, that love dissipated on my honeymoon the first time he abused me. No, there's no love for Scotty at all inside of me. The only thing I feel for him other than hate is void. He gave me my daughter, but she isn't his, never was. She's mine.

"Open this fucking door or I'll beat it down. I really don't want to wake up Stella right now," Bates' low rumbling voice vibrates through the door. I take a step away before I turn around and twist the knob.

The door opens and Bates takes a step inside before closing it behind him and locking the deadbolt. I don't want to know why he has a deadbolt on his bedroom door. Not right now. I don't care. My body trembles at the sight of him. When his downward eyes flick up to meet mine, I gasp.

"I'm pissed off at you, Brentlee," he announces.

"Bates," I whisper. He takes a step toward me and tangles his fingers in the back of my hair before he gently tugs my head back.

"But more importantly, I'm pissed off at myself," he murmurs before his lips crash against mine in a hard, punishing, bruising kiss.

"I don't want to be that girl again, Bates, but I don't think it matters. That's just who I was," I admit, closing my eyes.

Bates' fingers tighten in my hair and his other hand grabs a handful of my ass so hard I know I'll have fingertip bruises in the morning. Then he gives my body a gentle shake, forcing me to open my eyes and look up at him.

"You are not that woman Brent. That girl is gone, so is the woman who Scotty abused. Look how strong you are, you left him. You saved your baby," he grinds out. "Besides that, you plan on fuckin' my brothers? Any of them?"

"No," I murmur.

"You're mine, Brentlee. Your body is mine. Doesn't matter who's been inside it in the past. From this moment on, it's mine. Only cock you're allowed to fuck is mine. I don't give a fuck if you don't want to be my woman, but you won't take another man's dick. You hear me?"

I blink, unsure of what to say. This man in front of me is an asshole. He's not my sweet Bates, he's a giant dickhead.

"I'll do what I want, Bates." I announce. He throws back his head in laughter before he lowers it and his nose caresses mine, his lips just millimeters away from my own.

"You'll take no dick but mine, Brentlee. I'll fuckin' gut any man that comes near you, *tigritsa*," he says before his lips crash against mine and his tongue licks the seam forcing my mouth to open before he slips it inside.

He tastes like tequila and regret. Like the past and the future all rolled into one. My arms involuntarily lift and wrap around his neck, my fingers find their way into his thick, black hair, and I moan as he lifts me off of the ground and walks me toward the bed.

The backs of my legs hit the bed and I lose my balance falling and landing on the soft mattress. Bates kisses down my jaw to my collar bone, and then the tops of my breasts—licking and biting my soft flesh. His hands are still wrapped, one in my hair and the other on the cheek of my ass.

"Bates," I sigh. He sucks the top of my breast before he bites the skin, then sucks harder, marking me.

"No dick but mine, Brentlee," he mutters against my skin. Then his hands are gone. "You on the pill?" he nonchalantly asks as he begins to strip out of his clothes.

I nod my answer as my mouth goes dry at the sight of him. He's huge. Somehow, with his shirt off, his arms and chest look even bigger than they do encased in the too tight cotton. His pants fall to the ground, but I can't see anything past his thick waist and thicker thighs. There is so much to look at, I feel like I need an extra set of eyes. I gasp when his boxers are pushed down and his long, thick cock is on full display in front of me.

Bates wordlessly strips me out of my own clothes, tossing them behind him, leaving me in only my bra and panties. I hold my breath as his eyes wander over my body. I look nothing like the girl I did ten years ago. I'm rounder, softer—*fuller*, than I was as a teenager.

"Fuck me, but you're gorgeous," he murmurs as his eyes roam my body.

"Bates, I..." I begin, not knowing what exactly I want to say, but needing to fill the silence in the room.

"Spread your legs," he orders, ignoring my hesitation.

I do as he asks with shaky legs, thankful for my panties, which cover me so that he doesn't see *everything*. My breath hitches when I feel his hands encircle my ankles, he pulls my legs straight up, my knees locking, before he tugs me closer to the edge of the bed.

"Grab onto my thighs," he commands. Without thinking, I follow his orders.

My fingers grip the backs of his muscular thighs, which, because of the distance, causes my back to arch and my chest to push up.

"Don't let go. If you do, you won't be permitted to come," he grumbles. My already trembling body begins to shake even more.

I close my eyes tightly before I hear, then feel my panties rip. Then without warning, his fingers are inside of me. I gasp and open my eyes wide to find him smirking down at me. One side of his mouth lifted along with one brow, daring me to say something, anything. I don't. I keep my eyes locked on his and my mouth shut.

"You're so wet already," he announces.

He's right.

I am.

I have been since I saw him in that nasty as hell clubhouse. His fingers slide inside me again and curl, causing me to moan. I couldn't hold it in even if I wanted to. It's been so long since I have been touched by a man I wanted.

"Bates," I whisper. It seems his name is the only thing able to escape my mouth, other than a moan or two.

"I'll make it good, *tigritsa*. I'll always make you feel good," he murmurs as his thumb presses against my throbbing clit. "Don't take your hands or your eyes off of me. You need to watch as I take ownership of you."

I whimper as his fingers leave me and his cock replaces them. One quick thrust and he is completely seated inside of me, to the hilt. I gasp at the intrusion. He's huge. My fingernails dig into his thighs and he moans, dropping his head back, exposing his sexy as shit neck.

"Who owns you, Brentlee?" he asks as he slowly pulls out of me, centimeter by centimeter.

I sigh, trying to keep my eyes from rolling in the back of my head, or my hands from leaving his thighs and fisting in the sheets beside me.

"You do, Bates. You always have," I shamelessly admit.

"Fucking right, I have," he grunts before he slams back inside of me.

I cry out in surprise, but he doesn't stop. He repeats his move, but with speed and power, no longer slow. No, now he is taking possession of me. I am unable to move; he has me completely surrendered to him. Both hands now, wrapped around the outside of my thighs, holding them up, and out. His cock is so smooth and hard, as he pistons in and out of me. My eyes stay focused on his dark ones, owning every single piece of me—mind, body, and soul.

My pussy flutters with warning. I'm going to come. For the first time since before my marriage, I am going to come, and I'm scared. I want to so badly; I want him to give me something I haven't had in years.

"Don't come yet," he warns as sweat drips down his chest. *Fuck, I want to lick it off of him*, and just imagining that doesn't help me keep myself under control.

He releases my legs and leans over me, one of his fists landing beside my head as the other hand wraps around my throat. I hitch my legs around his back, my eyes never leaving his and my hands firmly gripping his strong thighs.

"Bates, I need to come," I plead. He shakes his head once, droplets of sweat flinging in all different directions from his forehead.

"Who's cock do you take *only*?" he asks as he continues to fuck me, with what I assume is close to all of his strength. It hurts, but it feels delicious at the same time.

I don't want to answer, but I want to come. *I'm his*. I have always been so; but what he wants, what he's suggesting isn't something I think I can deal with. It's sex—pure, raw sex.

How can I simply fuck the man I have been in love with for over a decade and not fall deeper into him?

I'm no good for him. I'm fucked from Scotty, damaged and unfixable. Scotty will always be in my mind, waiting to burst through at any moment and drive me further into the ground. Bates wants to own me. I'm not free from my last owner. I don't have much of myself left to give, and if he takes from me, and it doesn't work out, there will be absolutely nothing left.

"No," I weakly say.

I feel his hand tighten around my throat, his thrusts never slowing, never stopping, and his eyes boring into mine. He's trying to convince me with his stare and his cock. I groan when he pushes completely inside of me and stops, grinding against my clit.

It's too much.

My airway is constricted, not entirely blocked, but I can't

take a deep breath. Tears begin to fall from my eyes in panic. I lift my hands and claw at his arm to get him to release his hold on me.

"I won't hurt you baby, *never*," he coos, his voice softer than a few moments ago. My hands go back to his thighs, as his strokes continue but they're slower, softer, sweeter—I need to come. It's not a want anymore, it's a need, but my eyes are locked with Bates' and there's no way I can let go. He has me suspended and pinned in limbo.

"My dick only, Brentlee. No stupid shit, no other fucking men. I'll kill them. I've killed before and I'll do it again. No fucking hesitation. This pussy is for me only. *Should have always been mine, but I fucked up*," he murmurs before his lips touch mine and his hand loosens around my throat.

"Why do you still want me?" I ask against his lips. He doesn't kiss me, his eyes don't close, and his thrusts become slower, softer, sweeter.

"I haven't been whole since I walked away from you. I haven't slept peacefully since then, and I haven't lived. I've been surviving, just like you have, but in my own way. Besides, every piece of you was always meant to be mine, Brentlee. Denying it only makes us miserable. You don't have to be my Old Lady, but your cunt is only for me," he whispers. "Come on my cock, *tigritsa*," he grinds out before his tongue slides deep into my mouth and he shows me just how he does, in fact, *own me*.

I scream into his mouth as my pussy clenches and I come around him. Bates grunts as his cock grows and then twitches inside of me. He comes with a groan that I swallow. His hand tightens around my throat before he releases it completely and moves his fingers into the back of my hair. He nuzzles my neck with his bearded face and lips.

I start to move my hands from his thighs, but then I feel him nip my neck with his teeth.

"Don't fuckin' move a goddamn muscle," he mutters into my skin.

I freeze where I am, my legs wrapped around his lower back, my fingers still digging into his strong thighs. His heavy body resting on top of mine, the weight probably more than I should be able to bear—but with him, I welcome it.

"Tell me its mine, Brentlee," he murmurs before he licks my skin then gently sucks it into his mouth.

"I can't, Bates, I just… *can't*." I sob, my body shaking beneath him.

"I'll get you there, Brentlee. Swear to fuck, babe, I'll get you there. I'll get you where you were always meant to be and get you living again," he says as he begins to slowly fuck me, again.

My pussy is already sore, but when he tilts his hips and his cock hits me in just the most perfect way, I relax my body to accept more. I won't be able to walk tomorrow, but I don't care. All I care about is Bates inside of me, owning me. He does. I don't want to admit it out loud, but he owns every piece of me.

"Okay, only your big dick," I grumble. He laughs, his breath hot on my neck, and he continues his slow thrusts.

"Thanks, *tigritsa*. Now, take it again before we pass out," he grunts.

Bates' fingers tighten in my hair as his lips suck and bite my neck; but his cock, Jesus, his big, beautiful cock possesses me with every plunge. When I come, again, it is on a slow burn, a build that overwhelms me.

I don't scream, or cry, I simply tremble beneath him as my pussy squeezes around him. Bates comes again, inside of me, and I feel a closeness to a man, a closeness I didn't realize that had been missing for over ten years. I want to continue to try and push him away, but Bates won't let me. He sees me, and no matter how much I try to deny it, he's what I've been craving all these years. This is what was always meant to be. I don't know what will happen tomorrow, or the next day. I don't know if I will continue to accept him as my lover, but for now, this *feels* right.

Sniper

Once I've come for the second time, I allow Brentlee to release my legs. *Fuck,* having her all wrapped up in me, completely at my mercy, was fuckin' gorgeous. I tell her to stay where she is and go into the bathroom, grabbing a wash cloth and running it under water before I take it back to the bed to clean her up.

"I can clean myself, Bates," she murmurs as her face tints pink with embarrassment.

"Quiet," I grunt as I spread her legs and look at her swollen pink pussy. I groan at the sight of my cum leaking out of her.

It's one of the hottest things I've ever seen.

I ignore her protests and clean her, throwing the wash cloth toward the bathroom door once I'm finished. Then, I pick her up and gently lie her down on her side of the bed before I reach around and unclasp her bra. I'm disappointed in myself for not taking it off sooner so I could watch her pretty tits bounce with each thrust of my hips. Once I have pulled her bra off, I drop it on the ground and then cover her up with the sheet and comforter.

Walking toward the door I unlatch the lock and open it, so that when Stella wakes up she isn't frightened and can get to Brentlee easily. Then, I go back to my side of the bed and slip beneath the sheets myself before I turn to my side and gather her in my arms. *Fuck, she feels good there too.* Soft and warm, and her smell—*fuck*. She smells like her lotions, and me, and sex. The combination makes my cock stir.

"What are you doing?" she asks drowsily.

"Going to sleep," I murmur before I kiss her bare shoulder.

"You're naked and in bed with me," she points out.

"Yeah."

"When Stella wakes up, you're going to confuse her," she says. It irritates me. What did she think was going to happen when I claimed that pussy?

"You're livin' in a fuckin' dream world you think I'm going to sleep on the couch after I got back in that sweet cunt of yours," I point out. She lets out a heavy sigh.

"But Stella," she says in an urging tone.

"You think Stella don't know you're done with her daddy? You think Stella don't realize what's happening here? She's three, but she ain't fuckin' stupid, Brent," I tell her. She stiffens in my arms.

I tighten my grip around her, because if she gets out of my grasp, she might try and act crazy. Not tonight. I'm fuckin' beat. I just had the best sex I've had in over ten years and I'm sobering up. I need sleep.

"She'll see me jumping from one man to another," she announces like she knows what the fuck she's talking about.

"She'll see you leaving an abusive piece of shit you don't love and going to a man who will treat you right, is what she'll see. She'll see you taking care of yourself, of her, and getting stronger. She'll see all that shit because all of that is the fucking truth. You won't be hopping from man to man, Brentlee, because there is no other man after me."

"What if we don't work out," she whispers. I roll her flat on her back and crawl on top of her, my arms caging in her head.

"Do I need to fuck you again to show you just how right we are? Do I need to explain what it means when I tell you that only *my* cock sinks inside that tight cunt of yours?" I ask as I stare into those gorgeous honey colored eyes of hers.

"Okay, Bates," she says. Her husky voice washes over me as her hand comes up and cradles the side of my neck.

"Not losin' you again, Brentlee, not after all this time. I got you where I want you and we're gonna work this out. Eventually, you'll be my Old Lady. You'll have my name inked on this gorgeous body of yours, and *my* babies will grow inside of you. Might take years to get there, but babe, hear this—that's where we'll be," I announce. Her mouth falls open in surprise. I kiss her so she can't say anymore stupid as fuck shit.

"Now go to sleep before I fuck that hot pussy again," I grunt, which makes her roll her eyes.

Our serious conversation is on hold, *not over*, for the time being. She rolls out from underneath me and backs that sweet ass into my dick as she settles in. I wrap her up in my arms again and nestle my face into her hair, inhaling that scent of hers, before I close my eyes and pray that a dreamless sleep overtakes me.

Tomorrow is a new day. A new beginning, for us. It's not where I wish we were, but it's one step closer. Having her to myself will at least ease my frustration at the fact that she won't completely surrender to me. I don't think it'll take long, though. Once she's one hundred percent mine, I'm never letting her ass go.

She and Stella are *mine*.

Mine to protect.

Mine to care for.

Mine to love.

chapter ten

Brentlee

"Mommy," a sweet little voice stage whispers in my face.

I pinch my eyes closed tightly before I open them and find Stella about two centimeters away from my nose. Her eyes are wide and bright and she has a huge smile on her face. I, however feel as though I have slept about five minutes. I feel hungover, even though I didn't drink a drop last night.

"Stella," I whisper back. She giggles.

"Bates is sweeping," she says.

My eyes widen and my body stiffens. *I'm* naked, *he's* naked, and Stella is right there—her eyes wide and bright and focused on me. *Oh, holy shit.*

"Yes, he is. Why don't you go into the living room and get a toy out and I'll be there in a minute to make breakfast," I say, trying not to sound panicked, though panicked is exactly how I feel.

"Okay, mommy," she says before she shrugs and runs off.

"Told you she wouldn't give a fuck," Bates murmurs gruffly behind me.

"I need to get up," I say, ignoring his gloating.

"Sleep. You worked your gorgeous ass off last night, and this morning," he chuckles kissing my shoulder before he stands and walks to the dresser. It's his only piece of furniture, other than the bed in the room.

Wordlessly, I watch as he pulls on a pair of black boxer briefs, and I sigh at how freaking fantastic his ass looks in them. I have never been an ass woman, but Bates' ass, it's worthy of a swoon or two. Then, he pulls on a pair of low waisted sweats and grabs a black tank, covering his gorgeous chest, but luckily leaving his gigantic arms on display for me to ogle.

I hold my breath when he walks over to me and plants a fist and knee in the bed before he leans down and his lips brush my cheek. His beard rubs against me, and it makes me break out in a light sheen of sweat. I want that rough beard to rub against the rest of my body, *now*.

"Sleep, *tigritsa*," he murmurs. I close my eyes, falling asleep in a matter of seconds.

Hours later, I wake to a quiet house, too quiet. I sit straight up in a panic and grab Bates' shirt from the floor, throwing it on before I rush out of the bedroom. Stella should be playing loudly, the television should be on, and there should be noise everywhere.

I run to the living room only to find the television off

and the space empty. My next stop is the kitchen. There is evidence of breakfast scattered all around, but no Stella and no Bates. I rush out of the front door and stop dead in my tracks on the porch.

Stella is on a little bicycle, equipped with training wheels. Her hair is in pigtail braids, and she's wearing a pink helmet on her head. Bates is crouching down behind her, in jeans and a tight t-shirt, a smile on his face as he holds onto the bike seat behind her little booty. She has the biggest, happiest smile on her chubby cheeks as her feet peddle the bike forward, with the help of Bates pushing behind her.

The sight is so gorgeous, so absolutely beautiful, that I can't help but get emotional. I couldn't even if I wanted to. The tears fall, and I do nothing to try and stop them or wipe them away. Bates is teaching my daughter how to ride a bike on an old dirt road, in front of my dream house. He's doing something with her that her own father never once even tried to do. He's spending quality time with her.

I feel a pang in my chest. It hurts. It's too sweet. All I can think is that it's never going to last, and Stella will be destroyed. I'll be devastated and I'll never move on from him; but Stella, she'll be completely and totally destroyed when he finally leaves us. The thought makes me cry even harder.

"Mama, I wide," Stella yells with a smile.

"Good job, sweet girl," I call out, trying to keep my voice from wavering with emotion.

Bates' head comes up and I hold my breath when he smiles—full on bright with white teeth smile. I watch as his eyes scan my barely covered body. His gaze intensifies, turning even darker. Then his smile turns into a naughty smirk. I can almost see the dirty thoughts running through his head.

"Go get dressed, baby. LeeLee and the kids are coming over," he announces. My mood immediately shifts.

"Yeah?" I excitedly ask.

"Lee wanted to have lunch and do a playdate. I got some shit to do, but I'll have protection here for you," he calls out. I cringe at the language he uses in front of Stella, but I don't say anything.

"Okay," I say before I turn to leave.

"You look beautiful, baby," he calls out. I freeze before I turn to face him in surprise.

"What?" I ask, surely mishearing his words.

I can't look beautiful. My hair is a ratted, matted mess, and my makeup from last night is assuredly smeared under my eyes. I'm nothing short of a disaster.

"Heard me, babe. You look beautiful. Now go get dressed," he grunts.

A shiver runs through my body at his words. *Beautiful.* It's been so long since a man has said that word to me and meant it, truly meant it.

I don't respond. Instead, I hurry inside and get ready to see my sister. I don't bother looking at myself in the mirror. I don't want to see myself. Bates thinks I'm beautiful and I want to relish in that, soak that in. I don't want to see the truth looking back at me in the mirror.

Once I am dressed, I can hear that Stella and Bates are back in the house. There is a cartoon movie on television, blasting, and her voice is boisterously singing along to the song currently playing. I tip-toe past them and walk into the kitchen to clean it. I don't want Kentlee coming over and seeing a dirty kitchen. I would be embarrassed.

I gasp when two strong hands wrap around my waist as

I am washing the last dish. I moan when his lips touch that spot right behind my ear, and then when one of his hands slides up my belly to cup my breast—I melt.

"Bates," I murmur.

"Morning, beautiful," he whispers as he gently sucks on my skin.

"It's afternoon," I point out. He chuckles behind me, pulling me into his chest. "Thank you for doing that with Stella," I murmur.

"She said she'd never been on a bike before. Vault brought that over the other day; his daughter outgrew it," he announces. It makes my heart skip a beat.

That is so nice of Vault, and this club, for taking care of not only me, but Stella too. It's the sweetest thing that anybody has ever done for us. Bates and his club. I can't even put my gratitude into words.

"I don't know what to say. It's all so much," I whisper, looking out the little kitchen window in front of me.

"Nothin' to say, baby, except *thanks*. We take care of our own as much as we can," he states before his fingers squeeze my breast. I whimper.

"Bates."

"Want you again tonight when you come home, baby," he informs me as he grinds his hard, jean covered cock between my ass.

"It's going to be a late night again," I warn.

"I won't be home until after three, then I'm going to fuck you at least twice," he grunts before he plucks my hardened nipple over the top of my bra and shirt.

"You'll be at the strip club, then?" I ask as I turn in his arms to face him.

"I will. That's my job, Brent. I manage the club and the girls. I have to be there," he says, his face hardened and his eyes even harder.

"I know. I just…" I let my insecure words trail off. He doesn't need me acting insecure and totally bat-shit crazy.

"You just what?" he asks with narrowed eyes as his hands wrap around my ass.

"You'll be there with naked women all night long," I say on a sigh, turning my head to the side. I don't want to look at him. I don't want him to see my voiced insecurities.

"Think I can't keep my dick in my pants?" he grunts.

I don't answer.

I don't want to tell him even more truths about my life just a few short weeks ago. I don't want him to feel even more pity for me. He's already heard enough about my life—my marriage.

"Brent," he whispers. I turn to face him, my eyes shining with tears.

"He cheat on you, too?" he asks, reading me. He reads me so damn well. I should be angry, but I can't be. He knows me. He's always known me.

"Yeah," I croak.

Bates' hands cup my cheeks and his thumbs sweep the wetness from underneath my eyes before his lips gently touch mine. I sigh when his forehead rests against mine and his nose slides against my own.

"When I told you last night that your pussy takes no other dick but mine—that goes the other way, too, baby. I don't want anybody else, not when I have you at home. It's you, *tigritsa*. No other woman makes me feel the way you do. He's a fuckin' moron and an asshole. I'll never purposely do anything to hurt you or Stella, *ever*."

I let out a shaky breath at his words. Me. It's always been me. He's said them before, but the way he is looking at me now, like he sees me, like he knows exactly who I am—there is no more illusion that I'm this perfect, untouchable, mythical being from the past. He knows my ugly, he knows most of my secrets, and he knows what a slut I've been. Yet, he still *wants* me. I don't understand why.

"Why?" I ask what I'm thinking, but the rest of the words won't come. Fortunately, the most important does.

"If you can't understand why I want you, only you, then that just means I have to work my ass off to show you. I can't explain something like that, Brentlee. I have to show it. I'm your man, now. If you don't want to label that for the public yet, that's fine; but regardless, that's exactly what I am."

I blink and just look at him, really look at him. He's completely serious. He's my man. *Mine.* The thought is so foreign. It's been so long since I've thought of any man as my own. Since him, over ten years. Scotty was my husband, but he shared his body with whomever he wanted to, ignoring the ring on his finger. Bates was the last man who I called my own, and now he's telling me again, he's mine.

"I—I don't…" I can't finish my words. I shake my head in confusion. Bates shifts his forehead off of mine and captures my lips with his.

I fist his shirt with my hands and pull him closer to me when his tongue slides between my lips. He consumes me, as he always does, tasting me and tempting me all at the same time. I moan when his hands roughly squeeze my ass as he grinds his hard cock against my belly. I want him again. I'm still sore from last night, but that doesn't stop my body from craving more.

"Tonight, baby," he murmurs against my lips.

"Okay, tonight," I agree.

I can't deny I want him. I couldn't even if I tried. It's always been him, just as he says it's always been me. We're like magnets drawn to each other. I'm just not sure how we will end up.

Most likely, it will be in complete ruins.

Sniper

Brentlee is so fuckin' adorable as her mind races with about a million different thoughts. I want to fuck her to the point of exhaustion again just so she'll stop whatever bullshit she has going through that head of hers. But I don't have time. I have a meeting with Drifter in about thirty minutes, and then I have to go straight to the club.

I hate that I won't be able to drop her off for work tonight, but I'll be picking her up. Then, I'll be fucking her until she begs me to stop. I feel like an addict; I can't stop thinking about that sweet fuckin' pussy of hers.

"I gotta head out, babe. I'll pick you up at the clubhouse tonight, so don't leave with anybody else," I warn as I release her perfect ass and take a step back from her.

"Who's going to take me there?" she asks, chewing on her bottom lip.

"LeeLee is going to drop you off after you're done here," I inform her. She nods once.

"Okay, Bates," she murmurs. I nod once before I turn my

back to her. I hear her exhale loudly and it makes me turn around and take two long strides toward her.

I grip my hands around her hips and lift her to my height before I kiss her soft lips, fast and hard. She squeaks with her surprise, but soon her arms are wrapped round my neck.

"Now I'll see you tonight, yeah?" I ask after I've kissed her.

"Yeah," she sighs.

I place her back on her feet and press my lips against her neck, needing one more taste of her delicious skin as I swipe my tongue under her ear.

"Good god, you two are just the cutest couple I have ever seen," Kentlee says. We freeze before I turn to her.

"LeeLee, you shouldn't sneak up on me," I frown. She ignores me and smiles.

"I saw Buck outside, he's on full protection duty. I had to sneak in and see the two of you in action. I was honestly scared after Fury came home last night. I wasn't sure all of this would happen," she says, waving her hand around toward us.

"I'm out of here, ladies. Have a good afternoon," I say as I begin to walk toward the front door.

"You know I'm going to get all the details, right?" LeeLee calls out. I stop and turn to her before I smile widely.

"Anything Brent tells you isn't nearly as much as you've already seen," I tell her.

"You're disgusting," Kentlee cries. I can't help myself, I laugh.

In the living room Stella and Bear are seated and Bear is showing her some new toy of his. She's totally into it and doesn't even hear me walk up next to her. I sink to my knees and tug on one of her little blonde, braided pigtails. Those little fuckers were not easy to do. I hadn't braided hair since Mary-Anne was a kid, and it took me a few tries to remember how.

"Bye, *malyshka*. You be a good girl for your mama now, okay?"

"I will, Bates," she says as she looks up at me with her pretty blue eyes, and her mother's perfect smile.

"Take care of your cousin, Bear. You're the man of the house," I say before I ruffle his hair and stand.

"Yeah, I will, Uncle Bates," he says, trying to sound bigger with his little boy voice, his chest puffed out. Such a big man, he is.

I leave the women and kids, nodding to Buck as I pass by him on my way to my bike. I take a good look around, making sure there are no signs of Scotty or *whoever-in-the-fuck* he has had watching Fury and Kentlee's place. It looks clear, and I know Buck will keep an eye on the girls and kids. He's a good guy with kids of his own; he knows the importance of protection.

I take a deep breath and then smile as I start my bike.

Tonight, Brentlee will be on the back, holding me close to her, her sweet tits pressed against my back as we ride from the club to here—our home. My dreams are finally coming true, dreams that I didn't even know I wanted anymore. I thought they were long gone, buried and forgotten, but they aren't. Nope. They're alive and right in front of me, ripe for the taking. I'm going to take them, too.

My girls.

They're mine.

All fucking mine.

And if that prick Scotty thinks for one goddamn minute he's going to get them away from me, he's got another thing coming. I killed for LeeLee without hesitation. But for Brentlee and Stella, I'll fucking torture, and I'll do it with a fucking smile on my face.

chapter eleven

Sniper

I pull up to the *Devils Club* and see that Drifter is already waiting for me. Today isn't so much a meeting about the club as it is about Brentlee and that fuck face Scotty Corbin. I need information, and Drifter has it.

I give him a nod as I take my keys out and open up the club. Once we're inside, I lock the door behind him and grab him a beer from behind the bar, along with one for myself. I have a feeling I'm gonna need this shit.

"It's ugly, brother," he murmurs as he slides the manila envelope toward me. I take a pull from my beer and open it up, sliding the papers out carefully and setting them in front of me.

ROUGH AND RAW

Medical records. Pictures. Notes. They are all stacked neatly. They are all *undocumented* but kept by the family physician Brentlee said the Corbin's sent to her after the horrific beatings Scotty gave her. Things that she didn't have to be admitted into the hospital for.

"Yeah, I heard some of the shit," I admit, taking another pull before I open the file.

"Hearin' it and seein' it. Totally different, brother," he grunts as he drinks his own beer.

I open the first page and see a younger version of Brentlee. The date says she's nineteen, one month after their marriage. She's got a black eye, swollen shut, and bruising on her neck. *Choked.* I close my eyes. No wonder she freaked out on me last night. I'm surprised she didn't go into a full blown panic attack.

The report says she fell. *Don't they always?*

I scan the document and at the bottom in fine print it says that there's vaginal tearing and bleeding after a complete physical. It makes my stomach turn. Rape. He raped her. One month after their marriage, it had already begun.

I flip through the pictures, watching them like watching a movie, each one more brutal than the one before. Bloody noses and lips. Swollen eyes, concussions, vaginal and anal bleeding and tearing. All photographic evidence of her hellish nightmare of a life. I also notice the light leaving her eyes more and more as each year passes. In the last picture, her honey-brown eyes look completely dead—void of all emotion.

"How'd you get them?" I demand.

"Snuck in when the fuck was sleeping. Held a gun to his head," Drifter chuckles.

What I asked him to do is definitely below his pay grade, since he's the vice president of the club, but he's the best at sneaking in and getting shit handled.

"Retaliation?" I ask, finishing off my beer in one gulp.

"He couldn't get that shit to me quick enough. Said the Corbin's are an entire family of sick fucks and anything he could do to help, he would. He can't, of course, go against him in court, seeing as he'd be thrown in the pen for hiding it the way he did. But he said he'd cooperate with us anyway we want him to," Drift explains. I nod.

"Thanks, brother. I appreciate it," I mutter, my eyes focused on a picture of my beautiful Brentlee looking so fuckin' broken.

"He would have killed her, had she stayed any longer," Drifter says. I nod.

I know he would have.

Drifter leaves and I can't help my thoughts from being consumed by my own past. Instead of Brentlee's beautiful battered face, I see my mother's. Blood and bruises littering her face, arms, neck, and legs. I can't remember how many times my dad brought her to near death with his fists, let alone when he would use his feet and other objects around the house.

My mind takes me back to one horrible night in particular. I was seventeen, almost finished with high school. Already bigger than my old man, I had decided enough was enough. He walked in on me begging my mom to just pack her shit and go. I was almost through with high school, I could work and take care of her and Mary-Anne. We didn't need him anymore. Once he heard me say that, he started to wail on me. He wasn't as big as I was, but the old fucker was strong. Once the shock wore off, I was able to stop him. I screamed at my mom to go while I held him down. The old man just smiled and winked.

"She ain't goin' nowhere, boy," he sneered.

"Mom… go," I yelled.

"I… I can't, Bates. I love him," she whispered.

That was the moment I lost all hope for my mom. She *loved* him. *Loved* him so much she'd let her kids get beat by him; she'd let herself get beat by him. Nothing else mattered but her sick and twisted love for an abuser. I stayed until it was time to leave for boot camp. I stayed for only one reason. Mary-Anne. My baby sister. I didn't want to leave, but I needed to get the fuck out. I needed a good career so that I could take care of myself.

In the end, it didn't matter.

My career didn't fuckin' matter. Killing dozens of people in the name of country didn't matter. Not in the end, not when it consumed me and fucked me up and made it impossible to go back. The nightmares that plague me are sometimes more than I can bear. I've buried myself in weed, and booze, and pussy to try and forget, but I always remember—*I'll always be haunted.*

I put all the papers back in the envelope before I grab another beer and go into my office. I take a swig and shove the envelope into my desk drawer. I could live my whole life and never see it again. I can't, though. Scotty Corbin needs to be taken down. Brentlee can't live holed up in my house or the clubhouse her whole life. She needs to have her freedoms.

I pick up the phone and call the attorney.

"Bates Lukin, I was just getting ready to call you, myself," Stan says.

"Got a file I ain't supposed to have, Mr. Jones," I confess. He chuckles.

"Lay it out for me, then."

I do. I tell him everything in detail. He asks me to make copies and forward them to his office. He can't use them, of course, but what I love about Mr. Jones is he isn't afraid to scare the piss out of people.

"He is being served with the intent to divorce this evening. Make sure you keep a close watch on Brentlee and Stella in the next few days. You never know when guys like that are going to strike," he warns. I nod.

He doesn't know that I fully comprehend what he's saying. My father drug me out of bed once, by my ankle, because I didn't put a dish in the sink. I set it next to the sink. He beat the shit out of me for twenty minutes straight before he made me go back to bed. I was nine at the time. I never left a dish on the edge of the sink again. *This is probably why my housekeeping skills leave something to be desired.*

"I got a man on the house at all times when I'm not home. They're safe," I assure Stan. He hums.

"Honestly, I don't think the divorce will be much of a problem. He might turn into a bit of an asshole, but I have proof of his extracurricular activities, and Brentlee isn't asking for anything, so he won't really have much of a say in the matter. Custody, however, *that* is what I'm concerned with."

I agree.

I wholeheartedly agree.

Scotty might accept Brentlee leaving him, he won't like it, but he might be able to deal with it—*but having his child taken away*—he won't accept. Whether he cares about her or not, it won't matter. He'll do whatever he can to win. He'll do whatever he can to hurt Brent. My poor *tigritsa* is going to have to fight.

Brentlee

"You had s-e-x with him, didn't you?" Kent asks as she plates the sandwiches she brought with her for the kids.

"I'm not talking about this right now," I say as I widen my eyes and look down at Bear and Stella who are watching with rapt anticipation as Kentlee loads their plates with chips.

"They are more concerned with these chips then what you're saying," she shrugs before handing them each a plate. "Go into the living room. You guys can camp out in front of the T.V."

I roll my eyes at my sister.

"Now, tell me," she orders as she sits down. I watch her take Ellie and place her onto her little portable high chair.

Ellie is beautiful. Blonde hair and blue eyes, she looks like the perfect combination of both Fury and Kentlee. I see a little bit of Stella in her as well. I know she's going to be gorgeous, and I can only hope that she is brave enough to stand up to her father, or the poor thing will never date, *ever*.

"We slept together last night," I confess as I watch Kentlee place some goldfish snacks in front of Ellie on the little tray.

"*Ha!* I knew it. I could tell," she says with a huge smile on her face.

"What do you mean by that?" I ask, plating our sandwiches.

"I mean, you look happier. Less stressed, and freshly laid," she grins. I roll my eyes.

"Shut up," I mumble.

We spend the rest of the afternoon talking about the kids and playing with the kids. Luckily, she doesn't ask any real details about Bates and me—or our reunion. I leave her to watch the kids while I get ready for work, and I can't hide my smile once I walk inside of the bedroom. I look around at Bates and my comingled things, and it makes me feel at peace. How on earth I can leave one tyrannical crazy person and practically hop into another man's bed and be happy about it is beyond me. But I am. I'm so happy.

If Bates was expecting me to carry that Old Lady status he speaks of, I don't think I would be feeling quite as peaceful as I do. It would come with all kinds of emotions. But the way it is now, a physical exclusivity with nothing more—that, I'm okay with.

"Brent!" Kentlee yells. I open the door with a towel wrapped around my body, in pure panic.

"What," I cry as I run into the living room.

"I forgot to give you this." She hands me a bag of clothes and my heart slowly chills the hell out.

"First off, you scared the crap out of me. Secondly, what's in here?"

"I'm sorry, Brent, I just didn't want you to get dressed without it. Its stuff you can wear down to the clubhouse. Things my fat ass will never be able to wear again," she grunts. I roll my eyes.

My sister is curvier than I am, but she's incredibly gorgeous. I wish I had all those curves she's got going on. Boys and men have always admired her body over my more stick-figure-ish one. That's just one more reason why I threw myself at so many boys after Bates left—*validation*. I wanted to be the one all the boys looked at, not my beautiful sister. I was young, and jealous, and hurt, and so very dumb. I shake my head of the past and thank Kent for the bag before I go back into the bedroom and finish getting dressed for the clubhouse.

I slide on a pair of Kentlee's skin tight leggings, they keep everything exactly where it needs to be and come up past my belly button. I put on a bralette top and sigh at my stomach. Not as flat as it used to be, but good enough for a room of hard-assed bikers. On my feet I slide on a pair of wedge booties. I keep my hair long and straight, and my make-up dark. I smirk after I've painted my lips red with lipstick. Scotty would really hate, I mean truly despise, what I'm wearing. I feel a wave of victory at that thought. I can do and wear what I want now—*I love it.*

"Hot mama," Kentlee says as I walk out of the bedroom.

I roll my eyes but it doesn't stop the smile on my lips. I haven't felt *hot* in a long time, so I happily accept the compliment.

A few minutes later, there's a knock on the door. Buck announces that its Tammy to watch Stella for the night. Kentlee opens the door without hesitation and wraps Tammy in her arms. We spend the next few minutes talking as I help Kentlee pack up the kid's toys and then kiss and hug my sweet Stella goodnight.

"You'll be good?" I ask.

"I aways good, mommy," she says with a smile. I shake my head and hug her one last time, inhaling her sweet little girl scent, and then I leave.

I thank Tammy and tell her I'll be home much later.

"I got nothin' else going on, honey. You just do your job; providing for your family is what's most important." I smile sadly and nod. I'm not really providing for Stella, yet.

I hope that one day I will be. I hope to be a woman she can be proud of. But, for now, I'm going to keep going, keep working, and keep us both safe. Keeping us both happy and safe is all I really care about right now. Everything else will eventually work itself out.

Kentlee drives me straight to the clubhouse. I'm lost in my own thoughts and not very talkative. When she pulls up in front, I tell her thank you. Before I can leave, she wraps her hand around my forearm.

"I'm so proud of you, Brent," she announces.

"Not much to be proud of, but thank you," I say sadly.

"You're getting out. You're taking care of yourself and Stella. I'm so proud," she whispers.

"I'm just so thankful and lucky to have you and Fury and the club," I say.

"Those other people, our biological family, they can kick rocks, babe. This family, this family is the one that's going to help you, be there for you, and, in the end, have your back."

I nod, noticing a fierceness in her eyes. I don't know details of my sister's life these past six years, but there's something that has happened to her, or something she's seen. She isn't the same Kentlee she was all those years ago. There's something else there.

"What happened?" I ask, thinking out loud.

"That, little sister, is a story for alcohol and dessert," she smiles.

I leave her in the car to go inside of the club and start my night.

I have to make this dessert and booze night soon. I need to know exactly what my sister has been through. I need to understand everything. Maybe we aren't so different, my sister and me.

chapter twelve

Sniper

I watch her from the corner. She didn't see me slip in and I'm grateful for that. I'm not spying to be a dick, not really, I just like to watch her. She smiles at Grizz, who takes the offered shot glass from her hand and downs the jack. I can tell some of the heaviness is beginning to lift from her. Her smile is brighter. I feel like a fuckin' pussy, but all I have ever wanted was for Brentlee to be happy.

My phone rings in my pocket and I slip it out. *Mary-Anne.*

"Little sister," I greet as a smile tugs on my lips.

"I heard you have some news for me," she says. I can tell she's smiling on the other end.

"I do?" I ask, knowing damn well she's referring to Brent. Odds are, Kentlee called her the minute Brentlee moved in with me. Knowing my sister, she bided her time and now she wants details.

"Don't be an asshole," she murmurs. It makes me laugh.

"Don't act like you don't already know," I point out, which causes her to chuckle on the line.

"Okay, how about I just ask this. Are you happy?"

I pause for a moment. Taking in the question. Truly thinking about it.

Am I happy? *Fuck yes, I am.*

Could I be happier? *Always.*

That doesn't mean that Brent doesn't make me happy, because she sure as fuck does. But having her with my name inked on her body, my ring on her finger, and my baby inside of her—that would make me happier. For now, though, yeah, I'm fuckin' happy.

"Shit's goin' good, Mary-Anne," I admit.

"Be good to her, Bates. She deserves everything you can give her. But don't let her hurt you, either, because you deserve the best," she says.

"I'm not as good as I used to be, Mary. I don't deserve her anymore," I confess. She sighs.

"You're too hard on yourself."

"How's Cali?" I ask, changing the subject.

I don't want to talk about how undeserving of Brentlee I am. Mary-Anne doesn't need to know all of the truths that hide inside of my head; all the nightmares, and horror I've seen.

"Awesome. I met someone. We're going to come out there in a few months. I want you to meet him," she says excitedly.

As much as I want to warn her off of him, mainly because he has a dick, I can't. She sounds good, happy, and after the hellish childhood she's endured, she deserves all of the happiness she can get.

"Can't wait," I say before we say our goodbyes and I hang up.

My eyes go back to Brentlee, who is serving a beer to Torch. He grins at her, but he doesn't look anywhere but her face. He doesn't touch her or flirt, he just talks and laughs. I don't mind that. I have to let some shit go. So she fucked him ten years ago, what kind of asshole am I to hold that over her head? As long as he keeps his dick away from her now, I can't get too fuckin' pissed about it. Even though I want to beat the shit out of him, nobody can predict the future, and how would he or I have known this is where we'd end up?

"Hey, baby," a sweet voice from my left whispers.

I look down and notice it's Star. Long dark hair, big fake tits. The girl I've fucked so many times I've lost count, mainly because she reminded me of Brentlee. Though in reality, Star couldn't hold a candle to Brent in any way, shape, or form. She just resembles her, *slightly*.

"Star," I grunt.

Star, aptly named because she became a star in the clubhouse within days of her arrival. She sucks good cock, spreads everything, and she's good at it all. She also rivals anything Kitty, our old clubhouse slut star, ever did. She loves giving us a show with the other sluts, and is always down for whatever. She's my favorite whore.

"She's really pretty," Star says, wrapping her red painted fingernails around my forearm. I can't help my cock from stirring. Those fuckin' fingers always feel good on my dick; he totally knows what's up.

"She is," I grunt.

"You know I'd be willing, Sniper," she offers. I look down at her, lifting a brow.

"Yeah, that's kind of your job," I say, smirking.

"You want us both, right here, in front of everybody. I know your kink, baby. Does she?" she asks. My back goes straight.

My eyes go back to Brentlee, who is busily serving drinks to my brothers, oblivious to this conversation I'm having with Star. I turn my head back down to look at her. Innocent looking, but far from it, Star is one of the dirtiest bitches I've ever fucked.

"You won't be able to have that sweet closed-door-bedroom fucking for very long, Sniper. What happens when you have a nightmare? Is she going to let her use you the way I do?"

"Shut the fuck up," I grind out, hating the fact that she's right.

I can't do to Brentlee all the things I want to. She's been violated and hurt, no way is she going to let me use her body to cope with my own hell. I would never ask her for it, either.

"You know where to find me when you need me," she purrs as she slides her hand down my arm and over to my dick, cupping me and squeezing over my jeans. I couldn't hide the semi I'm sporting even if I wanted to.

"Yeah, I know exactly where you'll be," I grunt.

Star walks away from me, her ass swaying in her mini skirt. Every now and then, one of her cheeks peeks out the bottom and I can't stop my groan of appreciation. She's pretty, not as gorgeous as Brentlee, but there's no denying Star isn't a hot piece and a hot fuck.

"Playin' with fire, brother," Dirty Johnny says, walking up to me with a cigarette hanging from his lips, as always.

"Yeah?" I halfheartedly ask.

"Star wants to be your Old Lady. She sees Brent livin' in your pad. She's gonna try and get between you both and she's going to try her damndest," he says, blowing out a cloud of smoke.

"Don't matter. I only want Brent," I say, not believing my own fucking words, and feeling like a prick for it.

"Yeah, okay," he says, taking a step away from me. He stops and tips his head to the side, his cold eyes focused on mine. "Brentlee's eaten shit for a while, brother. Give it to her straight. You want her, that's cool, make sure she's getting all of you at the same time."

I watch Dirty Johnny as he walks away from me and toward another whore. He grabs her hand without missing a beat, and then they disappear toward the rooms. I shift my gaze back to Brentlee, who is now looking at me, a look of confusion plastered all over her features. My breath hitches and I panic at what she could have seen.

I push off of the wall and make my way toward her.

Apparently, I have some fuckin' shit to come clean about. This conversation is better had in my room here, not at home, and not in front of my brothers.

Brentlee

It's hard not to feel Bates when he walks through the door.

There is a charge in whatever room he enters. It follows him. I know the exact moment he slips inside of the clubhouse, and I can feel his eyes on me, watching me. I pretend not to notice him leaning against the wall. It's hard, but I succeed for the most part. My eyes fail as they keep drifting over to him for a glimpse every so often.

I watch as he talks on his phone. He's all smiles, and it makes my belly quiver. How can he be so damn gorgeous? Then, my belly falls to the floor when one of the clubwhores walks over to him. *Star.* I've heard her praises sung throughout the clubhouse the past two days. She's their pride and joy, or at least her mouth, pussy, and ass are.

I hold my breath as she talks to Bates, her hand on his arm. He's looking down at her, conversing. He smirks at her and there is a familiarity I hate in their actions. *They've fucked.* Of course they have. She's a whore and that's what she's here for. I grind my teeth together as her hand goes to his dick. Bates makes no move to remove her from his body. I hate it. I am so jealous that I see nothing but red.

"That don't mean a fuckin' thing, darlin'," Grizz says to me. I turn to face him, willing myself to get some fucking control.

"I don't know what you're talking about," I lie.

"These whores, you'll learn, they don't mean shit," he states. I gape at him.

"So Fury? Even though he's married?" I ask in shock.

"Fury? Fuck, no. Kentlee wouldn't be down for that. Me? Shit's happened. My wife has always known the way it is. Kind of like Vegas around these parts. What happens in the clubhouse stays in the clubhouse. Maybe you think that's wrong? But here, the rules are different. This isn't like civilian life out there," he motions at the doors that lead outside to the parking lot.

"My soon-to-be ex-husband fucked who he wanted, when he wanted," I admit.

Speaking that out loud is still hard for me. But there is also something freeing in accepting that he cheated on me. He fucked around, and he fucked me up, and I'm still here to tell the tale. I close my eyes for a second and try to gather my thoughts. Can I live to tell the tale if Bates fucks around? He wanted exclusivity, but how long will that last? *A week, a month, a year?*

"Then you know the score right, dalrin'? What happens in here, it doesn't mean he don't love you. It doesn't mean he don't want only you. It just means he needs to get laid. Can't fault a man for having a good time," Grizz shrugs before he taps the bar top and walks away.

I hate his words.

Every single one of them.

I look back at Bates and our eyes lock on each other. I can't read his expression, but I don't care. I don't want to. I'll never be more than a burden, dependent on him, on any man. I'm Bates' whore at home. Nothing more. He'll come here when I'm not working and fuck Star, and there's nothing I can do about it. I'll have to accept it. Take it. My price for protection against Scotty.

"C'mon," Bates murmurs to me, holding out his hand. I don't respond as I place my own hand in his. There's nothing to say, not really.

I let him lead me toward the bedrooms without protest. Once we're inside of his room, I look around. It's messy and unkempt. Clothes strewn about and trashcans overflowing. A complete bachelor's pad. It even smells, and I wonder when the last time he cleaned was. *Gross.*

"We have to talk," he says, locking the door behind him and wrapping his hands around my bare waist.

The touch of his warm hands on my sides sends a thrill through me. His touch, anywhere on my body, will always do that to me. It doesn't matter how my brain and my heart feel, my body will always want him.

chapter thirteen

Brentlee

*T*alk.

That word. It never means anything good.

It never has. And it never will.

"Is this about Star?" I ask out of pure need. I don't want him to beat around the bush.

"What about Star?" he asks, looking down at me. He's too close, he smells too fucking good. I want to lick and bite and suck.

"I saw her touching you," I admit. His body goes rigid. "It's okay. I know you said we're exclusive, but I also know about the clubhouse and what happens here with the whores and you guys."

"What do you know?" he growls, shaking me a bit. I look up and focus on those gorgeous dark eyes of his.

"I know it doesn't mean you care for me less if you fuck them," I whisper, unable to look away.

"Brent..." he starts. I put my finger up to his lips.

I don't want to hear any promises that will surely be broken. I don't want to hear how he'll take care of me—I know that he will. I don't need to do anything but accept what he's offering, his protection against Scotty, and a chance to allow me to be free of that.

"Bates, I get it, okay? I'm a big girl..." I start. I am interrupted when his lips touch mine, effectively shutting me up.

"Shut up," he grunts before he backs my body toward the bed. I fall back as soon as my legs crash into the side, and Bates lands on top of me.

"I don't want what you think I do," he starts. I open my mouth to ask him a question, but he narrows his eyes on me. I quickly shut my mouth and wait for him to finish.

"I have nightmares. I wake up and I need to fuck. It isn't gentle and it isn't sweet. It's rough and I don't want to hurt you," he confesses as he moves one of his hands to cradle the back of my head. "I would rather die than hurt you like that, Brentlee. I, uh, also... I have certain appetites and I don't know that you'd ever be okay with it."

"Like?" I ask wide eyed. I need the whole truth before I can say this, whatever we have, can really continue. I need to know.

"I like to have threesomes in public," he says in complete seriousness.

I look at him for a long beat. This is Bates. I can't believe he's telling me this. The man who didn't want anybody to see me stripping at *Devils* is telling me he wants to, instead, fuck me in public.

"So, what? You want to fuck Star and me in the clubhouse for everyone to watch?" I ask, trying not be be defensive, even if that is exactly how I feel.

"You and Star. You, another brother, and me," he shrugs.

"Get off of me," I grind out. Bates shakes his head, unmoving.

"Baby, I told you I wasn't the same boy. I'm a man now. I know what I like." I look into his eyes, waiting for an apology to cross his features, but it doesn't. He is completely unapologetic for his kinks.

"So you're telling me, you chastised me and became angry with me for fucking a couple of your *brothers* ten years ago, but you're okay with me fucking them as long as you're doing it, too?" I ask, trying to keep my voice low and even. Probably failing miserably.

"I meant it when I said you'd take no other dick in your pussy or your ass," he grinds out. I push him off of me and he goes willingly.

"What do you want, then? What's the point of this conversation? Do you want to fuck me roughly? Hurt me? Do it. I don't care. You can't do anything to me that hasn't already been done, Bates. Do you want me to perform a threesome with you and some whore? Do you want permission to fuck whores? What exactly do you want?" I scream out in frustration.

"*I don't know,*" he yells back. "I don't know. I want you, Brentlee. I want every part of you. But I have needs and I don't know when they'll surface. I also don't know what exactly they'll entail," he admits.

"I don't know that I can fulfill them," I shakily admit. I watch as he props his elbows on his knees and cradles his face in his hands.

"I know," I admit. "I shouldn't have fucked you. I shouldn't have, but I did and I can't let you go," he murmurs before he lifts his head and turns his neck to face me.

"What does that mean?"

"It means you're mine."

"This cannot work. It will destroy us both," I whisper as I stand.

Bates doesn't let me get far. His arm shoots out and his hand wraps around my waist pulling me between his legs. I stumble and have to put my hands on his shoulders for support. He looks up at me, the haunted eyes I'm so afraid of staring at me. His demons are so fucking dark, it frightens me.

"You leave me, and *that* will destroy me, Brentlee," he mutters.

"Bates…" I say.

He shakes his head and stands before he moves around me, his front to my back. I feel his lips on my shoulder. I feel him pepper kisses from my shoulder to my spine and then I gasp when his hand swiftly and intensely pushes my chest onto the mattress. I gasp when I suddenly feel him rip my pants down to my thighs.

"No more, Brentlee. You're not even going to think about leaving me. I won't let you," he grinds out, his breath fanning the bare skin of my ass.

I cry out when I feel his hand make contact with my left cheek.

"Shut up," he growls. I snap my mouth closed. "You even

think about leaving me again, about writing me off, I'll do more than spank this gorgeous ass of yours."

He spanks my other cheek before he repeats the move again, only in a different spot. Tears begin to fall down my cheeks when he's on his eighth blow against my backside. He pauses behind me, and I think that it's over, that he's finished, but the burning sensation of his hand meeting my upper thigh proves me wrong.

"No more," I plead through my sobs.

"One more," he promises as his hand connects the top of my other thigh.

I whimper when I feel two of his fingers slide through my center. I hear him hum behind me before he thrusts those fingers deep inside of me.

"You're crying, but your pussy's wet, baby," he whispers against my shoulder before he nips my skin.

I don't respond to him. I don't tell him that I'm used to pain with sex. I'm used to always *hurting*. He's like Scotty, in a way; except, he doesn't hide his brutish activities behind a suit. No, he's a walking advertisement for it. I was fooling myself to think he was any different.

I feel my hips being tipped, and then, before I can take another breath, he's inside of me. I hear him sigh above me once he's fully seated, and I pinch my eyes closed, waiting for his brutal forceful fucking. I can take it—I've taken it all before.

"Brentlee, you're my *tigritsa*. Don't ever forget that. I am *me*, I can't change that. However, I'll always be good to you, baby, *always*," he murmurs before he sweeps my hair to the side and tips his head to look at me in the eyes. "You're mine."

I don't try to stifle my tears or to look away from him.

Bent over his bed, my pants halfway down my thighs, the rest of me fully clothed, with a bright red ass from his hand. I'm embarrassed, and mortified, and angry. He wants to control me, own me, and *possess* me.

There is no way out, either.

If I leave, I open myself up and paint a big red target for Scotty—and not only will it effect me, it'll also effect Stella. I have to choose the lesser of two evils. Bates is good to me, he's given us a safe place and he's taken care of Stella and me without batting an eyelash. I can endure his forceful hand, as long as it doesn't leak outside of the bedroom door. I can take what he's giving, for protection and safety.

Bates doesn't say anything else as he begins to slowly slide out of me before he sinks back inside. It's achingly slow, and I moan at how good it feels, how surprised I am that he isn't being rough. He fills me up completely. I want to hate him. I want to tell him to fuck off, but I can't. Not when a simple touch from him ignites me. I'm too weak to turn away from him, and I hate myself for it. *Weakness*, my downfall, always.

"It's only you, *tigritsa*. You're the only one I want," he vows as one of his hands slides from my waist to my clit. He begins to gently stroke me.

Bates' other hand wraps around my hair as he begins to thrust harder, and *faster*, in and out of me. His fingers stroke harder and faster against my clit, as well. I can't stop myself from grinding back against him, and when he pinches my clit, I arch my back up with a cry as I come. My pussy clamps down around his hard cock, and my whole body stiffens.

"Fuck, yes," he moans before he releases me. Dropping his hands to my hips, he uses my body to fuck him.

I am limp and lifeless as he guides me up and down on

his hard cock. Then, he pauses, seated inside of me, and with a roar he comes—*hard*.

I pinch my eyes closed as he falls on top of my back, his forehead pressed into the crook of my neck. I want to cry, but I can't. I feel exhausted and completely wrung out. I have nothing left.

I thought by coming to the *Notorious Devils*, that by coming to Fury and Kentlee for help, I would feel empowered. I left my abuser, I left him before he killed me—I left him to save Stella. Instead, I've becoming spineless, again. I'm completely and totally dependent on a man, a man who I want to love so much, yet he's not giving me much of a reason to. He's saying some of the right things, and yet not committing. *What kind of woman leaves her husband and jumps into bed with another man and expects commitment?* I'm so fucked up, I don't know which way is up or down.

I want Bates, but I want my freedom. The way he is now, I can't have both. There's no freedom that comes with being in his bed. Only more control. I feel like I'm choking, suffocating. My independence and freedom is within my grasp, but I can't have it.

I do know that Bates will protect Stella. He'll make sure no harm comes to her and that—that has to be my main focus. So if I have to be with other people, if I have to put on some kind of show to ensure her safety and mine—I'll do it.

"I don't want to fuck you in front of anybody, baby," he murmurs.

"It doesn't matter. I'll do whatever you want, Bates," I resign.

He slips out of me, but he doesn't walk away from me. Instead, he picks me up like a child, my pants still halfway down my legs, and he lays me down in the center of his bed. I look up at the ceiling, waiting as he wraps his arm underneath me and pulls me into his side.

"It matters, Brent," he murmurs.

"You have different tastes now, I get it. I'm yours, so I need to fulfill those. I need to turn a blind eye if you want another woman, and I need to be waiting in your bed when you come home to me. I have a place. I can deal with that. I've done it all before," I ramble.

I'm just me and I won't be enough. I'll never be enough for any man, let alone him—a man who has cravings and needs that I can't fulfill on my own. I want to think that I'm strong enough to take him as he comes, but who could do that? Who could watch the man she has longed for, for a decade, be with another woman? I'm not that strong. It'll kill me, slowly.

My inner thoughts are interrupted when I feel his fingers tangle in my hair. I'm not prepared when they pull and my neck arches back, my wide eyes meeting his pissed off ones.

"One taste will never change, baby, and that's you. The other shit, my nightmares, what *I* think I need, we'll figure that out as we go. Only want your pussy. Only you," he murmurs before his lips crash against mine, taking them in a brutal kiss. His tongue forces its way inside of my mouth and his fingers tighten even more in my hair. He's owning me, all of me, and I'm letting him. I can't stop him; I'll never be able to.

I surrender to him—I'm his, it's all I have ever wanted and now I have it. I just hope that it's what I need.

Always and forever.

Sniper

Asleep in my arms, her lips swollen from kissing me, her brown hair tangled and matted, I wonder if this will truly last. I enjoy watching her for a moment before I have to wake her up and take her home. She looks so young, the horrors of her life gone from her face while she rests.

She's everything, my Brentlee, but *is she enough*?

I want her to be.

I want her to be enough so damn bad.

I'll ruin her. She thinks she's already ruined, but she's not—*not yet*.

I wake her up and together we leave the clubhouse in silence. We're on my bike, so luckily the trip to my place is quiet. Nothing but the wind whipping by us. Once we're inside and Tammy leaves, Brentlee quietly walks back to the bedroom. I follow, but not before I peek my head into Stella's room and see that she is indeed safe and sound for the night.

Once I make it back to my bedroom, I suck in a breath. Brentlee is stripped down, her face free of makeup and her bare skin exposed as she stands next to the bed. She doesn't say anything, she just stares at me, and I wonder what she's thinking for about two seconds before the blood leaves my brain and goes straight to my rock-hard cock.

"Brent," I grunt.

She's chewing her bottom lip and then she speaks.

"This is me, Bates. I'm nothing special. I'm just a woman who has been hurt one too many times. If you want me, you are going to have to take all of me. I'm insecure, I can be selfish, and I may not ever be what you need me to be. If you want me like you say you do, I have to be enough. I don't want to live the way I did with Scotty. I can do it, I can sit and take whatever you're willing to give me, but that's not what I want," she says.

It's the most honest she's been with me since I heard her nightmare of a life in that attorney's office.

I don't speak. I can't. She's being too raw.

Instead, I take the few steps over to her and wrap my arms around her, burying my face in her neck. I need her. I need to bury myself inside of her, to feel her around me, to know that she is real and mine. All fucking mine.

I'm never letting her go.

Sniper

"Mornin'," I murmur wrapping my arms around her from behind as she pours milk into a bowl of cereal.

"Good Morning," she says stiffly.

"What you doin' today?" I ask, trying to figure out just what in the hell is wrong with her.

"Nothing, resting," she shrugs. I watch as she slides out of my arms and takes Stella her breakfast, avoiding me and eye contact at all costs.

"I got some shit to do for the club today, I might not be home until tomorrow morning," I announce as I watch her.

"Okay," she shrugs as she busies herself in the kitchen.

"Okay, fine," I grunt.

I leave her in the kitchen, the awkward everything that filled the space behind me. But before I go, I crouch down in front of Stella who is munching on some sugar crap cereal.

"You be good for your ma, yeah?"

"Okay," she says, grinning up at me as she chews her food.

"Yeah," I murmur before I stand up and leave them.

I get on my bike and ride. I ride toward the clubhouse. I have shit to do and I need to get away from Brentlee. She's cold as fucking ice this morning and she's pushing me away. I'll give her a little space while I work for the MC, something I've been neglecting lately, to be available for her. I've been doing the minimum, working at the *Devil's Club* but not pulling my weight with my brothers.

"You good?" Drifter asks as I walk up to the bar.

"Yeah, what's your plan for the day?" I ask.

"Gonna go and watch some activity that's hit Fury's radar," he shrugs.

"Want some company?" I ask.

"Fuck, yeah. Hate scoping shit out alone; boring as fuck-all," he chuckles.

I follow Drifter out to our bikes and continue to follow him through the center and then to the complete opposite side of town, the outskirts.

"What're we watching?" I ask after we back our bikes into some brush to keep them hidden. Drifter holds his finger over his lips to quiet my questions as he walks down a hill crouched down low.

"See those guys?" he asks, lifting his chin to a group of men in leather, in a circle talking.

"Yeah."

"They ain't flyin' any colors, but they're fuckin' trouble. Just don't know what they're here for, yet. So we watch, and we wait."

I look at the men, trying to place them, but I can't. I have no fuckin' clue who they are and I don't see any tattoos marking them or affiliating them with another club. They're blank. They aren't one race either, so I can't figure them out. At all.

"You get anyone else on this, try and figure them out?" I ask, not taking my eyes off of them.

"No, just you, me, and Fury know about it," he mumbles.

They don't do anything. A couple of them take phone calls, and then about two hours later they leave. They don't drive into town, though; they head out and leave Drifter and me in a mass of confusion.

"What is their purpose? *Territory*? What?" I ask as I think aloud.

"No fuckin' clue, but we'll figure it out," he shrugs. Together we walk back to our bikes and then ride to the clubhouse.

Without a thought, I walk up to the bar and grab a bottle of booze for myself. I'm getting fucked up tonight. I jog to my room and grab my stash of green before I turn and go back to the bar. I sit down by the pool tables and light my smoke before inhaling deep, letting my head fall back and my eyes close.

My mind fills with visions of Brentlee. *Fuck*. She needs so much from me and I don't know if I can deliver. Not the way she needs. She's asking a fuck of a lot from me.

Fidelity.
Commitment.
Monogamy.

I want to give all of it to her. She deserves it all. But I don't know if I can. When push comes to shove, when it all becomes a reality and not the fantasy I've had in my head for years, can I do it?

I take a swig of booze before I open my eyes and look around at my brothers, my family. Fury is standing at the bar, his hand wrapped around LeeLee's hip, and she's got her head tipped back in laughter. I want that, I want that with Brentlee. I don't know if I'll ever have that.

I spend the rest of the night playing pool, drinking, smoking and trying to forget the dark haired beauty living in my house and sleeping alone in my bed.

My dick aches with need as I lie down in my bed. The room spins and I chuckle to myself. I feel like a fuckin' teenager all over again and it fuckin' blows. I throw my legs over the side of the bed and jump a little when my feet hit the cold floor.

My eyes shift toward the door and I give it a good long stare. I could walk right out that door and without a single fucking word make the ache in my cock go away. I could drain my balls down some bitch's throat.

Visions of Brentlee flash through my mind. The look on her face if she ever found out, the sadness that would consume her, as if she hasn't had enough of that the past ten years. I don't want to be the cause of more, all because I want to get off. I don't want her to hurt another fuckin' minute, and yet, that's all I seem to do—hurt her.

I lie back down and stare at the ceiling as the room continues to spin. I reach for my phone and stare at the numbers, I want to call her, tell her that I'm nothing but a fuckin' dick. I grip my phone and throw it. Pissed off at myself for treating her the way that I have. I don't even want these other whores and I can have them, right here and right now. Yet, my cock only wants one cunt—Brentlee's.

The next morning, I wake up and go with Drifter again. This time, the group of men are met by another man. He pulls up in a shiny, expensive car. When he gets out, my eyes narrow. It's Scott Senior, Scotty's father.

"That's Brentlee's father-in-law," I announce to Drifter.

"The fuck?"

"Bet these are the fuckers that have been watching Fury's place for any sign of her. He said someone'd been watching their comings and goings."

Without hesitation we both stand. I'll not have Brentlee terrorized a second longer, she's had enough. Whatever she wants from me, she has it. I'm fucking done with everything. She's what's important. Her and Stella. No more women, ever. Its only her for me.

"Hey there, assholes," I chuckle as I pull my gun out from my shoulder holster. In my peripheral vision, I see that Drifter has done the same. He also pulls his favorite knife out of its holster at his hip.

"What…" Scott Sr. tries to sputter. I point my gun to his head.

"These fucktards need to leave. You don't need to know where Brentlee is, she's not your concern anymore," I announce.

"That little whore is my son's wife, and her daughter is my granddaughter, so it seems she is very much my concern," he says, standing up a bit taller. He's trying to appear bigger, taller, but he's still a pencil dicked shrimp.

"Your son's a piece of shit. Call your men off of Brentlee

and pretend she never fuckin' existed," I grunt.

"Or what? You can't do shit to me, you thug. There are witnesses to your threats," he points out.

I turn to Drifter and ask if he's heard me threaten anything. He shakes his head, saying he hasn't heard a thing. Then I eyeball every single one of his wannabe goons, all of which have yet to stand up to bat for this asshole.

"Call everybody off, and leave Brentlee alone. She's suffered long enough."

"My son wants her, for whatever reason, he'll have her," he states.

"You're not calling these men off?" I ask. He shakes his head in defiance. I lift my chin to Drifter. In less than a minute, all four men are lying dead in pools of their own blood, and Scott Corbin Sr. is screaming like a woman.

"You killed them," he screeches.

"I did," I shrug. "Wanna be next?" I ask with a grin.

"N-N-No," he stutters.

"Leave Brentlee alone, and get your piece of shit kid to grant the divorce she's asking for," I demand.

"Yes, yes I will. I'll advise him," he says shakily.

"Now, get the fuck out of my sight," I bark.

I watch as he scrambles to his car and then takes off like a bat out of hell.

"I just called some prospects to clean this shit up," Drifter announces. "Do you think there'll be backlash?" he asks.

"That guy's so fuckin' scared, he just about shit his pants. There won't be backlash, at least not from him."

Once the prospects arrive, Drifter and I leave.

I text Brentlee once I'm back at the clubhouse, but hours go by and she doesn't respond. I want to throw my phone across the room. I miss her. I miss Stella. I miss my girls. I know what I want, what I need. The other shit—the fucking nameless bitches just because I think I need it—it doesn't compare to Brentlee.

There's a void now that I recognize when she isn't around, a void that she and Stella fill. They're what's been missing in my life, they are exactly what I need. I just need to figure out how to make her see that. If I could somehow *show* her that she's the only one I want because telling her won't be enough. I have to prove it to her, I have to find a way.

Brentlee

I stare at his text. It's not much, just a few words, words that mean so much more than I wish they did.

I miss you.

I miss him, too. So much. But he's not giving me what I need. I need more than a few words typed into a phone. I need him to talk to me, to tell me that he can be with only me. That he can accept me and all of my flaws.

I have to go to the clubhouse to work tomorrow, all day long, and I'm not looking forward to it. He'll be there and I don't know if I'm strong enough to resist him.

Physically, there's a magnetic pull between us that can't be denied. I want to give him what he needs, what I need, and what we both want. I wish I could be whatever he needs me to be.

"You look tired," Kentlee comments as she walks into the house.

"I am," I shrug.

"Saw him last night," she murmurs.

I wait for her to tell me more; there has to be a catch—something.

"He was drinking and playing pool. It seems you've tamed the beast." She grins victoriously.

"I highly doubt that," I snort.

"Don't. Before me, I don't think Fury had ever been in a real committed relationship. When they finally fall in love, Brentlee, when it's real, they'll put their all into it. I see the way he looks at you; the way he's always looked at you."

I roll my eyes at my sister.

My tender-hearted, romance-loving sister. Just because her life has turned into roses and rainbows, she thinks that everybody's life can be the same. I'm a testament to the fact that it doesn't work that way. I sigh and turn to the kids playing on the floor.

"Don't write him off yet, okay?" she urges.

I shrug, unable to answer. I haven't seen him for two days, and I have no clue where we stand. One text message, that's what I've received. I don't know what the future holds for us, but at this moment, it looks bleak.

"He's all fucked in the head, Brent. He'll get his shit together, just like you need to as well," she says, arching her brow.

"He's Bates," I sigh.

"When he opens up to you, take it, relish it," she murmurs.

I think about my sister's words. I want that. I want him to open up to me, to tell me that he's mine, to tell me his fears and admit his weaknesses. Then maybe, just maybe, I'll be able to begin to start trusting him with my heart.

chapter fifteen

Sniper

My head is pounding when I finally wake and I find that I'm alone, in my room at the clubhouse. It's been days since Brentlee and I had our moment. The space between us it's almost a living breathing thing. I don't know what she wants, and she doesn't know what she wants, either.

I can keep putting myself in her life, in her face, and in her bed, but that doesn't mean she's going to let me in. *Fuck, I don't even know if I can truly let her in.* I'm not the same boy I was all those years ago; and even then, even back then, she didn't know all of my truths. She knew my dad was a bastard, but I never told her details. I shielded her from the hell I lived. I didn't want her to feel sorry for me. I didn't want her to see me as weak.

I still don't.

"Sniper, baby," a sweet voice calls from the hall. I look up to see Star standing in my doorway.

She's wearing a tank top and a pair of thong panties. Nothing else. My eyes scan her bared skin, and when I get to her tits, I can see her nipples are hard under the thin top. Her hair is a little wild and her usually caked on makeup isn't there. She looks younger, *sexier*. I can't help my cock from twitching.

"Star," I grunt.

"Missed you around here," she murmurs before she walks through the door, closing it behind her.

I should stop her advancement. I should tell her to fucking *go*. I should do a lot of shit. But I don't.

"Yeah," I shrug, not moving, just watching her as she crawls up my body. "What're you doing?"

"Thought we were something," she whispers as her lips glide up my neck and her hot pussy presses against my stomach.

"You know we ain't," I murmur as my hands wrap around the outside of her thighs.

"I can give you everything you need," she purrs as her tongue snakes out and tastes my skin.

"But you can't give me what I want," I state. She sits up and looks down on me.

"What do you want? I'll give it all to you. I'll proudly wear your name, I'll have your kids, I'll fuck anywhere, everywhere and *whoever* you want me to. Whatever you want, it's yours," she says. My stomach rolls in disgust.

"Brentlee," I say shoving her off of me and standing.

"Have us both, then. Take me when you need what I can give you, what she can't. I'm not a jealous woman, Sniper, I can share. For you, I'd be willing to."

I stare at her lying on my bed as I stand above her. Any man's dream on a silver platter. She's pretty and her skills are unbelievable between the sheets. Brentlee's already said she'd deal if that's what I wanted, but I don't want Brent to *deal*.

I want her to be happy.

It's important to me that I make her happy; her and Stella. No matter what she claims, Brent's not going to be cool with me fuckin' another woman. In all honesty, yeah, Star makes my cock hard and fucking her would get me off, but she couldn't make me feel the way I do when I'm inside of Brentlee. Nobody has ever been able to match the way I feel when I'm with her, or inside of her.

"No, thanks. You need to go," I say, grabbing my jeans from the floor and lifting them over my hips.

"Whatever you want, Sniper. *Anything*," she almost pleads. It annoys me. Beggin' ain't fuckin' cute when the other person don't want you.

"I said no. You're a whore here, Star. I don't even know your real name, and I could give a fuck what it is. I took your ride a few times, but that don't make it more than the few fucks it was. It's over now. You need to get that and get the fuck out of my face," I growl before I step inside of my boots and grab my shirt from the floor. Once I am dressed, I snatch my cut off of the dresser and slide it over my shoulders. *Watching.* Waiting for this bitch to do something.

"You'll be back, wanting me again," she mutters before she stands up. I watch her walk out of my room without another word.

Crazy bitches. I'm surrounded by them.

Brentlee

I watch Star walking out of the hall where all the bedrooms are. I wonder whose bed she's coming from in just a tank and a g-string. I shake my head at the thought. Today I'm doing inventory and placing an order for the bar, so as much as I'm curious, I honestly don't have time. I'm exhausted.

Bates walks out of the hall a few minutes later and my mouth waters at the sight of him. He looks rumpled and has serious bedhead—he's so fucking sexy. I haven't seen him in three days. I'm trying to keep my distance from him. That last fight and fuck fest was too much. *Too much emotion. Too raw*.

I offered myself, me, and he hasn't responded. Sure, we fucked and the next morning he was semi-affectionate as always, but I can't read him. He didn't verbally respond. There was no promise of fidelity, and I don't know how I feel about that. No, I do. I feel shitty. I want him to be able to promise me that he won't be with anybody else. He has the power to break me, shatter me, and I'm so weak that it wouldn't take much to do that.

"Baby," he murmurs when he's right in front of me. His hands wrap around my hips and his face nuzzles my neck. His lips caress me in a gentle kiss before his teeth nip me, and I melt.

"I need to get this done and get back to the house," I murmur, stepping away from him. He lifts his head but his hands stay planted on my hips.

"Sorry I ain't been around…" His words trail off and I shake my head.

"You don't need to explain. It's not my place to question. You come home when you're ready," I say, looking down at my feet. His fingers slide under my chin and he tips my head back so that my eyes are forced to connect with his.

"Working, drinking, and smoking, baby. That's all I been doin'. I had the feeling you didn't really want me around," he shrugs. The nonchalant move doesn't match his serious gaze.

"We really need to get our shit together and get on the same page," I mutter.

"*Fuck*, no kidding," he grunts as his arm slips around my waist and pulls me closer to his hard body.

"Mr. Jones called me last night," I say before I hurriedly finish my thought. "Scotty signed the divorce papers."

"Huh," he grunts. I look at him in question before he begins to talk. "That seems too easy. For everything you went through with him, it just doesn't make sense."

"Custody hasn't been agreed upon yet. Just the divorce. Maybe he's ready to be rid of me, too," I shrug. Bates squeezes my waist with his strong fingers.

"Lived with an abusive asshole my whole life, baby. He'd kill her before he let her just walk out the door. It ain't as simple as it seems. Don't let it fool you. He wants you to get comfortable, to stop looking behind you, to feel safe," he murmurs. It makes a cold shiver run through me.

"I don't know what to do anymore," I say as I twist my fingers into his t-shirt.

"Lean on me, trust me, and let me take care of my girls," he whispers before his lips gently brush mine.

It's been days since he was inside of me, and I ache for

him. I was fooling myself if I thought that I could live a life without Bates in it. *No way.* I need him. I need his strength and I need his support. I bared myself for him and he hasn't verbalized his response, but maybe him offering for me to lean on him, to let him take care of us, maybe that's the only verbal answer I need.

I was also fooling myself into thinking that I could live with only having *part* of him. The past three days, I've been trying to distance myself and it's been killing me. My imagination has been going wild with jealousy. I can't handle him being inside of another woman. I can't handle another woman's hands on him.

"I… I need to get to work," I blurt out before I tell him everything I'm thinking. I'm not ready to admit what I really want from him, what I *need*. Maybe someday soon, but not today.

"Yeah, okay, baby. We got church in ten minutes. Afterward, I'll take you home and we'll just hang out the rest of the day," he announces. He presses his lips to my forehead and spins around, walking away from me. I take a few moments to appreciate his spectacular ass before I shake myself out of it and get to work.

The next hour, I find myself in the storage room, counting bottles of beer, when I feel the presence of another person behind me. I turn around and see Star in the doorway. She's wearing a pair of daisy duke cut offs and a bikini top. Her dark hair is pulled into a high ponytail, and her face looks like she spent about an hour applying and reapplying makeup, it's so thick.

"Star," I murmur, wondering what in the hell she's doing here.

"What is it about you? I don't get it," she states, eyeing me with a look of disgust on her face.

"What do you mean?"

"He wants you. Like he's willing to give up what he needs to make you happy," she says, narrowing her eyes.

"I don't even know what you're talking about," I sigh, annoyed with her and this conversation. What Bates wants or needs is up to him, not me, and certainly not her.

"He told me in bed this morning that he wants you. He won't even consider anyone else but you."

I stare at her. Completely fixed on her words—*he told me in bed this morning.* Visions of a rumpled Star and then Bates walking out of the hallway immediately flash in my mind and my stomach lurches. He fucked her and then he lied about it. *Fucking lied to my face.* It was bad enough when he told me he might need things I couldn't give him, that he would seek it elsewhere, namely Star over here. Now, he's lied to me.

Fuck. Him.

"Well, if he wants you, Star, he can have you. I'm not holding him back," I announce before I walk past her, deliberately bumping her with my shoulder. *Bitch.*

I don't wait for her response. I don't care enough to hear it. She obviously wants Bates, and if he, for whatever reason, feels like he needs to have her, then I'm not going to stop him. He can fuck that nasty bitch until his dick rots off.

When I walk back into the clubhouse bar, all the guys are out of their little meeting. My eyes scan the room and land on Bates, who is playing pool with Drifter.

Fuck him.

I ignore his beautiful, big, gorgeous, ass and go straight toward Paxton, who is sitting at the bar talking to Johnny.

"I need one of you to take me home," I announce. They both swivel their heads over to me.

Paxton smiles and Johnny grins.

"He piss you off?" Paxton asks. I roll my eyes.

"It doesn't matter. I'm ready to leave and one of you is taking me." I lean in close and whisper, "*Now.*"

"I got you, babe," Paxton says, setting his full beer down and wrapping his arm around my shoulders. "You want to make him jealous, babe, I'm your man," he announces as we walk out of the clubhouse.

I hear a shout behind me, but I ignore it. By the time I'm wrapped around Paxton's back, I look up and see Bates charging out of the clubhouse.

"*What the fuck!*" Bates screams from several feet away.

"Go," I cry. Paxton doesn't think twice, he takes off down the gravel road as his bike roars, and I hold the hell on.

Luckily, since I'm on the back of his bike, the entire ride is in silence. I don't want to talk. I want to curl in a ball and cry. I am so sick of making one stupid mistake after another. I immediately decide that it's time to contact Connellee. We aren't the closest, never have been, but I think he'll help me. As his sister, I pray that he will.

I can't stay with Bates another minute. I'll fall into his bed again and hate myself that much more. I'll keep doing it until there's nothing left of me but a shell. I need to be done with him completely. When we arrive back at the house, I see that Kentlee's car is here and Buck is on the front porch just hanging out. *Protecting.*

"Thank you," I murmur as I slide off of his bike. Paxton wraps his hands around my waist to keep me from walking away. I look down at him with wide eyes.

"You want more from me, I'll gladly give it to you, Brent. You're a good woman and nothing would please me more than to have you at my side. I'll take care of you," he murmurs.

I stare at him in surprise. Paxton Hill is hot. Dirty Johnny Williams is hot, too. But Bates is gorgeous and he owns every part of me. I could never be with another man aside from him. If anything, I'm just going to be alone. *Scratch an itch every so often, but relationships? No.* I've fucked those up too many times. It's obvious I don't choose men very well. I don't need to fuck my daughter up more than she's already going to be, either. Stella's going to be devastated when I inform her that we're leaving.

"I like you, Paxton, like a whole lot, but…" I begin. He holds his hand up.

"I get it, babe. I do. Just think about it. You want someone to just take care of you, I'm willing. Keep it in the back of your mind, yeah?"

I nod, unable to speak. He gives me a wink and waves at Buck before he starts his bike. Then my breath hitches. Barreling down the drive is Bates. I can almost see the anger that radiates off of him. Paxton doesn't turn his bike off or say a word. He leaves. He leaves me standing in the dirt drive waiting for Bates to turn his rage on me.

Great protector.

chapter sixteen

Sniper

I watch as Torch's bike passes me. I want nothing more than to block him and beat the ever lovin' shit out of him. How dare he take my woman and put her on the back of his bike without my permission. And Brentlee—*the fuck*! Not two hours ago we were gonna get on the same page. *Fuck*, I thought we already were. I don't want any other bitch but her, and I want to take care of her, of Stella—my girls.

Now, I don't know what the fuck is goin' on.

I kick the stand down on my bike and quickly get off. She's standin' in the drive, sexy as fuck, lookin' like a deer caught in headlights. Her honey eyes are round and wide, her hair mussed from the back of Torch's bike, and her chest is heaving with her labored breaths. She looks so fuckable right now, I can't stop my dick from pressing against the zipper of my jeans.

"The fuck, Brent?" I roar, vaguely aware that Buck is on the porch and LeeLee and the kids are inside the house.

"I'm going to Conn's," she announces, lifting one arm and planting her fist on her hip.

"No, you ain't," I tell her, wrapping my hand firm, but gentle, around her bicep and dragging her to the unattached garage.

I never use the garage for anything, except in the winter when I want to work on my bike or my truck. It sits empty, other than some tools and boxes and shit. I lift the door and flip the light on before I guide her inside, closing the door behind me. I have a feeling whatever this fight is, it's about to get messy; and though I don't mind fuckin' her into submission in the front yard, she might get pissed if LeeLee and the kids see.

"What bug crawled up your ass within the last hour?"

I watch as her gorgeous eyes narrow and she plants both of her fists on her hips. *Oh, she's fuckin' pissed, and I can't stop my lips from twitching.* This, right here, *this* is my *tigritsa*. Makes my dick so fuckin' hard when she gets that tigress attitude goin'. Makes me want to slay her, own her, force her submission to me. Only me.

"You fucked Star," she announced. I just look at her, cocking my head to the side.

"Yeah," I say slowly.

"You told me you were drinking, smoking, and working. Never in there did you add—*fucking nasty ass, trashy, fucking whores*," she screams as her fists come up and pound my chest. I let her. This is all a misunderstanding, or a ploy by a clubwhore to snag a brother. It ain't the first time.

"Quiet," I demand, my voice even and low.

"Fuck you, Bates," she yells, hitting me once more.

I wrap my fingers around her wrists and walk her backward. I don't stop until her back hits the dirty garage wall.

"Didn't fuck Star last night," I murmur, dipping my head to look into her eyes.

"That's not what she said, and you two came from the same hall this morning, looking awfully tired," she snaps. My lips twitch again. Fuck, she's a gorgeous being when she's got her claws out.

"She's a whore, babe. I wouldn't believe her if she told me the sky was blue. I didn't fuck her, not last night, and not since you been in my bed, baby. Whatever I gotta do to prove to you that *this* is what I want—*you* are what I want—I'll fuckin' do it. But this shit, this ain't gonna do nothin' but piss me off," I say. I then watch as her eyes narrow to little slits.

"What *shit*? The fact that I feel like I can't trust you because you already told me you'd be fucking whores whenever you saw fit, whenever you *needed* it?" she spits.

"Told you that, then I recanted it. My dick's yours, babe. You don't use it, I might have to go elsewhere, but I'd be informing you of that before it happened. I want you. I want Stella. I want my family," I growl before I smash my lips down onto hers.

Brentlee whimpers when I force my tongue inside of her, and I know I've won as soon as her hands leave my chest and her fingers tangle in my hair. This bitch, this fucking *tigritsa*, she undoes me.

I grab the hem of her shirt and yank it up. *I need her.*

I need that perfect cunt wrapped around my dick. I don't bother unhooking her bra, instead I just yank the cups down and free her gorgeous tits. Then my hands travel down to her jeans, tugging on the zipper before I push them over her hips, along with her panties, stopping when they've reached her thighs.

"Bates," she purrs. I know I need to fuck her hard. I have to. That purring shit she does, *fuck*, it kills me.

"Get on your knees," I growl before I pinch her pretty pink nipples. She whimpers again, and my dick's two seconds from exploding inside of my jeans.

"You can't force me," she says softly. I shake my head.

"Get on your goddamn knees, Brentlee. I'm gonna fuck that pussy while I stare at your perfect ass. I'm going to remind you that I own this sweet body of yours. Because sometime in the past three days, you've somehow forgotten," I growl. She shivers in my arms before she sinks to her knees.

"I haven't forgotten," she murmurs as she undoes my jeans and shoves them down my thighs.

"I'm still pissed at you," she grumbles.

"You shouldn't be. I only want you," I grunt.

"Why am I so weak?" she murmurs.

I cup her cheek in my hand and I look at her. My cock is hanging out, and she's half naked, but all I see is the vulnerability shining in her eyes. She needs to know that she isn't weak; nothing about her is weak. She's so fuckin' strong.

"You're my *tigritsa*, so fucking strong, Brent," I say, meaning every single fucking word. Her eyes sparkle and she gives me a small smile before she kisses the tip of my cock. Then, I groan as soon as her mouth wraps around the head of my dick.

"Can you take it, baby?" I ask, unsure of exactly what her tolerance is, the conversation of her strength on hold—for now. I need to know exactly how rough I can be with her. I know some of the things that piece of shit did to her, but I don't want to traumatize her more.

"Whatever you give me, Bates. I can take it. I want it," she says as her eyes connect with mine. Her fierceness radiates through them. *Fuck me,* my woman is strong. So goddamn strong.

I cup her cheek before I slide my fingers through the side of her hair. My eyes completely focused on hers.

"Then open your mouth, baby. I'm going to own it. I'm going to fuck it," I say. She obliges. Her lips part and her mouth opens wide.

I don't hesitate as I slide my cock down her throat. I keep my eyes on her, our connection deep. I'm watching for any change in her features, any stress, any pain—*anything.* She can't handle it and I'll stop, no hesitation, no bullshit, I'll stop. But as I thrust my hips, my cock sliding deeper and deeper down her perfect throat, the only thing I see shining in her eyes is pure, unadulterated, fucking *lust.*

I bite my bottom lip and keep my pace, even and strong. I want to fuck her mouth so hard she sees stars, but not right now. *Not for a while.* That's something we need to work up to. Honestly, she needs to trust me a whole hell of a lot more than she does right now.

"I want to come down your hot, wet, throat," I announce, my voice guttural.

Brentlee only hums, and it makes me shiver. It feels so damn good. "But I want my cum dripping out of that sweet cunt more."

I pull out of her throat and slide to my knees in front of her before I take her swollen lips with mine. Sliding my hand between her legs, I moan when I feel how soaking wet she is. Back in the day, Brent would get off on giving me head, but I figured shit had changed. *Luckily, it hasn't*. My lips travel along her jaw to her ear as I shove two fingers inside of her swollen pussy.

"You gonna let me sink inside this sweet pussy, baby?" I ask before I nip her earlobe. I make a come hither motion with my fingers, avoiding her clit, but touching that rough patch inside of her.

"Fuck me, Bates. *Own me*," she moans as her hips move, searching for more, searching for friction against that greedy clit of hers. I give it to her, grinding my palm against her, and she whimpers.

I pull my soaked hand out from between her legs and move around so that I'm positioned behind her. I trail my wet fingers through the crack of her ass and press two of them against her tight asshole.

I don't invade her entrance, not yet at least. Instead, I massage it. Her body goes taught for a moment before she relaxes and drops her head between her resting elbows. I know I'm the victor when she pushes her ass against me. Searching. Wanting. Needing.

"I want this ass one day, baby," I announce before I lean down and inhale her pussy, my fingers still massaging her back entrance.

"Bates," she gasps as my tongue snakes out and laps at her clit. It's so fucking engorged, and hot, and *sexy as shit*.

"Say I can take it, baby," I murmur against her wet center. I don't wait for her answer before I slide my tongue inside of her cunt, tasting her arousal.

"Yes, Bates. Whatever you want, baby, it's yours," she whispers, grinding that sweet pussy against my mouth and my beard.

"Not right now. Later. Now, I just want to sink my cock into this sweet pussy—my pussy," I murmur as I rise. Without warning, I slam inside of her wet heat.

"Bates," she screams, arching her back.

I wrap my arm around her tits and pull her up farther. I bury my face into her neck while my other hand goes straight for her clit. I had plans on fucking her like the animal I am, but now, now I just want her to come. I want to smell her and taste her, and just be *hers* while she does it.

"This body belongs to me, every piece of it, Brentlee. Don't fuckin' ever think about taking it away from me again. Lived over ten years without it, baby, and lived those years in a black hell. You walked into that clubhouse and brought me out of it. Don't put me back there again," I whisper against her neck while I thrust my hips, pushing my dick deeper into her cunt while I play that clit the way she likes it.

"It's yours, Bates, but I don't know if I can stay," she murmurs wrapping her arm around my neck while she grinds down on my dick and my fingers simultaneously.

"You're never leavin' me again," I growl, nipping her neck.

"You don't fuck any whores, you don't hit me, you don't treat me or my daughter like shit, and I won't leave you, baby," she whimpers.

I roughly squeeze her tit before I thrust inside of her with all of my strength. She cries out, but I feel her pussy grow wetter. My bitch likes it rough.

"Would rather kill myself then hit you, Brent. Never gonna treat Stella like shit. Never gonna fuck around on you. And baby, I do any of that shit, and I won't stop you from leaving me. Let me claim you, let me mark you, ink you," I ask. She screams out her release as her pussy clamps down around me.

Brent doesn't answer me, but that's okay. By the end of tonight, she'll agree to have my name on her body, and she'll be my woman one hundred percent. I thought I could ease her into this shit. I thought I could handle it, but I can't. I need her to be mine, and for my world to see it.

Maybe it's my ego, maybe my pride. I don't fuckin' know—but I need her to have my name permanently inked on her smooth, olive colored skin. I close my eyes as I continue to thrust up into her cunt, and I imagine the ink. It'll be feminine, a scroll, maybe some flowers. SNIPER will be on her, but so will Bates. She'll have them both branded onto her body. I come as soon as I think of my names forever marking her as mine.

"*Tigritsa*," I murmur, licking the sweat from her neck, tasting her skin on my tongue, smelling the combination of our bodies coming together.

This woman is perfect. I can't fuck this up, and I refuse to allow her to fuck it up, either. Even when we're fighting, I've never been so goddamn happy in my entire life.

Brentlee

I straighten my clothes and try to fix my hair a little by running my fingers through it. I have a feeling that nothing will make me look anything but freshly fucked. I look over at

Bates as he stands by the now open door. He's watching me with this glazed look in his eye, and a smile tipping his lips.

"I still don't think all of this is a good idea," I huff. His tipped smile turns into a full-fledged grin.

"It's happening, baby. There's no way around it. Can't go another day without you as completely mine," he announces as I walk through the door. I wait until he lowers it and he joins me, throwing his arm around my shoulders and pulling me into his side.

"We're a mess. *I'm* a mess," I announce, as if he doesn't already know.

"Yeah, babe, figured that out when you were fourteen. Didn't care then, and sure as fuck don't care now," he chuckles.

"I wasn't a mess at fourteen," I say defensively.

"Baby, you were so worried about what everybody else thought, you didn't think about what you wanted. You were a normal fourteen-year-old, but gave yourself these high expectations of constantly being perfect, all of the damn time. That shit had to be exhausting," he says. I sigh.

Fuck, I've been trying to be perfect for almost fifteen years. It's extremely exhausting. I nod, unable to agree with him verbally.

"Come on, *tigritsa*, let's so see our girl," he murmurs, planting a kiss on the top of my head before we are greeted by Buck. He smiles widely and shakes his head.

"Hey, follow Kentlee home, yeah?" Bates asks. He nods.

"Glad to see y'all worked your issues out," Buck mumbles.

I turn to him, red creeping up my neck. He winks before he bursts out laughing. Bates flips him the finger before we walk inside.

My sister is sitting on the sofa and her eyes meet mine before she gives me a knowing smile. I blush, a-fuckin-gain.

"When do you go to the tattoo parlor?" she asks before she giggles.

"Shut up," I say. At the same time Bates grunts, "Tomorrow."

Kentlee can't help herself, she doubles over with laughter.

"I love it. One fuck in the garage and you're gonna be a claimed woman," she says, wiping tears from her eyes.

"Do we want to go there big sister?" I ask, arching a brow at her.

I know most of her story with Fury. It didn't take more than a fuck and a few sweet words to get her own ink.

"Nope. I'm good. Gotta jet. Fury says he wants pulled pork tonight, and if I don't start it immediately, he's not gonna get it and then… well, let's just say I won't get it either," she frowns, pinching her brows together.

I roll my eyes before I help her gather the kids' belongings. Stella sits quietly, watching the entire exchange, and I have the feeling my girl needs a little talk.

Bates walks Krentlee out and I take Stella's hand in mine before I guide us toward her bedroom. I settle down on her bed and she snuggles up next to me. There's something bothering her and I want to find out what it is. We've gone through so many changes in such a short amount of time, I need to know that she's handling everything all right.

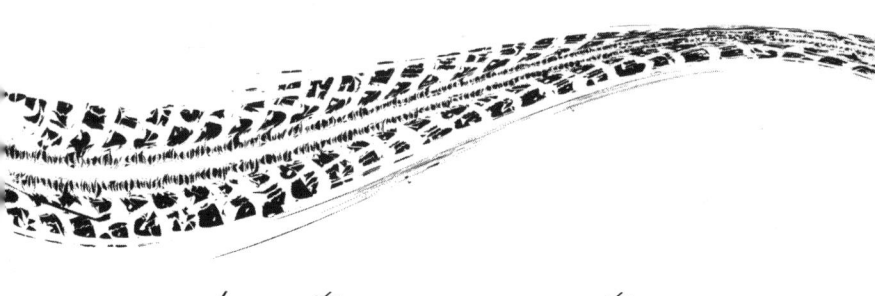

chapter seventeen

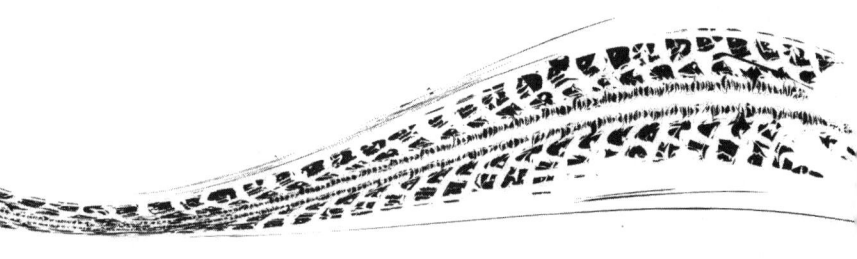

Brentlee

"What's the matter, sweet girl?" I ask as I run my fingers through her blonde curls.

"Bear said I wasn't never gonna see my daddy again," she blurts out. My hand stills in her hair.

"That's not true, Stella. I wouldn't ever keep you from your daddy, but it could be a while before you do see him again," I say.

"I don't wanna see him," she shouts.

"Stella, he's your daddy," I say in surprise. She may not be a daddy's girl, but I've never seen her act out this way before when it comes to Scotty.

"He mean. He hurt us," she whispers.

"He hurt you, when?" I ask.

My heart is suddenly pounding in my chest.

My breathing short and sporadic.

I can see stars in my vision and my chest hurts. *It fucking hurts.* What did this asshole do to my baby?

"Only last twime. But he hurts you all the twime," she murmurs. I let out a long exhale.

Holy fuck. Holy Jesus.

"He's never going to hurt me again," I say.

"And you ain't seein' him again," Bates growls from the doorway.

I open my mouth to say something, to *correct* him, but he puts his hand up before he sinks to his knees in front of my daughter.

"Daddy's aren't supposed to hurt mommies or sweet *malyshka's*. I will not let him hurt you or mommy again," Bates says. My daughter's eyes grow wide. She looks at him as though he's a super hero. And isn't he? He's my super hero. Always has been.

"Pwomise?" she asks quietly.

"He would have to get through me first, Stella," he says, wrapping his big hand around the back of her neck.

"You're stwong," she points out. Bates chuckles.

"I'm a beast," he grins.

The rest of the day we spend together, the three of us as a family. *It's glorious.* I make lunch for everyone and we eat it on a blanket outside, under a shade tree. Stella practices riding her bike while I lie my head in Bates' lap. I purr when his fingers run through my hair.

"Meant it when I said I wanted my name inked on you tomorrow, baby," he murmurs.

"Bates…" I don't know what to say. *What do you say?* This isn't a piece of jewelry. This is permanent.

"I want Sniper and Bates both. I want your name on me, too," he says. I look up at him in surprise.

"Is that normal?" I ask.

"Nope, but I want it. I don't want it hidden either, I want it somewhere where no matter what, it's seen," he grunts.

"Like where? Your forehead?" I ask, trying to hold back a giggle.

"Side of my neck," he says before his eyes turn down to meet mine.

"You don't have any ink at all, Bates. Why would you do that?" I ask.

I've never asked him why he isn't tatted up like the rest of the guys. Maybe I should.

"I need the Devil's insignia on my back; been needin' that shit for years. Been slackin'. Tats aren't my thing, never were. But I like the idea of having your name where the world can see who owns me."

"I thought *you* owned *me*?" I ask, arching a brow.

"Haven't you figured anything out yet, baby?" he asks, his voice gruff but sweet.

"Like?"

"You're the one in control here. You fuckin' own every part of me. Sure, I own your body, but *fuck, baby*, you still own my heart," he murmurs.

I look at him in surprise, remembering that conversation from so many years ago where he said I had his heart. He's had mine, too. *Always.*

"Okay, Bates," I breathe.

"Yeah?" he asks, giving me a boyish grin.

"Tomorrow, before our shifts," I confirm with a nod.

"I'll get my fuckin' back piece, too. Fury will be so pleased," he chuckles. "He's been on my ass for years for that shit. Bugs the fuckin' shit out of him that I haven't fallen into line like everybody else."

"Why haven't you?" I ask, trying to dig deeper into all that is Bates.

He's still the same person he was ten years ago, but now, he's more closed off to the time we've spent apart. He never talks about it. Never mentions anything about his past. All I know is that he did some things in the Marines that now give him nightmares.

I want to know everything about my man. He is that too, there's no sense denying it or trying to discourage it. He's mine and I'm his. Soon, we'll be permanently branded with each other's names and the world will know just how deep we are in with each other.

"Why haven't I gotten the Notorious Devils club ink?" he asks, repeating my question. He turns from me, but only to watch Stella, then he speaks.

"I had plans on getting ink in the Marines. All my brothers and I were going to get matching shit. Eighteen and stupid and all that. We had plans to do it as soon as we returned to the states. One of the guys was an artist. Drew it all out, looked fuckin' badass. I was the only one that came back to the states from that group alive," he says. My heart breaks for him.

No wonder he has nightmares. He lost his friends—apparently all of them. I don't say anything. I want him to continue. He's never been so open with me.

"Got the design still, but I'll never put it on my body.

Maybe I should in memory of them. Fuck if I know. Anyway, I never wanted *Notorious Devils* on my body because the last time I planned shit out, everybody got blown the fuck up."

I can't stop the tear that trickles down my cheek, or the next one that follows. I sit up and crawl on top of him, straddling his legs and cupping his cheeks with my hands, forcing his head to face me. I look into his deeply haunted eyes and I smile sadly.

"Let's create new memories with ink. Let's do your Devil's tattoo and our names. I'm so sorry you lost your friends," I whisper unable to speak any louder. His hands wrap around my thighs and he squeezes.

"The nightmares, sometime they're about them," he says. I feel blessed he's opening up to me.

"Yeah, baby, I'd imagine that's not something a person forgets."

"Never."

I bury my face in his neck, inhaling his scent and just holding him. My poor man. The hell he's seen. The hell he's endured. I'll never be able to make him forget that shit from his past, but hopefully one day, the memories won't be so vivid.

Hopefully, I can help create such a happy and wonderful life that he's unable to dwell on all that other shit. *I hope that I can.* I pray that with each other we can help ease the hurts and hells we've endured. That in each other we can find a peace and live a happy life. I know that with Bates by my side, it's entirely possible.

Sniper

Family day.

It's not something I know much about. But this afternoon, I truly experienced it. After Stella rode her bike until she was exhausted, dirty, and ready for dinner, we all went inside. It felt good, my woman cuddled up against me and my daughter playing in the warm sunshine. Stella is that, too. *Mine.* My daughter, as she always should have been.

Brentlee gets Stella bathed while I BBQ our dinner. I don't cook, never learned, but I can man a grill, so that's what I'll do for them. Burgers, grilled corn, and potatoes.

"That smells awesome," Brent says, carrying a clean pajama clad Stella in her arms.

"Brambugers," Stella cries before she wiggles out of her hold to dash to the table. I chuckle as I plate her food for her.

"Thanks, baby," Brentlee murmurs, taking Stella's plate and setting it down in front of her.

Once we're all seated, I wrap my hand around her upper thigh and squeeze. She turns and gives me a cute lopsided grin.

"Today has been perfect," I grunt. She smiles even wider.

"It has," she nods.

I don't think about this morning, how I almost lost my entire life in the blink of an eye. I don't think about my stubbornness or hers. All I can think about is fuckin' her in that dirty garage of mine; then spending the day with her and Stella.

I think about how I opened up a bit more, telling her a little of my past. In all honesty, I want to bury it all, but I can't.

Shit like that always has a way of rising to the surface.

I don't let Brent clean up dinner when we're finished. This is my night to take care of her. I plan on doing that, from the dishes to the bedroom. It's all for my woman—to show her how happy I am that she's agreed to be solely mine, agreed to wear my name. Tomorrow, she's going to be branded, and I couldn't be happier.

"Bates," she calls out from the bedroom just as I'm putting the last piece of silverware in the dishwasher.

I don't answer her call.

Instead, I close down the house and walk into our bedroom. I let out a groan when I see her. She's on her knees in the middle of the bed, her body completely bare. Not one stitch of clothing covering her. I turn and close the door behind me, flipping the lock. I take off my cut and hang it on the door handle before I quickly strip out of my clothes.

Brentlee doesn't move. Her eyes are fixated on me. They roam over my body and I can feel them on my skin like a caress. Just her hungry gaze turns me on.

"Spread your legs. Touch yourself," I order. She visibly shivers.

I watch as her hand travels down between her tits, down her stomach, and between her thighs. She's hesitant, and I stare as she begins to gently touch herself. I wrap my own hand around my cock and squeeze. Her small gasp fills the room, her eyes focused on the hand squeezing my dick.

"Are you?" she asks.

"Yeah, baby. I'm gonna stroke my cock while you play with that pretty pussy," I grind out.

It's taking everything inside of me not to throw her down and pound inside of her with all of my strength. But I want her worked up. I want her on the brink of insanity. I don't say another word as I watch her, as I stroke my dick at the sight of her. I know when she starts really getting into it. Her fingers shove up inside of her cunt and she grinds down against her palm. I love it when she does that against my hand. I moan as her tits sway.

I close the distance between us, on the edge of blowing my load.

"Open up, baby," I murmur. I watch as Brent's eyes open wide. "Suck my cock and finger-fuck yourself."

She wrinkles her nose slightly at my gruff words, but she doesn't protest. Instead, she leans over, wrapping her hand around my thigh and keeping the other between her legs. She opens her mouth and I shove my dick down her throat. I don't give her time to acclimate, like I did earlier.

I wrap my hand in her hair and hold her face still. I don't need her to move a muscle, I just need her to take me. I fuck her mouth—her throat. Her hand is moving hard and fast between her legs, and I groan.

Fuck, she's so hot.

When she starts to whimper and buck even harder I know she's close. She's tipping over the edge. I'm close, too. I thrust into her hot mouth a few more time before I yank her head back and pump my hand along my dick. I come in long, white spurts all over her gorgeous tits while she cries out her own release, her body stone still and her eyes rolled back inside of her head.

I hold her upright until her eyes open and meet mine. She has a little smile on her lips as I maneuver her to lie down on her back. I don't lay down next to her. I straddle her hips and look down at my woman. I take my hand and rub my cum into her skin—across her gorgeous tits and even around her nipples, making them hard with my calloused touch.

"You're so fuckin' pretty," I murmur as I continue to rub my cum into her body.

"What are you doing?" she asks, her voice sounding tired.

"Branding you," I shrug. She chuckles softly.

"You do know once I take a shower this will all be washed away, right?"

I grin shaking my head once before I stand. She's given me an idea.

I walk over to my jeans and snag my phone. Turning around, I make my way over to her. Brent's eyes are nothing but slits, her lowered lids watching me.

"Now I can look anytime I want to," I murmur before I start snapping pictures. Her eyes widen and she reaches up to snatch the phone away from me, but I jump back.

"Bates!" she cries.

"Smile pretty, baby," I laugh.

"What are you going to do with them?" she whines. I shake my head before I snap a few more.

"When I have to go out on a run, these are what I'm gonna use to jack off," I announce, tossing my phone onto the floor before I pick her up.

I carry her to the bathroom and start the shower for us.

"What?" she breathes.

"Can't fuck anyone else, don't want to either. Just gonna whack it to my *tigritsa*," I say.

It's the truth, too. Losing her would end me. Free, easy whore pussy ain't worth it. I want my woman to be so fuckin' happy she can't remember the past ten years, not a single fuckin' day of them. That means I gotta keep my dick in my pants. Ain't that much of a fuckin' hardship to do that.

I wash my seed from her tits, frowning as I do it. I want it to be as permanent as the ink she's going to get tomorrow. I want every part of her to smell like me. I want every person who crosses her path to know that she's mine.

I dry her off with a towel before I carry her to the bed, all of it in silence.

"I love you, Bates," she whispers as she settles her ass into my crotch and her back against my chest.

"Always been you, baby. You have my heart. I've always loved you," I admit before I kiss her shoulder.

We sleep. Unaware of what the future will bring, but willing to face it head on—together.

chapter eighteen

Brentlee

The sound of buzzing needles fills the space, and I shiver at the idea of getting these tattoos. Bates doesn't want just one tattoo branding me as his. No, he wants two. One of his road name, *Sniper*, the other of his legal name, *Bates*.

How I let him talk me into this, I don't know.

That's a lie. I do know. It was the look in his eyes when he asked me, the happiness that filled them. I couldn't deny him, not when he looked so fucking happy and then relieved.

Now, I'm standing in a tattoo parlor waiting for my turn. I still don't know exactly what I want. I honestly don't care. Whatever makes Bates happy, that's what I want. It may sound silly, naïve, and passive, but it's what I want. His happiness.

"Bates, brother," a man says walking up to us. He's got long hair pulled up in a man-bun, just the way Fury wears his, and he's covered from neck to knuckles in black inked tattoos.

"Hey, man," Bates grins as he shakes the man's hand. "This is my woman, Brentlee," Bates introduces. The man grins.

"You're the famous Brentlee. I've heard of you," he chuckles. "They call me Dragon," he says, shaking my hand.

"Are you a Notorious Devil?" I ask quietly. He chuckles.

"Naw, but I do all their work; so I guess I'm kinda honorary, you'd say," he laughs before he turns and walks to the back of the parlor.

Bates wraps his hand around mine and pulls me behind him as he follows. We pass people getting work done—arms, legs, hips, backs and chests, all on display and getting adorned with what will hopefully be masterpieces.

We follow Dragon into a little room, and Bates closes the door behind me.

"What and where, babe?" Dragon asks.

"I have absolutely no clue," I confess with a shrug. He starts laughing.

"You want Sniper somewhere, yeah?"

"Sniper and Bates. Script, girlie, but that's all I know."

"Snipe, you want a tramp stamp of that shit? Great viewing pleasure," Dragon chuckles. I scrunch up my nose at the idea of a tramp stamp.

"Fuck, no. How about Sniper on her hip and Bates across her ribcage, wrapping around where her heart is?" he murmurs. I gasp. It sounds so pretty.

"How you want me to weave that shit in, flowers? If you say butterflies, I'm kicking your ass out," he announces. It makes me giggle.

"I hate butterflies. How about a pretty feather, Bates, and an arrow underneath? The hip I'll just make black scroll, girlie and delicate?" Dragon asks. I smile widely. It sounds so cool. I look up to Bates and he grins.

"Fuck yeah," he grunts.

That's what I spend the rest of the afternoon doing, getting my man's name inked on two separate places of my body.

The tattoo needle feels like hundreds of little ant bites; it's annoying, but it doesn't hurt. I've had worse pain inflicted on me, so this is nothing. Dragon finishes the hip piece in what seems like mere minutes. Then he has me sit up and lift my shirt on the opposite side.

Bates growls when I have to remove my bra, but I just roll my eyes. This is what he wanted, where he wanted it. He really has no room to complain to me. There's more pain when the needle goes into my ribs, but I just close my eyes and breathe. I listen to Dragon and Bates' voices float throughout the room as they talk. I have no clue what they're saying, as I can't concentrate on their words, but their voices sooth me.

"All right, babe, all done," Dragon says, patting my thigh.

I open my eyes and smile at him. I watch as he walks over to a table and grabs a mirror, bringing it over to where I'm sitting. He holds it out and my eyes scan the reflection. The tattoos are simple. An arrow with a feathered end on one side and a point on the other. The word Bates in scroll and then a feather above that right under my breast.

It's beautiful. Simple. Elegant. Girlie.

It's me.

"I love it," I whisper before I turn to Bates. "Do you like it?"

"Love it, baby," he murmurs, his eyes focused on his name, his name permanently branded to my skin. Though nobody will likely see this piece, it's there, and he'll see it, and that's all that matters.

Dragon hands Bates the mirror and he holds it up so that I can see the tattoo on the other side of my body, on my hip. The script is high on my hip so that it can be seen when I wear low waist jeans, but it's pretty. It's simple and the same font as Bates' name on my ribs. I like that they match.

"Can't wait to show this shit off, baby," Bates mumbles, his eyes fixated on my hip. I shake my head and smile.

"I love them both, Dragon. Thank you so much."

"Now it's the big man's turn," he chuckles as he rubs gel on my new ink and wraps them up with cellophane.

"Bates'll tell you how to care for it, babe. But just keep 'em clean, and keep puttin' this shit on it. They're gonna itch in a few days, and then you'll be good to go." I nod, taking a tube of gel from him as I stand up. I pull my shirt down, unable to put my bra back on. No way in fuck is that thing touching my skin anytime soon.

"What're you gettin'?" Dragon asks as Bates takes his shirt off and settles in the chair, his broad muscular back on display.

"Need my Notorious ink, then I want my woman's name on my neck," he states.

A shiver runs through me and my nipples pebble at his voice and the meaning in his tone, the way he said *my woman*. All of it combined makes me want to jump him right here and now. I don't, though I'm sure he wouldn't mind, based on a few things he's said about people watching him. I'm sure Dragon wouldn't mind in the slightest, but it's not something

I could do. No matter how comfortable I am, that to me is private, or fairly private. A dark corner, a supply closet—yeah, okay. The middle of a room with an audience? No way. I close my eyes and try to shake all those images running through my head away.

"Babe, wakeup," I hear Bates' voice. I blink my eyes open.

He's crouched down in front of me and I look over to his neck, seeing my name in dark scroll. The font matches his names on my body. It starts with the B right below his ear and runs diagonally, ending with the E at the hollow of his throat. Right between his collarbones. I don't touch it, as badly as I want to. I also want to lick it, which I don't do, but I can't wait until it's healed so that I can.

"You like it?" he asks, his eyes bright and shining as a smile plays on his lips.

"Yeah," I breathe. He bites his bottom lip before he leans over and brushes his lips against mine.

"My back," he stands and turns. The back tattoo is massive. We must have been here for hours.

The word *Notorious* is written across his shoulder blades. There is a skull in the middle with devil horns. The eyes are completely blacked out. It's huge, taking up the majority of his back. It looks so lifelike, 3D, as though it could jump out at me. Across his lower back is the word *Devils*. The words are in block lettering, and the massive tattoo is all black. No color. None is needed. The statement is made. He is a Notorious Devil. He's not to be fucked with.

"It's badass," I state. He turns with a jerk of his chin and a wink.

"It fits me then, yeah?"

I roll my eyes but smile as I do it. He *is* a badass. *My* badass.

"Let's get outta here, babe. We both gotta head into work." He takes my hand and we walk toward the front door. We pass Dragon on the way, and I tell him thank you with a wave.

"Anytime you need any new ink, babe, you just come on by. No appointment necessary," he calls out.

"You don't go in there without me," Bates says as we climb into his pickup truck. I'm grateful we didn't bring the bike. I would feel horrible having to be pressed against his back the entire ride.

"What? Why?"

"Just don't," he grunts. I grin, looking over at him.

"Are you jealous?" I ask.

"Of Dragon? Fuck no," he mutters as we continue toward the clubhouse.

"Then what's the big deal?"

"He's seen your tit. He don't need to see nothin' when I ain't there," he grinds out. I giggle, which quickly turns into a full on laugh.

"Bates," I gasp, trying to catching my breath.

"It isn't funny," he mumbles.

"You're around naked strippers every single night. One tattoo artist sees half my boob and you act like he tried to seduce me."

"I don't look," he states. I just stare at his profile, not understanding his words. "At the strippers. I don't look anymore. I go into my office and I do my paperwork. I have cameras and I can see the audience through my surveillance. The tits, the ass, the pussies, I don't look."

"You don't look," I repeat. He nods as he pulls into the clubhouse parking lot.

"Only tits, ass, and pussy I want to see are yours, babe," he says as he parks, throwing his wrist over the steering wheel.

"Seriously?" I ask, unbelieving of his words. How can he be surrounded by all of that bare skin and not look?

"Serious. Nothin' any other bitch has that I wanna see," he murmurs before he lifts his hand and slides it around my neck. I hold my breath when his face dips down and his lips press against mine.

"Meant it when I said I loved you, babe. Meant it when I said I'd stay faithful to you. Meant it all. I'm yours," he whispers against my lips.

I melt.

Every part of me turns completely to goo. This man owns me. He has always owned a piece of me, but now, right this minute, he owns every single part of me.

"I love you, Bates," I murmur, unable to say anything else.

"Now, try to keep from giving the guys a free show with your tits while I'm gone, yeah? Really should have thought about placement of your tat better," he grunts. I giggle.

I'm wearing a cropped oversized shirt that hangs off of one shoulder, but shows off my belly. My shorts are cut offs, short and low cut; you can see the *per* of my Sniper tattoo perfectly. I dressed super casual today, mainly because I wasn't sure how much the ink would hurt. I'm glad I did, too. I'm pretty sore.

Sniper

I watch her cute little ass walk into the clubhouse, jealous as fuck that my brothers are going to have that view of her all night long. She bends over in that loose fitting top, and they'll have the perfect view of her lush tits.

I should have made her go home for the night, but I already knew she'd raise hell with me. She needs the job. She needs to feel useful and to keep her mind off of her ex. Though she hasn't mentioned him much since she came here, I can sense her unease about the prick. She's constantly searching her surroundings for a sign of the bastard.

My eyes scan the parking lot once she's left and I see Drifter on his bike. He gives me a head nod and I dip my chin before I take off. I look in my rearview mirror to make sure he's behind me and am pleased to find him there. I drive toward my destination. It isn't the club. I fibbed to Brent, but only to keep her safe.

We drive down the street of a fancy as fuck neighborhood. Brent's old neighborhood. It's lined with trees and huge houses. We park five houses down from our destination and I jump out of the truck. It's dark and quiet.

"You sure you wanna do this, brother?" Drifter asks.

"Fuck yeah. This prick needs to be warned. I know he's planning shit. No way did his daddy warn him off completely, he's too cocky to take heed anyway," I say.

"He is, no doubt about that," Drifter says. I follow behind him.

We walk around the back of the house and slip inside undetected. *This asshole should really have an alarm system.* We wordlessly, and quietly, stalk up the stairs and toward the only light on in the house. The master bedroom. I hear moaning and grunting coming from the closed door. Drifter turns to me and lifts his brows with a grin on his face. I shake my head.

I watch as Drifter lifts his boot and kicks open the door. A woman screams. I walk in and see that she's sitting on Scotty's cock. Reverse cowgirl style. I look at her face and cringe. Fuck, she's young, real young.

"Get the fuck out of my house," Scotty screams. His face turns red and he throws the young bitch off his lap.

"Don't think I will," I state as I point my gun at his head. Drifter has his out and pointed at the naked bitch's head on the floor.

"What do you want?" Scotty asks, narrowing his eyes on me.

"Give my woman an easy divorce, sign over your parental rights, and pretend like your marriage never existed. Pretend *she* never existed," I say.

"You're fucking crazy. You want the bitch? You can have her. Worst lay I ever had," he grunts. "But my daughter is a different story. I'll be taking her and raising her properly. No way would I let trash like you and the likes of her whore mother raise her."

"You really shouldn't talk about my woman like that," I tsk.

"I really don't give a fuck what you want. I'm Scotty Corbin, I'll do what I want," he huffs. I chuckle.

"Scotty, little dick, Corbin. Thinks he's somebody, Drifter. What do you think?" I ask Drift without taking my eyes off of Scotty and his little dick. Fuck me, it's small, too.

"I think nobody would miss his scrawny ass. I think he's a wife beater, a rapist, and the scum of the earth," he snaps. Scotty's eyes go wide, traveling from Drifter to me in panic.

"She's a selfish bitch and a liar," Scotty cries. I shake my head, unable to respond immediately as I clinch my jaw tight.

"Brentlee doesn't lie. She doesn't have to. I have the medical records and photographs to prove exactly what and who you are. Do what your daddy advised and grant the divorce, sign the agreement to give up all custodial rights, and pretend you never met Brentlee Johnson," I grind out, taking another step closer to the piece of shit.

"You don't have shit," he boasts. I chuckle.

"Man, I got it all. Every bloodied picture of my gorgeous girl; every documented piece of evidence you could think of. I fuckin' got it. Your money can cover up a lot of shit, but there are still some good people in this world, and they keep shit like that for a rainy day—just in-fuckin'-case. Lucky for me, I got originals of it all, you dumbfuck," I laugh.

"They can't be used in court," he says, puffing out his chest a bit.

"They can't. You're right. But when the cops come sniffing around because they find your cold dead body, I can show them just what kind of man you are. They'll drop the search for your killer because, believe it or not, most cops—they ain't gonna give two fucks about some piece of shit that beats and rapes his wife for years. They'll figure he had it comin' to him. Pissed off the wrong person," I say, talking completely out of my ass.

"Do you know who my father is?" he shouts. I full on belly laugh at his rich-boy tantrum.

"Yeah, met the pencil dick the other day. Killed some of his lackey's in front of him, too; so I'm thinkin' he won't be a fuckin' problem. I'll tell you who my daddy is, though. He's a wife beater, a rapist, and a full on piece of shit. So forgive me if I don't give a fuck about you or your daddy. I give a shit about the women men like you hurt. Women like Brentlee who couldn't deserve that shit if they fuckin' tried."

Luckily, Scotty doesn't say another derogatory word about Brent. Maybe he can tell I'm holding on by only a thin thread. I want to put a bullet in this fucker's head so badly I can taste it. His eyes drift down to the barely legal girl naked and shaking on the floor before they come back up to me.

"I'll sign over rights," he mutters.

"Good. I'll have my lawyer send them right over," I say with a smile.

"You better watch your fucking back, biker," he grinds out. I laugh wholeheartedly. What a dick.

"I don't have to watch shit, Corbin. I find out you even breathe the same air as my Brent, I'll cut your dick off and feed it to you—that's after I saw your balls off and shove them down your throat. You're nothing, you little punk, asshole. You even attempt to retaliate, and I'll have my whole fuckin' club here. We'll make a party out of disemboweling you. It'll be great fun," I grin and the little girl starts to sob.

"You're such a big talker with a gun in your hand," he yells.

"Want me to get my knife instead?" I ask arching a brow. He doesn't respond and I can't help but smile. I lift my chin to Drifter, whose eyes are fixed on the girl curled into a ball on the floor.

"You need a ride, babe?" I ask. She looks up at me with terror.

"Come on, honey, you need to get away from this crazy man," Drifter mentions with a grin.

"I—I'm scared," she whispers, her eyes darting between the three of us men.

"How old are you?" he asks. He's completely focused on her, but my gun is still aimed right at Scotty's stupid head.

"Nineteen," she murmurs.

"Grab your clothes, honey," Drifter murmurs. She nods once before she gathers her things and quickly dresses.

"Stay away from my woman and her kid," I reiterate to Scotty. He doesn't say anything. He just watches as Drifter throws his arm over the nineteen-year-old girl's shoulders.

"Just fucking leave," Scotty shouts. It makes me laugh.

Together, the three of us leave Scotty Corbin alone and naked in his bed. Dude's gonna have blue balls. I hope he takes my advice and stays away from Brentlee. It's doubtful, though. That asshole doesn't know when to stop. He'll fight until the death, and that's exactly where fighting me will land him—fucking dead.

I watch as Drifter and the young girl take off on his bike before I go toward the club. I do have a few hours of work before it's time to pick up Brent and head home for the evening. My back is sore and achy, my throat the same. I'm ready to wrap my arms around my woman and just sleep. I need some serious fuckin' shut eye.

chapter nineteen

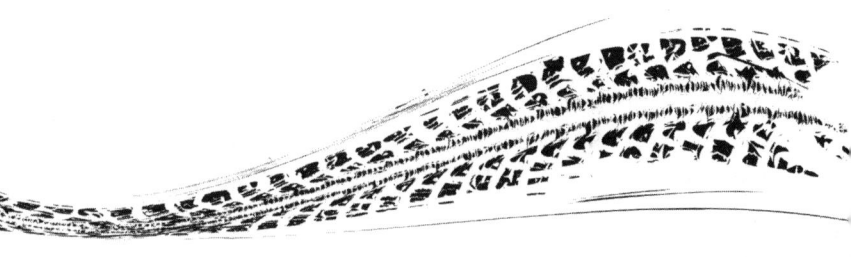

Brentlee

It's been a week since Bates and I marked our bodies with each other's name. I still surprise myself every time I look in the mirror. I'm not used to the ink on my skin. I love it, though; and Bates' neck piece, fuck, I can't wait until it's fully healed. I still ache to trace it with my tongue as I ride his delicious cock. I don't know that I'll ever get tired of having him inside of my body—anywhere inside of me.

"Babe, you ready?" he calls out from the living room.

Tonight, I'm not working; tonight is a party, the first party I get to attend as an Old Lady. Kentlee is beside herself with glee that we're going to be there together. Tammy is watching all of the kids over here for the night, Kentlee's two and my

Stella. Bates and I are going to spend the whole night at the clubhouse. I'm a little nervous, to say the least. Not only have I never left Stella overnight, anywhere, but now I'm going to be on Bates' arm as his woman—*officially* his woman.

"I am," I call out, taking one last look in the mirror.

My long dark hair is straight and sleek. I'm wearing a tight, black mini-skirt with a blue cropped top that's loose but shows off my entire stomach, ending just below my breasts. My Sniper tattoo is on complete display. On my feet are a pair of black high heels, so high that I know my feet are going to ache after the first hour, but they are so cute I don't care. I'll drink the pain away. I apply one last layer of bright red lipstick to my lips and leave the room.

"You can't go," Bates growls as soon as I step into the living room.

Fury, Kentlee, Tammy and the kids are all looking at me with wide eyes.

"Why?" I ask, feigning innocence.

"Too much skin," he barks.

I do a slow spin in my outfit, making sure to stop when my back is turned so he can see how short the skirt really is. It barely covers my ass.

"I think it's cute," Kentlee pipes up.

"You stay out of it, sugar," Fury murmurs.

I look over and see that my sister is wearing a dress. It shows off her ample cleavage and is tight on her spectacular curves. It's also not much longer than mine.

"I think it's cute, too," Tammy chimes in. Bates just growls.

"Then that settles it, three out of four," I grin walking over to him and placing a gentle kiss on the B of my name along his neck.

"That don't settle shit. You get drunk tonight, baby, and I'll settle this with some fantastic drunk fucking," he murmurs against my ear.

"Sounds like a plan. Let's get outta here," I practically yell, making both him and Fury chuckle.

We say goodbye to our babies and give them kisses before we load onto the bikes and head to the clubhouse. I wrap myself around Bates' body, though not too tightly, knowing his ink is still tender to the touch on his back. I feel one of his hands slide up my thigh and give it a squeeze.

Once we arrive at the clubhouse I try to gracefully slide off of his bike, which isn't easy in the short skirt, high heel combo I have going on. Bates gets off but wraps his hand around my waist, stopping me from walking inside immediately.

"I love you, baby," he murmurs before his lips brush against mine.

"You okay?" I ask, furrowing my brows.

"These parties can get crazy. It's a free for all and I just, I love you," he shrugs.

This isn't my first Notorious Devil's party, but apparently it's going to get crazier than a normal party would be. There are a few other charters here visiting, passing through town on runs with men I've never met before.

"You'll stay with me the whole time?" I ask.

"I'll be fuckin' glued to you, baby," he grunts as his hands travel to my ass and squeeze.

"Then I'll be fine," I say brightly. He just shakes his head as he disengages his hands from my ass and wraps one around my waist to walk me into the clubhouse.

"Let's party, babe," he grunts.

We walk inside of the clubhouse and the smoke is heavier, the music louder, the smell of sex and booze stronger than I have ever witnessed before. There are at least twice as many people here as I've ever seen, and suddenly I understand exactly why Bates has been a little worried. It's complete chaos.

We wind and shove our way to the bar. I need a few shots before I can shake the unease of the atmosphere away. It's a complete crush of people, and it has my anxiety on high.

A prospect slides two shot glasses toward us along with a bottle of tequila. Bates doesn't hesitate to pour two shots, and I don't hesitate to down my first one. Together we shoot at least four shots a piece and then ask for beers.

"Who in the fuck is this bitch?" a guy yells. I turn in Bates' arms to see a very tall, handsome, longhaired man standing right behind me.

"Snake. This is my Old Lady, Brentlee," Bates chuckles. The man looks me up and down, then his eyes stop on my hip and narrow before he breaks out into a big smile.

"Fuck me sideways, you got an Old Lady. Inked and everything," he chuckles before he pats Bates on the back. "Well, gorgeous, you got stuck with this ugly fucker for life. Sucks to be you," he laughs. Bates joins him.

"Snake and I go way back," Bates chuckles. I can't help but smile.

"It's nice to meet you," I say holding out my hand. Snake grasps my palm and pulls me in for a quick hug.

"Any woman who can tame this cranky ass motherfucker deserves a fuckin' medal," he says. Bates gives him the finger.

We spend another hour talking to Snake. Well, Bates talks to him and I snuggle into his side, happy to just be held by my big mountain of a man.

As the night drags on, I notice that more and more people are losing their clothes. Most of the clubwhores are completely naked, and even a few of the Old Ladies have lost articles of clothing. I'm sitting on Bates' lap, my beer on the table in front of me, and he's talking to somebody. I'm so drunk, I can't remember his name. I can't even focus on him. I have my face turned to the side buried in Bates' neck, my lips gently grazing my tattoo. I purr when I feel his hand slide between my legs.

"Bates," I whisper.

"Quiet, feel me *tigritsa*," he growls. I spread my legs a little as his finger slide my panties to the side before it enters me.

I'm wet. So fucking wet. I wrap my hand around the back of his neck and grind slightly against his hand. I need more, so much more from him. I can feel his chest vibrating behind me and I know that he's still talking to whoever is next to him. I can't seem to give a shit. All I feel is him touching me, filling me—*owning* me.

I gasp when a second finger fills me and he slowly begins fucking me. It's so damn slow, I think I might actually explode, or scratch his eyes out, or cry.

"*Please*," I whimper. He ignores me.

Bates continues to slowly torture me. He makes even strokes with his fingers, filling me, making that come hither motion I love. When his thumb presses against my clit, I groan. I can't stop my hips from meeting his thrusts. I grind my ass against his jean covered cock.

"You don't stop, and I'm going to take it out and fill you with it right here in front of the whole damn bar," he grunts.

"Do it," I dare.

"Fuck," he hisses. Before I realize what's happened, he

picks me up and throws me over his shoulder.

I hear whoops and hollers, but I can't take my eyes off of his gorgeous ass as he walks. I can feel his arm around the hem of my skirt, keeping my body from the view of the people surrounding us. He walks us inside of his room and I cry out when my body bounces on the bed.

"Want all of you tonight, baby," he murmurs as he strips his clothes. I nod as my mouth waters. He can have me, all of me. I'm so turned on, he can do what he pleases. As long as I come, I don't give a shit.

"I want your ass, Brentlee. I want to slide my cock in your gorgeous, tight ass. Will you give that to me?" he asks. I take a gulp of air before I look up to him. His hand slides into my hair and his eyes are focused on me, solely focused on me. Suddenly, I don't feel drunk.

"Erase all the bad memories I have, Bates. Replace them with you," I murmur.

He bends down, his lips crashing against mine, his tongue forcing its way inside of my mouth. I'm filled with his tongue and his moans. I wrap my hands around the back of his neck and thread my fingers through his hair, slightly tugging.

"Gonna make you feel good, baby. Never gonna hurt you," he mumbles as one of his hands slides up my side and cups my breast.

"Make it good, Bates," I whisper against his lips. He nods once before he steps away from me.

"On your stomach, baby," he commands. I shiver before I roll to my stomach.

Bates grabs my skirt and yanks it down my body before I hear it hit the floor somewhere behind me. He orders me to remove my shirt, and then he unclasps my bra before he yanks my panties down my legs. I'm completely bare for him, with the exception of my black high heeled shoes. I hear a thump behind me before Bates' mouth sucks my clit between his teeth. I moan when his tongue flicks me, and push myself closer to him. I'm on my hands and knees, and his glorious mouth is between my thighs.

"I'm gonna bring you close to the edge, baby," he warns before his tongue slices through my core and enters my pussy. I moan shamelessly loud as I grind on his face.

Fuck, this man and his beard are going to be the end of me. Thank god he's branded me and is keeping me, because I have a feeling no other man could ever make me feel this way again.

I feel myself climbing toward my release when he pulls away from me. I whimper and slide my hand between my legs, but he slaps me on my pussy. I cry out, but the bastard just laughs. Luckily, he only lightly slapped me so it doesn't hurt—but it's throbbing and aching and I need to come.

"Sshhh, *tigritsa*," he murmurs.

I hear him fumble around and then a cool liquid slides through the crack of my ass. I gasp when I feel his finger enter me. It doesn't hurt; I feel as though it should, but it doesn't. When Scotty took my ass, he just shoved himself inside of me and did as he pleased. Bates isn't doing that, he's taking his time and he's being gentle.

"Bates," I moan, meeting his thrusting finger, enjoying the feeling of him in that forbidden part of me.

I groan when a second finger fills me. Bates wraps his other hand around my hip and begins to play with my clit. He's all around me, inside of me, filling me and it's so much, yet not enough.

"You feel so good, baby," he murmurs as two fingers slide

inside of my dripping pussy.

"I need more," I demand. I'm drunk and I need him, I want him, I want all of him.

"Yeah, baby, you got it," he says, keeping his fingers in my ass.

Then I feel the head of his cock position against my pussy and he slowly pushes inside of me. I whimper before his lips touch my lower back and his fingers continue to play with my clit.

"Relax, my *tigritsa*, don't be scared, baby. Take me inside of you, push back now and accept me," he coos.

I should be fucking terrified, but I'm not. I'm glad it's only his fingers, I don't know if I would survive his cock. I close my eyes and will my body to relax. I focus on his fingers strumming my clit, the smell of him surrounding me.

"Just feel me filling you. Feel my fingers on that gorgeous pussy, my dick deep in that tight cunt. My gorgeous girl, my *tigritsa*," he murmurs against the back of my neck as he places sweet kisses. I sigh and begin to slowly rock against him.

"I want more, Bates," I whisper.

He returns my whisper with a groan and starts to slowly fuck my ass with his fingers. I never thought I could enjoy this act, even just this little part of it. Scotty used it to defile me, demean me at one time, but now—it feels beautiful. I sigh as I meet his fingers' thrust with my ass—offering myself willingly to him.

I cry out when his hips thrust harder, slamming his cock inside of me, filling my pussy. I scream when I come and my whole body goes stiff before it starts to shake. Then the most beautiful guttural sound of my man's release fills the air and he comes inside of me, filling me with his climax.

After a quick shower down the hall, we hurry back to his room and lock ourselves inside. I can hear the bass from the music at the party, but it seems far away. Curled up and in the arms of my lover, my man, my Old Man, we're in our own cocoon.

"Thank you for that, Brentlee," he whispers into the dark.

"No, Bates, thank *you*. I wish I could give it all to you," I say.

"You will; one day you'll be ready. I knew you weren't," he murmurs before he places a kiss to the top of my head.

"Well, anyway, thank you," I sigh.

"Sleep, my *tigritsa*," he grunts. Without further prompting, I close my eyes and I fall into a blissful sleep.

Sniper

I see the explosion and it is as if it is in slow motion. All around me, there is fire and mayhem. Men are screaming and crying out, and I'm frozen in my tracks. This shouldn't be happening. We've done this a dozen times, and this shouldn't be happening. I grab my gun and shake myself out of the daze. I need to save my friends, my brothers.

I look down and fall to my knees when I see a kid, Morgan, screaming and holding his stomach. I take a closer look at his stomach and notice that his insides are completely missing; there's nothing but a big hole there.

"Daddy," he calls out in his southern accent.

"Morgan," I grunt.

"Are you proud of me now, daddy?" he asks. I wrap my

hand around the back of his neck. I meet his eyes with mine and I smile.

"So fuckin' proud, son," I say. He smiles before his whole body goes limp. He dies, right there in my arms, he fuckin' dies.

"Bates" a woman screams. I stand up, running across the bloody sand. It's Brentlee. She's kneeling and there's a man in front of her. He turns around and it's Scotty.

"Say goodbye to your whore, Bates Lukin," he hisses before he pulls the trigger.

I sit straight up, sweat dripping off of my face and my chest. The dark room is too much, I search for Brentlee and sigh when I find her warm body curled next to mine. I need her. I need her to chase my dreams away. I don't bother waking her up. I roll her onto her stomach and wet my dick before I push myself inside of her pussy. She's not as wet as she usually is, but I don't care. I just need to feel.

I know the moment she wakes because her body stiffens before she lets out a moan and then relaxes again. I kiss her neck as I continue to fuck her. I yank her hips back a little higher and slowly slide in and out of her heat. She's getting wetter and wetter with each slide of my cock, and I can't help the groan that escapes my lips.

"Harder," she grunts. I don't hesitate.

I slide to my knees and roughly grab her hips before I pull her onto my cock, hard. I hold her still and I fuck her with all of my strength. I can't say anything, except grunt and moan at the way she feels around my cock. The room is filled with the sound of slapping skin, grunts, and Brentlee's cries.

"Make yourself come," I order. I'm pleased when her hand dives between her thighs.

I'm so fucking close. I'm two seconds from tipping over

the edge, and when I feel her pussy squeeze my cock as she screams my name, I finally let loose. I come so hard, shooting my release deep inside of her.

"Baby," she whispers when I pull out of her.

She tries to roll away, to clean herself up, but I can't let her leave my side. I never want her to leave me. Ever. I wrap my arms around her and pull her back into my front, spooning her.

"Just let me clean up," she murmurs. I grunt before I dive my hand between her legs and shove two fingers into her wet cunt.

"No, I want my cum inside of you when I sleep," I say.

"Did you have a nightmare," she whispers when I finger her. I almost sigh at how wet and warm she is, our mixed release helping guide my fingers in and out of her pussy.

"Yeah," I murmur, kissing her shoulder. She begins to move her hips with the rhythm of my hand.

"Tell me about it?" she asks, her voice breathy and her hips thrusting harder, searching for more.

"No, I just want to fuck you into exhaustion. That sound good?"

"Yeah, baby, that sounds good," she sighs.

I don't fuck her from behind this time. Instead I instruct her to climb on top of me. I let her ride me. I tell her to take her time, torture me with a slow as fuck pace. I want her to get herself off, but in no hurry.

I want her to build herself to a point where she explodes. I want to watch every little detail, every little expression on her face. I want to make sure she's real, she's here, and she's mine.

When she comes, she screams. I know she must be heard

throughout the entire club, but I don't give a fuck. It's the most beautiful thing I have ever witnessed in my entire fucking life. Her whole body is shaking, her pussy squeezing the life out of my cock. I thrust up inside of her a few times before I tip over the edge and fall, more of my cum filling her body.

I'm finally exhausted.

I leave her in a pile of bones and flesh in my bed as I go over to the bathrooms and get a cloth to clean her up. She's asleep by the time I make it back, but I don't care. I clean the remnants of our evening from her pussy and I crawl in behind her. I wrap her in my arms and I finally drift off to sleep.

Peacefully.

My beautiful woman in my arms.

My *tigritsa*.

chapter twenty

Brentlee

My head is pounding, and so is my pussy. Jesus, it feels like we screwed all night long—mainly because we did. I groan and roll over, but Bates' strong arm tightens around my stomach and pulls me closer to his chest. I feel him bury his face in my hair, and then he inhales. I'm sure I smell like sex, sweat, and tequila, a combination that cannot be in the least bit sexy.

"Stop, I'm gross," I grumble. He doesn't stop. Instead, he kisses my shoulder.

"You okay, baby?" he murmurs his voice deep and husky, gruff and sexy.

"Sore, but yeah, I'm okay," I admit.

"I'm sorry I hurt you. Knew I would soon enough," he grunts before he releases me and rolls onto his back. I turn to face him and throw my arm over his stomach, resting my chin on his chest.

"You didn't hurt me. We just had a lot of sex last night and I'm a little sore. I never told you to stop, I liked all of it," I admit.

"You remember it all?" he asks as his hand comes up and tucks a few strands of hair behind my ear.

"What, you mean when you fucked my ass with your fingers? Or when you started fucking me from behind when I was asleep? Or how about when you commanded me to ride you for what felt like hours?" I ask, arching a brow.

"Yeah, you remember," he grunts, his voice lower, gravellier—sexier.

"I loved it all, baby. Every time you touch me, I love it, Bates. Don't ever think I don't," I admit. His eyes darken, and they look so black.

"Now I'm hard again and your pussy needs to recoup," he murmurs, making me laugh.

"I could ride you slow again," I whisper, placing a soft kiss on his nipple before gentle nipping it.

"Not gonna turn my woman down when she offers to take my dick. But I don't want you hurting," he groans as I wrap my hand around his already hard cock.

"Then you better make me nice and wet Bates, so you slide right in." I feel him shudder and then his hands wrap around my waist and he pulls me up to my knees.

"Ride my face before you ride my cock, baby. I wanna taste that pussy. My pussy," he hums.

"I haven't showered," I warn. He chuckles as I spread my

thighs over his face.

"Think I know that, baby. Now get that pussy up here and ride my face," he commands.

I gently lower myself onto his lips and cringe at how gross I must taste to him. I can't believe I'm doing this. *Though, I would do just about anything for this man.* When his tongue slides between my swollen lips, I moan. When his teeth graze my aching, sensitive clit before he sucks on it, I throw back my head and cry out his name.

All thoughts of how I taste go completely out the window as his hands grab onto my thighs and he pulls me down hard against his face. His beard tickles and scratches and feels so damn good, I can't breathe.

I'm close, so fucking close.

Then, he stops.

I growl, but he only laughs as he pushes me down his body. I want more of his mouth, but when I reach his dick, I shiver.

Never mind. I want *that* instead.

He aligns himself with my entrance and I slowly sink down on his hard cock. We both groan when I am fully seated.

"Don't move yet," he orders. It's so hard not to just ride the hell out of him, I'm so turned on, *so close.*

I close my eyes and just feel him inside of me, stretching me. He's warm and hard. I gasp when his thumb starts to rub against my clit.

"Bates," I warn. His eyes are completely focused on his hand between my legs. "Bates, baby, I'm going to need to move," I warn.

"Not yet," he says, sounding completely distracted. I

grind my teeth together, forcing my body to stay still. I want to move so badly, it aches. I feel like I'm going to crawl out of my skin, I want it too damn bad.

"Please," I whimper. I'm not above begging; I don't know if I ever will be when it comes to him.

"No," he barks roughly.

It should piss me off, but it doesn't. It makes me shiver, the way his harsh command washes over me.

The way he so obviously owns my body.

"Baby, I feel like I'm going to die," I whine as I ball my hands into fists and dig my nails into my palms.

"Just wait," he says harshly.

I growl in annoyance. He doesn't react to my obvious irritation. He doesn't say a word, his focus only on my clit and the way his thumb is working it. I feel my thighs shake against his waist as I bite down on my bottom lip, tears welling in my eyes. I can't stop them, no matter how hard I try. Tears fall from my eyes, down my cheeks and onto Bates' stomach. I need to come, it physically hurts.

His other hand slides up my side and wraps around my throat. He massages my throat, his thumb making the exact same pattern on the side of my throat as the other one is making on my clit. The tears continue to flow, and then suddenly his eyes meet mine and he grins.

"Lean forward on my hand, baby, and make yourself come," he murmurs. I don't hesitate. If he wanted me to cluck like a fucking chicken at this point—I would.

I lean forward and feel my airway being slightly restricted as his hand moves out from between my legs and wraps around one of the cheeks of my ass. I raise my hips and let them fall, grinding down on his gorgeous cock. Then, as if something inside of me snaps, I ride him. I ride him like I am a woman possessed, like I need a priest to come in here and perform an exorcism on me.

Bates' hand on my neck tightens and I feel as though I'm floating. My body is not my own, and I'm thinking of nothing but seeking my own pleasure. When I come, it's an explosion of epic proportions, and if I had my voice to scream, everybody within a ten-mile radius would hear me.

Bates doesn't allow me to relax after my climax; instead, he flips me to my back and he fucks me with all of his raw strength. His hand is still on my throat, squeezing and releasing as his cock slams inside of me. When he finally comes, I feel him explode and twitch inside of me before he collapses on top of my body. His weight is heavy, pushing me into the mattress, but it feels divine.

"You all right, *tigritsa*?" he asks once his breathing has evened out. I wince when he pulls out of me and rolls onto his back.

"Yeah, I'm okay," I sigh, turning my head to look at him.

"I gotta go on a run in a couple days. I'm gonna be gone a week, maybe two," he announces out of the blue.

"Where to?"

"Can't really tell you. Buck will stand watch, so will a couple of prospects, and Fury's gonna be takin' you to and from work," he says.

"You're really leaving? Just like that?" I ask as my breathing starts to increase and panic starts to fill my body.

"It's club business. Not much I can do about it. Scotty ain't gonna bother you. Honestly, I'd pull the brothers off of you, but I just want to be extra careful until the divorce and custody papers are finalized." He shrugs as he stands and gathers his clothes.

"I don't understand why you can't tell me what you're doing, and I really don't understand why you aren't concerned about Scotty anymore," I say, sliding off of the bed and gathering my own clothes.

"It's been weeks, babe. He'd have tried something by now, that's all," he says, avoiding my gaze. He's lying, or omitting something, I just don't know what.

"Maybe," I murmur as I finish getting dressed.

I'm ready to go home and take a shower. Our fuck fest has me feeling gross, and this conversation is doing nothing but irritating me.

"It's club shit. Women aren't told anything," he says, wrapping his hand around the back of my neck and dipping his head down to place a gentle kiss on my lips.

"My sister doesn't know anything?" I ask, arching a brow.

"Your sister knows what her man tells her. I can guarantee it ain't much, if anything. There's a reason we don't tell the women; we don't tell anybody, Brentlee. What we say when we go into that room for church, it stays there. The less people that know our shit, the less liabilities we have. You're going to have to deal with that," he says before he turns and sits on the bed to put on his boots.

"I don't know if I can deal with a bunch of secrets," I say, crossing my arms over my chest to try and protect myself.

"My business with the club can't be shared with anybody," he states.

"What else will you keep secret?" I ask, biting on my bottom lip.

"What's the real question here, babe?" he asks, standing and sliding his cut on over his arms and shoulders.

"Are you going to screw around and everybody just keeps it a big secret?" I blurt.

God I am so damn insecure; it's pissing me off. I don't know how Bates doesn't slap the shit out of me for it. Maybe I'm pushing him on purpose. Maybe I'm trying to goad him, to push his buttons and test him. Maybe I want him to lose his shit, so I can prove that he's just like Scotty, that he'll beat the shit out of me and expect me to take it.

I am so fucked up.

"This is the last time we're having this conversation, Brentlee," he announces before he grabs my hips and roughly pulls me close to his body. One of his hands slides up my spine and fists in my hair, yanking my head back. I let out a surprised cry, but stay quiet otherwise.

"For the last fuckin' time—your name is branded on my fuckin' throat. I'm yours and you're mine. My dick only gets wet inside your sweet cunt, ass, or mouth. Nobody else, no matter where I am or what I'm doin'. I'm yours, baby. Every piece of me is yours. Shit goes down in the club and you can't know anything. It's for your protection as much as it's for the club's. I go to jail or some shit and you can't testify against me because you don't *know* anything. My main focus is the club—keeping my brothers safe and all that shit—but it's also you, keeping you and Stella safe. You'll always be taken care of because my names on your body," he growls.

"What?" I breathe.

"Anything happens to me, this club will take care of you, baby. They'll have your back, they'll help you and Stella, no questions asked, because my name is right here on your hip." He squeezes the Sniper tattoo for emphasis.

"Don't you leave me," I whimper.

"Never gonna leave my *tigritsa* willingly," he murmurs before his lips slam down on mine and he takes me in a hard, swift kiss.

"Now, tell me you get what I'm sayin', babe. Tell me you understand. I'm yours, my cock's yours, and my heart, it's always been yours," he whispers before his teeth nip my earlobe.

"Yeah, baby, I understand," I sigh. And I do.

I understand.

I finally understand.

He's in this about as deeply as I am.

I only hope that he stays this way.

I don't know if I'll ever be one hundred percent comfortable with this relationship. I think because of my marriage to Scotty, I'll always be sitting around *waiting* for the other shoe to drop. But for now, I'm going to try and push those thoughts out of my head and be happy. I have a man who loves me, who loves my daughter, who is willing to take care of us, no matter what. How can I possibly bitch about that?

Sniper

After relieving Tammy from kid duty, I leave my girls. Brent is exhausted and Stella is bursting with energy, ready to tell her all about her evening with Tammy and her cousins. I haven't seen Stella this excited since our little Target shopping spree for Elsa sheets. A grin tugs on my lips as I make my way back to the clubhouse. As much as I'd like to curl up with my girls on the couch, I can't. I have shit to prep for.

It's my turn in rotation to make a run from here to Salt Lake City and then up to the Canadian border to do a hand off. It's a hard run, but the payout is fuckin' phenomenal. Working with the Cartel hasn't been nearly as fucked up as working with the Aryan's was. Those assholes were fuckin' terrifying. I shiver just thinking about them.

"You ready for this run?" Fury asks as soon as I walk into his office. He looks about as exhausted as I do, and I wonder if LeeLee kept him up all night, too. I chuckle at the thought.

"What's funny?" he grunts.

"I'm fuckin' beat to shit, brother," I admit. He sighs before he leans back in his chair.

"Christ, that woman is going to be the death of me. She's too young. I can't keep up, and if I admit that, she'll laugh at my ass and call me old," he grumbles.

"Bitches," I grunt. He looks up at me before he grins.

"Bitch with the most fuckin' addictive pussy I've ever had the pleasure of being inside of," he chuckles. I nod in agreement.

"Fuck, yeah. And thank fuck for that, too," I laugh.

"Canadian brothers are gonna stay here until you guys get back from SLC. We're just gonna do the handoff here for this time around," I narrow my eyes slightly.

"That why they're here to begin with?" I ask.

"Some shit about one of their brothers losing his shit and getting locked up when he was visiting his Mama in Texas. They had to bail his ass outta jail," Fury shrugs.

"Took the whole charter for that shit?" I ask in confusion.

"They had to make the fucker who caused the whole scene *fade away*," he says. I nod.

"Hey, thanks for helping Drifter with that issue the other

day," he murmurs.

"It was my issue anyway," I shrug.

"It's family, nobody's single issue, Sniper. Now, go and get this shit done and over with. We'll keep your girls safe."

I nod and leave, wondering just what kind of cluster fuck they caused in Texas. The downfall with this life is that it's a hard life. Sometimes people get caught up in shady shit and this situation is just that, real fuckin' shady. I don't say anything else, though; mainly because it ain't my business. Plus, I don't really give a fuck. Me not having to make the trip up to Canada just means I can be inside of my woman that much sooner.

chapter twenty-one

Brentlee

I roll over and reach for Bates, but find his side of the bed empty. I sigh. He's gone. I knew he was leaving, so I don't know why I'm surprised to find him actually gone. Maybe I thought if I pouted enough, he'd be able to stay. I feel badly for being bratty about him going. I'm scared, though. Things with Scotty have been way too quiet for way too long. Plus, he didn't give me much time to prep for him leaving. He just announced it and then left.

Yesterday I received a call from my attorney, and he said that Scotty has agreed completely. He signed the paperwork granting the divorce, and he's willing to sign over full custody of Stella to me. He wants nothing in return. He's going to completely terminate his rights. This also means I won't be getting child support, but who cares? I don't want a dime from him. I want to believe that these are answered prayers, but in all honestly, it feels like a trap of some kind.

My phone rings and I pick it up, noticing that it's Kentlee.

"Are you sure you want to go there?" she asks without even saying hello first.

"I need to talk to them. It's been weeks," I say.

"You make sure that you take protection. I would honestly prefer if Fury took you," she says.

I roll my eyes. Yeah, taking Fury to talk with my parents would really go over well, or absolutely not.

He despises them for their treatment of Kentlee, and I don't blame him one bit. They're Kentlee's past, and odds are, they will be mine as well after this little get together, but I need to talk to them. I need to explain things, for my own peace of mind, if nothing else.

"Johnny Williams is taking me," I inform her. She giggles.

"Oh, mom and dad are going to just *love* Dirty Johnny. I kinda want to go just to see the look on their faces when he walks into their pristine house with a cigarette hanging from his lips," she howls.

"It'll be fine," I grumble, knowing damn well it won't be.

Johnny is on babysitting duty today, so he's the one who is going to have to take me, and he's the one who is going to have to hear my mother be a total bitch to him, with no regard to his feelings or anybody else's.

"I'll be over in about an hour to watch Stella," she informs me before she hangs up.

I groan and hurry into the shower. Stella will be up any minute, and I want to at least be showered before she starts asking for breakfast and requires all of my attention.

Once I'm showered and dressed, I make breakfast and nervously wait for Kentlee and Johnny to arrive. I don't know what my parents are going to say, how they're going to react to not only my leaving Scotty, but also to my relationship with Bates. I'm not going to hide it from them. They'll find out soon enough, if they don't already know, and I want them to hear it from me.

I close my eyes for a moment and remember how they treated Kentlee, how horrible they were to her. They told her to abort her baby if she still wanted to be in their family. She was so brave, my sister, so much braver than I have ever been.

I hope that one day I can be half the woman she is.

DIRTY JOHNNY

I'm not the kind of guy that does nice shit for anyone, but there's something about Kentlee and Brentlee that makes me want to help them. Maybe it's their perceived innocence, the way they look up at you and you just know they're good girls. Sure, Brent used to be a little slutty back in the day, but her wide eyes and coy smiles always, *always* made my dick hard. Still do.

I don't want her like that anymore. She's a nice ride, but Sniper is in love with her and she him. I like her for my brother, they're good together. I don't think I'd ever seen the bastard smile before she came barreling through his life again.

I pull into the drive with my classic 1970 Chevy Chevelle and notice that Kentlee's badass SUV is parked in the drive. I have to say, I miss seeing her blonde hair flying in her sweet

Camaro, but the SUV is safer for her and the kids; plus, Fury had it tricked out so it's fuckin' tight. I get out of my car and walk up to the front door, knocking before I turn the knob and walk right in.

"Hey, Johnny," Brent says, throwing her purse over her shoulder.

I give her a chin lift before I make a beeline for the only girl in this room that truly holds my heart. Ellie Duhart.

"You spoil her," Kent says as she hands her over to me. I hold her close to my chest and just enjoy the way her head rests on my shoulder. She's not a tiny baby anymore and it fuckin' kills me, she grows every single time I see her.

"She deserves every second of it," I murmur, trying not to wake her.

She's gorgeous. Little Ellie. Never thought I wanted a family of my own until I held this sweet thing in my arms. Now, I want a whole fuckin' litter. All girls. Don't ask me why. There's something about her, sweet and innocent. I want to protect her from everything bad in the world, and she ain't even mine.

"You can't keep her," Brentlee says, standing right in front of me.

"I know," I sigh as I place a kiss on her forehead and hand her back to her mama.

"You need to find a nice girl and make one of your own," Kentlee says as she takes her daughter from me.

"Doubt that shit'll ever happen, babe," I grunt as I turn to walk toward the front door. I hear Kentlee hum behind me, but I ignore her.

These bitches, once they tie down a brother, they think we all want to be tied down. Sure, I'd love to have a family, a whole fuckin' houseful of angel girls, but settling down completely? *I shiver.* I don't know if my dick could handle one pussy for the rest of its life. It might retaliate, shrivel up, and hate me forever.

"I saw the way you looked at Ellie," Brentlee says as she buckles her seatbelt across her lap.

"Yeah?" I grunt, putting the car in reverse.

"You want one. A baby, a family," she announces.

I roll my eyes as I reach for a cigarette. *Fuck,* I should quit these things, but I don't think I could. Raised on them. Been smokin' since I was nine. "It's okay to want those things, Johnny."

"I do, but I don't want all the shit that comes with it," I say, shrugging my shoulders.

"Like?" She laughs softly and I let her sweet voice wash over me.

Sweet.

Haven't had sweet since I had her ten years ago. Not that I harbor any feelings for Brent. I never did. I want sweet, though. Unfortunately, sweet chicks run from me. The tattoos, the hardened angry face I sport, the dirty way I fuck. Yeah, no sweet girl would willingly stay in my bed.

"Commitment, stability, fidelity," I murmur as I drive toward her parent's house.

"You never know what you're willing to compromise for the right person," Brent says, giving me a wide smile.

We ride the rest of the way to The Johnson's in silence. I think about being tied down; it comes with restraints, but it could be good, too. It comes with an opportunity to have a family. I shake my head as I turn down the Johnson's street.

I smirk over at Brentlee as I throw the car into park. I

want to laugh. Don't think I could compromise on any of that shit I mentioned. No, my dick likes to roam, and I let it. No sense in tying a noose around it. No way. I couldn't have one pussy for life.

Brentlee

Johnny looks a little like he's going to hyperventilate at the thought of settling down, but I saw the truth. I saw the way he held Ellie; the way he looked at her. He may not realize it, but he's ready for more. I can't wait until love knocks him on his ass. I'm going to replay this little conversation of ours for him and laugh.

As soon as I reach my parents front porch, my stomach flips. All thoughts of Johnny and his future fly out of my head, and the only thing I can focus on is my fear and nervousness.

Johnny knocks on the door and I shoot him a dirty look. His response is a shrug.

"Brentlee, oh my god, where have you been?" my mother dramatically cries. I ignore her outburst and push my way past her and into the house, Johnny right on my heels.

"What's happening, who is *this*?" she asks with disgust laced in her tone.

"I need to talk to you and dad," I murmur. She nods before she leaves to get my father.

Once my parents are in the living area, I sit down on the sofa. Johnny slouches in the chair in the corner, and my parents sit poised to perfection on the loveseat. My mother can't take her eyes off of Johnny. He's a hot, rugged dude, but that's not why she's looking at him. She's completely disgusted with him, and she's probably watching to make sure he doesn't jack her silver.

"Well, where have you been?" my father demands.

"I left Scotty," I begin before taking a deep breath. "He hurt Stella and I couldn't stay."

I don't tell them where I've been on purpose. I don't know what their reactions will be, but I do know what they've been in the past. My parents have turned a blind eye to every single bruise and broken bone I've suffered. Money and status have taken precedence over my health and safety.

"I'm sure it was just a misunderstanding. You'll just go back and ask his forgiveness. Tell him you were premenstrual," my mother coos. I hear Johnny growl, but he doesn't need to stand up for me. I can do it myself.

"It wasn't a misunderstanding. He hurt me for six years, and he was escalating. I left him before he killed Stella and me," I say. My mother frowns.

"You need to make it right, Brentlee," she says.

"I did make it right. I walked out and left," I reiterate. It's clear to me that my mom isn't going to change her mind. She thinks I've made a grave mistake.

"He loves you, Brentlee. You can't hold a few bad things against him like that. He has a highly stressful job," my father explains, cajoling me, talking to me like a small child.

"You two are batshit crazy," I point out as I stand up. Johnny snickers next to me, but I ignore him.

"Brentlee, do not talk to us that way," my father booms.

"I'm not going back to him. I'm not allowing my daughter anywhere near him, either. If you two can't accept that, then you can go kick rocks," I shout.

"You are more like your sister than I thought. You were always our good girl. What happened?" my mother cries with fake as shit tears falling down her cheeks.

"That's probably the nicest thing you've ever said to me, comparing me to Kentlee," I smile. My mother's eyes narrow.

"You don't go back to your husband, then don't come back here looking for our help," she shouts.

I want to act shocked, but I'm not. I knew this would be how our conversation would play out. My mother only wants things done her way. I'm not a little girl anymore, she doesn't really get a say in my life, and I'm not going to put my daughter in jeopardy to make her happy. Neither am I going to give up Bates. I love him. For the first time in ten years I'm happy, and I'm not going to let anybody change that.

"Let's go, Johnny," I murmur. He nods once before he walks toward the front door.

"Do you realize what you're doing, young lady?" my father asks. I stop at the opened door and turn to face him.

"I'm doing what I should have done years ago when you pulled this shit with Kentlee. I'm leaving. I don't need assholes like you in my life."

I don't wait for their response. I turn and leave. They can be bitter and angry all they want, but I won't allow them to control my life, or my daughter's life. They aren't acting like loving parents. Their only goal is to control and manipulate, and I for one am done with it. I love my daughter too much to subject her to anymore of the living-hell we were in months ago. No, it's time I stood up—not only for me, but for her.

"You did good in there," Johnny says after we take off down the road.

"They're fucking crazy," I murmur.

"They are. I'd say they love you and they want what's best for you, but to be honest, I have no clue what their agenda is," he chuckles.

"No shit. You know they just pretend Kentlee was never born? They took down every picture of her in the house. I bet my mom's doing that with me now, too. Connellee doesn't even visit anymore. They've officially isolated themselves from their own children. If Stella wanted nothing to do with me, I think I'd die," I say looking out the passenger side of the car.

"You're a good mom, Brent. You're a survivor. Most importantly, you'd never threaten to disown her for making a decision you don't approve of," he says.

"I wouldn't. Not ever. I love her too much," I vow.

We ride back to Bates' house, my house, in silence. Once we pull into the dirt drive, my anxiety disappears.

This is where I was always meant to be.

This place feels like home.

I've never been happier than in this little country house, surrounded by nothingness, but filled with everything—Bates and Stella. How can I ever want anything else? I can't. This is where I plan on staying, forever. This is my happily ever after.

chapter twenty-two

Sniper

The road to Salt Lake City is boring as *fuck*. Torch and I ride together, and it feels as though we're going at a snail's pace. Maybe it feels long and lonely because I have something to get back to now. I have my Brentlee and Stella waiting for me. I also have a bad feeling in the pit of my gut that shit could go down with that fucktard, Scotty.

"You okay, man?" Torch asks me once we park our bikes at the SLC clubhouse.

"Got a bad fuckin' feeling. I'm sure I'm just being paranoid." I shrug as we walk through the doors.

"Dirty Johnny'll take care of your girl," he says, clapping my shoulder. I narrow my eyes at him, which only makes him laugh at me. "You know what I mean," he grumbles.

"He's had his dick inside of her," I announce as if he doesn't know.

Torch doesn't say a damn thing. He's had his dick inside of my woman, too. Though I'm annoyed by those facts, I can't hold it against any of them. It was over a decade ago.

"Hey," a booming voice shouts. I look up to see Rain, the charter's vice president standing in the middle of the bar.

We greet each other and then go over to a table where a cute, little, curvy redhead brings us some beers. I watch her plump, little ass sway as she goes back behind the bar. I look around for Blow, the club's president, but I don't see him anywhere.

"She ain't a whore," Rain barks. I turn back to him as I take a pull from my beer.

"Got a woman; just enjoyin' the view," I say. He narrows his eyes at me before he laughs.

"You got a woman now?" he asks, disbelieving.

"Branded her a coupl'a weeks ago. Bitch branded me, too," I chuckle, arching my neck so he can see her name scrawled along its length.

"Fuck man, you really are taken," he grunts.

"I am. Happily," I admit. He shakes his head.

"Pleased as fuck for you. Good woman is hard to find in our world." I nod and Torch snorts.

"She's not from our world, but she's in it now. Our president's wife's little sister," he speaks up.

It's my turn to snort. Brentlee might be LeeLee's little sister, but she's always been her own leader. Never acted her age, and has always taken center stage, no matter where she's at.

"I like that. Keeping families together and shit," Rain

says. We all laugh.

We spend the rest of the evening drinking and shooting the shit. When the party really starts to get into full swing, a couple of bitches try to cuddle up next to me, but I shoo them away. It's easier than I thought possible, turning easy pussy down. Brent would never know if I fucked someone else, but I would.

I don't need these other women, not when all I can think about is being inside of my own. I decide to leave the party earlier than I normally would. Its late and people are starting to really get wild.

I make my way to my room for the night and slide my phone out of my pocket. There's a new text waiting for me, and I grin. It's from Brentlee. I bite my bottom lip in hopes it'll be something for my spank bank, but it isn't.

Instead, it's a selfie with her and Stella. Brent has atrocious makeup all over her face—bright red lipstick that's more on her face than her lips, purple eye shadow, and hot pink blush. She's also wearing a tiara. Stella has the same look going for her, and it makes me laugh. Underneath Brent's message reads—*playing dress up, aren't we beautiful princesses?*

I decide to shoot a text back, even though it's late and she probably won't see it until the morning— **the most beautiful I've ever seen.**

I shed my clothes and fall into the shitty, little bed they have set up and sleep. Tomorrow, I'll collect what I'm here for and we'll be gone again. On our way home, back to my girls. I can't wait.

Brentlee

It's been one week since I have seen Bates. He texts me at least once a day. I try not to be that clingy, crazy girlfriend and get upset when I don't hear from him, but it's a struggle. I wish that he would call me while he's away, but I'll take the one text I do get *happily*.

Tonight, they're supposed to be back, and Fury is having a big party for their return. Then tomorrow, the Canadian charter is going to leave, and the whole club is going to have a family BBQ. Kentlee is so excited to spend some time with the other Old Lady's and enjoy the evening later, kid less. I'm excited to be on the arm of Bates at the family day. I would be lying if I said any differently.

I have to work at the party tonight, but I want to look sexy for Bates' return. I put on my shortest shorts; they're black, skin tight, and low waisted. On top, I pull on a black leather bustier, tight bralette crop top, and then slide into my bright red high heels. I curl my hair, making it big and fluffy, before I apply my makeup, dark and sultry with bright red lips.

I want him to drool at the sight of me—fall to his knees and declare his undying love for me. *Okay. That's not going to happen*, but I want to make him hard in an instant and for him to fuck me like he missed me—*for hours*.

"Ready?" Fury asks. I nod.

I give Tammy a hug goodbye and kiss Stella on the cheek before following Fury out of the front door. I'm nervous. I don't know why; it isn't as though a week is a terribly long time. Maybe I'm not sure how he handled us being apart? Did he give in to temptation and screw around? Did he think about Stella and me and decide that we're too much trouble to keep around? I have made a mess of things in my head, and until I see his face, until I look into his haunted eyes, I won't feel settled.

Luckily, Fury doesn't talk on the way to the clubhouse. He wordlessly parks the SUV, and I follow him inside of the building. The music is thumping and smoke is already filling the air. I make my way behind the bar. A place I have discovered is the absolute safest place for me to stay.

Earlier in the week, I ventured out into the floor area to pick up discarded bottles of beer, and one of the Canadian members mistook me for a clubwhore. Johnny had to beat the shit out of him for grabbing me and refusing to let go. It had to have been one of the scariest things in my life. Granted, the things Scotty did to me were horrendous and terrifying, but this man was a stranger. I shiver just thinking about his hands on me.

I spend the entire evening watching the door, waiting for Bates to breeze on through. When two in the morning rolls around, I give up. *He's not coming.* I tell the prospect helping me serve the men, that I'm going to the restroom, and I leave the bar. The hall to the restrooms is dark, as all bathroom hallways seem to be. I wonder offhandedly why that is.

The bathroom smells, even though I just cleaned it the day before. The women in this club are a bunch of dirty bitches. I should show the guys just how truly disgusting their whores are. If I were a guy, I wouldn't put my dick in women that are as dirty as these chicks. I giggle to myself as I wash my hands, wondering how many of them have crabs. I always hover over the seat, just in case. I'd rather have a little pee splash on my thigh then some incurable disease.

"Always knew you were a whore," the cool calculated voice of my husband says as he walks through the door and flips the lock behind him. I look up and freeze, my eyes completely focused on him.

"You need to leave," I say shakily.

"I don't think I will, *wife*," he snarls.

"Not for long," I say squaring my shoulders.

"But you still are, very much, *my wife*," he says, approaching me. I shiver in disgust when his finger trails my shoulder and down my arm.

"Bates will be looking for me," I say, using all of the false bravado I can muster.

"No, I don't think that he will. You see, he walked in after your bathroom trip, and right around that time, one of their whores began giving the heathens a show," he chuckles, letting his hand wrap around me and travel up my spine.

He's too close. I can smell his aftershave, his cologne, his detergent. It's too much. Too painful and too debilitating. A whimper escapes me, but my eyes are locked in on his cold, dead blue ones.

"You could have been such a good wife, Brentlee. Why couldn't you just accept everything? I gave you a nice place to live, the finest clothes, and a child to keep you entertained during the day. I gave you *everything*, but you took it all for granted. You're such a selfish, little bitch. And now you're nothing but a slut. I should have whored you out all those years. I had men asking after you, you know?" he announces.

I press my lips together, trying to keep from crying out, sobbing, and showing any true emotion. He feeds off of my reactions.

"Speak," he shouts in my face. I blink, keeping my cool,

trying not to freak out.

"What would you like me to say?" I ask quietly.

I don't realize what's happened before I feel the pain radiating off of my cheek. With one hand tangled in my hair, the other makes a fist and he punches my cheek.

"Suck my cock like the whore you are," he demands as he pushes me down to my knees. I reluctantly have no choice but to land on the concrete floor. My bare knees connecting hard with the dirty, ground.

"No," I say. He doesn't own me anymore. Bates does. I'm a whore for no man. I'm Bates' woman, his *tigritsa*. I am no longer Scotty's punching bag.

"You don't suck me off, Brentlee, I'll kill you and then I'll kill that little fucking brat you pushed out of your dry as fuck pussy," he grinds out.

I close my eyes and think of Stella. He'd do it, too. The sick fuck would kill his own daughter. He had no qualms beating the shit out of me until I lost our first baby.

"The only dick that comes near me is Bates'. I'm not your whore, Scotty," I say, staying firm, standing my ground—on my knees.

His arm comes out and he backhands me. I can feel blood trickling from my lip. The whole left side of my face aches, but I don't care. He's not going to torture me, not without me giving him a fucking fight.

"I should mutilate you. He wouldn't want you if you were hideous. Nobody would," he laughs. It comes off as maniacal and completely creepy. How I ever fell for him, how I ever *married* him, is beyond me. Looking at him now, all I see is a disturbed and disgusting individual.

I hear something behind him, but the music is so loud

I'm not sure what it is. I don't want to alert him in case it's nothing. I can only pray that somebody has found us.

"Do it," I challenge.

Fuck him.

Scotty opens his mouth to surely spew more shit, but there's a loud sound. I cover my mouth with my hands, finding my face completely covered in blood. Scotty's blood, and brains, and everything that goes along with it.

When his body falls to the ground, I look past him and see Bates standing stoically. His eyes are transfixed on Scotty's lifeless body. I let out a sound that's only described as a mix between a cry, a sob, and a shout. Bates' eyes leave Scotty and come to me. I'm sure I look scary, covered in blood and brain, bruises forming on my cheek.

"*Tigritsa*," he says. It sounds animalistic, guttural.

"Bates," I whisper.

He doesn't come for me. He doesn't console me or pick me up and tell me everything is going to be *okay*. Instead, he turns from me. He leaves. He walks away, leaving me on my knees surrounded by my husband's blood.

Immediately, tears fill my eyes—not because Scotty has died, but because Bates has left me. I'm under no illusion that he needs a moment to collect his thoughts. No, I saw the light dim; the horrors return in his eyes. He's gone.

"Come on, babe," Paxton says, crouching down next to me. I watch as a Prospect and Johnny drag my husband out of the dirty bathroom. I look up to Paxton with tears in my eyes.

"He's gone," I whisper.

"Yeah, babe, and he ain't never comin' back," he grunts.

"No, not Scotty. *Bates*," I mutter.

"He'll come around," he says. The look on his face is telling me what I already know.

Bates is *gone. Done. Out.*

I let Paxton guide me toward the bedroom's when Fury stops in front of us.

"Take my room, it has a bathroom attached, you can clean up there," he mutters, handing Paxton the key.

I turn around to thank him and see Bates leaning against the wall, a joint in his hand and his eyes focused on me. They aren't dead, heated, or full of horror, no he looks—*bored*. I turn back around, unable to look at him another second.

How did this happen?

Why did this happen?

Haven't I suffered enough?

I finally find my happiness and now it's all fucked up. All fucked up because of Scotty, because Bates had to kill for me. I hate that it happened, and I wish he would talk to me, hold me, assure me that everything is going to be okay, instead of staring at me with that bored expression on his face.

Paxton locks us inside of Fury's room and I'm glad for it. I don't want to be around anybody, but I need this fucking blood off of me—*now*.

"Will you, can you…" I begin.

Thankfully, he understands and nods. I stand against the locked door as he checks out the bathroom.

"All clear," he says softly.

I nod once and make my way toward the bathroom. Once I step past him, he takes the door handle and starts to close it. I put my hand up, stopping his movement.

"Please, leave it open. I just can't. Can you stay in here? I don't care if you see me, I just can't be alone," I murmur.

"I'll do whatever you want me to, Brentlee," he whispers. I

have a feeling he means more than just helping me right now. I don't care, though. Right now, I can't think.

I quickly strip out of my bloodied clothes and completely disrobe. I look in the mirror, but avoid my face. Instead, my eyes focus on the reflection of my *Bates* tattoo. My fingers trace his name when I hear Pax clear his throat.

"He'll get his head outta his ass, babe," he states.

"I don't think he will," I murmur. "Not unless I fight for him."

Paxton doesn't say another word as I step into the hot stream of water that he started for me. I use Fury's soap and what appears to be Kentlee's fruity shampoo. I let the clean smell envelope me. I close my eyes and wash away the blood and the hurt from my marriage with Scotty.

After this shower, I never want to think of him again. I'll tell Stella about him when she's old enough. For now, she knows enough, more than enough. I want to move on with my life. I want my daughter to live in a world where she isn't afraid of anything—ever.

"Babe," Paxton's voice floats through the shower.

"Yeah," I call out.

"I need to get you home," he murmurs. I turn the shower off and he thrusts a towel through the curtain. I dry off and wrap it around myself.

"I need something to wear," I say, standing in front of him, fresh faced and wrapped in a towel. I feel better. At least my body does. My mind, however, is a completely different story. I'm a jumbled up mess.

"Come on, I'll take you to my room, get you some clothes," he murmurs. I bend down to grab my bloodied clothes and he presses his hand against my back. I look up into his coffee colored eyes and he shakes his head.

"I'll take care of all that later tonight. Let me get you outta here, babe," he says, his voice soft, sweet, and even. I nod and allow him to guide me toward his room, his hand on the small of my back.

When we arrive at Paxton's room, I look up and tears immediately well in my eyes. Standing with his back against the wall is Bates. His dazed eyes are on me, completely focused on me. When I trail the length of his body, there's Star.

On her knees, sucking his cock.

My stomach turns at the sight. He's *mine*. His *dick* is mine. I look back up to him and my eyes connect with his. A smirk tugs on his lips, but his eyes, they're still dazed and bored. I don't see his fire. I don't see anything of the Bates I know and love. It makes my heart ache. It pisses me off.

What a fucking asshole.

chapter twenty-three

Sniper

I wrap my hand in Star's hair and pull her off of my dick. She looks up at me with wide eyes, hopeful eyes, and it makes me sick. I release her and slide away from the wall, tucking my semi-hard cock in my pants. I'm surprised it's even a semi. I'm not in the least bit turned on.

"Sniper," Star whines from her place on her knees.

"Get the fuck outta here," I grunt.

Star opens her mouth to say something else, but I can't muster a fuck to give. I turn and walk away from her, straight to my room. I slam and lock the door behind me before I walk over to the bed. I sink down and reach between my legs for a bottle of Jack. I say a silent thanks when I find a completely brand-new, unopened bottle.

I open it and take a long drink of the amber liquor. I'm such a fucking *fuck-up*. I lean against the headboard and I continue to drink.

One pull after the other.

I close my eyes and think back to earlier tonight. I was so fuckin' excited to see my woman, my Brentlee. A week being away from her was excruciating. I didn't want to ever do it again. I missed her, not just her pussy, but *her*. I missed her smell, the way she smiled up at me, the way she looked at me.

I walked into the clubhouse and asked the prospect behind the bar where she was. When he told me the bathroom, I thought it was the perfect opportunity to get my dick wet before she went back to work. When I tried the handle and the door was locked, I knew something was wrong. Hearing a man's voice on the other side sent a shiver down my spine. I pulled my gun out of my shoulder holster and kicked the flimsy as fuck door down.

He had her on her knees. *Scotty had my woman on her knees for him.* I pulled the trigger. One shot was all I needed, and I took it. I added another soul to the notch on my belt in hell. *I killed another human.* I didn't want to think about what that made my number. The devil is keeping a tally; I don't need to.

The look of shock on her face, I'll never forget it. *I ruined her.* I sullied her. I killed in front of her.

Brentlee was covered in blood because of *me*.

I'm not good for her.

I'm not good for her daughter.

I'll keep making her dirty.

I'll continue to ruin her.

I ruin everything.

There's no way around it, she's seen a portion of the evil I can inflict on another person without batting an eyelash. No way in fuck is she going to want me anywhere near her or her innocent child. I'm the piece of shit my dad always said I was, useless and fucking dumb.

I close my eyes and all I can see is her face covered in another person's blood, as a result of me. I'm not sad I killed Scotty. I should have done it earlier. I'm pissed at myself for doing it in front of her. For giving her more brutality in her life. She should be living easy now, I should be making her shit easy, not fucking her up even more.

***

I wake the next morning and take a sip from the Jack, swishing it around my mouth before I spit it out on the floor. No reason to keep my room clean. I could live in my own filth, because that's what I am—filthy.

I look off into the empty space and think back to the night before. Brentlee is gone. I made sure she wouldn't come back and fight for me, too. I would give in to her pretty honey colored eyes in a heartbeat.

I spend the day in solitary. *Alone.* Drinking. I don't want to see another person. I don't want to see the look of pity in their eyes, and I don't want to give in to my own temptations and go to Brentlee. I need to be alone.

Brentlee

I wake up, my eyes swollen, my head hurting like hell. I roll over and crash into a hard body. For a split second, I think it's Bates, that he's come home, but when my hand flies to his chest I discover it's covered in a shirt. Bates doesn't sleep next to me with clothes on. I open my eyes and see Paxton Hill looking down on me.

"I'm sorry," I mumble. He shrugs sitting up.

"For what, Brent?" he asks as if he hasn't a care in the world. How nice that must be. I couldn't remember a time I was carefree.

"Everything. Making you stay," I sigh, standing. I look down and realize that I'm in Paxton's shirt and gym shorts. I'm surprised I didn't catch fire wearing another man's clothes in Bates' bed.

"I'll always be here for you, babe," he murmurs.

"Pax…" I start. He puts his hand up.

"I know you're in love with him, Brent. But he ain't here. I'll help you anyway you'll let me, but I ain't gonna slide into his bed, babe. That ain't me. You're a good woman and you need a man that's gonna take care of you," he says.

I nod, unable to say another word. All I can think about is the fact that Scotty's dead and Bates doesn't want me anymore, or he's just fucked up about what's happened. I don't know what he's thinking. He killed for me and then went to the arms of another woman. *Who does that?*

"Go take a hot shower. I'll get Stella some breakfast started," he murmurs.

I'm so fucking thankful for him right now, I don't question his motives for helping; instead, I nod and practically run into the bathroom.

Once I am finally under the spray of the warm water, I cry, again. Everything is shit. Bates is gone. I can't even think about Scotty and what almost happened. All I can focus on is Bates and how he doesn't want me anymore. God, I'm so fucking pathetic and needy. I shake off the doom, the pain, and the feelings of desperation.

Bates doesn't want me.

So what?

Even if my heart and body want him, it doesn't matter. I've marked my body with his name, I gave all of me to him. All of his talk was nothing but bullshit. Something major happens and he runs instead of talking to me, instead of dealing with it together.

I don't understand him.

Fuck Scotty and fuck Bates.

I dress in a pair of cut off shorts and a loose oversized t-shirt. I have to tuck it in in the front so that it doesn't look like I'm going pantless. I glance in the mirror and cringe at my face. I look pretty beat up. Not the worst I've been, but certainly not the best. I gather my makeup and begin to apply it. I know how to minimize bruises with contouring and layering. I've studied at length how to look flawless. Hopefully this is the last time I ever have to use this knowledge I have.

"Hey, pretty girl," Paxton says as I walk into the kitchen.

He's sitting at the table, shoveling scrambled eggs and toast into his mouth. Stella mimics him, doing the same. She turns to me and gives me her huge bright smile. I know in this moment, no matter what happens in my love life, she's what's most important—her and her happiness.

"Hey," I say shyly.

I take a plate and load it with eggs and toast before I join Paxton and Stella at the table. It should feel awkward and uncomfortable, eating breakfast with another man, but it doesn't. It feels friendly, like eating breakfast with Fury.

Paxton is hot, but he doesn't make *me* hot. Only one man can do that. But Paxton is comfortable, and there is something to be said about comfort. Don't we always love our most comforting clothes, or our food? Paxton is like Mac & Cheese, comfy and warm.

"What are you planning for the day?" he asks.

"Nothing," I murmur.

"You're free now, babe. No reason to hide out. Go and do whatever you want." He winks. I suck in a breath. He's right. I'm not stuck. I'm completely free to go about my own business.

"What'll happen to his house and all his things?" I murmur.

"You want anything from there?" he asks, his eyes darkening.

"No, just curious," I shrug, taking a sip from my orange juice.

"When his body's found, they'll probably, *eventually*, contact you. It could all be yours, but his parents will probably fight it because you guys were in the middle of a divorce," he shrugs.

"Makes sense," I say.

"So you didn't answer my question. What are you planning today?" he asks, smirking at me before he winks.

"No clue," I say.

"Spend it with me and Stella," he suggests. I look down to Stella who is looking at us with confusion. "At the BBQ. Did you forget?" he asks chuckling.

"I shouldn't go there," I mutter. Paxton lifts his hand and cups my uninjured cheek.

"You should. That's your family. Fury, Kentlee, Bear, Ellie and all us brothers, we're your family, babe. Have a few beers, eat some good food, and just relax," he says. I give him a shaky smile.

"Okay," I agree with a nod.

"I'll take you two, but we gotta leave soon so I can get changed into some clean clothes before the party," he says.

I spend the next thirty minutes getting Stella and myself ready while Paxton watches television on the couch. I change my top, leaving my short cut-offs on, since it's warm outside. I put on a loose fitting, flowing tank top. I style my hair in a simple side braid and slide a pair of converse on my feet. I touch up my makeup and hope that it holds in the heat.

I dress Stella in a cute little girl maxi dress, putting her blonde curls in pigtails and giggle at how adorable she is. I take her hand and guide her to the living room, where Paxton is focused on the television. He turns to us and smiles widely.

"Prettiest girls I've ever had the pleasure of laying eyes on," he says dramatically. I roll my eyes.

"You're cheesy," I grumble. He chuckles as he wraps his hand around my waist.

"I am. But you are pretty," he says softly.

"Pax…"

"Don't. I know," he says, dropping his hand from my waist and stalking out the door. With a heavy sigh, I follow him.

"Where Bates?" Stella asks a few minutes later as we wait outside of Paxton's apartment while he changes.

"I don't know," I answer honestly. "He is… away," I lie.

"Miss him," she murmurs. She hasn't mentioned her actual father once, yet she misses Bates after just over a week.

"Me too," I whisper as I watch Paxton descend the staircase of his apartment complex.

We drive in silence to the party. I'm nervous, and my stomach is in knots. Bates is going to be there and it's going to hurt to see him. Just yesterday, I was his woman, and he's walked away from me.

Could I forgive him if he asked for it? I probably would, without question.

I'd throw myself at him because I love him, and I'm committed to him. Committed to make it work, at whatever the cost. I've seen him kill, and yet I still love him and still want him. Nothing could make me love him less, nothing but his betrayal of me or Stella.

Betrayal I'm not sure he hasn't already committed. I knew it was too soon to get into this with Bates. I should have listened to my heart and not let my body rule my decisions. Here I am dependent on him, waiting for him to tell me what's going to happen next.

I feel a warmth squeeze my hand, and I look down and then over to Paxton. He's comforting me. He's so fucking sweet, I don't deserve him. Not when I know we'd never be anything more than bed partners, if that.

"You should just leave me alone, Paxton. I'm a mess," I whisper.

"Yeah, know that. You're a gorgeous mess, though. Also, I'm a big boy, I can handle being fucked around a little," he chuckles before he gets out of the car and shuts the door behind him. I try not to think about his words. I need to ignore them—ignore him.

Stella and I climb out of the pick-up and quickly walk over to a waiting Paxton. He's got a grin on his face as he takes Stella's offered hand. She may not know what's happening, but I like the fact that she's comfortable around Paxton. Regardless of what goes down in my personal life, I know that Paxton's a good man, always has been.

When Kentlee see's us walking toward the party as a unit, her eyes widen and her mouth falls open. Then, she's on me. She's charging me like a bull. It's a little frightening, but I know she's probably just worried and confused. Paxton rests his hand on my back and leans down so that his lips are practically touching my ear.

"I'll take Stella to the other kids," he murmurs.

"Thanks," I croak.

Kentlee reaches me as Paxton straightens. He winks at her and guides Stella ahead of us. I watch as he drops her off with her cousin, Bear, and a bunch of other kids playing on a little playground gym they have set up.

"Tell me everything," Kentlee urges.

I don't look at her. I can't. Instead, I keep my eyes on Stella as I replay my horrific evening.

"That *asshole*. I'm going to beat the shit out of him. No, I'm going to have Pierce beat the shit out of him," she cries out. I can't help myself, I start to laugh.

"He's an asshole and I'll have it out with him, but not today," I say, shaking my head.

"It's really not okay. I'll stand up for you if you refuse to stand up for yourself," she says. She then looks into my eyes and I see something akin to pity there. "You can't be with Paxton, or anybody else, until he announces that you're available to the club," she murmurs.

"*What?*" I ask in shock.

"It's archaic. They're a bunch of fucking cavemen. But Brent, you aren't a free woman and you aren't free to leave him until he cuts you loose," she whispers.

"But he can do who and whatever he wants?" I balk. She doesn't answer. Instead, she shrugs.

"Let's just relax. He's only been stupid for one day so far. He could pull his head out of his ass any second. My man's head was up his for three years," she says with a grin. She reaches down into an ice chest and pulls out two bottles of beer.

"Not that I'm going to go hopping to another one of these guys again, but that rule is insane," I grumble. She giggles.

Then, my sister, knowing exactly what I need, begins to introduce me to wives, not clubwhores, wives.

"You're one of us, babe, we got your back," a sweet woman named Rosie says with a wink.

"Well, for now at least," I grunt.

"Forever, hon. You're Kentlee's sister. You'll always have a place, no matter who your man is," she grins. I shake my head.

I rub the center of my chest as the women talk, trying to get the aching feeling to leave me. It's been bothering me all day and I know what it is. It's my heart. It's broken. I remember the feeling from ten years before when Bates left me.

It's suddenly sinking in, it's real, he's not going to wrap his arms around me and tell me he loves me, apologize for being an ass, and take me away into the sunset. I've been here for hours and I haven't seen him once. I just want to go home; I don't want to be here anymore. I want to crawl into bed and cry. Then, I need to figure my shit out. Figure out what exactly I'm going to do. Obviously, I've made another mess. I've relied on a man when I shouldn't have, depended on him, and now I don't have a place to live—yet again.

The hours tick by and we all drink a little more. Tammy comes by to collect Stella, Bear, and Ellie. I promise her that I'll be by to pick Stella up before the end of the night. I don't plan on partying at all. In fact, I really just want to catch a ride home with the kids.

"You deserve a night off," she says, her meaning clear. She knows all.

"Kentlee fill you in?" I ask. My lips loose from beer.

"I was worried when you came in last night, looking the way you did. Your gentleman friend filled me in," she admits. I nod.

"Thank you, Tammy, so much," I gush. She just wraps her arms around me in a motherly hug.

"My husband was a good man, he never treated me the way you've been treated. You're so strong, honey," she whispers before she turns away, gathering the children without another word. I feel a heat at my back a second later and lean back. I can tell it's not Bates, but it's comforting and warm just the same.

"You okay?" he asks, wrapping his hand around my hip.

"I will be," I admit.

"You will, babe," he agrees, squeezing my hip. I turn around to face him. I'm so drunk, I sway slightly before I can focus on him.

"Kentlee said that Bates has to announce my freedom before I can be with another guy," I announce with a slight slur.

Paxton chokes on his gulp of beer and coughs a few times before he looks down and focuses on me.

"He does," he nods.

"But he can get blowjobs in the hallway and I have to accept it?" I ask, planting my hand on my hip.

"Way of our world, babe," he grunts.

"Lame," I huff.

Paxton laughs before he wraps his arm around my neck, pulling me into his side. It's not sexual at all, it feels very—brotherly.

We start to walk over to where Fury and Kent are cuddled together on a now empty picnic table. I turn my head to say something to Pax when my gaze collides with the angry face of Bates. He's glaring at us, Paxton's arm thrown over my shoulder, looking cozy—*comfortable*. Yet, not as comfortable as Star looked on her knees the night before.

I want to flip him a bird, but instead I turn my head—before I cry again. I'm on the verge of tears just by seeing his face—his gorgeous, angry face.

At least he doesn't look indifferent today.

chapter twenty-four

Sniper

I close my eyes and try to tamp down my anger. I shouldn't give a fuck; I shouldn't care that Torch is touching what's mine, but that bitch has my name stamped on her. She's branded as *mine*. I take a drink from the bottle of Jack that dangles from my fingers.

"Hey, baby," Star rasps next to me.

Her cool fingers wrap around my forearm, and as much as I want to fling her off of me, I can't. Not now that I'm staring at my woman—*my* woman who has another man wrapped around her.

I grunt at the bitch, unable to form words. I'm so fuckin' drunk, having her next to me is kind of a relief. At least her fake tits'll help break my fall—help me bounce a little instead of landing on the hard as fuck ground. I chuckle as I imagine it in my head. She'd scream like a banshee.

"All the kids are gone. How about we have some fun?" she purrs. It isn't sexy. It doesn't make me hard. Although, I don't think much could at this point. I've been drinking non-stop since I woke up this morning.

"Why don't you do what you do best? *Be a fuckin' star*," I suggest. She giggles, and it's grating on my ears, like nails scratching a chalkboard.

I find an empty chair and plop my ass down. I have a great view of whatever Star plans; but more importantly, I can see every single move Torch and Brentlee make right in front of me. My *brother*. What a fuckin' joke. He's nothing but a backstabber. A traitor, ready to move in as soon as he can—before my side of the bed is even cold. *Fucktard*.

I look over Star's shoulder as she dances seductively in front of me. She's recruited another whore, and they're grinding on each other. Something that should be sexy as fuck, but leaves me cold and my dick limp. *No*, my focus is on anger, and it's directed at a slut and a backstabbing asshole.

I hear her laugh reach my ears and it makes my dick twitch. Then Torch's hand slides down to her hip; he's not touching her skin, but he's touching the place my tattoo is stamped on her.

My *Sniper* brand.

I finally completely lose my shit. I stand and stagger toward them. Kentlee's eyes widen and she opens her mouth, but before she can warn Brentlee, I have my hand wrapped around her bicep and I turn her around.

"Bates," she gasps.

Paxton takes a step toward me but I glare at him, making him back down. He can't interject at the way I handle my woman. She is still that, too. Until I say otherwise, she's fuckin' *mine*.

"You like his hands on you?" I ask squeezing her arm.

I'm probably handling her too roughly, because I'm so drunk I can't tell my own strength. She doesn't speak, her lips clamped tightly and her eyes full of fire. *Fuck*, my cock goes hard at the sight.

I grab her loose-fitting shirt and wrench it up, exposing her stomach and her tits. I can hear that conversation has ceased around us, everybody is watching and waiting for the drama to unfold. I've been a ticking time bomb since I shot her good for nothing ex-asshole in the back of his head.

"Everybody take a fucking look. This is my name, right here. This bitch is mine. This other one," I yank her body around to expose her *Bates* ink. "Is my legal name. She's mine. My Old Lady, my woman. Any brother thinks he can touch what's mine has another thing coming."

"Snipe," Vault murmurs from behind me.

I spin around to see his sweet wife Rosie wrapped in his arms. She's looking at me with concern, but Vault is looking at me with disgust. I don't give a fuck. They can shove it up their asses.

"Shut the fuck up," I bark. "This cunt is mine until I say otherwise. Any brother thinks about getting his dick wet in my snatch will have to deal with me; and trust me, you won't be leaving the fight walking," I slur staring at Torch.

"That's enough," Fury announces.

It's only then that my eyes leave Torch's and I see that LeeLee is crying. When I look down at Brentlee, she's crying as well, her fingers covering her lips and her body shaking. I push her away from me and she falls to the ground. Nobody makes a move to help her. Her shirt is still askew and one of her bra-clad tits is hanging out, but she's frozen to her spot, her horrified eyes on me.

"You share your cunt with any other man, I'll slit your throat," I growl before I turn around and walk away.

I need to get away before I actually do something instead of just threaten. I walk past Star and she's looking at me in horror.

"Still want to ride my cock for life, bitch?" I spew. She shakes her head. *Good.* I didn't want her nasty ass anyway. *Maybe now she'll stay away from me.*

I go straight to my room and I drink until I finally pass out.

Fuck everybody.
Fuck my life.
I'm such a piece of shit.

Brentlee

Paxton reaches down to help me up, but I bat his hand away. I'd hate to get my throat slit for looking funny at him. Bates is such a fucking asshole. I fix my shirt and look around. Everybody is staring at me, their eyes wide—some concerned, but mostly curious.

"It isn't the first time I've been threatened with having my throat slit, carry on," I say, waving my hands around.

I hear a few chuckles and the music is turned back up.

People go about their business and I turn to my sister who is sobbing.

"Brentlee," she mutters.

"I'm fine," I assure.

"I've never seen him like that before. Never," she blubbers.

I've never seen Bates like that, but I've seen his father like that. *Once.* I snuck over to try and get Bates to hang out late one Friday night. I hadn't seen him at school, and I missed him. When I approached their house, there were lights on, so I peeked into the kitchen and I saw his father beating the shit out of his mother. He called her every name in the book, then I watched as Bates tried to interfere. His father knocked him around a little and sent him to his room.

Then, his mom and dad fucked right there in the kitchen. She had blood and bruises all over her face. I ran away and was sick for days about it. When I tried to talk to Bates about his father, he closed down. He just told me he was a mean drunk and that he couldn't wait to leave.

This is the first time I have ever seen Bates resemble his father. It's terrifying. I don't want that. Not again. I've been there; except Scotty didn't have an excuse. He didn't drink, he was just a douche in general.

"Pax, can you take me home?" I ask.

"You sure you want to go back there?" he asks, furrowing his brows.

"He can't even walk straight. He won't be coming back tonight." *If ever*, I think.

I promise Kent that I'll call her in the morning and I leave with Paxton. We don't speak the whole ride home. I look out the window, watching the darkness fly by, catching a glimpse of a tree every so often.

"If I could have stopped him, I would have. I hate that he treated you like that," Paxton says.

I shake my head. If Paxton was passionate about his feelings for me, he would have stopped him, but he isn't. Which is fine. I don't want him to be. I'm not passionate about him, either. He's my friend, nothing more. Well, he's a friend I fucked once when we were young, nothing more.

"It's fine. It's your world and your rules."

"It's not fine. He didn't need to be such a damn dick," Paxton growls. It makes me laugh.

"I have a thing for dicks," I shrug.

"You really need to pick better men, babe. I'd like to say I wouldn't be a dick, but let's be honest here," he laughs.

"Thanks for the ride; and thank you for everything last night," I say softly. Pax wraps his hand around my neck and squeezes lightly.

"You deserve the best, babe," he murmurs.

"So do you," I whisper.

"It ain't you?" he asks, cocking his head to the side.

"No, it's not me. I'm a damn disaster. I need to get my head on straight before I think about anything. Plus, I have this crazy bastard that thinks he owns me. He's even tattooed his name on my body," I smirk.

"Crazy fuckin' bikers," he grunts. I kiss his cheek and thank him for the ride.

Paxton waits while I walk inside of the house and lock the door behind me. I lean against the door and sigh heavily. *What a fucking horrible couple of days.* I can't even wrap my head around everything that has transpired.

I don't even want to think about Bates' crazy, jealous,

drunk rant. *What a dick*. I don't need that shit in my life. I definitely don't need it in my daughter's. Maybe it's good that I saw it now, rather than later. When he said he'd changed, he was not wrong. Hard liquor is not his friend, and I have no desire to be around him when he's like that.

Once I've cleaned my face of my thick makeup and have taken a hot shower, I change into a pair of panties and an oversized shirt that smells way too much like Bates. I crawl into bed and I look around at the room. I can't be around his things and in his home. It will only give him more of a hold over me. I need to be as free of him as possible.

I close my eyes and will myself to sleep.

I need to rest.

I need a few hours of nothingness.

I need for my brain to shut down. I need a few hours just to breathe.

The future terrifies me.

I have no clue what's coming, and it seems like something new is being thrown at me at every single turn in my road.

chapter twenty-five

Sniper

I blink my eyes open and look around. *Fuck,* it's daytime already. I grab my phone and try to focus on the numbers. It's noon, on a Friday. Too bad it's a week later than I thought it was. I've lost a whole fucking week, and I have no clue what happened in that timeframe. I scrub my hand over my face. My beard is longer and my hair is probably a fucking train wreck.

I stumble into the bathroom down the hall from my room and step into the shower. I turn the water on cold. I need to sober the fuck up. I wash quickly then get out.

I walk back to my room and throw on a pair of jeans and a t-shirt before sliding my cut on. I've probably missed at least one church meeting, and god knows what the fuck else. I don't give much of a fuck. My hand itches to grab the bottle of Jack on the floor, and that's how Fury finds me after he slams my door open.

"My office, now," he barks. There's nothing friendly in his tone. He's fuckin' pissed.

I follow behind him quietly. I know when to shut up, and now's the time.

"Sit the fuck down," he barks as I walk through the door. He closes the door behind him and flips the lock.

"What's up?" I ask, knowing damn well what's up.

"You're a pussy," he says, his gray eyes focused on me. They're swimming with anger and it pisses me off.

"Fuck you, man," I say. In this office, in this conversation, this is my friend—not my president.

"You fight like hell for her and then you bounce? What the fuck man? Don't even get me started on that shit that happened at the BBQ. Do you know how long it took me to talk Kentlee out of barging into your room and sawing your nuts off with a dull knife?"

Instinctually, I grab my balls at the thought and hiss.

"She don't need me," I say, shrugging my shoulders.

"But you don't want her with anyone else. That makes perfect fuckin' sense." He rolls his eyes and anger creeps up my neck.

"It's complicated. I killed her husband. In front of her. No hesitation. I didn't even fuckin' blink. And you know what? I haven't even thought twice about it. That piece of shit deserved to die. But all that did was show her what kind of monster I am," I say, looking down at my boots.

"So you're making decisions for her, then?" he asks, repeating my words from year ago. I look up to him and he grins. "You need to get your head on straight. You think I deserve Kent? You think Vault deserves sweet little Rosie? Fuck no, we don't. But pushing her away—you ain't a martyr, man. Don't make yourself and Brent miserable because of some fuckin' pedestal you have her on.

"And if you're really done with the bitch, cut her loose. Torch wants in there somethin' fierce, but he ain't gonna step on the brotherhood—on you. He respects you too much for all that shit. You can't keep her at arm's length, it ain't fair to you, to her, or to Stella. And for fuck's sake, if you want her back you better go back crawling, that shit was not cool."

I look at my friend. Fuck, I'm a prick. I'm the biggest kind of prick. I've abandoned not only Brentlee, but Stella, too. Because of my own issues. They didn't do one thing to deserve any of it. Not one thing, except love me.

"I see it's sinkin' in how much you fucked up, brother."

"I fucked up. Fuck, the way I was at the BBQ? I acted just like my old man," I confess. Fury nods.

"You did. But you didn't do anything you can't apologize for later," he says. I grimace.

"The fuck did you do?" he asks.

"Made sure Brentlee saw Star suckin' my dick," I begin. Fury clears his throat. "About twenty minutes after I blew her husband's brains out," I finish.

"When you fuck up, you do it big," he whistles. I nod. "It might take you a minute, but you'll get her back. Before you even try, sober the fuck up, and make sure she's exactly what you want. I can't survive any more family fuckin' drama. My woman's been way too involved in this shit, and she's stressin' me out about it. I honestly don't give a fuck what you all do, but Kentlee does, and I want my baby girl happy—so fix this shit," he barks. He then lifts his chin toward the door, signaling that our meeting is officially over.

"I'll fix it, brother," I murmur as I leave the office.

I walk into the clubhouse and instead of going toward the bar, I detour to the kitchen to get a bottle of water. Fury's right. I need to sober up. I don't want to become my father. I've worked way too fuckin' hard to be everything he isn't to throw it away now. I hear footsteps enter the room. I turn around and see Torch standing a few feet away.

"We cool?" Torch asks as I remove the cap and take a gulp of the cool liquid.

"You gonna try to fuck my woman again?" I ask.

"You gonna cut her loose?" he returns, arching a brow.

"Fuck no."

"You gonna fight for her, get her back?" he asks, smirking.

"Fuck yeah," I admit, returning his smile with one of my own.

"Go get her. She's hurtin'. Don't give up without a fight," he says, shaking his head once before he turns to leave.

"Why're you bein' cool? I was a dick to her, and you," I admit.

"Don't get me wrong. You fuck with her again and I'll get in there so fast, your head'll spin. But she loves you and I know you love her. Make that shit right, you two look damn good together," he mutters before he leaves.

I stand in the kitchen, alone and sober for the first time in at least a week. Maybe longer. I really don't remember how long it's been. It feels like a fuckin' month.

I'm just tired.

So fuckin' tired.
I miss my woman.
I miss my kid.
I miss my house in the country.

Brentlee

I look at my phone for probably the tenth time. Every time I try to call my brother, I cancel the call. He doesn't need my shit showing up on his front porch. I haven't even talked to him since leaving Scotty. He's broken away from our dysfunctional family, and I should just leave him alone and let him live his life.

I shake my head and continue folding laundry. I've never cleaned so much in all of my life. Bates' house sparkles, and every piece of laundry is clean and folded, aside from what I'm working on and what's on Stella's and my body.

I sigh as I load the clean, folded laundry in the basket and pick it up to head down the hall to Stella's room. She isn't home. Kentlee took one look at the dark circles under my eyes this morning during our coffee date and snatched my baby from me.

I'm supposed to be taking a nap, resting, per her orders, but I can't do it. Every time I close my eyes, I see *him*. I see Bates and the look of indifference that crossed his face. I don't want to think about him, but I can't help myself. When I close my eyes, he's all I see. I hate it.

I hum as I put Stella's laundry away, trying not to think about the clusterfuck that is my life. I need to move soon. I can't stay here at his house. Though he hasn't been back, I just can't be here. I can't see his things and smell his smell without going completely crazy.

Once I have her clothes put away, I turn around and scream bloody murder. Not that anybody would hear me, there's nobody around for miles. The basket falls to the floor and my eyes collide with the gorgeous face I have been dreaming of and dreading to see again.

"Brentlee," he rasps.

I don't move.

I can't.

I want to run to him, to wrap my legs around his waist and bury my face in his neck. But I can't.

I'm too fucking broken.

"No," I whisper as tears fill my eyes.

"I fucked up," he practically moans. It breaks my heart.

I look into his eyes and see nothing but devastation there. It breaks my heart, but not enough to welcome him back with open arms.

"Yeah, you really did," I whisper. His eyes shoot to mine, his brows furrowed, and his jaw clenching beneath his thick beard. He looks rumpled and unruly, but thank goodness, *sober*.

"Tell me how to fix it," he demands, though his voice is low and even.

"You can't. You turned your back and walked away from me again. You embarrassed the hell out of me."

I shake my head, unable to look away from him. Memorizing his face, his strong jaw, his furrowed brow, the way his nose slopes and his lips—god his lips, so tempting.

"You aren't leaving me," he grunts, taking a step toward

me just as I take a step backward.

"I wasn't the one who left," I say. He stops in his tracks and gives me a slight nod before he opens his mouth to speak.

"You don't know where my head was at, baby. Let me tell you. Let me explain," he pleads.

I don't say a word; I walk right past him. I can't do this in Stella's room. I can't look at her gorgeous furniture and bedding and have the memories of how sweet this man can be surrounding me. If I do, I'll make a decision based on emotion and not based off of what I know. I hear him following behind me and I stop in the middle of the living room and turn to face him, crossing my arms over my chest. I need protection, and my arms are all I have.

"*Explain*. Explain turning away from me when I needed you; explain why Star was sucking your cock two seconds later; explain why you humiliated me in front of your friends? Because from where I stand, there's not a damn excuse good enough to warrant all you've done." I demand.

Bates looks at me, regret shining in his eyes, and I'm glad; but it doesn't change a thing. He did all of those things. He can swim in regret—drown in it for all I care.

I'm angry, hurt, and sad.

Nothing he could tell me would make me change my mind at this point. Maybe after I calm my racing heart. Maybe after I think about whatever it is he'll explain. Maybe after I miss him a little more. But right now—*I hate him*.

"I killed a man in front of you. I covered you in his blood, Brentlee. And you know what? I didn't feel a fuckin' thing when I pulled that trigger. Not remorse, not sadness, not adrenaline, not anger, not regret. Not a single fucking thing. I never do. Killing means nothing but the end of the man breathing my air. How fucked up is that? How fucked up am I? *Do you really want my blood soaked hands all over you?*" he shouts before he runs his hands through his hair, tugging on the ends.

"I made you dirty, baby. You watched as I ended a life. Doesn't even matter who it was, you should have never seen that shit. *Not ever.* I'm going to hell when this life is over, there's no hope for me. You're too fuckin' good for me, and that's the truth of it. Whores like Star are what I deserve. I was letting you go, saving you." He groans.

Obviously his head and heart are at war with each other, and all I want to do is wrap him in my arms. But I can't. Not when I still have questions that I need answered.

"Then why humiliate me?" I ask.

"Because no matter what I think is best for you, my jealousy and my heart never want to let you go. You're my *tigritsa*," he murmurs.

"I can't just let you back in, Bates. You devastated me. You did exactly what I feared. You let me go. Without a backward glance, you just walked away," I whisper as the tears that have been building in my eyes finally fall.

"I'll make it up to you," he promises. I shake my head.

I can't. *It's too late.* I don't know if there is anything he could do to make up for how he walked away— the way he so callously grabbed a warm body minutes later, and then the way he humiliated me.

"No," I whisper.

I gasp as he takes the few steps toward me to close the distance between us. His hands are cupping my cheeks, his eyes completely focused on mine and nothing else.

"I love you, baby, *please*," he begs.

I can't stop the tears. Even if I wanted to, they continue to fall. A sob escapes my lips as I shake my head and pinch my eyes closed tightly.

"I'll win you back, my *tigritsa*. Swear to fuck, I'll win you back," he vows as his lips crash hard against mine, taking me in a bruising, owning kiss.

"Just don't," I sob.

"Never letting you go. Never walking away again. You could deny me for years, and I'll be right here, waiting, trying, and begging for you, baby," he says.

My shoulders shake with my sobs and his hands drop from my face only to wrap around my back and pull me into his chest.

"I'm so tired," I admit.

"I know, baby, me too," he confesses.

My hands fist in his t-shirt when he picks me up and carries me to the bedroom. A bedroom we shared just weeks ago. He lies me down on the pillow, but doesn't join me. Instead, he places a gentle kiss on my forehead and tucks a strand of hair behind my ear.

"Sleep," he murmurs as he stands. When I blink, he's gone.

I stare at the bedroom door as I hear the front door open and close. My mind is spinning a million miles an hour. I don't know what has just happened. His vows don't mean anything without action.

Can I forgive him? Can I accept him back in my heart? Can I trust him ever again?

I don't know the answer to any of that. But his promises of never letting me go, I'd be a liar if I didn't think it flattering and almost sweet. However, the proof is in the pudding. I'll be watching and waiting.

chapter twenty-six

Sniper

I leave Brentlee alone. It takes everything inside of me not to lie next to her in bed and show her just how much I want her, only her. She isn't ready; and frankly, neither am I. I need some time. I need to stay sober for a while and get my shit together. I need to work it all out in my head, get shit straight before I really dive in deep. Right now—right now I want to see Stella. I've abandoned her and it was a dick move; not my biggest dick move, but a dick move nonetheless.

I pull up to Fury and Kentlee's house, knowing this is probably exactly where the little curly blondie is at, since she wasn't with Brent. I park my bike and walk up the front steps of the little house. Knocking, I wait.

The door opens and a pissed off, curvy blonde stares back at me. She narrows her eyes before she steps aside and wordlessly lets me walk past her and into the living room.

"How may I help you?" she curtly asks. I want to laugh. The Johnson girls, full of piss and vinegar when they need to be.

"Cut the shit, LeeLee," I say.

"You better not come in here saying that to me, Bates Lukin," she growls, putting her hands on her hips.

"I messed up. I get it. I've sobered up and I'm fuckin' sick over it all," I admit.

"Have you told my sister that?" she asks.

"I have. I just left her. She's not forgiving me anytime soon, as she shouldn't. I'll work for it. I'll work my ass off to get her back; but what's going on between us is between us," I say.

"Not when you treat her the way you did in front of me," she says. I sigh.

"Touché," I chuckle.

"What are you doing here?"

"Aside from seeing one of my favorite blonde bombshells?" I offer with a smirk. Kentlee rolls her eyes but with a smile tugging on her lips. "I came to see Stella."

"She misses you," Kent says. I nod.

"Fucked up with her mama, but fucked up with her, too," I admit.

Kentlee nods toward Bear's bedroom and I turn to walk in that direction. I can hear her following me, and when I step into the doorway, I can't hold back my smile. Stella's sitting in front of Bear, her blonde hair in curly pigtails, and a row of motorcycles lined up in front of her.

"Stella," I clear my throat, unable to watch her a moment longer without giving her a hug.

She looks like she's grown in the few weeks I haven't seen her. I watch as her head whips up and her blue eyes widen. Then she gives me the greatest gift of all. She smiles.

"*Bates*," she cries as she scrambles to her feet. She runs toward me, barreling into my arms at a million miles an hour. I chuckle and lift her up before I plant a kiss on her cheek.

"I missed you," she whispers as she takes my bearded cheeks with her tiny, little hands.

"I missed you, too, *malyshka*," I easily admit.

"You come home now," she demands.

"Yes," I say. Kentlee clears her throat.

"Don't make promises you can't keep," she mutters under her breath. I prop Stella on my hip before I turn my neck to face Kent.

"I'll be there. I may not be sleeping where I want to be, but I'll be there," I say, keeping it PG.

"Yeah?" she asks, not giving anything way, keeping her face hard.

"Yup. Meant it when I said I was gonna work for it, babe," I grunt.

"Good," she nods.

I spend the next hour playing with Stella and Bear, spending much needed time with my little *malyshka*. Kentlee announces lunch for the kids, and I decide that it's my time to leave them. Before I walk out of the door, her hand is wrapped around my forearm.

"Treat my sister right, Bates. You both deserve happiness," she says, grinning at me.

"I want her to be so happy." I admit.

"Then work for it, prove it, and do it," she says. I nod and leave them.

I drive to a sandwich shop and pick up some lunch for Brent and myself before I go back to my house. When I walk inside, she's exactly where I left her, except she's sleeping and it takes my breath away. She looks so young, innocent, and so fuckin' gorgeous.

How could I ever even think about leaving her?

I'm such a goddamn fool.

I leave her asleep and put her food in the fridge before I head to the garage to work on my truck a little. I don't want to wake her up, and I need something to do with my hands.

Brentlee

I hear a noise and it startles me awake. I lie in bed for a few moments and wipe the sleep from my eyes. Looking over at the bedside clock, I notice that it's four in the afternoon. I get out of bed and wash my face, take care of business, and head out to the living area. Stella will be home soon, and I should eat a little something. My stomach growls in agreement.

When I step into the kitchen, I chance looking out the window, and am surprised by what I see. The garage door is open, but that isn't what surprises me. No, Bates, *shirtless* and working under the hood of his truck is what makes my mouth water. I watch as his hands work on the engine. Each muscle in his back moves, bunching and relaxing. I shiver. He's so freaking big, it still surprises me, still turns me on— though, I don't think any red blooded American woman could look at him and *not* be turned on.

I grab a plastic cup from the cabinet and fill it with ice and water. Surely, he'll want something to drink, and I want to know why he's still here. I slip on a pair of sandals and walk out to where Bates is working.

"I brought you water," I say, clearing my throat.

He lifts his head from the truck and squints into the sunlight. He has sweat and some grease on his face. I have to clench my thighs together at how freaking sexy he looks.

"Thanks," he sighs, setting his tools down and taking the cup from my hands.

I shamelessly watch as he drinks the liquid, working it down his throat. I have to bite back a moan.

"You're welcome," I mumble.

"I bought you a sandwich, it's in the fridge." He lifts his chin toward the house and I look at him in surprise.

"What are you doing here?" I blurt out. He shakes his head once, but when his eyes meet mine, I am taken aback by the depth, the longing, and the sadness I see shining in them.

"Gonna work at getting you back, baby. I don't have to sleep in your bed to do that, but I won't be sleeping anywhere but this house, either," he announces.

"Bates…" I exhale.

"Ain't givin' up, *tigritsa*," he murmurs. I sigh and turn from him, stopping before I take even a step away, whispering a thanks for the lunch.

"Thank you for the water." He winks, and I leave him to work on his pickup outside in the warm sunshine.

A few hours later, Kentlee is at my door with my Stella. She smiles at me knowingly, and I roll my eyes.

"He came to see me," she murmurs when she gives me a

hug goodbye.

"And?" I ask.

"He said he's going to put the work in to fix everything," she says, almost repeating his words verbatim.

"Yeah," I sigh.

Kentlee leaves and I can't help but sigh. He isn't going to give up easily, but he'll give up eventually. Bates has already proven through a hurdle that he'll bail. I just need to remember that and not let my vagina or my heart take control of me.

I'm not very good at that—at controlling myself—but for my sanity's sake, I need to. I don't want to watch him walk away again, and I don't want to be on the receiving end of a drunken rampage. I'm too fucking tired for it.

"LeeLee just leave?" Bates asks, walking through the backdoor.

"Yeah, she was dropping off Stella," I say with a shrug.

"Hey, *malyshka*," he offers, pinching her nose slightly.

"Hi," she grins before she runs off to her room.

I expected more of a reaction from her, since it's been weeks since she's seen him. The look on my face must show my confusion.

"Went to talk to LeeLee after you fell asleep earlier this afternoon. Spent an hour hanging with Stella and Bear. Played cars and shit," he shrugs as he washes the grease and oil from his hands. I blink in surprise.

"Missed her, too," he whispers. I close my eyes before bowing my head. "Missed both my girls," he continues as he wraps his hand around my lower back.

He's in front of me and I can smell him, smell his scent, his sweat, his oil and grease. I want him. I want him to take me and own me all over again. One day in his presence, and

I'm ready to spread my legs for him. *I am such a fucking idiot.*

"Bates," I say with a shaky voice.

"Let's just relax tonight. No talking, no drama, just you and me and Stella. Maybe watch a movie?" he suggests.

I look up at him. He's grinning and he looks so handsome, so unbelievably handsome. I nod, unable to speak.

"You spend some time with Stella, I'll make dinner."

I open my mouth to protest, but he shakes his head once, effectively shutting me up. I step away from him and look at him for a beat. Neither of us speak, we just take each other in.

I'm soaking in the fact that he's here, in front of me, offering to make me dinner and take care of me. I can already tell that he's going to be working hard for me to accept him back. I'm already wavering, already wondering how long I can keep him at arm's length.

Bates makes Stella and me ribs, corn on the cob, and fries. It feels like a very manly meal—starch, meat and potatoes—but I don't complain. It's sweet. After the week of no sleep I've endured, it's nice to be taken care of a little bit. We settle in on the sofa, Stella in between us as we watch a cartoon movie. *Princess and the Frog*, chosen by Stella, of course.

Bates' arm rests along the backside of the sofa, and I almost moan when I feel his fingers tangle in my hair and gently begin to massage my neck and scalp. He doesn't tug on the strands; he just massages me.

I try with everything inside of me not to look over at him. I can only hold off for about five minutes, and then I quickly glance over at him. He's just watching the movie, completely unaware of how turned on he's making me. Or maybe he knows, but he doesn't care?

I bite my bottom lip and try to keep from moaning, or

sighing, or making any noise at all whatsoever. He spends the entire length of the movie torturing me, and by the small smile tipped on his lips, he knows it, too.

Once the movie is finished, I jump to my feet and announce that it's time for Stella to go to bed. Bates follows behind us and offers to read her a story before bedtime. I'm surprised, but I let him. I sit on the bed and listen to his sexy gruff voice read about princes and princesses. I close my eyes and just let his voice consume me.

"C'mon, mama," he murmurs as I feel my body being lifted into the air.

"What…" I exhale, opening my eyes. He's carrying me toward my bed.

"You passed the fuck out," he announces as he sets me down on the soft mattress.

"I haven't been sleeping well," I admit.

"Get some rest, baby. I'll be on the couch if you need me, yeah?"

I nod and watch him go. He closes the door behind him and I just stare. He didn't try a thing, not a single thing. Granted, this is only night one, but I expected something. A kiss—something. I don't understand my disappointment; I should be glad that I didn't have to fight him off.

I'm a complete disaster.

I huff before I change into my pajamas and open my bedroom door before I slip into bed. I like to have the door open in case Stella wakes up. I want to be able to hear her. I sigh as I curl into a ball and close my eyes.

I want to be able to trust Bates, but I don't think that will ever happen, and that—*that* is why we will never work out. I need to trust him and he needs me to trust him. Without trust, I can't be in his life, I can't be by his side. Kentlee trusts Fury one hundred percent. You can see it in just how they look at each other.

I want that, he needs that.

We're a freaking disaster.

chapter twenty-seven

Sniper

I watch her from afar. She can see me. I'm not hiding, just watching.

Brentlee is working, and I'm waiting until her shift is over to take her home.

It's been a week since I came back to her. Apologized to her. Started sleeping on the couch every night.

A week since I've had hard liquor.

It's been hands down the best week of my life.

I didn't think I could have a week with no sex be the best. But it has been. I've been spending every waking moment with my girls, in one way or another, and I couldn't be happier. Well, *I lie*. Sex would make it just that much better, but

I can wait. I want Brentlee sure of me, of us, before we go there again. I shouldn't have pushed it the first time; it was too soon, for both of us.

"You cool?" Vault asks as he takes the seat next to mine.

"I am. The coolest," I joke.

"You back in there?" he asks, lifting his chin to Brent. She is serving Buck a shot of tequila and laughing at something the dirty old fuck has to say, no doubt.

"No, not yet," I admit with a shrug.

I don't need to be back there, though. I'm good. Real fuckin' good. Slow is something both of us need. I haven't had a nightmare since my shit's calmed down, and Brentlee seems better, healthier. She's put on some weight, and the dark circles are gone from beneath her eyes. She's never looked more beautiful.

"You will be," he says. I tear my eyes away from Brentlee to look at him, arching a brow in question.

"You two are like fuckin' magnets, brother," he grunts before he slaps my shoulder and walks away. I turn back to Brentlee and our eyes connect. She doesn't move, except to offer me a shy smile.

Magnets.

Two people that have a powerful attraction.

We are that.

Magnetic.

I'm drawn to her and she to me.

"Hey, baby," the sweet voice of Star says. It makes me cringe. I take my eyes off of Brentlee to face her. I don't say a word.

"Haven't seen you much lately," she says, taking Vault's vacated seat.

"What do you want?" I bark, annoyed with her.

"I'm here for you. Anything you need, I'm yours," she says, pushing her tits together and leaning forward to give me a view—a view I don't fuckin' want.

"I don't want anything of yours, Star. Don't you fuckin' get that?" I ask.

"Well, I just wanted to tell you. It doesn't seem like Brentlee is really all that into you anymore," she shrugs. Her eyes shift up to where Brentlee is, proving she's calculated, as if I didn't already know.

"Wouldn't matter if Brent didn't want me. I don't want you. Never did," I grunt as I stand.

"I know the score, Sniper. Brand me and I'll make sure you're always happy, no matter who your cock slides into," she pleads.

"Thought you didn't want me?" I ask arching a brow.

She shrugs, not giving me a verbal answer.

It's pathetic, needy, and just plain sad. She's searching for somebody, for something, but it ain't me. I've found my somebody. Brentlee.

"Doesn't matter what you offer me, Star. I don't fuckin' want it. Got everything I want right there behind that bar," I state. She opens her mouth, but I don't give her a chance to spew any shit.

Instead, I turn toward Brentlee and see red at the sight in front of me.

She's leaned over the bar, her tits on full view for Dirty Johnny as she says something to him with a huge smile on her face. He reaches over the bar and touches her shoulder. I charge, without a fuckin' word, and walk behind the bar, picking her up and throwing her over my shoulder.

Fuck. This. Shit.

"Bates," she cries as her hands grab onto my belt.

"Shut the fuck up," I grind out before I slap her ass. Then, because I can't help myself, I grab a handful of her perfect ass.

I open my truck door and throw her ass inside. I grin when she bounces in her seat. Then, I slam the door closed and run over to the driver side. I start the truck and speed out of the parking lot. She's saying some shit to me, but I'm completely tuning her out. *I'm just happy she's talking.* Even if it is screaming. She's been like a scared pussycat the past week, afraid to say or do anything. Then she openly flirts with my brother, my friend, and a guy she's fucked before.

Hell.to.the.fucking.no.

I drive out to the country, nowhere near my house, just a big open field I've gone to to think before in the past. I put the truck in park and stare out the windshield into the darkness ahead of us. I know there's a pond out there somewhere, but I can't remember how far. There are also trees and rocks and all kinds of shit.

"What the hell?" Brentlee screeches.

"You let him touch you," I simply say, not looking anywhere but straight ahead.

Brentlee

"You let him touch you."

His words ring throughout the quiet pick-up cab and I look at him in surprise.

"Bates," I murmur.

I'm afraid to say anything else. I don't know what to say. Star was talking to him, and I got jealous as hell. I started flirting with Johnny. He told me I was playing with fire; he knew what I was doing immediately, but I didn't care.

"I'm fine with not being able to touch you right now, Brentlee. But that doesn't mean I can stand to watch another man anywhere near you," he grumbles.

"You were talking to Star," I begin. His hand flies up and wraps around the back of my neck, startling me. I stare at him in shock and surprise.

"I didn't let that whore touch me. I wouldn't. Not now, not ever again," he says.

I search for the lie in his eyes, except I don't find it. *Truth*. His eyes are swirling with nothing but the absolute truth.

"I…"

"You need time to trust me, that's cool, baby. I get that. You don't get time to get off with another dick. You're still mine," he murmurs, resting his forehead against mine.

"It was innocent," I whisper.

"*Bullshit*. You were showin' him your tits and flirting with him," he barks. I back up, but don't get far as his hand is still on the back of my neck.

"Fuck you. You had your dick shoved down Star's throat. You don't get to tell me anything," I snarl. He grimaces.

I lift my arms to hit him, but his other hand wraps around my wrists and he pushes me down onto the seat. His hips between my legs.

"I love you, my *tigritsa*," he whispers as he gently pushes his hardened, jean clad cock against my panties.

"I'm so fucking mad at you, Bates," I cry as tears begin to leak from my eyes and down into my hair.

"I know, baby," he murmurs before his lips crash against mine, his tongue forcing its way into my mouth.

I fight him for about two seconds, maybe three. Then I shamelessly moan and roll my hips up to meet his rough jeans.

"Forgive me for fucking up, baby," he murmurs, kissing my jaw and neck.

I want to forgive him, but I can't. A week of being a *good boy* doesn't take away the way he treated me. I can't forgive him, not yet, if ever.

"I can't," I truthfully admit. I feel his whole body sag on top of me before he sits up and rights himself.

"How can I make you?" he asks. It almost makes me laugh.

He was the exact same way when we were young. Anytime we fought, he'd try and force me into telling him how to fix it. Some things never change about people.

"I don't think it's anything I can just *do*. It's going to take time. It's only been a week," I say. Bates takes my hand and wraps his warm, strong fingers around it, giving me a gentle squeeze.

"Time," he nods. "I'll give you as much time as I can, but please, for my sanity, don't fuckin' flirt with other men."

"Okay," I agree with a nod.

Wordlessly, Bates starts the truck and we head back home to his house. We walk inside and relieve Tammy. I thank her for staying with Stella, and for being wonderful in general. Once she's gone, I check on Stella and then walk toward my bedroom.

I turn around and look at Bates.

He's standing in the middle of the living room, looking

hopelessly lost, and so damn sexy it makes me ache. I want to just invite him into my room, tell him it means nothing, lie to him and to myself. I want to, but I don't. I turn away from him and close the door before I do something stupid. Something that would clearly ruin what we're trying to build—what we're both desperately trying to fix.

The next thing I know, there is screaming coming from the living room. It's animalistic and guttural and so fucking scary, my heart practically leaps out of my chest.

I don't think.

I do.

I jump out of bed and run to the living room. Bates is on his knees on the couch, his pillow wrapped in his arms, his eyes wide as he looks at it, screaming with tears running down his face.

I take a deep breath to calm my shaky nerves and I slowly walk toward him. I don't want to startle him. I start to call his name, hoping it will wake him from his dream. I call his name louder and louder. I'm afraid to touch him, so when I'm right in front of him, I dip down to get in his view and say his name sharply, with purpose.

His eyes flick to me and he inhales suddenly, but he doesn't see me. I don't know what he sees, but it isn't me. His eyes are wild and his movements jerky. He stands and scoops me into his arms, holding me close and tight as he stomps loudly to the bedroom. I'm thankful that Stella is a hard sleeper. This, right here, would terrify her.

The bedroom door closes and he locks it before he throws me onto the bed. His heavy weight shortly follows, and I gasp for air. He grunts in return. I feel his hand slide beneath the cotton shorts I'm wearing, and then two fingers roughly enter me. I cry out in pain and tears soon follow; then I watch as he wakes. His eyes slowly focus and he looks down at me, horror replacing the wild before he quickly leaps from me.

"I... *fuck*," he growls.

"Bates," I say, sitting up and reaching for him. He shrugs me off and heads for the door.

"I won't stay here anymore. I'll go back to the club," he murmurs, leaving the room before I can speak.

I sit quietly for a moment, then I hear his bike start. I quickly scramble to my feet and run to the front door. By the time I get there, he's gone. I close my eyes and I cry. Not because he's abandoned me; he hasn't, not really. He's going to protect me, that much I know. But I don't want him to. I want to help him. I want to hold him when he's had a nightmare, a flashback. I want to comfort him however he needs it, just like I want him to do for me.

I just want him.

All this push and pull, this internal struggle. It isn't because I don't want him, not in the slightest. I do want him, that's part of the problem. I want him so baldy, I never want him to leave me again.

I wipe the tears from my eyes and decide I need to get my shit together. He's fucked up. I've fucked up. Doesn't matter how or when, we've both fucked up over the years. But if we don't let that shit go, we'll never get back to each other and we'll forever be unhappy.

I don't want to be unhappy.

I want to fight and makeup and love.

I want to love him and he love me and show it however we desire.

I want it all.

The good, the bad, and the assuredly downright filthy and ugly.

chapter twenty-eight

Sniper

It fucking aches to stay away, but I have to. If I don't, I could hurt her. When I slept next to Brentlee, with her in my arms, my nightmares were almost nonexistent. I hadn't slept that good in years. I didn't even realize I was sleeping so well next to her until I started sleeping on the couch. I was sober, and the nightmares, they came in full force. I almost raped her. I would have, too, had her crying not woken me.

"Gotta head up to the border, you game for a few days?" Torch asks as he walks into the room. I'm sitting at a table drinking a bottle of water, thinking.

"Yeah, I need a few days," I grumble.

"Brentlee still giving you hell?" he asks.

"No, I had a nightmare," I explain. I don't have to go into detail with Torch. He knows and he understands.

"Let's roll," he grunts.

We ride together, to the border and then over to Canada. I think about the brothers we lost when Fury was in prison, the families that were destroyed by the skinheads and the Bastards. It was the saddest sight I had ever seen. It made me question the life, question my position. I would die if something happened to Brent or Stella because of my involvement with the club.

"What're we doin' here?" I finally ask once we've pulled through the clubhouse gates and start to get off of our bikes.

"Just doin' an accounting check and popping in," he shrugs.

"Who ordered it?" I ask. I've been checked out lately, so I don't know what the hell is going on with the clubs, apparently.

"*MadDog*," he says. Fury's dad, and the President of the original charter. This club must be in some deep shit.

"Hey guys, to what do I owe the pleasure?" Blow, the clubs President, hollers as we walk up to the building.

"Just out for a ride and thought we'd stop by and pay a visit to our brethren," Torch smirks.

"Well, come on in—fresh beer, weed, and pussy for you guys," he says with a chuckle. I watch his eyes as they shift from side to side. He looks cagey, uneasy, and that in turn puts me on alert.

Once we step through the clubhouse doors, I cringe. It reminds me of our club in Bonners Ferry before Fury came in and cleaned house. There are a couple of broke down, strung out whores lying on the sofa, barely breathing. Nobody is laughing, joking, or partying. They're separated and they all look pissed.

I walk over to a guy I've known for a while, Free. He's leaning against the wall.

"Got a minute?" I ask. He lifts his chin toward the door and I follow him out. "You guys in trouble?"

"Got more trouble than we know what to do with," he admits, looking off into the distance.

"Need help with that?" I ask.

"Might here shortly," he says.

"Whatever you need, here for you, brother," I say. He nods.

"I appreciate that. Give me a month to try and clean house. If I can't get it done, then I'll call in reinforcements," he murmurs.

"Got your back, Free," I confirm.

Free walks away, leaving me standing near the clubhouse, and I watch him take off on his bike. I turn around and head back inside. Torch looks at me in question and I shake my head. We spend the evening partying. Well, they do. I don't drink a drop. I nurse the same beer all night and I observe.

The drugs are flowing; cocaine is everywhere. The whores are junkies itching for their next fix, and most of the men aren't fairing much better. There's a problem here, and I have a feeling Free won't be able to fix it himself. I have a feeling that we'll be back soon and cleaning house with vengeance.

The next morning, we leave the clubhouse but we don't head back home to Idaho. Instead, we drive to California, to *MadDog*. We need to report what we've witnessed, who is definitely fucked up and fucking things up. Then we need to report on who definitely doesn't approve of the shady shit happening. There are a few on the fencers, but for the most part, there is a clean divide between the brothers.

The ride to California is going to extend our trip, but that's ok. I need some time away from Brentlee or I'll fuck it up even more than it already is. After a long day's ride, we settle into our hotel and I decide to call Brent and check up on her.

"Hello," she murmurs sleepily into the phone.

"Hey, baby, it's me," I say.

"Bates, I thought you were going to be back in town today," she yawns. I had text her the day before and told her where I was and when I'd be home so she wouldn't worry.

"Gotta go see MadDog in California, then I'll be home."

"That's a long trip. Be safe, please," she whispers.

"You too, *tigritsa*," I sigh.

It's been another week. A long fuckin' week. A week where I haven't been sleeping, and the flashbacks are coming regularly. Between riding to Canada, to Cali, and now coming home, I'm so fuckin' exhausted, I don't know which way is up. I should give in to the bottle of Jack that's underneath my bed, but I don't want to do that. I don't want to be my father.

I've been drowning myself in work at the club and the drama of the Canadian brothers. Now that I'm home, it's time for me to focus on the Devils Club. It's a place I have been neglecting for weeks.

"You haven't fixed your shit," Fury grunts as I walk from my room into the bar at the clubhouse.

"Nope," I reply, straightening my cut.

"You need to," he says. I want to roll my eyes.

"Doin' the best I can," I lie, knowing damn well I could do a fuck've a lot more to woo Brentlee back. I don't want to do that, though; I want her to come to me.

"Prospects gettin' patched in tonight. Party at *Devils* starting at midnight," he informs me. I nod.

Fuck. The girls hate getting last minute changes to the schedule. I roll my neck and stretch it out. *I'm gonna have to give some of these bitches a pay raise.* I grunt as my response and leave. I don't have time to waste telling Fury all the reasons he's an asshole. I have bitches to round up.

The club is already alive with music, strippers, and booze when I arrive. I quickly make my way backstage, where the girls are all applying makeup and changing into costumes for their next show. A few of them give me knowing smiles, because I've fucked them more than once. I try not to with the girls that work for me, but patch-in parties happen, and shit happens.

"Patch in party tonight. Who's staying?" I ask. I hear a few groans but about five of the girls raise their hands.

"Extra bonus included for the night, naturally," I chuckle. Another girl raises her hand. "I'm gonna call in a few of the girls that have the night off, then. I need more than six," I say. Nobody else volunteers and I turn to leave.

"Can't wait for tonight," one of the girls I've fucked in the past speaks up as soon as I step out of the door.

I don't respond to her. If I do, I'll say somethin' stupid. I want to wait for Brentlee, I want to wait for as long as she needs me to. I want to show her that I mean it, that I want only her. But my dick—yeah, my dick ain't so patient, and he wants some pussy.

I spend the rest of the night in my office doing paperwork

I hate so that I'll keep my eyes and my dick to myself. When the club shows up at midnight, it's time to kick the rest of the patrons out of the bar. Luckily, nobody gives us any hassle and the girls start the show right away. I make my way over to the bar and grab a beer for myself before I go to join my brothers.

I watch as two girls start to strip, doing their regular routine. I know It'll end up being much dirtier with the doors locked. When they're completely naked, the show really begins and they start to go at it on stage. Licking, fingering, pinching, and kissing. It's sexy as fuck, and my dick presses against my zipper at the sight.

One of the other stripers walks right over to me, already completely naked. I've fucked her. *Angel.* She's a fuckin' wildcat, too. I bite my bottom lip as she climbs on my lap, her thighs spread with her knees on either side of my legs.

I watch as her fingers trail between her tits and down to her waxed pussy. I almost whimper when she slides them between her folds and thrusts them inside with an exaggerated moan. I don't give a flying fuck if its fake, it's still hot as hell.

"Touch me," she demands breathlessly. My hand twitches, ready to roam over her naked body, but I don't.

I shake my head. I want Brentlee. I know the abstinence and the hard work will pay off eventually.

"*What—oh, my god.*"

I hear Brentlee's rasping voice from behind me and I stand, sending the naked stripper to the ground before I turn to face her. She looks horrified and sad all at the same time.

"Brent," I start. She shakes her head, backing away from me.

I didn't do a fuckin' thing wrong and I'm not letting her

out of here thinking I did. I take several quick steps toward her and pick her up without warning. She screams, but I ignore her as I take her to the closest private place. The strippers dressing room.

"What are you doing here?" I demand.

"What were you doing? You know what? It's not my business," she says as her head hangs.

"Why ain't it your business?" I ask.

"Because you're not mine. It doesn't matter. We aren't *together*," she says. It pisses me the fuck off.

"Fuck that, my names on your body—we're as together as it gets," I grind out, taking a step toward her. I watch as she backs up with each step I take, until her ass collides with the makeup table.

"Bates," she whimpers.

I don't stop until my hips are fitted between her thighs, my jeans making contact with her panty covered pussy. Her skirt is indecently short, and that's another thing that pisses me off, added to my fucking list. I slide my hand up her spine and twist my fingers into her hair before I tug her neck back. I scrape my beard along the length of her neck before I press my lips to hers.

"We shouldn't," she murmurs against my lips.

"We absolutely fuckin' should," I growl before my lips crash against hers. I shove my tongue deep into her mouth, tasting her, consuming her, showing her exactly who owns her.

I know the moment she surrenders. When her hips roll and her hungry pussy searches for more; when her fingers slide through my hair at the nape of my neck; and when she shivers in my arms, trembling, I know I've won. I slide my hand from her hip over her thigh and to the lace over her pussy. Fuck, she's soaked through, and I shiver myself before I slide it to the side and run my finger over her damp lips.

"Baby," she whispers, pulling her lips from mine and arching her body closer to me. I lick and kiss the column of her neck while I sink my finger inside of her hot core.

She feels so fucking good. *Warm. Wet. Tight.* I pull my finger out and rub her wetness onto her clit, rolling it between my fingers and enjoying the way she gasps when I pinch it lightly before I sink two fingers inside of her. She sighs as her body relaxes beneath my touch. My lips never leaving her neck.

This is the end of our separation.

I can't deny myself a moment longer. I need to have her at my side. I need to have all of her, *always*.

Brentlee

I resist him for about a second before I give in. Once he touches me, slides his fingers inside of my pussy and his tongue into my mouth, I'm done for. I need him. More than that, I *want* him.

I want every piece of him inside of me.

"I need you, Bates," I murmur. Within a second, I hear his belt clink and the sound of his heavy jeans rustling and then falling to the ground.

"Open your eyes, Brentlee," he demands.

I do; I open them and I focus on his gorgeous eyes. They're full of lust, longing. The counter is hard under my ass, but in Bates' arms, it wouldn't matter how uncomfortable I was—I'd take it. I'd welcome it.

"Bates," I moan when he wrenches my panties to the side and he presses his cock again my core and gently pushes in, until he's fully seated inside of me.

He pauses, just staring at me. His jaw clenched beneath his beard and his brows furrowed. I remove one of my hands from his hair and trail my finger over my name on his neck, my eyes never leaving his.

"Don't want anyone else," he states. I nod but she shakes his head. "Don't want anyone else, baby. Nobody, just you," he murmurs slowly, pulling out of me and then sinking back inside.

"But…" I start.

He continues his slow pace, his eyes focused on me until he pulls completely out and then tugs me to my feet. Wordlessly, he spins me around to face the mirror above the table. I squeak when he wrenches my hips back and then fills me from behind. His gaze meets mine in the mirror as one of his hands dips inside of my panties. His finger gently strokes my clit while the other hand wraps around my throat.

"Don't want anyone else, Brentlee," he repeats. I can't take my eyes off of his as I feel his cock's long, deep strokes.

"That's not the way it looked," I rasp as I tip my hips a bit more, shaking slightly in my high heels.

"She climbed on me and asked me to touch her. I didn't. I wouldn't. I only want you," he grinds out, squeezing my throat a little tighter.

"I can't trust you," I say, meaning every single word.

Bates growls above me and begins to fuck me a little harder, a bit rougher. I throw my arms up and wrap them around the back of his neck. Surrendering to him, letting him hold me up while his powerful body thrusts inside of me. I'm his, my heart and head can't trust him, but my body always will. I feel him pinch my clit before he taps it with his fingers.

"You're going to have to trust me, *tigritsa*. You're going to have to accept that you're mine, and I'll take care of you," he grunts.

"I can't," I whimper before he pulls completely out of me. I almost fall when he steps back from me. I whip around and look at him in surprise.

"You can't fuckin' trust me, then we can't do this," he roars.

I open my mouth as he grabs his pants and pulls them up. I can see the defeated look in his eyes. If he leaves now, there's no hope. I want hope. I want him. He's right. I need to let some of my shit go. He's been constant and consistent, but this place, this limbo, it isn't going to work for much longer.

"Wait, please don't leave me," I beg. He stops, his eyes wide.

"Brent," he sighs.

"Fuck this. Fuck the past. Fuck it all, Bates. I love you and I want you. The rest of the shit, I'm going to have to let it go. Because losing you, it would be my biggest regret," I confess.

A second later, I am wrapped in his arms and he's lifting me, his lips crashing against mine and my back slamming against the closed door. I don't register his fumbling hands beneath me as I wrap my legs around his waist, my lips attacking his with the same ferocity his attack mine. I cry out when he rips my panties completely off and then fills me again. This time, he doesn't fuck me slow. No, he pounds into me, his strength causing my back to bang against the door. I'll be bruised up in the morning, but it will be worth it—worth every second. I wrench my lips from him as I cry out in pleasure.

"Say you're mine," he grunts against my neck as he sucks at my skin.

"I'm yours," I murmur.

"I want that whole fucking club to hear it," he orders as one of his hands smacks the outside of my thigh.

"*I'm fucking yours*!" I shout as I feel myself on the verge of climaxing.

"Shit, yeah, you are," he groans as he slides his hand between us and pinches my clit, sending me over the edge.

I cry out as I come around him, my pussy pulsing, my entire body going still. Bates doesn't stop, though. He fucks me like the savage beast that he is. His fingertips dig into the sides of my thighs as he holds me up, and his cock pistons inside of my core.

I cry out with each and every thrust until he stills inside of me. His cock fills me with his release as he lets out a guttural cry into my neck. He doesn't move as he empties inside of me, then he begins to slowly slide in and out of me, his face nuzzling my neck.

"Bates," I whisper breathlessly.

"Never leaving. Not ever again," he states. I sigh. I hope he's telling the truth. I hope that he means his words. I'm so tired of fighting it, fighting him.

"Are you coming home?" I ask.

"I'm already home, baby," he grins, thrusting his hips slightly. It makes me laugh. I immediately stop when his hand cups my cheek and his thumb slides across my bottom lip.

"I love you so much," I admit. His eyes darken before he

kisses my lips softly, brushing them twice before he rests his forehead against mine and closes his eyes.

"I love you more than life itself, Brentlee. I'm so sorry I hurt you. *So fuckin' sorry*. I'll try not to do it again, ever," he murmurs. I tighten my legs around his waist and he lifts his head up, looking at me with confusion.

"You better not ever do it again, Bates. Not like that," I warn.

"Never." He nods once before his lips touch the tip of my nose and he slides out of me. I straighten my skirt and start looking for a tissue or something to clean up with when one of his hands cups my cheek.

"You're mine. *Always*," he whispers as his thumb slides along my cheekbone.

"Always," I whisper.

I gasp when his other hand slides between my legs and his fingers enter me.

"My cum stays here tonight," he murmurs.

"Bates," I breathe in surprise.

"Need you marked. Head-to-pussy," he grins. My heart stops for a second at how gorgeous he is.

"You know you're a disgusting Neanderthal?" I ask.

"I branded your body with my name permanently, babe. You can't seriously just be figuring this shit out now." I giggle at his words, unable to control myself.

"Now that's the sound I love—close second to the little sounds you make when you're about to come on my cock—your laughter," he says softly before he pulls his hand from between my legs.

"Let's go home," I suggest. He nods.

Together, we walk out of the dressing room, my arm

around his waist, his hand planted on the spot on my hip where his name is etched into my skin.

"Thank fuck," Fury barks as soon we walk into the bar area. I notice that he's bellied up to the bar, talking to a pretty bartender.

"Candy, get my woman here somethin' to drink, yeah?" Bates shouts over the loud music.

"What'll you have, honey?" she asks.

I ask for a bottled beer. I don't need anything special, and I really just want to go home, cuddle next to Bates, and sleep—god, I want to sleep so damn bad.

I sit on the barstool next to Bates, who is leaned down murmuring to Fury about only god knows what.

"You the reason he's been absent?" Candy asks. I shrug as my response, unsure of what to say.

"He looks happy, honey. Keep him that way, yeah? Makes my life a hell of a lot easier." She winks and I smile back at her. "You're Kent's sister?" she asks, changing the subject.

We spend the next thirty minutes talking about my sister, about her time working in the club serving drinks, and how close she and Candy became during those years. By the end of the conversation, I have an even higher opinion of my sister, a higher respect. My sister kicks ass and has to be the strongest woman I have ever known.

"Ready?" Bates asks as his hand wraps around my waist. I look around and notice that the party is pretty much dead. I missed it all.

"Yeah," I yawn. I'm exhausted. Completely shattered.

Bates and I head over to his bike. As I climb on behind him, I can't help but feel excited at being wrapped around him on the back of his bike again.

I close my eyes as we travel down the dark country roads. I think about how Fury claimed they needed my help tonight at the bar. The asshole was playing matchmaker. As I curl closer to Bates, inhaling the leather of his cut, I can't help but be grateful that he did. No telling how long we would have danced around each other and avoided each other. Possibly until it was too late. *That* would have been truly tragic.

chapter twenty-nine

Brentlee

The knocking on the door is forceful. I look over at Bates, who is completely comatose. I grab his t-shirt from the night before and throw it on over my naked body. Once we came home, we alternated between fucking and making love until the sun came up.

I glance at the clock and groan when I realize Stella will be waking any second, then the pounding on the front door begins again. I rush over to it, opening it without thought.

Standing in front of me are two uniformed police officers. I squeak at the sight of them. Honestly, I expected it to be Kentlee with coffee and a knowing smile, here for all the dirty details of Bates and my reunion. I did not, however, expect two uniformed officers of the law.

"Ma'am," one says with a grin as his eyes slowly travel the length of my body.

"Can I help you?" I ask, running my fingers through my ratted, matted hair. Hair I know Bates spent most of the morning tangling with his strong fingers.

"We're here about your husband, ma'am," the other officer says. My eyes widen before I nod and step aside, letting them into the house.

"The fuck is goin' on here?" Bates growls as he walks from the hall into the living area.

He's shirtless, wearing his jeans, zipped but unbuttoned at the top, and I know he's not wearing boxers underneath. I lick my lips at the sight of him.

"We're here to talk to Mrs. Corbin about her husband," one of the officers says, his eyes narrowing on Bates.

"What about that douchebag?" Bates grunts.

"Uh… we're sorry to inform you that Mr. Corbin's body was found yesterday afternoon. We've just identified him," the younger of the two officers says. I gasp in feigned shock and hold my hand over my lips. Afraid the truth will shine on my face.

"Where was he?" Bates grunts.

"A popular area known for…"

"*Billy*," the other officer interrupts.

"We'll need you to come down to the station when you can and give an interview. We understand you two were estranged, but it's just a formality," the older officer advises.

"Okay, I'll come down this afternoon," I murmur.

The police officers leave and I turn to Bates who is smiling.

"What did you guys do?" I ask.

"We put him where all the pros and druggies deal, in a hotel room filled with so much jizz and fingerprints they'd never figure a fuckin' thing out," he chuckles.

"You can't be serious." I wrinkle my nose and he wraps his hands around my waist, pulling me into his chest.

"They found him anywhere else, baby, and you'd be a prime suspect. I couldn't have that," he murmurs as his nose slides alongside mine. I sigh and melt against him.

"Wha happen?" Stella asks, rubbing her little eyes.

"Nothing, sweet girl," I say before I pick her up and hold her in my arms.

"My girls," Bates murmurs before he plants a kiss on my forehead and then Stella's.

Bates calls Kentlee over to watch Stella while he takes me to the police station to answer their questions. Luckily I'm not a suspect at all, thanks to Bates and the club. Then, we spend the day together, something we haven't done in what feels like months, and its lovely. Bates and I cuddle in the grass and watch Stella play in the dirt, something she would have never been allowed to do with Scotty. I lean my head against Bates' shoulder and sigh.

"You happy, babe?" he asks as his hand plays with the end of my hair.

"Yeah, I am," I sigh.

"But?" he prods.

"Our road has been so damn rough. I'm afraid at what's going to be thrown at us next," I admit.

"Look at me, *tigritsa*," he commands. I tip my head back to look into his eyes. "Nothing will be thrown at us that we can't handle. Our road has been bumpy as hell, but honest to fuck, baby, I've never been happier than I am with you right now. If I would'a kept you when I was eighteen, I wouldn't appreciate you for the woman you are. I would have taken you for granted, and, baby, you would hate me. I was not an easy man to love all these years."

"I was a spoiled brat princess before Scotty," I admit. He chuckles and places a soft kiss on my nose.

"Yeah, we'll get you back there again," he grins. I shake my head.

"I don't ever want to be that way again. I cut my sister from being Maid of Honor because Missy talked me into it, told me Kent was too fat to be next to me, that she'd ruin my pictures. Then, when my parents were so awful to her, I didn't defend her. She's never done a damn thing wrong and she was treated so horribly, and I'm one of the people who was horrible to her," I admit, that weight finally being lifted from my shoulders.

"Missy is a cunt. I never liked that bitch. She was so jealous of your relationship with Kent, she always tried to put a wedge between you. I'm sure Scotty was doing his own manipulating on that whole wedding shit, too. I can't answer for you standing up to your parents; I think you were young and scared. You were getting married and didn't want to rock the boat. You still lived at home, for fuck's sake."

I'm grateful that he's giving me an out for feeling so guilty, but it doesn't erase my shame, and it doesn't erase my actions. I turn away from him and stare at the grass on my left as I pick at it with my fingers.

"You feel badly, baby, then apologize. LeeLee is one of the sweetest women I know; she'll forgive you verbally, even if her actions prove that she's already forgiven you in her heart."

"I wouldn't forgive me," I admit, letting out a breath.

"Wouldn't you?" he asks, wrapping his fingers around my thigh and gently squeezing. I look up and he's smirking down at me. "You forgave me, and I was a fucking prick more than once."

"But I love you," I say. Then, suddenly, it all clicks together.

"And LeeLee loves *you*, babe."

I grin up at him, finally feeling freer and lighter than I have in years. My sister loves me, she'll forgive me, and like Bates said, she probably already has. I still need to truly apologize for my behavior in the past.

I can't change the way I acted, the way I tried to exclude my sister from my wedding. I can't change the way I just let our parents say such horrible things to her without standing up to them. But I can apologize and ask for forgiveness.

Kentlee already has moved on. She's healed from the hurts of our past; she's dealt with our parent's dismissal and betrayal. She's so much stronger than I ever could be, and her life is that much more beautiful for it.

Sniper

The last thing I want to do tonight is go into work. The next to last thing I want to do tonight is leave both Brent and Stella home alone. But I gotta make sure the brothers didn't trash the place too badly last night, and I have to get everything set up for tonight. A regular night at the club is just as chaotic and hectic as a night where the whole fuckin' MC comes over.

Brentlee is in the kitchen making dinner, some meat thing she stuffs into bell peppers. I do not fuckin' understand that shit, but she likes it, so I'll try it. I walk into the room and see her mixing the raw meat with her bare hands. I take it as my opportunity to fuck with her a bit.

I slide up behind her and wrap my hands around her stomach, thrusting my hips into her gorgeous ass.

"Bates," she hisses.

I ignore her as I gently caress her neck with my cheek, letting my beard rub against her skin. She shudders beneath me.

I let one of my hands drift between her legs while the other one slides up and under her shirt, cupping her tit. I pinch her nipple over her bra at the same time I apply pressure where her clit is beneath her jean shorts.

"Stella," she moans.

"Napping. Come to the bedroom and fuck me," I murmur into her ear. She shivers, which only makes me grin.

"Dinner," she protests. It's weak as fuck.

"Come on, *tigritsa*, I want you to ride me. I have a taste for watching those pretty tits bounce," I grunt, pinching her nipple even harder through the thin fabric.

"Okay," she whispers. I let her go so that she can wash the raw meat from her hands.

I watch her ass sway as she goes to the sink. Every single curve on the woman makes my dick hard. I used to love her lithe body, but nothing could have prepared me for the curves she now sports. Though still slight compared to some, she's got more than she did when she was a girl, and to be honest, I'd like to see some more added. She's so fuckin' gorgeous.

"C'mon, baby," I growl, holding my hand out. I tug her into the bedroom and waste no time locking the door behind us. "Strip," I order as I begin to take my own clothes off, tossing them around the room.

Brentlee quickly sheds her clothing, and she's only seconds behind me on the bed, crawling up my thighs faster than I've ever seen her move in my life. I moan when I feel her hot mouth close around my cock, and she sucks me in deep. I wrap her ponytail around my hand, twice, and hold her movements still before I start to thrust my hips, fucking her mouth from below her.

When her hand travels between her legs, I almost come down her throat. Instead, I pull her head up and order her to crawl up my body. I need in her hot pussy. I need to feel her wrap around me, squeeze me—own me.

I line my cock up against her wet core and groan as she slowly slides down on me, enveloping my whole dick with her wet heat. She shakes slightly, but she doesn't move. I don't want her to, either. Not yet. I slide my hands up her sides and gently cup her breasts. Feeling their weight in my big hands, loving how soft she feels against my rough, calluses.

"Bates," she murmurs. It's breathy and soft—so fuckin' sweet, too.

"Ride me, Brentlee baby. Show me how good I make you feel," I rasp.

Her moan fills the air as she slowly begins to ride my cock. I never urge her faster, I don't even move my hips. I place one thumb on her clit and pinch her tits with my other hand, but she's in control of this. She's the one who controls my orgasm today.

I grind my teeth together, clenching my jaw as my whole body tightens. Fuck, she's a sight to see above me. Her head thrown back in pleasure, her hands resting on my thighs, and her tits bouncing with each fall down on my cock. I can feel her pussy swelling, contracting around me, and I know she's close. She lifts her head slightly and her furrowed brows catch my eye.

"You okay, baby?" I ask trying to keep my shit together, knowing I could blow at any second.

"I'm so close, Bates, so damn close," she whimpers. It kills me. I want her to combust around me.

I take my hand off of her tit and bring my fingers to my mouth, wetting them before I slide them between the cheeks of her ass and gently massage her back entrance. She gasps, but not in anger—in pleasure. She whimpers as I work my fingers into her tight ass.

I begin to slowly fuck her ass with my fingers while her pussy fucks my cock. In seconds, she starts to buck harder, her heavy breathing filling the room. Then she cries out as her pussy clamps down around my cock, holding me in.

I take the opportunity to fuck her from underneath. My fingers firmly planted in her gorgeous ass. It only takes me a few pumps into her tight swollen pussy before I fill her with my release. She collapses on my chest seconds later, and I remove my fingers from her, but keep my dick in its home—in her cunt.

"I'm sorry I won't be home until the morning," I mutter into her sweat soaked neck.

"You leave me this satisfied and breathless every time, I won't mind you going to work," she chuckles above me. Unfortunately, I lose her heat at the motion.

"Does it bother you? Me managing the club?" I ask, unsure why I'm suddenly worried about her thoughts and feelings on the matter. She lifts her head and rests her chin on my chest.

"It really should," she admits with a smirk. "But it doesn't. I know you're coming home to me."

"Do you? Do you really know that?" I ask, tucking some wild strands of hair behind her ear.

"I'm trying to convince myself," she says with a shy smile as she bites her bottom lip.

"I'll prove it to you, Brentlee. I'm yours and you're mine. No man will ever touch you but me. No woman will ever touch me but you. It'll take time for you to trust me, and that's okay. We have all the time in the fuckin' world, babe." I smile up at her and she returns it, with a much bigger smile than before.

"I love you, Bates," she whispers.

"Always have, always will love you, *tigritsa*," I say. I lift up and take her lips with my own, sucking on them, nipping at them, and worshiping them as they deserve.

My *tigritsa*.

The woman who has always owned my heart in a way that there would never be anything for anybody else. She's finally all mine, and I'm going to do my absolute damnedest to keep her happy. Anything in my power to make her smile at me, every day, that's what I'll do for her. My honey-eyed dream.

chapter thirty

Brentlee

If I could pinch myself, I would.

This life of mine seems more like a dream than a reality. I'll take it with a smile, and I won't look back. It's been the best week of my life. Bates and I are finally more comfortable with where we are in our relationship. Without the looming threat of Scotty constantly hovering above us, it feels lighter than ever.

I feel lighter than ever.

I spent all yesterday morning inventorying the bar and ordering more alcohol, but unfortunately, I have to work tonight. The room is charged and the men are wired. It must be a full moon out, because it feels off. *Everything feels off—I feel off.*

"The Cartel was not happy with that last shipment, claimin' shit was missin'," I overhear Buck tell Vault as he takes a shot of whiskey.

"I'm tired of dealing with these shady, fuckin' bastards. First the Aryans, and now these pricks. I wish we were done with the whole lot of them. Do you think it could be the Canadian brothers?" Vault grumbles.

I turn my back to them and take a deep breath. The groups they've mentioned, I'm not an idiot, I know who they are and that they're dangerous as hell. I can't believe that Bates and the whole club are mixed up with people like that. I shake my head at my dumb self. I knew they weren't selling girl scout cookies to make ends meet. I knew they were criminals; I guess I didn't realize how lawless they really were.

I decide to take a moment to myself, so I walk into the liquor storage just to breathe for a moment. There's too much smoke and noise and people to even think, let alone to wrap my head around what kind of men these really are in this building.

"You know you won't last long. He'll come back to me when you can't satisfy him anymore. You're nothing but a blip," Star says from the doorway. She continues to walk inside and close the door behind her.

"That's why he's come back to me more than once?" I ask, lifting a brow.

"He's got some teenage obsession with you. Once he gets his fill, he'll be gone," she shrugs as she looks down at her nails, seemingly bored. I can tell by the quiver in her voice she's anything but.

"Why do you want him so badly?" I ask, switching tactics.

I want this bitch away from the door so I can bolt. She's coo-coo fucking crazy, and I want away from her—like, now.

"Because I've put in my time, dammit. I want to be an Old Lady. I want to be branded, and Bates is the one who will do it," she announces.

My eyes widen in surprise. She thinks—a clubwhore actually thinks any of those guys out in that room are going to want to marry her. She's been with almost every single one of them. This can't be news to her that she's nothing but a toy to them. She can't be that delusional.

"You know that's never going to happen, right?" I blurt out.

"Bates likes to share. He's the only one who it could be," she screams.

All right. She's completely crazy.

"Bates doesn't share me," I admit stepping to the side, hoping I can get over enough to knock her over and get free of the *President of Crazy Town*.

"He'll get bored of you soon. He has needs,"

I snort, unable to hold back. He has needs, all right, and I know exactly what they are. What they aren't is crazyville over here.

"He could. When he does, I'll make sure he comes right over to you," I say sweetly.

"Don't patronize me," she barks. I'm surprised by her word. It's a big one, and she used it correctly.

I don't know what to say, or how to say it in order to get out of this situation, so we stare at each other. A standoff of sorts. I have the man that she wants. The man that she thinks is going to save her from whatever demons she's got swimming around inside her head. She doesn't know the first thing about Bates. She thinks this is all sex. It's not. Sure, the sex is fantastic, but Bates and I... we're so much more than two bodies meeting. We're two souls meeting—two hearts.

A knock on the door and a grumble of a muffled voice makes me sigh. My savior, whoever that might be. A man mixed up in shady shit, but I'd take the whole room of them over this crazy person standing in front of me.

Star narrows her eyes at me and shakes her head, but I obviously am not good at following directions since I walked out of Scotty's house. I cry out for help. Two seconds later, the bitch goes flying as the door is shoved open. Star cries out as she lands on the floor, and I look up to see Dirty Johnny standing in the doorway. His cigarette is dangling from his lips, as usual, and his thin but obviously muscular body is completely bare from the waist up.

"The fuck is she doin' on the ground?" he asks, scratching the back of his head.

"She was informing me of Bates' eminent departure," I offer with a grin.

"What?" he asks, furrowing his brows.

"Apparently, he's going to leave me and run to her, make her his Old Lady, and share her willingly with whoever," I shrug. Johnny throws his head back in laughter.

"Oh, holy fuck. Bitch, you better gather your fuckin' shit. You're done now," he says. I look at him in surprise, but he just lifts his shoulder and grabs her by her hair, pulling her to her feet. I cringe at his rough handling of her.

"Johnny, baby," she coos. He shakes his head with a grunt.

"I ain't nothin', especially to you. You don't disrespect Old Ladies—you don't confront them, you don't even act like they exist. You are nothing but three wet holes to get off in, a fuckin' cum dumpster. Old Ladies are about a million levels above you. So get your fuckin' shit and get the fuck out of this clubhouse. You, *bitch*, are banned," he growls.

When she makes no motion to move, he guides her by her hair, dragging her through the club to where I know all of the whore's sleep. The music is cut and the brothers stop whatever they're doing to watch.

"What's goin' on here?" Paxton calls out from his place at the bar.

"This nasty bitch had Brentlee cornered in the supply closet and was spewing shit about Bates making her his Old Lady. This ain't the first time she's been mouthy with Brent, and I for one am sick of it. Brent's an Old Lady, nobody treats her with disrespect," he says. I blink in surprise.

Johnny Williams has always been a jokester, a funny guy. Right now, I see him in a completely different light. He's a serious badass, just like the other men that surround me. Although, I'm not scared of them. Sure, they're mixed up with some bad people, but taking a quick glance around the room, they're not bad people. They're rough and scary, but they'd never purposely hurt me, not unless I betrayed them.

"Get that cunt outta here," Drifter says.

The vice president of this club is a quiet man. He's never once said a word to me, just watched from afar. I've never been able to gauge him, and he's probably the only man in this club that truly intimidates me.

"No, call Bates down here. He can deal with her," Drifter suggests. I watch a smile cross Johnny's face that looks almost maniacal.

Star starts shaking her head violently, but Johnny already

has the phone to his ear. Once he finishes telling Bates the story, none of which I can hear, he grins again and nods. I watch in shock as he drags her out of the clubhouse.

"Where's he taking her?" I ask, turning to Drifter, who isn't too far from me.

"The shed, probably," he shrugs. I open my mouth to ask what that is exactly, and what that means. "Don't ask," he says, answering my unasked question. I nod before returning behind the bar.

"You okay, darlin'?" Vault asks, his voice laced with concern.

"Yeah, I guess. I don't know," I let out a breath and he shakes his head. I watch as he reaches over the bar and grabs a clean shot glass, filling it with the tequila that Buck had been pouring from all evening.

"Shoot it, babe," he grunts, pushing it toward me. I take the shot and down it quickly, feeling the burn of the liquor, letting it warm me from the inside out.

"You can't help people that don't wish to help themselves," he offers with a shrug.

"I just, I don't want anybody else to be hurt because of me," I murmur.

"Sometimes, shit happens. Sometimes, people don't heed warnings they're given and make stupid as fuck decisions. And sometimes, people are just fucking assholes."

Vault gives me a sad smile before he leaves the bar, and it makes me wonder exactly what he's talking about. I don't think it has everything to do with this situation, but I understand his meaning. He's right. You can't help people who don't wish to help themselves. I still don't wish any harm to come to anybody at all, but this world isn't full of sunshine and rainbows.

Sniper

I walk into the shed and see Star crying on her knees. Dirty Johnny is staring at her, smoking his cigarette like he's bored. The fucker is totally insane, but he's a good friend, and genuinely a fuckin' badass. He sees me and lifts his chin. I already know what happened, or at least most of it. Now, I have to deal with this cunt.

"What're you gonna do?" Dirty Johnny asks me as I walk up to him.

"Think she'll leave?" I murmur so the bitch won't hear me. Johnny chuckles and shakes his head.

"Fuck no. She has dreams, man. Big fuckin' plans. It's gonna be you and her and whoever you share her with. Forever, baby. The most fucked up perfect family," he laughs.

I hang my head a bit. This girl is clearly not right in the head; and like Kitty all those years ago, she needs to be put down. Though I probably won't torture her like Fury did to Kitty.

As much as I want to walk up behind her and just quickly slit her neck, I can't. I've done it enough times in my life, I should be an old hat at it by this point. I look over to Dirty Johnny. He's glaring at Star.

"You want to deal with her?" I ask. His head pops up and his eyes widen.

"You want her gone?"

"Yeah, but maybe just take her to another club somewhere else," I shrug.

"Can I play first?" he asks, lifting his brows.

"Go for it. I just don't want to see her face ever again," I say before I turn around and leave them alone.

I walk out of the shed's door just as I hear Star's excruciating scream fill the air. He isn't going to make it pretty, but he's going to get the job done, and that's all that should matter. I make my way toward the clubhouse bar and quietly slip inside.

Brentlee is behind the bar, and she turns to me, her eyes hooded. She smiles, and instantly, I know she's drunk. I can't help but laugh a bit at her inebriated state. My cock presses against the seam of my jeans and I know that I want that drunk *tigritsa* naked, *now*.

I walk over to her. Nobody else in the room fuckin' matters. I shrug off a few of my brothers on my quest to get to my woman, and when I reach her, I reach over across the bar and pick her up by her waist, dragging her legs over the bar top. I ignore the way she squeals and giggles, it only makes my cock harder, and me more impatient to get inside of her. As much as I wouldn't mind throwing her down right here, she would regret it in the morning.

"Bates," she sighs once we're safely locked in my room.

"I need your ass, baby," I murmur against her lips before I take her in a rough, hard kiss.

"I—" she pauses and I sigh. She's not ready, not yet. I need to stay patient.

"All right," I murmur as I quickly strip her clothes from her body.

"Okay, just… I'm afraid it'll hurt, like last time," she whimpers.

I shake my head before I take her lips again, slowly and gently until I move my lips to her ear.

"Never gonna hurt my *tigritsa*. Never." I vow.

She doesn't say anything else, her big honey colored eyes wide and a little scared. I run my hands down her sides until I reach her perfect ass and I pick her up, my hands squeezing her round cheeks.

"First, I'm going to make you come with my mouth; then, I'll make you come with my cock in your ass. You're my woman, babe. I'll never hurt you," I say.

She nods, and I smirk. Her words seem to be completely gone. I strip her naked, taking my time as I do. I want to see all of her, every fucking gorgeous inch.

I lie her down on the bed before I grab her hips and wrench them back. Then, I bury my face in her sweet pussy. One swipe of my tongue, and I shiver at the sweet taste of her. I suck on her clit, which causes her to moan and grind against my lips.

I fuck her with my mouth, slipping my tongue deep into her cunt. I shift my focus to her clit, alternating between flicking it and sucking. With a long moan, her thighs quiver and she bucks against my face as she comes, *hard*.

I don't wait for her to come down. Instead, I grab the bottle of lube and a condom from the nightstand. I let the cool liquid drip against her tight ass, which makes her break out in goosebumps. I quickly roll the condom on and coat my dick with lube. I pull her hips up again and press my dick against her tight ass.

"Bates," she warns. I feel her tense against me.

I slide one hand around her hip and start gently playing with her pussy, stroking her clit before I slip two fingers in her swollen cunt. Soon, she's forgotten about her fears and she begins to ride my hand as I slowly start to slide my cock into her tight entrance. She freezes, but I nip her shoulder, then kiss and lick the hurt I caused.

"Relax, baby. Let me in, yeah?" I coax.

Brentlee whimpers, but she forces herself to relax and even pushes against me, accepting me. I hum when I am completely seated inside of her tight ass. My dick feels like it's in a vice, the best feeling vice of my fuckin' life.

"How are you, baby?" I ask as I continue to play with her clit, rubbing and petting her.

"It doesn't hurt," she says, as though she's in awe. I want to chuckle, but it's all too fuckin' good and no laughing matter.

"Let me fill my baby up," I say before I slide two fingers into her cunt and press my palm against her clit.

I slowly fuck her with ease. I don't want to hurt her, ever. I've hurt her enough, and she's been hurt enough in her life. Never again will she feel pain.

Brentlee's moans fill the room as my cock and fingers fill *her*. I'm officially taking ownership of her in all ways. She's one hundred percent mine. I wrap my other hand around her hip, across my name permanently etched into her skin, and I fuck my woman. She gasps and throws her head back with a scream as her body begins to shake beneath me. Her hips slam back into mine, which makes me release a moan of my own.

When I feel her pussy begin to clench around my fingers with her climax, I lose it. I completely lose my shit and I slam into her ass with more force than I intend. *Twice.* Then I come. My entire body shakes with my release as I press my body into hers, surely suffocating her.

"Did I hurt you, *tigritsa*?" I ask, pressing my lips to her shoulder as I slowly pull out of her sweet as heaven ass.

"No," she admits. She then turns her head to look over at me as I rid myself of the condom. I notice the smallest smile playing on her lips, and I can't help but smile back at her.

"I liked it," she admits quietly.

"I'm glad, baby," I murmur, taking my shirt off of the floor and giving it to her to hide her body. I pick her up and carry her to the bathrooms.

I used to not give a fuck that we had communal bathrooms; but right now, I hate that I have to take care of my woman in a shared shower. I don't say a word as I take her into the bathroom and lock the door behind us. I don't bother starting the shower, I'm taking her right home, but I still want to clean her up a little bit. I get a cloth from the cabinet and run it under warm water before I gently wipe between her legs.

"You don't have to," she murmurs.

"Want to, babe. And when we get home, we'll take a bath," I offer. I'm glad I do, because her smile is so bright and gorgeous, it was worth it.

"Let's go home, Bates," she whispers. It goes straight to my dick. She looks down when she feels it twitch against her thigh and shakes her head.

"You really should have worn pants out of your room," she says.

"Yeah, wasn't worried about everyone getting jealous of my giant cock, babe. Was just worried about my woman," I grin. She awards me with a sweet giggle.

It's then that I can't wait to take her home to take care of her, to show her how much I appreciate what she's given me tonight. Another piece of her. I doubt there's much more of her left to give to me. She's already given me so much. I love her for it, too.

chapter thirty-one

Brentlee

I groan, rolling over to find Bates' side of the bed empty and cold. I'm so tired. My ass hurts, too, but I can't keep the smile off of my lips. It didn't hurt, and as he promised, he made me come. It was all so surreal. I was expecting the excruciating pain that Scotty delivered when he took me that way, but instead, Bates' gentility made it pleasurable.

I climb out of bed, still tender, and walk out of the room and into the kitchen. My most favorite sight in the world greets me. Bates and Stella are sitting at the kitchen table eating pancakes. Stella is talking, and her little girl voice fills the room, but I don't hear her words. Instead, I'm focused on Bates—more importantly, the way he's looking at my daughter. His eyes are kind, crinkled around the edges, and he's focused completely on her. It's as if what she's saying are the most important and intriguing words he's ever heard.

I shuffle my feet and Bates must hear me because his head shifts up a bit. He winks at me as Stella continues her story. I shake my head and continue over to the counter to get myself a cup of coffee, hoping it will cure the little bit of hangover I'm sporting.

"Mommy, Bates says we go shop today," she squeals. I look over at them in surprise.

"Get dressed, yeah, babe?" he asks, grinning at me.

"What are we shopping for?" I ask in confusion.

"Girlie shit. Now come on, get dressed," he grumbles. I look at him in confusion before I turn and do as he's demanded.

I dress in pair of dark blue leggings and a loose fitting white tank top. I know Bates wants to go shopping for *girlie shit*, but all I want to do is curl up on the sofa and watch sappy movies all day. My *everything* hurts, and my head is still pounding a little from my slight hangover.

"Ready?" Bates asks, popping his head into our room as I finish throwing my hair into a messy bun on top of my head.

"Yeah," I say before I yawn.

"How are you feeling?" he asks, sliding his hand around my hips.

"Okay. Sore," I admit with a shrug.

"Let's go get *malyshka* some pretty things and then bring you home to rest, yeah?"

"Yeah," I sigh, reaching up to cup his cheek. Running my thumb along his bottom lip, my eyes are completely focused on the path it makes.

"Come on, or I'm gonna fuck you right now," he grunts. It makes me laugh.

Bates snags my hand and pulls me behind him before he bends down and picks up Stella with his other arm. He doesn't say a word as he walks us to his pickup and shuffles us inside before he starts the engine and we take off in silence.

"Where are we going?" I ask.

He doesn't answer.

He pretends not to hear a word I'm saying. It's frustrating as hell, but also cute, in a gruff, badass kind of way. He obviously wants to do something for us as a surprise.

I recognize the road as we begin driving to the next town over. I don't say a word to Stella, now that I know what city we're going to, but I still don't know the reason why. I sigh and look over at Bates, so freaking happy right now. We're good, so good. I don't know if there's something terrible lurking in the shadows, but I don't care anymore. We will confront it together, and jump whatever hurdles are thrown in front of us.

I look at him in surprise when we pull into a car dealership—a *Ford* dealership, to be precise. I look over to him as he puts his pickup in park and jumps out. Quickly, and confused, Stella and I follow right behind him.

Bates shakes a man's hand and I watch as the man hands him a set of keys. He looks at me and winks as he lifts his chin and we follow him.

"Mommy, wha happening?" Stella asks, tugging on my arm.

"I don't know, sweet girl," I admit truthfully.

Bates stops at a huge black pick-up truck. It's lifted with gigantic tires, and its quite possibly the most massive thing I've ever seen.

"What the heck is happening here?" I ask, trying to keep my words PG for Stella's sake.

"Bought a new truck," he shrugs. I stare at him slack jawed.

"Bates," I hiss, knowing how expensive these pickups are.

"Got money, baby, got plenty of money," he assures me, already sensing my worry.

"How?" I ask.

"Don't matter. Just know I can take care of my girls, and that means getting a better truck for them. Also, gonna need to get you your own ride soon, too," he murmurs, wrapping his hand around my waist and pulling me into his chest. His head dips down and he places a kiss on my lips.

"You're too much," I sigh when he lifts his head.

"Ain't nothin' too much for my girls. Now let's finish this shit," he grunts as he helps us into his new pickup. It even smells new, like leather, and a little like Bates.

Stella asks a million and ten questions about the pickup, but all I can do is stare out the window. I hope that he isn't trying to break himself to live up to the monetary things that Scotty provided for us. I didn't care about them back then, and I don't care about them now.

I won't lie and say that the perfect, shiny life was exciting, but when I discovered the strings that came attached with it, I didn't want it anymore. I love Bates' little country house, his old pickup truck, and his bike.

I love him the way that he is.

I don't need shit to make me happy.

We stop at a Mexican restaurant for lunch, and I can't get the uneasy thoughts out of my head. Bates notices and he wraps his arm around me, nudging me slightly.

"What's up, babe?" he asks nonchalantly.

"Did you buy the truck because of Scotty?" I blurt out, then cringe at my words.

"The fuck does that mean?" he barks harshly, making Stella jump a bit. His eyes fly over to her sitting across from us and he grins, waiting for her to smile back. When she does, he focuses back on me.

"I don't want you to think you have to buy this stuff, spend money to compete with him. I like you and your truck and the house just the way it is," I explain. He throws his head back laughing. I'm momentarily mesmerized by the beauty of his deep rich laugh, but he stops and looks at me, completely serious.

"Babe, I could give a fuck what Scotty had. I bought the truck 'cause I needed it. Mine was old as hell and wasn't going to make it through the winter without some major work. Been needing the upgrade; but having you and Stella with me now, I needed it a bit sooner. Which is fine. Had my eye on that truck for a while now. Knew what I wanted.

"As far as the house goes, I'm not leaving it anytime soon. You can fix it up however you like, but I like the house and the land it sits on. I'm not rich, but, baby, I ain't scrapin' by either. We can have some nicer things, even if you want to quit and stay home, doesn't matter to me. We'll be just fine. I pull in plenty of cash regularly," he informs me. I just stare at him, shocked, and kind of impressed.

"Okay," I nod.

"You know it's never been a competition with him, right? I love you because I've always loved you. I want you because you're mine, and I'll provide for you the best I can. I can't give you what he could, but I can give you everything he couldn't," he murmurs. My eyes water.

Bates can give me everything Scotty couldn't, and more. I love him for that—every rough, ragged, raw edge of him. He's mine and I'm his, and this life—it's going to be perfect for us.

Sniper

After lunch, I take Brentlee to the mall. No way in fuck do I want to go to the mall, but they have one store I need to dip inside of without her noticing. I figure she'll get sidetracked with Stella in one of those clothes stores they always talk about when the mail comes. Some bullshit about *Janie and Jack*—I have no fuckin' idea.

When Stella see's the store, she begs to go inside, and I know it's my cue to get to where I need to be. I tell them I'm going to grab a soda from the food court and hightail it to the jewelry store.

I found what I wanted to get Brentlee online and cleared it with LeeLee before I made the trip here. I had the store hold it for me, and now I get to see it in person.

"How can I help you?" a man asks from behind the counter.

"Had a ring on hold for Bates Lukin," I announce as I walk up to the counter.

His eyes scan me, slowly, and he huffs before he walks through the door leading to the back of the store. I wait a few moments and he returns with a box in his hand. I wait for him to open the little velvety book and then take the ring out.

It's a huge, round solitaire diamond. Simple, yet beautiful. It's Brentlee. Classically stunning. The asshole prattles about clarity and quality, but I ignore him, too invested in imagining Brentlee wearing nothing but this fuckin' ring and a smile.

I know I'm rushing shit, but I don't care. I've been in love with this girl since I was a punk ass kid, and that shit ain't never changing.

"Now what we can do to dress up the diamond is accompany it with a ring guard," he suggests and pulls out a ring with a missing center but diamonds on each side of it in a row. I watch as he places the ring I've picked in the center and it makes my mouth drop at a bit.

It's blinged out and epic.

"Wrap it up," I grunt.

"Um, sir, maybe you should look at some of the less expensive sets just like this one," he gently suggests. It greatly pisses me off.

"*Wrap.It.Up*," I grind out between my clenched teeth.

"Sir, I don't think you understand. This set right here will be forty thousand dollars." He almost smirks and it pisses me off. He could say it was a hundred grand at this point and I'd buy it just to prove a point.

"Wrap the fuckin' thing up, man," I grunt.

"Fine," he mumbles.

I should have pulled cash out and shoved it in his face, but my bank card will have to suffice. I hand the piece of plastic over to the dickface and wait for him to run the card. To his surprise, it clears. *Of course it does*. I'm not some poor bastard off of the streets.

I take the little velvet box and shove it into my jeans pocket, ignoring the stupid as fuck tiny little bag he tries to shove at me. I grab the receipt and crumple it up to stick in my back pocket. Without a word, I turn around and leave him standing behind the counter, his mouth hanging wide open.

When I find the girls, Brentlee has about fifteen things in her hand, but she's looking around in worry, confusion, and maybe apprehension.

"That what you're buying?" I ask as I walk up behind her and wrap my hands around her stomach.

"No, it's all way too expensive. These are the things she wants, but I'm going to let her pick two items. She doesn't really need them."

"You two hardly have any clothes, babe. She needs it. We'll get it for her," I announce.

"Bates, this stuff is insanely priced. We can go somewhere a lot cheaper and get a hell of a lot more," she murmurs.

"She wants it, she can have it," I say.

"You're going to spoil her. She can have two items and then we'll go somewhere more reasonably priced if you want to get her more. She's three, baby, I don't want to spend thousands of dollars on her clothes," Brentlee says. I widen my eyes in surprise before I take something off the top of her pile.

I hold it up, a little white dress with pink bows on the shoulders. It's cute as hell, but when I look at the price tag, I burst out laughing. *Ninety fuckin' bucks.*

"This shit is insane," I say between my outburst.

"I know. She'd get it dirty in about two seconds, and then it'd be ruined," Brentlee says, looking at the dress before shaking her head.

"You want to get this for her, I'll buy it, babe," I murmur.

Brentlee shakes her head and smiles up at me before she sets the pile down on an empty table. I watch as she takes

Stella's hand and then walks for the entrance without looking back. I follow, trying to keep up. Once we are outside, she turns to face me.

"That store, that white dress that she can't get dirty, that is our old life, not our new one. We live in the country now. We're happy and we smile and Stella plays in the dirt and rides bikes. She needs clothes that represent that. *Fuck* that place," she practically shouts. I watch as her chest heaves.

"Okay, shit that represents us. *Walmart?*" I ask. I then watch as her nose wrinkles, which makes me laugh, and then the three of us begin to laugh—together.

We don't go to Walmart. She takes me to some fuckin' place called the *Gap*, then to about ten other stores. By the end, I'm regretting this little trip. But when I look over at my girls, fast asleep in my new ride, I can't help but feel my heart swell at the sight of their sleepy, slight smiles. They had fun, and that's all that matters.

I can't wait to give Brent the ring in my pocket. But I'm selfish and a dick. I'll want to fuck her after I do, and she's too sore tonight for that. So the ring will wait another day. But today, my girls had a good day, a *fun* day, and that's all I give a shit about.

chapter thirty-two

Brentlee

I slide my brand new skinny jeans up my legs and grin when I see myself in the mirror. *Legs for days.* They look long and lean, Bates' favorite part of my body, and these jeans make them look fantastic. I pull on a tight halter top and slide my feet into the red high heels that are my absolute favorite. Tonight I'm working. After spending three days with Bates and Stella, we need to get back to our work week.

I won't lie. As I was getting ready this evening, I thought that maybe, just maybe, I might like to be a stay-at-home mother again. But as enticing as that sounds, I also like to interact with adults, even nasty biker men. And I like knowing I have my own income. I don't want to be completely beholden to anybody ever again.

"Babe, we gotta head out," Bates shouts. I quickly grab my purse and run out of the bedroom.

Tammy is sitting on the floor, playing Barbie's with Stella, and Bates is standing by the front door, looking down at his phone. When he looks up, I watch as his eyes drag over my body, and he grins when they meet mine.

I quickly say my goodbyes to both Stella and Tammy and hurry after him out of the door. He's already straddling his bike when I close the front door behind me, so I rush to climb on behind him. We take off down the road and I wonder what he seems to be in such a hurry for. He doesn't usually drive this fast with me on the back. I hold on tighter than normal, and when we arrive at the clubhouse, I notice that the parking area is completely full of bikes.

"What's going on?" I ask, looking around at all of the bikes.

"Fury's dad is here. The original charter," he grunts. I tug on Bates' hand and make him stop walking.

"What does that mean?" I ask, looking up at him.

"Means we're gonna party tonight, probably end up at the *Devils* later on. Means I'm gonna have church tomorrow. It also means you make sure all those fuckers can see your ink," he growls, wrapping his hand around my hip.

"You aren't going into *Devils*?" I ask as I slide my hands up his chest and link them around the back of his neck.

"Candy's in charge until I get there. I'll be here, watching you," he murmurs, dipping his head down to place a gentle kiss on my lips. He releases me, but keeps one hand at the small of my back.

When we walk into the clubhouse, its wilder than I've

ever seen it before in my life. There are men and women everywhere. The women are either topless or barely dressed, and the men are in all states of action. Some are just sitting around talking, some are playing pool, smoking, and drinking, and some are actually fucking girls. It's even crazier than the patch-in party I attended.

Bates stops to talk to someone, but I need to get behind the bar. I have to help out the prospect who looks like he's two seconds away from crying as he quickly hands beers out to men. I leave Bates and make my way toward the crowd of people.

I feel a hand wrap around my upper arm and it halts my mission to the bar. I turn around and my eyes widen at the man in front of me. He looks exactly like Fury, except a few years older. He's a freaking hot as hell silver fox.

"Where are you in a hurry to, darlin'?" he asks, his voice smooth and slightly slurred.

"Behind the bar… to work," I offer shakily.

"You should stay with me," he murmurs, his thumb slightly caressing my arm and his eyes fixated on mine.

"MadDog, wanna take your hand off my Old Lady," Bates' deep voice growls from behind me. I jump as MadDog lets his hand fall from mine.

"Your *what*?" he asks with a chuckle.

Bates roughly shifts me so that my tattoo is in view. MadDog's eyes widen in surprise before he looks up at me and narrows his eyes.

"You're Kentlee's sister," he announces. I nod. "Fucking hell. Good for you, brother. And how the hell did I not notice that shit the last time I saw you?"

"We were a little busy, with all that drama," Bates says

with a smirk.

MadDog slaps Bates on the shoulder with a smile, and Bates returns the gesture, making me breathe a sigh of relief. I go to my toes and whisper to Bates that I need to get behind the bar, and his answer is a wink and a pat on my ass, whatever that means. I ignore him and hurry behind the bar, thankful for no new altercations.

I spend the evening slinging beer and shots. I'm so thankful nobody wants anything mixed, because my bartending experience is limited to only beer and shots.

The party is wild, so insane that I can't believe my sister is even here. But she is. I noticed her the second she walked inside. Now she's perched on Fury's lap as he talks to his father, who has a topless skank perched on his own lap.

When I get a minute to breathe, my eyes scan the room for Bates. I don't see him anywhere. Not playing pool, not at any of the tables, and I even scan the sofas where people are screwing and don't see him. My heart starts beating against my ribcage. I imagine him in his room with some clubwhore, and my head spins.

"Looking for me," a rough voice whispers from behind me. I spin around to see him grinning at me.

"Where were you?" I ask, my curiosity always getting the best of me.

"Outside hangin' out with Torch," he shrugs.

"What was Paxton doing outside?"

"Why do you give a fuck about Paxton?" he growls. I roll my eyes at his misplaced anger and obvious jealousy.

I don't even bother answering him, I just wait. I can tell by the way his lids are drooped, he's probably both high and drunk. No way am I going to get into it with him, he won't be reasonable.

"He was having a hard night. He said it's the anniversary of something. He didn't want to really talk about it," he shrugs.

"Paxton was in the military too, right? Maybe something happened with that?" I offer. Bates just shrugs.

"I don't think so; I think it's more. I think it's a woman. You bitches are always tying us up in knots," he grunts before he wraps his arm around my waist and pulls me into his chest. I giggle when he nuzzles my neck and his beard tickles my skin.

"Baby," I murmur. I feel his lips smile against my neck before he nips my skin and lifts away from me.

"Everyone's headed to *Devils*, but honest to fuck babe, I just wanna go home," he slurs, his eyes focused on me. Even bloodshot, they're beautiful.

"We can't take your bike," I say.

"No shit. Kent's driving us home before they head that way themselves. Old married people don't need to go to the club after hours," he states. It makes me laugh.

"I'm not old," I offer with a wink. He smacks my ass.

"You're my *Old* Lady, so there's that," he grins. I roll my eyes.

I'm exhausted.

Completely exhausted.

I've honestly seen enough people going at it tonight to last me a lifetime. I really don't want to see more, and I know that is exactly what's going to happen. I can have my own fuck-fest with Bates at home, I don't need to see everybody else going at it any more than I already have.

"Take me home, and fuck your Old Lady," I grin up at

him and he smirks before his top teeth sink into his lower lip, as if he's really thinking hard about us fucking.

I hope he is.

I'm tired, but I still want him. All of him. It's been a few days, and I feel like I might actually combust.

Once Fury drops us off and we thank Tammy for all of her help and hard work, I throw myself at Bates. I jump into his arms and wrap my legs around his waist. His hands wrap around my ass as he carries me into our room. I untangle myself from his body, but he doesn't undress me. Instead, he peppers my lips with kisses before he pulls away.

"Let's take a shower, yeah?" he suggests.

I know I smell, I have to, I've been sweating my ass off all night. A shower sounds awesome.

I strip my clothes, leaving them to liter the floor on my way to the shower. Bates is following me. I hear the heavy clink of his belt, the sound of his boots, and his heavy jeans hitting the floor. By the time we're both in the bathroom, we're both completely nude.

Bates starts the water and I watch his muscles work, every single move he makes is with ease as his massive muscles bunch. I want to run my fingers over his body, his warm skin. I want him to fill me, and make me smile like only he can.

"Come on," he murmurs. I follow him into the warm shower.

Quickly, he washes me—my breasts, my stomach and between my thighs. I hear the soap fall, but his fingers stay between my legs, sliding through my folds. Once all of the soap is washed away, he gently slides two fingers inside of me while his head dips and captures my nipple with his lips, gently sucking me into his mouth.

"Bates," I sigh as I arch my back, giving him more access to my breast as I shift my hips for more friction between my legs.

He doesn't say a word as he pulls away from my body and picks me up by my waist, pressing my back against the warm tile of the shower. His cock fills me with one quick thrust. I whimper as I dig my nails into his shoulders. Bates' tongue fills my mouth and he mimics the thrust of his hips with his kiss. He's ruthless, my back surely bruising as he slams in and out of me—but it feels fantastic. The warm water washing over us, and Bates' warm body pressed against mine as he takes me.

"I love you, *tigritsa*," he grunts between kisses.

I can feel myself fall over the edge, my climax full force, like a freight train as I cry out into his mouth. He continues to fuck me through my orgasm, and when he finally comes, it's with a roar after he wrenches his lips from mine.

He looks down at me and his eyes shift around slightly before he releases me. I don't know what it means, but I don't ask him. There's something he's waging inside of him. I wish I knew, but I want him to tell me when he's ready. It's as if I can actually see a shift happen in him.

We don't say another word as we dry off and head to bed. I'm sliding one of his black t-shirts over my naked body when there is a pounding on our front door. Bates is up and pulling his jeans on before I can finish wrenching the shirt over myself.

"What the fuck is up with people pounding on my fuckin' door?" he mumbles as I follow him to the door.

I watch as he looks through the peephole and his whole body tightens with what I can only guess is anxiety, worry, or both.

"Pop, to what do I owe this late night visit?" Bates asks as he wrenches the door open.

Sniper

My old man stares back at me and he looks like shit. He looks old and weathered and even a little frail. Nothing like the man who tormented me as a boy and teenager. I want to laugh in his face, but I'm too fuckin' pissed off he's even here to enjoy the Karma. He looks behind me and widens his eyes in surprise.

"See you're still with the little Johnson slut," he slurs.

"Go back to bed, baby," I murmur to Brent, not taking my eyes off of the bastard.

I feel her hands fist in the waistband of my pants, and I know she ain't gonna listen to me. I should be mad, but I'm not. Brentlee knows far too much about this bastard, yet she doesn't know half of what he's really like.

"What is it you want?" I ask again, my limited patience pretty much null and void at this point.

"Your old man's sick. I need some money," he murmurs. He even adds a convincing cough at the end.

"I haven't seen you in over ten years, now you want money?" I ask before I bark out a laugh.

"I'm dyin'," he says. I suppose I should feel sorry for him, but I don't.

The sick son of a bitch tortured his family, us, our entire lives. Both my sister and I ran away just to get away from him.

Mary-Anne's still gone; she'll never come back, and I don't fuckin' *want* her to.

"Get off my property," I demand. "You're a drunk and an abuser."

"I'm the only dad you have, *syn*," he says.

It pisses me off. Calling me *son* in Russian. Pretending I'm anything but a way to get more cash for booze.

"I'm not your fuckin' *syn*. Get the fuck off my property or I'll kill you myself," I grind out. He takes a step back.

I watch as he goes over to his piece of shit car and flips me off. He calls me a son-of-a-bitch and I laugh. I'm his fuckin' kid, and he's a little bitch, so if the shoe fits…

"Are you okay?" Brentlee asks as soon as he drives off. I close the door, securing the lock.

"I'm fine," I grunt as I walk toward our room.

I strip out of my jeans, leaving them in the middle of the floor before I slide between the sheets. Brentlee follows and even discards my shirt she had been wearing.

"What're you doin'?" I ask as she crawls up my legs. She doesn't answer me. Instead, she takes my cock in her mouth.

I lift my hand and slide it through the side of her hair, gripping it with the intention of pulling her off of me; but when she sucks hard, I can't. Instead, I thrust my hips up as my cock hardens in her mouth. She hums and I close my eyes, enjoying the vibration. When I feel like I'm close, I yank at her hair and pull her from me.

"I want to make you come," she pouts. It makes me laugh.

"You will, *tigritsa*, calm," I grin. "Hands and knees," I order. I watch as her body shivers before she turns over and presents herself to me—*hands and knees.*

"I hope that pussy's wet," I grunt before I slam inside of

her.

Zero warning.

I fully enjoy the gasp and yelp that escapes her mouth at my sudden entrance. Her body is mine. Her pussy is mine, and I feel it adjust to my cock perfectly. I wrap one of my hands around her throat while the other I wrap around her shoulder.

"Make yourself come while I fuck you," I say before I pull out and slam back inside of her heat.

I fuck her, *mercilessly*.

I take out my frustrations about my father on her pussy. I lose the ability to speak, my animalistic grunts filling the air as my cock fills her. My fingers tighten around her throat and her shoulder, surely bruising her, but I don't give a fuck.

I need this. I need her body to sooth my beast, and I'm not soothed, not yet.

I feel my balls slapping her fingers as she works her clit. Closing my eyes, I feel. I don't think—*I just feel*. I feel her pussy swollen around my cock, hugging me tightly. *My pussy*. No man will ever see it, smell it, or touch it again. *It's all mine*. She tightens around me as she cries out hoarsely with her release, but I'm not done. I don't know if I will be anytime soon.

When her fingers stop touching her clit, I remove my hand from her shoulder and slap her ass.

"Make yourself come again," I grind out through gritted teeth.

"I can't," she says shakily.

"Do it, or I'll do it for you," I warn.

The arm holding her body up collapses, but I don't stop ruthlessly fucking her. I just wrench her hips up and continue to take her. She's wet and warm, so fucking good. I never want to leave. I feel her fingers go back to her clit, and she works herself up again.

When she screams, I can tell there's a little agony mixed into her pleasure, and I can't help but smile. I feel like a sick fuck for it, but I am a sick fuck. Or I can be, at times. She'll learn. I slap her ass again and command her to keep going.

My cock is in no hurry to come.

I've fucked her already tonight, I've been drinking, and I'm good and pissed at my dad. It could take a while to get me off. While I wait, I want her to be boneless from her own orgasms.

"Bates," her muffled screams fill the air. Her face is buried into the bed, and I can't help but chuckle as I slide two fingers in her sweet, little asshole.

"This is going to be a big one when you finally come again, baby," I mutter.

"No more," she whimpers.

"Yes, baby, more. Give me more," I murmur. I feel a sob escape her throat. The vibrations move against my hand.

I fuck her pussy with my cock, and her ass with my fingers. When she finally does come, it's so fucking violent that I feel sorry for her. She squeezes me so tightly; it forces my own climax. I gently remove my fingers and my dick from her, not wanting to cause her any real pain. Her body has to be completely sore, tender, and an entire surface of nerves.

"I love you, my *tigritsa*," I whisper lying next to her, looking at her but not touching her.

I watch as her eyes open. Instead of the anger and hate I thought I might see shining from them, I see nothing but love.

"You needed that?" she asks, not one ounce of anger in

her voice.

"I did. I fuckin' did," I admit, feeling like an asshole.

"I'm glad I could give that to you then, baby," she whispers as her hand lifts to cup my cheek. I don't let her. I take her wrist and press my lips to her palm instead.

"You give me everything I need, babe. I never thought it was possible, that it could be possible, but you do, baby. You give me fuckin' everything," I rasp as a tear slides from her eye, down her cheek.

I don't let her speak again. Instead, I kiss her. I show her just how much she means to me with a long, deep kiss. Then, I pick her up, wrap her in my arms, and I hold her until she falls asleep. I don't sleep, though.

I think about that wedding ring I want to slide on her finger. The babies I want to plant in her belly. Then, I think about how happy she's made me. I knew I wanted her. When I had the chance again, I knew I was going to take it, but I honestly didn't know if she would ever make me happy in every aspect of my life, especially in the bedroom. She's exceeded my expectations; or maybe she's just my match and I don't need anything *but* her.

Whatever it is, she's enough.

She's *more* than enough.

I love her.

Every single part of her.

chapter thirty-three

Brentlee

It's been two weeks since Bates' father came by in the middle of the night and shook Bates up. He's been seemingly good, but I can tell something is bothering him. Something just isn't quite right.

Kentlee breezes through the front door, Ellie on her hip and Bear at her feet. He runs toward Stella's room, where he knows she's setting up toys for their playdate. I smile at my sister and take Ellie from her. She's already beginning to move too much, wanting to run around, instead of crawl, so I want to take my baby cuddles while I can.

Kentlee wordlessly walks over to the coffee machine and makes herself a cup. I take Ellie into the living room and sit down on the brand new sofa I had delivered the day before. It's a gorgeous dove grey, microfiber and I can only hope that Bates and Stella can keep it somewhat clean for a while.

"This is pretty," Kentlee murmurs as she sits down on the end.

"What's up with you?" I ask, noticing how distracted and tired she looks.

"I'm pregnant," she blurts out. My eyes widen. Then I look from Ellie, to her in surprise, as she wiggles down from my lap and hurries toward the other kids in Stella's room. We both watch her in silence until she's made it inside with her big brother and cousin.

"Don't you drink that coffee, Kent," I order. She laughs.

"It's tea, and I'm having at least one hot tea a day for my own sanity," she chuckles.

"I'm so happy for you," I say, trying to keep my excitement to a minimum. But I'm going to be an aunt again, and that is grounds for squealing. Nevertheless, I know how much Kent hates that.

"If you say the word *squee*, I'll slap you," she grunts. I don't hold in my laughter as I almost double over.

"Now, what's bothering *you*? Because I can tell it's something," she says, taking a sip of her tea.

"Something's wrong with Bates. He's acting funny," I say. Then I explain when it all started.

"Who knows? You know how men are." She shrugs as if it's no big deal.

"Maybe he thinks I want to get married or something," I say, chewing on my bottom lip. I don't know where the thought came from, but it's been brewing.

Marriage.

It's like a dirty word to me. I don't know that I ever want to do it again.

"And that would be bad because…"

"Scotty Corbin, need I say more? I'm happy just being Bates' Old Lady. I don't think I ever want to be another man's wife ever again." I scrunch up my nose, but Kentlee shakes her head in obvious disagreement.

"Bates is nothing like Scotty, absolutely nothing like him. And if you ever compare him to Scotty, he will flip his shit. Don't ever say anything like that again if he's around," she says. I nod.

I've accidently said similar things and, yeah, Bates loses his shit.

"And Bates loves you. He's going to propose eventually. If you don't want to marry him, be prepared to lose him. No man will stay with a woman who rejects him like that."

"Even if I tell him I don't want to marry *anybody*?" I ask. Kentlee looks at me like I'm certifiably insane before she speaks.

"*Pride*. You crush that man's pride, and your relationship won't survive. Besides, would being Bates' wife be such a hardship? You're already living together, his name is on your skin, your name is on his. In the eyes of the club, that means you're man and wife. Maybe he just wants to give you his last name, too? Do you know he still won't call you Brentlee Corbin? He hates that you have that man's last name. If for nothing else, maybe you should just do it to appease his delicately, fragile ego," she suggests before she giggles.

I think about Kentlee's words. As opposed to marriage as I have been since my horrendous life with Scotty, I can understand what she means. I hate having the Corbin last name as well. I don't want to be associated with Scotty or his family anymore. They're disgusting people.

Would being Bates' wife be so bad?

I love him, and he loves me. He also loves Stella and treats her as if she is his own daughter. I wouldn't ever want to lose him. If something that minimal could cause tension between us, I don't think it's really worth it.

Kentlee and I spend the morning and afternoon together. The kids play and she rests, something I don't think she's been doing a lot of. I think she's been stressing out about baby number three, as I would imagine I would be too if I had a six month old at home. Once they leave, I put Stella down for a nap and clean up before it's time to make dinner.

I'm making dinner when I hear the door open and close. A few minutes later, strong arms wrap around my waist. Bates' lips touch my neck as I stir the ground turkey in the pan, browning it for the enchiladas I'm going to make for us tonight.

"How was your day, *tigritsa*?" he murmurs against my neck.

"Kentlee came over and we hung out all morning," I say softly.

"Yeah, how's your sister?" he asks as he steps back from me and walks over to the fridge for a beer.

"Pregnant," I shrug as Bates chokes on his drink. I turn around and he's looking at me in surprise.

"What?" he asks.

"She's pregnant again," I say, looking at him in question. Why he's surprised, I don't know. Fury is always all over my sister.

"That fucker's too old to have more kids." He scrunches

his nose and I laugh.

"But Kent isn't," I point out. He nods.

"He's gonna be like eighty when those kids graduate high school," he says. I shake my head and shrug. "I'm totally going to fuck with him on this one."

"Be nice to Fury," I chide.

"I will, I will," he murmurs. I don't believe him, especially since he's smirking.

We spend the evening together with Stella, our perfect little family. The more I look at him, the more I watch how sweet he is with my daughter, the more I want to be his wife. I want more of this; I want it forever. I don't need it immediately, but now I want it. I never thought I did—but this feels so right. So very right.

I want a lifetime of this.

A lifetime of being held in Bates' arms. I never want him to let me go. I never want his kisses or soft touches to stop. He fills every part of me, emotionally and physically. There is no other man for me but this one who holds me every night.

Sniper

Brentlee is looking at me—*differently*. The apprehension that used to always stay deep in her gaze is gone. She seems lighter, the lightest I've noticed since we were kids. She's at peace. I'm not sure what has shifted, but I can tell she's completely—happy.

I have thought here and there that she was happy, but she was just happy for a moment. Now she's content.

It makes me smile.

I make her feel that way, and it makes me feel invincible.

I read Stella a story and tuck the little *malyshka* in bed. Her pretty blue eyes close, and her blonde curls spread out along the pillow of her *Elsa* sheets. The little princess holds a special place in my heart that nobody could ever fill or replace. It is solely hers. I leave her in dreamland and go in search of her mama.

When I walk into the bedroom, Brentlee is waiting for me, in the middle of the bed, completely naked, the way she knows I like her to be. My cock hardens at the sight of her, gorgeous and laid out, all for me. I want her, but not just as my Old Lady. *I want her as my wife.* I want my ring sparkling on her finger, fuckin' blinding me. I want her last name to be mine, because that's what she is—*mine*.

I turn from her and walk over to my dresser, pulling the little velvet box out. *It's time.* I open it, keeping my back to her, and take the rings from the box. I should just give her the one, the solitaire engagement ring, but I want her to have it all—*now*.

I'm not a man that waits.

I want to give her everything, everything I can, and immediately.

I strip my clothes, keeping the expensive diamonds in my palm before I crawl up her body. Her legs automatically spread to accept my hips between them. She's mine in almost every way. Now I need her to be legally mine, too. I want Stella to be my daughter in name as well. Corbin, even in death, doesn't deserve to have his name live on through that gorgeous little creature.

Keeping the diamonds in my fist, I slide my fingers

through her wet folds and she shudders beneath me, her whole body breaking out in a shiver.

I kiss her.

Sliding my tongue through her lips as I slide my fingers through her wet center.

I love her.

She's raw and beautiful and all mine.

Made just for me.

I pull my fingers from her body as I pull away from her lips. Then, without uttering a word I slide the rings on her finger before I guide my cock into her waiting entrance.

"Bates," she gasps looking down at her hand, ignoring the fact that I'm inside of her. I almost laugh.

"Marry me, my *tigritsa*," I murmur as I pullout and then thrust back inside of her welcoming heat.

"Bates," she whispers as she wraps her hands around my cheeks.

I rest my forehead against hers, closing my eyes as I continue to make love to her. I'm not fucking her or having sex with her. No, right now, I'm *making love* to my woman.

"I love you so much, baby," I murmur as I continue to take her body, slow and gentle.

"I love you, too, so very much. Yes. *Yes*, I'll be your wife," she cries out as she lifts her hips to meet my thrusts.

I smile wide, happy as I make love to my fiancé.

The woman should have always been mine.

I made a mistake that changed the course of our lives when we were just teenagers. Never again. I'll never lose her again. I won't even chance it. This road, it's been fuckin' rough to get to where we are, but I wouldn't change a fucking thing about it. Not now. Not now that she's agreed to be my wife.

Not just my Old Lady, not just my woman, but my wife.

When I come, I do it looking into her gorgeous, honey colored eyes, and she soon follows behind me, her climax making her entire body shake. I will never get tired of this, never get tired of her. She's mine, one hundred percent my life. Without her, I'm a lost soul. I've proven that shit. I never want to be that man again. I will forever be the man she needs me to be—the man that makes her happy, and the man she can trust.

I love her.

My tigritsa.

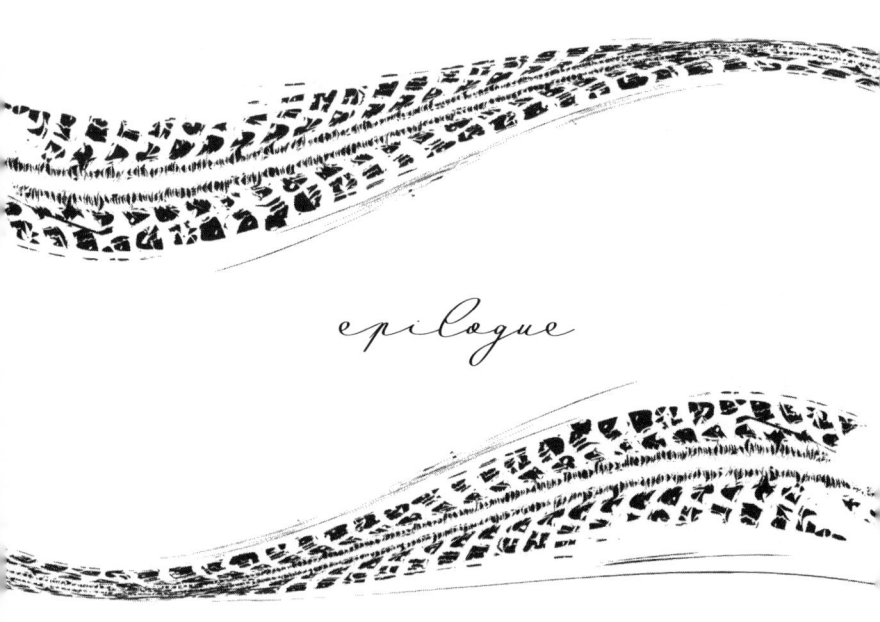

epilogue

Seven Months Later

Brentlee

"It's time." The words come out in a panic. I look over to Kentlee, whose face has turned bright red, and she looks like she's going to explode.

"Oh, shit," I murmur before I grab my phone and dial Fury's number.

Nobody answers, of course. They're all in church, and nobody has their damn phones on. I gather the kids and load them up into Kentlee's SUV before I help her into the car. She screams, holding her gigantic belly with one hand, the nails of her other digging into my arm.

"Shit," I curse.

She ignores me. I continue to re-dial Bates and Fury, over and over, as I drive like a bat out of hell to the hospital. When neither of them answer, I give up and call Tammy.

"What's going on, honey? I haven't heard from you in a while," she says.

Tammy hasn't heard from me in a few weeks. I haven't needed her. Bates and I eloped the weekend after he proposed. We ran off to Vegas and had a quick, *quiet* ceremony, just the two of us. Kent watched Stella. She and Fury were the only ones who knew of our nuptials. We had a huge party at the club the weekend after, but the private ceremony, it was perfect and exactly how I had always envisioned marrying Bates.

When we came home, Bates informed me I wasn't going to be working anymore. It was the control I had feared would happen had I ever married again. After we talked, I discovered his caveman tantrum was really because he wanted to have a baby with me. He didn't want me tending bar around all the booze, sex, and smoke while we were trying or while I was pregnant.

I understood his rational, but I still gave him plenty of shit about it.

We fought and made up and I quit.

Two months later, I found out I was pregnant. I'm now five months pregnant with our first child together. We discovered just this week it's a girl. I thought he would be disappointed, but to my surprise, he was excited.

Another little girl to add to our house. Another *malyshka*. He told me he was so excited to have another princess to spoil, and maybe the next one would be a boy, but maybe not.

He didn't care. It didn't matter to him either way. I smile just thinking about his excitement.

"Brentlee," Tammy says, breaking me from my reminiscing.

"Kentlee is in labor. I can't get ahold of the men, we have all the kids," I say as I frantically drive toward the hospital. Kentlee is turning about fifty shades of red, and she looks pretty damn terrifying.

"I'll meet you there and take the kids back to my house," she says before she hangs up the phone.

Tammy is the best. I don't know how Kent found her, but I never want her to leave us. I wouldn't survive without her.

When I pull up to the hospital, I park in the emergency parking and jog inside as fast as I can, yelling that my sister is in labor. She was panting and breathing funny. I know she has to be close, and she's scheduled to have a C-section in a few days. She's not supposed to have him naturally.

Luckily, a nurse takes me seriously and she and some other staff follow me outside. They take my sister with them in a wheelchair, and my stomach turns at the blood that's on the leather seat of the SUV. My eyes water and my mind goes over a million different scenarios. Only one thing consumes my thoughts though—fear.

I clean the seat as best as I can and get the kids out of the SUV just in time for Tammy to come barreling around the corner like a bat outta hell. We don't exchange two words to each other as I transfer all the kids' things to her car. When she wraps me in a hug, I try my hardest to stay strong. I'm so scared.

"Go be with Kent," she says softly. I nod.

"Thank you," I say before I hurry toward the hospital. I

dial Fury's phone again and, thank Jesus, he picks up.

"The fuck?" he barks into the phone.

"Kentlee's in the hospital," I cry as I run.

"*What?*" he breathes.

"She went into labor, you need to get down here, now. Tammy has all the kids," I say.

The phone call ends. Seconds later, my phone rings, and it's Bates.

"Baby, what's happening?" he says, sounding out of breath.

I explain the situation to him as I ride the elevator to the floor where they have my sister. He curses and assures me they'll be here to join me as soon as possible.

When I make it to the floor where my sister is, the nurse tells me I can go inside, but they're prepping her for surgery. I run into her room and she's high as hell. She smiles lazily at me and reaches for my hand.

"What's happening?" I ask.

"He's breech. Of course he is. He's Pierce's." She chuckles before she pulls me down to her level and whispers, "I'm so high, I can't even feel my brain," she giggles.

Luckily, Fury bursts into the room at that exact moment. When he falls to his knees at her bedside, I take that as my cue to leave. No way do I want to see that big ass scary man breakdown. I walk out and find Bates sitting in one of those uncomfortable waiting chairs.

"Hey, baby, how is she?" he asks wrapping his hand around my belly as soon as I stand between his open thighs.

"Kentlee or your daughter?" I ask with a smirk.

"Both," he murmurs as he places a kiss on my belly.

"Kentlee is high as a kite. She says she can't feel her brain.

Your nameless daughter is good," I smile.

We spend the next four hours waiting, just waiting for anything. I've asked the nurses about a thousand times for updates, but they don't give me a damn thing. Then Fury charges through the room with a huge ass smile on his face. I sigh in relief.

"He's so fuckin' perfect. Come on," he calls. I quickly follow behind him.

We walk into the hospital room, and the tiny little baby cradled in my sister's arms takes my breath away. I walk right up to him and sit next to her on the bed. Without a word, she hands me the little bundle. I look down on him and smile at the bright gray eyes that stare back at me.

"He's perfect," Bates murmurs from behind me.

"He is, so beautiful," I say. "What's the little guy's name?" I ask, unable to look away from him.

"Danger," Fury grins. I wrinkle my nose.

"It isn't my favorite, but I named Bear," Kentlee shrugs. I look over at my sister.

She's looking at Fury, who looks so damn proud. I would let him name my baby just about anything, too, with that look on his face. He is completely smitten, in awe, and so fucking proud.

"Danger Duhart it is, then," I murmur. Bates squeezes my shoulder.

I look around the room. Fury, Kentlee, Bates and me. Aside from our children and Mary-Anne, this is our family, our real family. I have never been prouder of these people, and I've never been happier. I'm so grateful and thankful to have my sister back in my life. And Bates—words cannot describe how I feel about him.

This world we live in can be a hot mess, but it can be beautifully breathtaking, too. Sometimes, you have lived through complete hell to come out on the other side, to appreciate all of the beauty it does hand you later in life. Had I not gone through my hell, had Kentlee not gone through hers, perhaps we wouldn't feel as incredibly blessed as we do right now. I know that I wouldn't be as appreciative of the man at my side had I not gone through my marriage with Scotty.

"I love you, Kentlee. He's just so beautiful," I murmur as I hand him back to her.

"I love you, too, Brent. Thank you for being here for me," she says. I want to brush it off, but I don't. Instead, I take her hand in mine and I give it a squeeze.

"We'll keep the kids for a week. Longer if you need," I offer. Fury blinks once before he grins.

"Thanks. 'Preciate that, sister-in-law," he says. A new thing he's started calling me. *I love it.*

Bates and I leave the hospital hand-in-hand and walk over to his truck. He helps heft my ass inside and we head over to Tammy's to gather the rest of our family.

I never thought I would be this happy.

When I would run and hide from Scotty, praying that I would just disappear, I never thought I would smile again. Now, I do nothing but smile, and it's Bates, Kentlee, Fury, and the entire Notorious Devils family that has made it possible.

I love all of them—with all of my repaired heart.

ROUGH & RUGGED
Notorious Devils MC Book 3

prologue

DIRTY JOHNNY

The clubhouse is wild tonight. I should be inside fucking a whore, maybe two, but I'm not. Instead, I walk outside and inhale the crisp air. Fall is coming to an end, and soon the snow will be on the ground. We'll all be forced to drive cages instead of our bikes. I fuckin' hate winter.

"Those things'll kill ya," Torch says, pushing off of the wall and walking toward me.

"Yeah? No shit," I grunt, taking another drag from my cigarette.

"I gotta go into *Devils*, wanna join?" he asks.

The Devils Club is the only strip club in town, that our Motorcycle Club owns and runs. Sniper is the manager, but with a new baby at home, we've all pitched in helping him out until he and the family get settled. I look back at the party behind me, but it doesn't call to me. I have no desire to fuck any of the whores in there, to watch their shows, or to get shit-faced drunk.

"Sure," I shrug, following him toward our parked bikes. We don't say a word as we start our engines and take off down the road.

A few minutes into my ride, I notice I need gas and signal

Torch toward the station. He nods, but we're only a few miles from the club, so he rides on ahead of me. The gas station is isolated, as usual for this time of night. Our little town rolls up their sidewalks when the sun goes down.

I walk into the station and pay the attendant. His eyes shift from side to side and nervousness is visibly apparent on his face.

"You all right there, bud?" I ask, taking some bills out of my pocket.

"Yes, everything is great," he stutters. That's when I know that nothing is *great*.

I hear a soft whimper from behind his counter, and I pull my gun out of the back of my waistband. I train it at his head before I order whoever is behind the counter to come out.

A girl stands up from behind the counter, she's a slip of a thing. Her hair is light brown and long, her eyes big and green, staring back at me wide and innocent. Her innocence is overshadowed by the fear on her face, and I wonder what this fat fucker behind the counter has done to her.

"You okay, sweetheart?" I ask before I shift my eyes back over to the fat-fuck.

"No," she whispers. Her sweet voice washes over me. Fuck it's sweet, too.

"What'd he do to you?" I ask, cocking my brow as the fucker starts shaking his head.

"He… he," she stutters before her big green eyes fill with tears.

"C'mon, let me get you outta here," I grind out as I hold one hand out to her. She doesn't hesitate. Instead, she crashes her tiny body into my side and buries her face in my shoulder.

"He told me I could use the phone, then he shoved me

down and told me I had to suck his dick first. Then you came in," she whimpers against me. Instantly, instinctually, I wrap my hand around the back of her head, holding her closer to me, keeping her face against me.

I pull the trigger on the fat-fuck. I watch as his brain explodes against the cigarettes that line the back of the counter. *It's a shame, all those smokes are ruined now.* Then I point my gun at the camera and pull the trigger on that too. The girl screams against me.

Quickly, I guide her out of the convenience store before pulling my phone out and making a call to a prospect. They're going to have to get rid of possible evidence and clean up fat-fuck's body. Once we reach my bike, I pull her away from me and look down into her frightened green eyes. My dick hardens at the sight of her. Fear fills her features and I fuckin' love it.

"Get on," I grind out.

I don't wait for an answer. I get on my bike, and once I feel her fumble around and her arms slide around my waist, I take off down the road. I don't have enough gas to go far. So I go back to the clubhouse. Once we pull into the lot, I nod to the prospects that are straddling their bikes to take care of my shit. I pull the little thing behind me toward the bar, past all the partiers and into the hallway. We walk into my room and I lock the door behind us before I turn to face her.

Hattie

I blink, looking up at him. I'm not sure how I got into this situation. No, that's a lie. *I know exactly how it happened.* I got into a fight with Willa and she kicked me out of her car—told me to walk my ass home. She was just mad that Brandon was flirting with me at the party. She's had a crush on him since we were in kindergarten.

When I walked into the gas station to use the phone, I thought it was the smart thing to do. I was going to call my big brother to come and get me. He was going to be pissed that I was even in Bonners Ferry. I don't know why we all came up here to party, except that Brandon's parents had a vacation cabin up here. I was supposed to be spending the night with Willa and she was spending the night with me. I was almost an hour from home. I couldn't walk, so I was going to call my brother, Andy, to get me. He'd give me shit, but he wouldn't rat me out to mom and dad.

"Who were you gonna call?" the sexy as hell biker asks me.

He's tall, thin but muscular. I felt his muscles beneath his t-shirt as I held onto him. Abs. Real abs. Not like the boys I go to school with. No, this is a man. He looks rough, rugged, and mean, but sexy as sin all at the same time.

"My brother," I murmur.

"Yeah?" he asks before slipping his hand into his pocket and pulling out his phone, handing it to me. I take it from him and look from it to his dark brown eyes.

"Call'em," he grunts

I don't hesitate.

"Andy?" I ask when he picks up the phone.

"Hattie?"

"I need a ride home," I whisper. He asks me where I am and when I tell him Bonners Ferry, he starts screaming into the phone.

"Stop shouting," the stranger says after he takes the phone out of my hand.

"I'll keep an eye on her until you get here. She's warm and safe, at the Notorious Devils clubhouse," the stranger says. I don't know what it means, Notorious Devils clubhouse. My brother must, because the stranger's eyes turn black before he speaks.

"You better calm your shit before you get here, partner." Without listening for my brother's reply, he ends the call. "Your brother's a dick, sweetheart."

"Yeah," I agree, nodding my head.

Andy is a dick, but he's dependable and reliable and he'll drive the hour to get me without telling mom and dad. Sure, he'll make sure I pay him back somehow, but his payback is less than mom and dad's punishment would be.

"How long's he gonna take to get here?" the stranger asks, his dark eyes roaming over my body. I shiver when they meet my eyes and I watch him smirk.

"An hour or so," I whisper. He smiles before he takes a step toward me.

His phone rings and he steps away from me for a while as he talks to whoever is on the other end. I am not where I should be, I should be at home, and I should be tucked into bed. This has to be the absolute worst night of my life. Luckily the stranger stays on the phone for at least thirty minutes and I sigh out an exhale of relief. Andy will be here soon, so soon, then I can go home and stop allowing Willa to drag me into her crazy shit.

"What's your name, sweetheart?" he murmurs as he steps into my space and tucks my long hair behind my ear. I look up into his eyes and gasp at the darkness swirling in them.

"Hattie," I whisper as he bites his bottom lip.

"Gorgeous," he whispers before his lips touch mine.

I gasp when one of his hands grabs my ass. He chooses that moment to slide his tongue into my mouth. He's warm and the stroke of his tongue is firm. He's not sloppy, like the boys I've kissed. He's not unsure—no, he is controlling this kiss. Controlling me. I lift my arms and wrap them around his neck, pressing my body closer to him while I tangle my tongue with his. I feel the vibration of his chest before I hear the moan that escapes his mouth into mine. His other hand tangles in my long hair and grips it tightly.

"You should get out of my room," he mumbles against my lips. Yet, he makes no move to untangle himself from my body. I don't want him to, either. I want more of his lips on mine. More of his hands gripping me tightly.

His lips crash against mine again and the hand on my ass moves up to my waist and slowly works its way under my shirt to my bra. I've never let anybody touch me before, but I want him to. When his fingers curl around my breast, I inhale as my body shivers beneath his touch.

"Need to fuck you, sweetheart," he murmurs against my neck between kissing and licking my skin.

I freeze.

What in the…

"Ummm," I say, unsure of how to respond. Who says that? He's known me all of two seconds.

"Let me in, baby," he mutters before he sucks on my neck.

I quickly step away from him, my chest heaving and my body filling with fear. Why did I come in here with him? Why did I kiss him? I shake my head, knowing the answer to that. He's hot, and bad, and a man, and he looked at me like I was a woman, not a child.

"What's wrong, sweetheart? You got at least ten more minutes before your brother gets here," he shrugs. It makes my stomach roll.

Ten minutes.

He wants me for ten minutes, and then I'll just be that girl he fucked once who was waiting for her big brother to give her a ride home. I shake my head before I quickly adjust my shirt.

"No," I shake my head.

No way am I telling this guy that I'm a virgin. No way am I telling him that he's the first guy to put his hand up my shirt. He's a man, he's hot, but no way am I embarrassing myself any further.

A loud pounding on the door interrupts us and I'm completely grateful. He swings the door open and there's a huge bear of a man that fills up the doorway. He's huge and hairy. He looks like a giant grizzly bear.

"Your girl's brother is here," he rumbles. My eyes widen. Holy shit, Andy is going to freak the fuck out at me being alone in this stranger's room.

"What the fuck is going on here?" Andy shouts, pushing past the grizzly bear man and into the room.

Andy is tall, wide, and built like the college football player that he is. I look like a teacup poodle next to him. Though our hair and eyes are identical, other than that, we are completely opposite. I watch as his green eyes go from the hot stranger to me and then back.

"Just hangin' out until you got here," the stranger smirks as he throws his arm around my shoulder and pulls me into his side.

"Hands off my sister," Andy grinds out.

"Or what?"

"I'll call the cops, you asshole," Andy warns. The guy laughs.

"I didn't do fuck all," he says between his chuckles. I don't tell him that he killed a man right in front of me. In fact, I don't say a word.

"My sister is sixteen, you idiot," Andy growls. The man beside me stops laughing. He looks down on me for confirmation and I nod once. Immediately, his heat leaves me and he takes a step away.

"Get the fuck outta here, girl," he grinds out. He looks so dangerous, so menacing, so unbelievably hot.

I can't move.

Andy grabs my hand and pulls me; but as my feet move, my eyes stay pinned to the handsome devil of a stranger. His angry eyes don't leave mine until we're out of each other's sight. Andy doesn't stop dragging me behind him, and once I'm in the car and we're safely on the road, he grills me. I tell him nothing of the convenience store, the murder I heard, or the way the man kissed me, owned me—made me want so much more than I have ever wanted.

I keep his kiss a secret.

A memory for just me.

Something special that I can think back on fondly.

I'll probably never see him again; I don't even know his name. But that doesn't stop me from putting my fingers against my lips and thinking of him.

also by
HAYLEY FAIMAN

MEN OF BASEBALL SERIES—
Pitching for Amalie
Catching Maggie
Forced Play for Libby
Sweet Spot for Victoria

RUSSIAN BRATVA SERIES—
Owned by the Badman
Seducing the Badman
Dancing for the Badman (July 25, 2016)
Living for the Badman (Winter 2016)
Protected by the Badman (2017)

NOTORIOUS DEVILS MC—
Rough & Rowdy
Rough & Raw
Rough & Rugged (Fall 2016)
Rough & Ruthless (2017)
Rough & Real (2017)

Follow me on social media to stay current on the happenings in my little book world.

Facebook: https://www.facebook.com/authorhayleyfaiman

Goodreads: https://www.goodreads.com/author/show/10735805.Hayley_Faiman

about the author

As an only child, Hayley Faiman had to entertain herself somehow. She started writing stories at the age of six and never really stopped.

Born in California, she met her now husband at the age of sixteen and married him at the age of twenty in 2004. After sixteen years together, he's still the love of her life. Hayley's husband joined the military and they lived in Oregon, where he was stationed with the US Coast Guard, before they moved back to California in 2006, where they had two little boys. Recently, the four of them moved out to Hill Country in Texas, where they adopted a new family member, a chocolate lab named Optimus Prime.

Most of Hayley's days are spent taking care of her two boys, going to the baseball fields for practice, or helping them with homework. Her evenings are spent with her husband and her nights—those are spent creating alpha book boyfriends.

acknowledgments

My Husband —The man whose endless support is unwavering. What would I do without you by my side? My biggest cheerleader and my best friend. Thank you babes. Always.

My mom— How do I thank the woman who is everything? The words THANK YOU are not enough. Ever. I appreciate the way you love me, and the support you've always given me. Thank you for always, always being the best.

Rosalyn— There are no words. God brings people into our lives for a reason, when we need them the most. Our friendship is a true testament of that and I will forever be thankful and grateful.

Nisha — My sister from another mister. Thank you for always being my friend, for the past eighteen years of laughs!

Cassandra Searby— My boo! Thank you for always being there, day in and day out! You're such an inspiration!

Cassy Roop—Thank you for the gorgeous cover—AGAIN!

Crystal Snyder— Thank you so very much for all of your help. I truly appreciate everything you do for me!!

Stacey Blake— Your work is gorgeous from front to back. Thank you for always making my books so beautiful. I appreciate all of your hard work and dedication. You're truly a treasure and I'm lucky to have found you! You're seriously the best!!

Enticing Journey— Ena and Amanda— THANK YOU! Every single book that's released I have full faith that things will go swimmingly because of you two! Thank you for all of your hard work. You are truly appreciated.

To all the Blogger babes that have taken a chance on me...

Thank you from the bottom of my heart.

My fans, every person who decided to see what was beneath the covers of my books. I appreciate you. Thank you so very much for joining me on this wild ride.

Printed in Great Britain
by Amazon